THE
MAGISTRATE'S
SON

Xessus I

THE
Magistrate's
Son

Mike Thexton
Illustrations: Johanna Gousset

Copyright © Lanista Partners Ltd, 2016
All rights reserved
The moral right of the author has been asserted
The moral right of the illustrator has been asserted

First published in Great Britain in 2016 by
Lanista Partners Ltd

45, Leyborne Park
Richmond – TW9 3HB
United Kingdom
www.xessus.com
ISBN 978-0-9553185-1-1

A catalogue record for this book is available from
the British Library.

Designed by Luisa Hiromi Yatsu Simon.
Printed and bound in Great Britain by Clays Ltd, St Ives plc.

For Zoe,
who asked me to write some more

1
APPRENTICE

Nothing could spoil this day. He'd been waiting for so long. 'You have to be sixteen,' his da had said. Time had never dragged as slowly as it had to this birthday.

Lebasi stood to attention by his lead animal, ready for the order. Rabor the donkey-master walked down the line with a lantern, tugging and pushing to make sure all was secure. He stopped in front of Lebasi and put his face close. Lebasi was surprised to smell alcohol on his breath this early.

'You were late. You go last. I don't care whose son you are.'

Lebasi put his hand on his heart and lowered his head in respect. He knew better than to answer back to an apprentice-master, especially one with Rabor's reputation. 'Move out!' Rabor shouted. The donkeys started to walk, kicking up dust. Lebasi breathed in a lungful and began coughing, his eyes closed. He felt someone barge into him. He looked up to see Sammas leering down at him in the lamplight. He turned sharply, knowing that where Sammas was, Ruffur would be close behind, and what Sammas did, Ruffur would do twice as hard. He dodged the bigger boy's shoulder, and the movement blew out the candle in his own lantern.

Even so, nothing could spoil this day, not even having to walk thirty thousand paces with those idiots, when he'd normally run a good distance to avoid them.

Faya came past with the third string of donkeys. If she was there, he could put up with Ruffur and Sammas. She ignored him now, as she had since the previous summer. She'd been one of the last to stop talking to him, but for today, he would put that to the back of his mind. They were going out, free of the crowded streets, beyond the walls, further than the town fields where he'd worked at planting and harvest, all the way to the border. Today he could imagine it was possible to keep walking, to go somewhere they wouldn't know who he was. Wouldn't know, or wouldn't care.

Faya's fifth donkey trotted past him. He was left standing in darkness. He gave a gentle tug on the rope and clicked his tongue, as Rabor had told him. Nothing happened. He pulled harder and clicked louder. The donkey snorted and shook its head. The end of Faya's string of animals was turning out of the yard. He tugged again.

Rabor's words ran around his head. Don't hold us up. 'Hey, now, Beauty,' came a man's voice from the shadows, followed by a low whistle. The donkey made a noise like a gentle laugh, and started to walk. Lebasi set off in front as fast as he could, encouraging Beauty onwards. There was enough light from the dawn sky for him to make out his rescuer, a man taller than Lebasi and slimmer than Rabor.

The man put a hand on Lebasi's shoulder. 'I'm Perra, Rabor's deputy.' He laughed. 'That means I shovel dung and I pick ticks off donkeys. Twenty years of that and I might be the guildmaster myself.'

Lebasi grinned. 'I'm Lebasi.'

'I know.' Lebasi's smile faded. Of course he knew. Everyone knew.

✻ ✻ ✻ ✻ ✻

They caught up with Faya at the turning to the gate. Rabor was waiting. 'I told you —'

'It's all right,' said Perra. 'Beauty was just playing her tricks.

We're here, and the gate's not open yet.'

Rabor snorted like one of his own animals, and strode back up the line. Perra ruffled Lebasi's hair and followed the donkey-master.

Lebasi had never been in the gate-street before dawn. He could see why Rabor was in a hurry. The strip of sky between the walls above him was already bright blue, so the rising-bell must be about to sound. People were lining up beside the wall, men carrying spades or forks over their shoulders, women with bundles balanced on their heads. No one spoke. No one looked at Lebasi. Each new arrival stopped at the end of the queue and leaned on the stonework, closing their eyes as if they could sleep a little longer standing up.

One of the gate-keepers marched down the line with Perra. He spoke briefly to Faya, then walked slowly past her donkey-train, putting his face up close to each load and squinting at it as he counted. Lebasi could see his lips moving. He stopped and peered at Lebasi.

'Who're you, then?'

'Lebasi of Xela, apprentice to –'

The man took half a step backwards. Lebasi was used to it. The gate-keeper composed himself, determined to show that he was in charge. 'What's in your loads, then, boy?'

Perra started to speak, but Lebasi was quicker. He pointed to each animal in turn. 'Dried spices and medicinal herbs. Dyed cloth from the weavers. Charcoal. Leather from the tannery. Cooking pots.' Perra nodded and smiled. The gate-keeper moved on to the line of farm-workers.

There was movement ahead. The donkeys were kicking up dust again, but the cloud couldn't hide the bright gate-shaped patch of daylight beyond them. Faya was walking. Lebasi tried to imitate Perra's whistle, but Beauty didn't need any encouragement now. She seemed to have left her mischief behind in the stables. He entered the tunnel through the walls, ten paces of gloomy stone. There was a hold-up – Faya had stopped – a man pushed past into the town, leading a line of sheep, another man at the back with a dog driving them. Lebasi closed his eyes, starting a story in his head. A long, long journey, one that went to the capital city and beyond...

Perra nudged him. 'Move on, lad, before Rabor catches you dozing.' The animals in front were already twenty paces on, as keen as he was to be in the open air. As he stepped out into daylight, a flight of pigeons rose up, silhouetted against the sun. Lebasi watched them as they circled overhead, then set off to the south-east. He took a deep breath, determined not to look back. Ahead, the road led straight into the distance, shining white between green fields, shaded by lines of trees on either side. Maybe it went on for ever.

Lebasi was grateful for his boots. He'd woken to find Marrak, his father's agent, standing by the bed, holding them up – 'It is a long walk, you will need them.' Lacing them had made him late, and being late had made Rabor angry. Five thousand paces of stony road later, he knew that Marrak had been right: his feet were tough from running around the town, but this was much harder going.

They crossed a wooden bridge over a slow-moving river. The donkeys ahead turned off the road onto the grass verge and started grazing. Rabor beckoned the apprentices to him. He walked up and down, prodding each one with his finger as he spoke, making no distinction for girl or boy, bully or magistrate's son.

'We're out beyond the town fields now. Most people don't go this far. Your mothers may have told you' – he paused and stared at Lebasi, who felt his face get hotter – 'that there are wild animals out here, lions, who knows what kind of monster.' Rabor bared his teeth. 'But I promise you there's nothing in the wide world more dangerous than me. You remember when you were little and you thought those stories about dragons were real? A dragon's a little kitten beside me.' He stepped back and banged his fist into the other palm for emphasis. 'So. You keep on the road. You don't talk to the country folk. You don't talk to outsiders at the border. And you stay back from the line. Is that clear?'

They all nodded meekly, even Ruffur and Sammas. That wasn't good enough for Rabor. 'I said, is that CLEAR?'

'Yes, sir, Rabor, sir,' they all replied.

'Now eat your breakfast quickly and let's get to the border before the day's too hot.'

Lebasi sat on his own, staring back across five thousand paces of neat, flat farmland, still able to pick out the gate where the road met the wall. The town seemed too small: how could all those people spend their whole lives inside it? Roofs crowded together above the wall, layer on layer like a cake, circle after circle up to the bell tower. The land outside spread out from horizon to horizon, hills and woods, the blue glint of the river where its banks were low, the mountains towering up to the north, black rock faces rising to white points. The early workers were out in the fields by now: Lebasi could see flocks of wild birds following the plough. Those people would pass back through that wall before nightfall, like pigeons returning to their roost.

He'd come half this distance before, when he was apprenticed to a shepherd; but turning the other way, everything was new. He could see that the road wound into a valley between wooded hills, rising in the distance to a col. He guessed that was as far as they would go. But there was a promise of a view beyond, a view that he had never seen. People he had never seen, who would collect their loads and give them something in return. Things they didn't make or grow in these fields, in this town. Already his mind was running ahead towards that horizon, imagining how different it would be from everything he knew so well.

He didn't expect the other apprentices to sit with him, but it annoyed him to see Faya talking and laughing with Sammas and Ruffur. He didn't think she liked them – she was clever and they were stupid, she was kind and they were mean. It was worse when he realised that they were laughing at him – at his boots. Faya and Ruffur were wearing sandals. Sammas's feet were bare. It hadn't occurred to him before that no one else in town, at least no one his age, had a pair like them. And while Ruffur was chewing a lump of meat his father the butcher must have given him, Faya and Sammas were sharing what looked like stale bread and rank cheese. Marrak had packed Lebasi's bag with dried fruit, nuts, a couple of little cakes, and some ham. He wanted to offer it around, but he knew they'd sneer at him for patronising them. He ate a little, then put the bag away. He felt his neck reddening, not from the sun.

He was glad when Rabor shouted that it was time to go.

He tried to put the others out of his mind. Everything else about the day was as good as he had hoped. Every step of the road was fascinating. The country was wilder than the town fields: uncultivated meadows covered with spring flowers, woods of tree varieties he'd never seen before, the sky full of strange birds that he didn't recognise. He was aware of people living here – he spotted a village away to the north, a collection of houses that might be home to ten families. A herdsman sat on a rock on the far side of a stream running beside the track, chewing a long stem of grass and watching them. Lebasi waved to him, but he made no sign in return.

Perra fell into step beside Lebasi. His smile seemed friendly enough, but Lebasi was wary. Sometimes boys at school would pretend to include him in something and then laugh at him for thinking they meant it.

'So, the great Xela's your da, is he?'

Lebasi nodded.

'What's he like? To live with, I mean. We all see him doing his job.' He sounded genuinely interested. Lebasi studied him more closely. He'd seen Perra around the town, of course – he'd seen everyone. He guessed he was about twenty-five, maybe one of the oldest boys in school when Lebasi started. He wasn't as tall as Rabor, but he had broad shoulders and strong arms. His black hair was cut very short, and he was clean-shaven, which was unusual in the town.

Lebasi considered the question. All the legends he'd ever loved told him that it was right to be loyal, and wicked to say bad things about someone when they weren't there to defend themselves. He wished he could still describe Xela as he'd been years ago, before Lebasi went to school – playing games, telling stories, laughing. It was always sunny in his memory, and Xela always smiled at him, although even then he seemed sad underneath. He couldn't remember when he'd last heard his da find anything funny.

'Busy,' he said at last. 'I don't see him much.'

Perra shrugged. 'And what about the southerner? There are some wild stories about him.'

'Marrak?' He thought about the agent's neat beard, his bald head, his face fixed in one stern expression. 'He's not wild. He helps my da with his work. He's busy too. But he runs the house, because...' He glanced ahead again, and pulled on the rein to narrow the gap that had appeared between him and Faya's last donkey. 'Because my ma died when I was a baby.'

Perra nodded. 'I know. Sorry. I don't mean to pry.'

Lebasi twitched as if flicking off an insect. 'It's all right. It's a long time ago. I don't remember her.' He kept his eyes on the road.

'But kids are unkind, right?'

Lebasi turned and stared at Perra. 'How do you know?'

Perra scratched his chin. 'Because my mother died when I was six. I was the only one my age at school who didn't have a ma at home, and they teased me for it. As if it was my fault.'

He clapped Lebasi on the shoulder and walked on to talk to Faya. It wasn't the greatest thing to have in common, but it was something. Lebasi realised he was smiling.

2
BORDERLINE

They climbed steadily for a long time. The shading trees ended and the road levelled off into a shallow saddle between steeper slopes. The sun beat down on his head, and he wished Marrak had suggested some shade as well as the boots. Faya had put on a broad-brimmed straw hat.

Ahead on the road, Perra stopped and waited for him to catch up. He nodded towards the skyline. 'See if you can spot the high wall that keeps us in.' He laughed to himself, then dropped back to bring up the rear of the procession for the last hundred paces.

The other apprentices led their donkeys off the road and tied them up. Lebasi did the same, but while they sat down to rest, he followed Rabor towards the highest point. A white stone stood on each side of the road, taller than a man. A low wall that ran to left and right up the grassy hillside petered out after fifty paces. On the road itself there was nothing: no gate, no guard, not even a line in the chalky surface.

Rabor stood with his hands on his hips, muttering under his breath about the menkers being late, they'd be baking in the afternoon sun, why did he always have to deal with idiots, but Lebasi guessed he was pleased to have reached the border first. From two paces behind the guildmaster he stared at a world he had never seen. There was another valley, running down to the west like a reflection of the one he had climbed from the east, to another town on another hill in the distance, fifteen thousand paces further on. Coming over a rise in the foreground, he saw a line of men making their way uphill with four apprentices and another twenty laden donkeys. As they came nearer, Lebasi realised that they were the same and not the same: they had a blue square tattooed on the back of the right hand. He was used to seeing people over the age of eighteen with a tattoo of a red circle on the left hand. Everyone he knew had one, apart from Marrak.

Rabor turned, almost bumping into Lebasi. He gave him a hard shove in the chest. 'What did I say about staying back from the line? Go and unload your animals.'

The others were already half finished, and Lebasi had to hurry to catch up. Sammas was untying packages and handing them to Ruffur to carry to the line. Ruffur didn't seem to have noticed that this meant he was doing three times as much work. Lebasi smiled. It was always the same: Sammas had the brains, as far as they went, and Ruffur provided the muscle. Faya was doing her own unpacking, staggering under one of the heavier loads. He took a step towards her, but a flash of her eyes told him she didn't want any help, from him or anyone else.

The apprentices carried the packages up and set them down five paces from the line, telling Rabor and Perra what was in each one. The men handed them over to the outsiders. Lebasi watched as he worked: never a tattooed hand, never a finger crossed the line that wasn't there. He glanced around to see if there was a watchman somewhere. They would have to be a long way away, because there was no cover on the open hillside above them and no one in sight. Watched or not, Rabor and Perra and the men from the far town obeyed the law exactly.

It was hot and tiring, but at last their loads had been passed across and the other side's goods were fastened into the panniers, the new contents memorised in their turn. Rabor grunted that they had done a good job. They could have a rest and some food before starting back. After lunch Lebasi followed the donkeymen's example and stretched out on the short grass. They were taking a nap before heading home, but he was staring up into the blue sky and watching a pair of eagles soaring. No worries about boundaries for them – wheeling in rising circles, then with an effortless flap of their great wings heading off in a straight line to the north, towards the distant mountains.

A shadow fell across him. He twisted his head, squinting against the sunlight, and jumped up in a hurry. Ruffur was leaning over him, grinning. Lebasi braced himself for a punch, and stepped backwards into Sammas. He turned around and found Faya completing the triangle, arms folded across her chest.

'Any food left, Basi?' Sammas didn't wait for an answer but reached down and snatched up his bag.

'Help yourself,' Lebasi shrugged.

'Nice boots, Basi,' Ruffur growled. His voice seemed to get deeper every time Lebasi heard him speak. He seemed to get taller, too – Lebasi only came up to his shoulder.

'Marrak told me to wear them.'

'Marrak told me, Marrak told me,' chanted Sammas in a sing-song voice, still poking around in the bag. 'Basi always does what he's told.'

'Didn't see any reason not to put on some boots if someone gave them to me.' He stared at Faya. Surely she wasn't going to join in? She said nothing, but glared back. Her eyes weren't friendly.

Sammas held up the bag and shook the last crumbs into his mouth. He ran his tongue round his lips, making sure he hadn't missed anything. 'Wish my ma baked cakes like yours, Basi.'

That was hard to take. Lebasi turned to walk away, but Ruffur grabbed his wrist. His hands were huge, his arms like hams. The only way to escape would be by calling for Rabor or Perra, and Lebasi wasn't going to do that.

Ruffur sniggered. 'Sammie, that's not nice. You know Basi hasn't got a ma.'

'Ooooh yes, I forgot. Just that funny southrat who doesn't speak normal, and his big powerful da.'

Ruffur put a finger under Lebasi's chin and made a show of studying his face. 'No ma, and no granma or granda either. I've got two of each. Any uncles or aunts? I've got nine. Any cousins? Can't count mine.'

Lebasi decided not to encourage him by answering. It crossed his mind that Ruffur had never been good with numbers bigger than ten, and he almost laughed. This wasn't going to be funny, and he didn't want to make it worse.

Sammas shook his head, leaning in close to inspect Lebasi's face. 'D'you think it's a human at all, Ruffie? D'you think it might be a vegetable, grown from a seed?'

Lebasi turned towards Faya, trying to ask her with only his eyes whether she wasn't above this. She shook her head, her red curls catching the sun. 'I don't know what you do in class, Sammas, but you ought to know that's not possible. Lebasi is his father's boy, no doubt about it.'

Lebasi tried to pull his arm away, but Ruffur only tightened his grip.

'What do you mean by that?' His voice came out louder than he intended. He expected meanness from the two boys, but he'd thought better of Faya.

'Xela makes everyone keep the law, and you would never dream of breaking the law.'

'That's not true.' He knew that it was.

She smiled at him. He remembered how pretty her green eyes were, when they weren't narrowed in a knowing smirk. 'You'd never do anything wrong, not the smallest thing. When did you ever?'

He hardly noticed Ruffur and Sammas joining in. He could only hear Faya taunting him. He couldn't look away from her mouth laughing at him, her eyes, her hair.

'I tell you what, Lebasi of Xela,' she said, turning her head to the side. 'If you're not just your da's good little boy, fetch me that nice stone.'

She stretched out her arm to point. He followed her finger. A smooth black rock the size of a grapefruit lay on its own by the chalky roadside, flecked with crystals glinting in the noonday sunlight. It was fully fifteen paces away, but she could only mean that one.

Five paces the other side of the line.

'Don't be silly, Faya,' he started.

'Vegetable,' said Sammas.

'Scared vegetable,' grunted Ruffur.

'Xela's little boy,' muttered Faya.

Their voices seemed to swell and fade. His tongue stuck to the roof of his mouth as he tried to say something. He stared at the black rock. He shook his arm, and this time Ruffur let go. It wasn't what he wanted to do. It wasn't what he intended to do. His mind had stopped working. He took a step, two steps, quicker and quicker. Past Rabor, who still had his eyes shut – Perra sitting up, scrambling to his feet – he was between the white stones – he was beyond them.

It felt no different. The air, the breeze, the sunshine were the same. The same view of the valley running down to the other

town. Two donkeymen snoozing in the grass, four apprentices getting their animals ready for loading. He reached down and grabbed the rock. It was cool and heavy in his hand. He turned, walked ten paces back, and tossed it to Faya. She put her hands up but missed the catch – she was staring at him, the whites showing all around the green centres of her eyes, her mouth a perfect circle. For a moment he smiled, fixing that picture in his memory.

But then Rabor's roar brought him back to what he'd done, and everyone started shouting.

3
TROUBLE

There'll be trouble. You'll be sorry.

The words ran around Lebasi's head for the whole of the long walk home. There were no other words to listen to. No one spoke to him. Rabor put Lebasi's team in front, as if to keep an eye on him, but the donkey-master walked ten paces ahead, eyes fixed on the distant town. He never looked round in fifteen thousand paces. Lebasi kept his face forward as well. The back of his neck was burning – he knew it was the sun, but it felt as if the others were still staring at him.

There'll be trouble. You'll be sorry.

The strange thing was that the men had shouted at each other more than at him. Rabor had squared up to the leader from the other town as if they were going to fight. They jabbed their fingers and shook their fists, but nothing more than words crossed the line. Rabor had told the man, 'If the magistrate finds out, I'll see you regret it.' He replied, 'Who are you calling a reporter, then?'

Lebasi turned it over and over. It seemed trouble would come for them, as much as for him, if the magistrate heard that they had allowed such a thing to happen. When he turned back to his own side of the line, Rabor could hardly speak to Lebasi, but he had made his orders clear to Perra and each of the other apprentices: silence.

Perhaps he wouldn't be in trouble at all, not if the threats worked and the magistrate never found out. And as the magistrate was his da, he thought that whatever happened to the men, trouble for him would probably mean being yelled at over dinner.

It would make a change from being ignored.

The gatekeeper counted them in without saying anything. The people passing in the avenue acted normally. They unloaded the donkeys and stacked the goods in the storeroom without watchmen arriving. No one spoke a word more than they had to. When Lebasi made the sign of respect to Rabor before leaving, he received a sharp jab of the man's forefinger in his shoulder, but that was all. He knew what it meant. *If there's trouble for me, you'll get worse.*

When he got home he asked Marrak where his father was: out of town, not due back until tomorrow evening. At least a day before he had to worry, then. He ate his dinner alone, in the usual silence. He'd been on the road before dawn and travelled a long way in the hot sun, further than he'd ever walked before. By the time he lay down on his bed, the possibility of his da's anger the next evening wasn't enough to stop him falling asleep in a moment.

⁂ ⁂ ⁂ ⁂ ⁂

He was woken by a finger and thumb clamped over his nose. As he opened his mouth to gasp, something was stuffed between his teeth. He bit down on a piece of cloth. The fabric tasted of sweat, sour and salty. It soaked up his saliva and swelled so there was no room for his tongue. Hands gripped his arms and legs and lifted him off the bed. He seemed to be standing up, but his feet weren't touching the floor. There was no sound. Only the fingers digging into his limbs told him this was more than a nightmare. He felt other fingers scrabbling at the back of his neck, tying the gag in place. It stretched his lips into a grin and bit into the corners of his mouth.

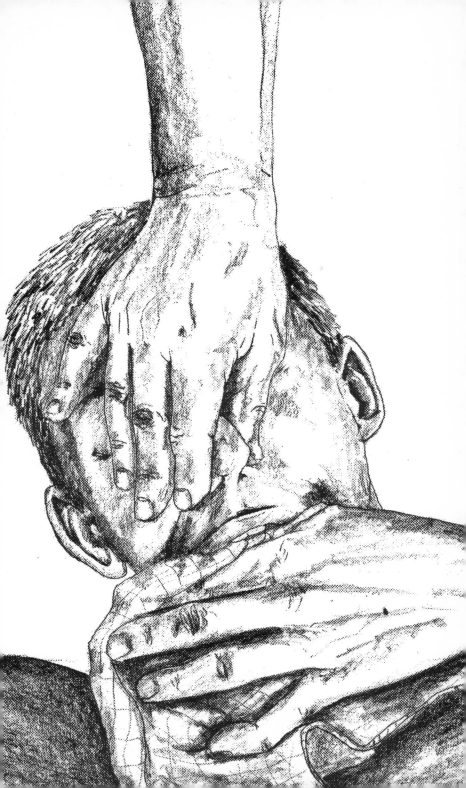

He turned his head to try to see who was there. In the dim light, the little room seemed full of black cloaks: they merged into the shadows. He followed the glimmer back to its source – a man standing in the doorway, a hood hiding his face, a shuttered lantern held high. Lebasi struggled, but there were too many hands, too strong. He drew in a breath to shout. Even through the gag, surely he could make enough noise to wake Marrak. A fat palm clamped over his mouth and pinched his nostrils. His chest was too full. His head started to spin. The lantern-man wagged a finger, his message clear. The fingers released his nose. He choked against the gag. He wouldn't try that again.

A cloth slipped over his eyes. His hands were pulled together behind his back and tied. He felt himself being lifted over someone's shoulders, his face pressed into the rough material of the man's cloak. He was moving. They must be going through the doorway – a hand on his head guided it past the frame. Still there was no noise. He wondered if something had gone wrong with his hearing, or if this really could be a dream. No, he could smell the sweat of the man carrying him, that was too real – and one sound broke the hush: the wheeze and rumble of Marrak gently snoring in his bed, ahead on the right, level now, falling behind him...

His sleep-muddled mind wandered for a moment. The jolting of the man's silent tread descending the stairs, the blindfold, the dizziness – he was three or four again, playing his favourite game: his da, wrapping him in a blanket, spinning him around, carrying him over his shoulder, setting him down and making him guess where he was. The garden, the bedroom, the chicken house. The man stumbled and banged Lebasi's arm against the wall. The pain brought him back to the present.

How could they walk into the magistrate's house and do this? Carry the magistrate's own son like a piece of meat past the room where his agent was fast asleep?

The cool air brushing his face told him they were outside the front door. They stood him on his feet and turned him three times, just as his da used to. He couldn't tell uphill from downhill.

He was out in the curfew for the second night running. On the way to the stables, a watchman had stopped him, but had let him go as soon as he said 'Lebasi of Xela'. The watchman had been afraid of his da's name. These men weren't afraid to come into his da's house. Who were they? Where were they taking him? Why?

Someone pushed him in the back to make him start walking. Uphill. A hand on each arm to keep him moving. The cobbles were slick with dew under his bare feet. The sloping stones gave way to smooth, flat earth – they must be crossing the eighth avenue. Then cobbles again. He counted the avenues as they went up: seven, six, five... they were going straight to the top of the town. He could still play his da's game. The sharp vinegary smell of the tannery on the right, just above the fourth avenue. The cheesemaker's shop on the left, unmistakeable. The butcher's at third. A waft of stale beer confirmed they had crossed the second avenue. Still there was no challenging watchman. They were climbing the main eastern downstreet in the middle of the night: surely someone would see them. Even if there were too many in the gang for one man to tackle, they would go for Marrak, bring help. Surely...

He wondered again if his ears had failed. He knew there were five or six men walking around him, but the only sounds he could hear were his own heartbeat and laboured breathing through the gag. On his way to the stables before dawn he'd picked out the noises of people stirring in upper rooms, babies crying for a feed, dogs growling at his passing scent. He'd felt the houses crowding close, watching, listening, in the night-time as in the day. Now, it was as if the buildings themselves had stepped back, averting their eyes. He remembered the threats again – 'if the magistrate finds out...'. Was this to stop him telling his da? Was everyone on the eastern downstreet in on it? How could he let them know that he wouldn't? How could he make them believe it?

Several times he stumbled, but his escorts caught him before he fell. The stones dug into his bare feet. He wished for his boots.

The ground levelled again. The silence somehow opened up and became larger. They must be out of the downstreet by now, standing on the first avenue, facing the Town Space. Through his blindfold Lebasi could imagine it all as if it was daylight: the bell tower on the right, the lines of trees in the centre giving shade for lessons, the open space on the left for games. Today would be a school day. Would he be missing from class? What would happen if he was? His da was due back that evening. Marrak would wonder where he was at breakfast time.

They turned left. Lebasi tried to count his steps, to picture the buildings they must be passing. They stopped and turned to the left again. Eighty paces – maybe a third of the way along the southern side. He searched his memory. There was a door in the rough stone wall, a door he had never seen opened, in a wall with no windows.

A gentle rapping of knuckles on wood startled him. It wasn't loud, but it was the first noise he had heard from outside himself since he had left the house. Then the scrape of something opening – a small sound, not the door itself. A spy-hole?

A hoarse whisper: 'Who goes?'

'Snatch squad with a prisoner.' Lebasi guessed this was lantern-man. He strained his ears to try to recognise the voice. At least that proved they were men, not ghosts.

'Who is it?'

'Lebasi of Xela.'

A coughing fit erupted, muffled quickly as the spy-hole

snapped shut. Maybe his da's name had an effect on some of these men, whoever they were. Lebasi heard the clicks of bolts being drawn back and the squeak of hinges that needed grease. As the door swung open, the guard muttered, 'I hope you know what you're doing, Dem –'

Lantern–man's voice cut him short. 'No names, idiot.' A hand on Lebasi's shoulder steered him through the opening. The earth of the first avenue gave way to cold smooth tiles. The door thudded shut behind him, heavy and thick. There would be two hundred children out there later, just the other side of the avenue. Could he make himself heard?

He heard the click of boots on a hard surface, the room seeming large around them. After twenty paces the noises changed. Lebasi turned his head from side to side, trying to guess what it meant. There was less echo now: had they entered somewhere smaller? They stopped. Fingers fumbled with the knots at his wrists, then he felt the cold touch of a blade against his skin. His heart thumped. Had they brought him here to make absolutely sure? He tried to say something, but only a grunt came out.

A new voice cut in, low and angry. 'What're you doing? That's a decent bit of rope –'

A different one, nervous and defensive: 'You should learn to tie better –'

'Shut up!' A roar from lantern man. Lebasi felt the knife cut the cord, but his mind had raced elsewhere. He opened his eyes wide. He was sure he recognised the voices, but he couldn't place them – they sounded blurry and distorted, bouncing off the walls. *That's why they're not speaking. I know them, and they know I know them.*

Someone placed his left hand on a railing and pushed him forward. He guessed there would be steps. He sensed the curve of a spiral staircase leading down and started counting. After twenty-four, they must be so deep underground that no one on the Space would hear, however loud he shouted. But maybe he could put the fear of his father into these men, if he could just get a look at a face.

There was only a guiding hand on his right arm now. His left brushed against a rough stone wall. Even without his eyes, he could feel that they were in a narrow corridor, damp and mouldy. They stopped again. His head was pulled back as someone tugged on the knots securing the gag. At last he could spit it out and take a proper breath. The blindfold fell away. After complete blindness, the dim candlelight was bright: he was standing in front of a low doorway into a tiny stone room. He turned around to protest, to plead, to argue – they didn't need to silence him about what happened at the border, he wouldn't tell anyway – he knew who they were, and they'd have to answer to Xela for what they'd done tonight.

The man held up his lantern. As the flickering light showed the face beneath the hood, all words left Lebasi's mind; any idea of identifying him, saying his name, or threatening him with the magistrate. A skull leered at him from the shadows, pale bones with blank spaces where the eyes should be. He started backwards and hit his head on the lintel. He felt a hand in his chest, a firm push. He stumbled and sat down hard on the stone floor. The door slammed shut. For a moment he still saw flashing lights from the bang on his head, but they faded. He opened and closed his eyes. It made no difference at all.

4
CELLS

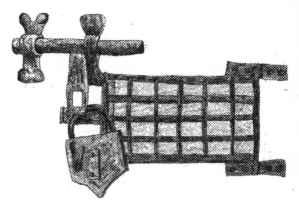

Lebasi hugged his knees to his chest and gently probed the back of his head with his fingers. A little blood, warm and sticky. He wiped his hand on his shirt. His brain was still jangling from the shock and the blow, but now he listened hard: there was utter silence, as well as darkness. Cautiously, he stretched out his hands and met rocky walls at the edge of his reach. The floor sucked the warmth out of his body. He rubbed his legs to try to stop the cold spreading, but suddenly he was shivering uncontrollably. He clamped his arms around his chest to try to hold still.

Who were they? He told himself the death's head could only be a mask. They weren't ghosts, they were too physical. They had voices. They smelled. Their leader had a name: it began with Dem. Lebasi started to run through the people of the town in his mind, looking for someone who fitted. He only had to wait for Xela to get back. Xela knew everything that went on, or so he said. Usually that was a reminder to Lebasi to behave himself, because there would be consequences if he didn't. Now, it gave him comfort. Lebasi believed it, too. There were a few hiding places in town where he reckoned he was out of Xela's sight, but his da often made comments across the eating-table to show that it was hard to keep secrets from him. Masked men taking his son up the main eastern downstreet and into a building on the first avenue

– someone would have seen, someone would tell. If he could just keep himself going until evening... He needed something to fill the darkness until then.

He tried telling himself a legend, one of the stories of the hero Xessus overcoming impossible dangers. That was a good way to pass an empty afternoon on a freeday if he couldn't find a game that the others would let him join. He knew all the tales – he would put himself in the adventure, close his eyes and let his imagination take him away. But daydreaming in the open air was different from passing time in the dark. The words were slippery in his head. Maybe the walls were too thick for even his thoughts to escape.

Instead he turned his mind back to yesterday afternoon, the shouts, the threats. *There'll be trouble, you'll be sorry.* He hugged himself closer, remembering the heat and the glare of the noonday sun. Yesterday he would have been glad of some shelter from it. Thinking about how hot he'd been, how sweaty, seemed to make the cold even worse.

The memory of those raised voices faded into the silence of the cell. When he opened his eyes, the sunshine at the border was replaced by blackness. But he was sure something had changed: there had been a sound from outside the room. When he blinked, he could see a faint line of light where the foot of the door must be. There were footsteps in the corridor. Timid, tiptoeing footsteps. They stopped outside. The light was clearer, but it was still not enough for Lebasi to see anything of the room he was in.

'Are you all right, boy?' It was the door-keeper's voice.

Lebasi was about to answer, but he stopped himself. If he said nothing, the man would have to open the door.

'Boy?' There was definitely worry in that tone. 'I hope you know what you're doing,' he had said to Dem. Was the man afraid of Xela's reaction, or was he concerned for his prisoner's well-being? Either way...

Lebasi waited as the bolts were drawn back. He pressed his hands against the wall behind him and got ready to spring, to fight, to run. A new line of light appeared at the side of the door as it began to open.

The lantern came first, followed by an arm, then a head. The face was old. Lebasi didn't recognise the man, which surprised him – he thought he knew everyone in the town. He wasn't tall, but he filled the small doorway. Still, Lebasi had to try – he sprang for the narrow gap between the man and the door, took him by surprise and pushed his way through. He turned to the right – that was the way he had come, the way out – and ran straight into a second guard. This one blocked the whole corridor. He hardly seemed to notice Lebasi crashing into him: he just stood there, solid as an extra wall.

Lebasi turned and looked the other way. The tunnel disappeared into darkness. He took two steps, then realised it was hopeless.

'Come on, lad, there's no use in trying to get out. Best get used to the idea.' The smaller man was leaning out of the cell, holding up the lantern. Lebasi walked slowly back in and sat down against the wall.

The guard didn't seem to mind that he had tried to escape. 'There now, I've brought you a blanket, and a bucket, in case you need it.' Lebasi's brief action had driven away the cold for a moment, but now it took hold of him completely. He wrapped himself in the rough cloth and tried to stop shaking.

'I'm Bennek,' the man was saying. His skin was pale in the candlelight, as if he didn't see much sun. Lebasi tried to focus on his words. 'Lodder, give me that drink.' The light swayed towards the door and back. A wooden mug was pressed into his hands. 'Go on, it'll warm you up.'

Lebasi gulped down what tasted like warm tea, with an after-

kick of something else in it – something much hotter – that spread through his chest and made him cough. The shivering stopped.

'Thank you,' he gasped, handing the cup back.

Bennek closed the door and sat with his back to it. He put the lantern on the floor and gazed evenly at Lebasi.

'So, Xela's son, what did you do?'

'Nothing.' He knew what this must be about, but how could it be? What could it matter if someone walked five paces over an imaginary line and came straight back again?

'Come now, the snatchers don't go out in the night unless someone's broken the Mercy. If you'd been stealing fruit or playing truant or being rude to an elder, you'd have your da to answer to for sure, but not this.'

'I don't know what you mean.'

Bennek snorted. 'I'm trying to be friendly. Don't lie to me.'

'I'm not lying. What's "broken the Mercy?"'

The man stared at him. The silence lengthened. Lebasi didn't see the point in adding anything else. At last, Bennek blew out his cheeks. 'You don't know the law, and you the magistrate's son?'

'I know the law. They teach it in school. But what's the Mercy?'

'It's the reason we have to keep the law. Don't they tell you that in class?' Lebasi shook his head. Bennek rubbed his chin. 'No, I guess they don't, do they? Your ma and da tell you, when you're little and naughty, and when you're bigger and awkward. Big bad King Rednaxela will come get you, but not if you obey Riadsala's Mercy.'

Lebasi shook his head. He knew that Rednaxela was the king – they taught that in school – but Riadsala? He had never heard the name. 'My da's never told me that. And my ma...'

Bennek sighed. 'Yes, I know. You've got no ma to tell you anything. You have to make do with that southerner. He ought to be the one to explain it, for sure. He never did?'

Lebasi thought about it. He knew that Marrak never used two words where a nod would do instead. 'He doesn't tell me anything much. He just looks after the house.'

Bennek's 'Ha!' suggested he didn't agree with that, but Lebasi couldn't tell why.

'Well, your da's coming, so maybe he'll explain it now. But it's a pity you'll be hearing it for the first time in front of the council of elders.'

Lebasi's first thought was *good, my da's coming*. Then his heart speeded up. 'My da's coming – here?'

'Well, not here, he doesn't like it underground. "Bennek," he always says, "I'll live and die in the open air, thank you very much, and you can have the tunnels for yourself." But the courtroom's upstairs, that's where the council will be meeting, and he'll be there.'

'So he knows about this place?'

Bennek stared at him again, his frown deepening. 'This is the town jail, boy. Of course he knows about it, he's the magistrate.'

Lebasi's mouth was dry. His voice didn't sound right. 'And the snatchers –'

'Come because Xela tells them, yes. Just because he's out of town, doesn't mean he can't keep an eye on things, give orders if something needs doing. Somehow he can be in the next town and he still knows what's happening here, and tells people what to do about it. Doesn't have to send a runner, no one knows how he does it. And he's coming back in a hurry, they say. You must have done something really wrong.'

Lebasi leaned his head back against the cold stone wall. His father. His own father had ordered him to be taken while Marrak slept. Whatever it was couldn't wait until he came home, couldn't be dealt with by shouting across the eating-table.

There was a knock on the door. The voice of the second guard interrupted them. 'Bennek, it's daybreak. Better get him upstairs for the hearing.'

The keeper's knees clicked as he pulled himself to his feet. 'Come, lad. Maybe not knowing will make a difference, if they believe you.' He picked up the lantern and waited while Lebasi straightened his stiff, cold legs. 'Maybe it will, maybe it won't. We'll see.'

5
HEARING

As he filed along the corridor with one guard in front and one behind, Lebasi realised he didn't know Lodder either. He hadn't managed a good look at his face, and his broad back could belong to anyone, but the name meant nothing to him. Did the two of them live the whole of their lives in here, prisoners as well as keepers?

Dem... Demika, Demmor, Dempirren... there were quite a few names that could fit. His da would know. He shook himself. Of course his da would know. His da sent them.

They climbed the spiral stairs to a large room lit by many candles. He had counted to twenty-four, so this must be where they came in, on the same level as the Space. As he had remembered from the outside, there were no windows. He shivered, realising that night and day made no difference here. It was barely warmer than the cell. He only knew it was dawn because Lodder had said so.

Lodder led Lebasi towards a group of people at the far end of the room. It struck him that there had been raised voices a moment before and now there was silence. An argument had stopped and the arguers were watching him approach. He scanned the faces. No masks here, and no strangers. White hair or no hair, walking sticks, bent backs – they were the town elders, all twelve of them. Regular visitors to Xela's house, every one. Men and women who nodded to Lebasi in the street, greeted him by name. Now they were all staring at him. Lebasi recognised the way Marrak looked when he came across a large spider in the house – a mixture of fear and horror.

Bennek's question echoed in his brain. 'What have you done?'

The answer was still 'Nothing – I walked across a line that wasn't there, and I came back again'.

Lodder pointed to a chair on the left. As Lebasi sat down, the elders turned away from him and started talking again, discussing him as if he wasn't there. Lebasi looked for Tannaka, the oldest of all. He always joked when Lebasi asked him if he was really eighty years old, said he had stopped counting when he ran out of fingers and toes. But Lebasi knew he was clever, and he had always seemed kinder than the others.

He recognised the old man's voice, his words punctuated by wheezing. 'I tell you it isn't right. He's not of age. He should be represented.'

At this moment, he certainly seemed kinder than the rest. Lebasi could tell from the way they were standing, the way they were shaking their heads, that in this argument there were eleven against one.

'It is a clear breach of the Mercy, and he has to answer for it. An example must be made, a message sent.' It wasn't obvious who had said that, but it was apparent that the others agreed.

Tannaka raised his palms to call for quiet. The candlelight shone on his bald head. He glanced towards Lebasi, his deep-set eyes hidden below his bushy eyebrows. He tapped his stick on the ground and wagged a finger at the other elders. 'I do not dispute it. But a sixteen year-old boy, he should have his mother or his father to speak for him. And this boy cannot have either. And the punishments for breaking the Mercy – will you inflict them on a child?'

Lebasi pulled the blanket tighter. *An example, a message.* What were the punishments for breaking the Mercy? Who was the message for? Where was his da? Even if he had sent the snatchers, surely he would understand that it was nothing. Surely he would put it right.

Some of the elders nodded, but a woman's voice snapped, 'He is not a child. Look at him. He is old enough to know what he is doing, he is old enough to be punished for it as anyone else would be.'

Tannaka's eyebrows waggled. His mouth worked as if he was chewing something. Eventually he spoke, evenly and slowly, as if he was explaining something to a group of infants. 'We stand for the law, do we not? That is why we are here, is it not? If there is no law, there is no need to punish him. And in law, a youth is not a man until he is eighteen and has the tattoo.'

'Even so, Tannaka, there must be a hearing.' The voice came from behind – the elders looked up, Lebasi looked round – Xela had arrived. Even in the candlelight, Lebasi could tell that he had come straight from the road – his boots were dusty, he was wearing his travelling cloak. Lebasi caught a glimpse of pale daylight as Bennek closed the door behind him.

Xela did not meet Lebasi's eyes or return his hopeful smile. He handed his heavy coat to Bennek and stalked across towards the group of elders. He waved a hand impatiently. 'Places! We must do this quickly.'

As the elders arranged themselves on benches, six on either side of the room, Lodder gripped Lebasi's arm and manhandled him into another chair in the centre. Xela sat on a raised platform opposite him. Tannaka continued to protest.

'Magistrate, you cannot sit in judgment on your own son.'

At last Xela looked at Lebasi. He leaned forward, his elbows on his knees, and rested his chin on his hands. He rubbed his beard. 'You are right. I cannot. The decision must be made by the elders alone.'

There was an outbreak of muttering. Lebasi felt his stomach churning. Unless Tannaka was very persuasive, he was unlikely to overturn a majority of eleven to one. If Xela wouldn't even try to help... Lebasi opened his mouth to speak to his father, but could not think of any words. Xela lowered his eyebrows and shook his head, so slightly that it could have been a tic, but Lebasi took it as an order to be silent.

The second eldest, Sendra, stood up. She always spoke to him when she visited, asked him how he was, told him how much he'd grown. He guessed she was something like a grandmother would be to him, or even a great-grandmother.

She was questioning him now. Lebasi recognised her voice as the one that had argued with Tannaka. In the lamplight, Lebasi thought her nose resembled the beak of a hawk. He realised he was not concentrating properly: the cold, the lack of sleep, the shock had made his brain slow. Or else the something in the drink Bennek had given him.

She was speaking again, slower, impatiently tapping her palms together. 'Lebasi of Xela, do you understand the charge?'

'I'm sorry, I didn't hear. I haven't slept. I was taken from my bed in the middle of the night...'

There was a murmur of concern from some of the elders, but not from Sendra. She interrupted: 'Lebasi of Xela, it is reported that yesterday shortly after noon you stepped across the borderline between this town and the town to the south-west. Is this true?'

'Yes, but...'

'That is all.' She turned towards Xela. 'It is proven by his admission. We move to decide the sentence.'

'But it was nothing!' Lebasi protested.

He stared from face to face. Some of them were shaking their heads, some were studying the floor. Sendra carried on addressing his father. 'There is the possibility of making allowance for his youth, but nevertheless the law requires an example to be made.'

Lebasi turned to look at Xela himself. He had not moved. He was still leaning on his knees, staring at Lebasi. He gave no sign of having heard Sendra. After a long pause, she started again, 'Magistrate, we – '

He sat up straight and raised his hand. His words seemed to struggle out of his throat. 'I hear you, Sendra,' he croaked. 'But I will also hear what my son has to say.'

Several of the elders stood up – not quickly, given their age, but the effort they made underlined the strength of their objections.

'It is irregular –'

'It is an admitted breach –'

'There is no defence –'

Tannaka's low voice cut across their babble. 'Blood and bone, you are Xessans, are you not? Will you impose the king's law over common justice? Let the boy speak.'

As they sat down, muttering to each other, Lebasi tried to order his thoughts. His mind was usually so sharp, so ready with the answers in class, so able to remember the smallest detail of what happened when or what someone had said. This was only yesterday, but how could he explain it? Who could he blame but himself? He wasn't going to point the finger at Faya. She had teased him, but he had risen to it. He wouldn't mind if Sammas and Ruffur got into trouble, but he wasn't going to be the cause of it. And anyway, they had done less than Faya. On their own, they could never have goaded him into crossing the line.

Who had told Xela? The thought formed in Lebasi's mind and got in the way of the words he wanted to find.

'I... I just walked over for a moment and straight back again.'

There was silence. Lebasi realised how lame it sounded: one of the elders had said there was no defence, and this was hardly even an attempt at one.

'What does it matter? It's just a line, there's nothing there. One side's the same as the other.' He almost added, 'That's what Perra said,' but decided to leave him out of it.

There was still silence, but it was different. It was as if sound had been sucked out of the room, as if a thunderclap in the room would disappear into the hole that he had made. The elders all stared at Lebasi, including Sendra and Tannaka, both standing. Then, one by one, they turned towards Xela. Lebasi remembered Bennek's words: his da should have explained. Maybe they would blame Xela for not telling him, instead of him, for his lack of understanding. But that was a crazy thought.

Tannaka spoke first, his voice sounding thin and old in the overpowering hush. 'Xela, how can he not know?'

Xela rose from his chair slowly, stiffly. He looked down at the floor, then ran his eyes along the two lines of elders. 'History is forbidden, you know that. We do not dwell on the past. Perhaps I apply that more exactly than many of you. He knows the law, and he knows that he is required to obey the law.'

Tannaka protested again. 'But a citizen must understand the consequences of breaking a law, to know what is serious and what is – '

Xela made a chopping motion with his hand. 'All law is serious. All breaches have consequences. That should be enough.'

Tannaka spread his hands in mute disagreement. Xela stepped down from his dais and took two steps towards Lebasi's chair. He shook his head. 'I am sorry, Lebasi, but the law applies to all citizens equally. The court must decide on a punishment.'

Lebasi reached out his hands towards his father, his eyes watering. Xela turned his back and returned to his seat.

The elders gathered in a group at the side of the room and

argued. Lebasi sat staring at his father, who rested his forehead on his fingertips, his eyes cast down. He found his mind wandering to how Xela had been when he was little: taking care of him – picking him up when he fell, cleaning grazed knees, plucking splinters out of his hands. Spending time together, playing games. Xela had even taught him a special language for secret conversations. It sounded nothing like the ordinary speech that people used in the street, but it wasn't nonsense. There were particular words for everything: Lebasi had to put them in the right order, use different forms for singular, plural, past, present and future. He loved it: apart from anything else, it was something that existed just between the two of them, a demonstration of his father's full attention. He didn't get that any more. Except perhaps now, when he didn't want it... what if he said something in that language, to remind Xela of how things used to be? He tried to call some words to mind.

Tannaka turned from the group with a grunt, waving his hand dismissively. That wasn't a good sign. Sendra stayed standing as the others took their places on the benches.

'Magistrate, we must send a message that we are upholding the law, a message that will keep the soldiers away.' Xela nodded. 'We have taken into account the fact that he is not of age. If he was older, then we would recommend six moons in the cells, or fifty strokes of the stick.'

Lebasi bit his lip. Consequences. For walking over a line, five paces of ground there and back, half a year in the dark? Or a thrashing that severe? He'd seen a man being given ten strokes for stealing, and that was horrible. Fifty...

Sendra turned to face him. 'We say that for a sixteen-year old, the punishment is two moons in the cells, or twenty strokes. It is for the boy to choose.'

Xela was balling his hands into fists and releasing them, but he said nothing. Lebasi's fear gave way to anger. 'Da, how can you –'

'I have no choice.' Xela's anger matched his, overwhelmed it. 'I cannot say to another citizen, "here is your punishment, accept it," and then say to my own son that he doesn't have to do the same. The elders have decided. You must choose.'

His fist hitting his palm made a sound like a whip cracking. Lebasi flinched at the image it conjured, but the beating would be done and it would be over. Two moons in Bennek's care, fifty-six days and nights not knowing which was which?

He stood up and spoke through clenched teeth. 'I'll take the stick.'

'Very well,' said Sendra. 'Lodder, you know what to do.'

A strange, wordless noise came from Xela's mouth, somewhere between a groan and a roar. Everyone turned towards him. He growled, 'I am not going to stand here and watch that animal beat my son.'

Lebasi took a deep breath, filling his lungs with hope. No one moved. The moment seem to stretch on and on.

Xela broke the silence, his quiet voice now empty of emotion. 'I will do it myself.'

6
SENTENCE

Lebasi could not speak. Even if he could have found a voice, he would not have been heard over the babble of the elders' protests. 'Magistrate, you cannot –' 'Surely you will not –' 'It is not –'

'Not,' was all Lebasi could think. His own da was going to beat him, twice the flogging the thief got. For stepping over an imaginary line.

Xela was pushing through the elders. 'I know the force the law requires. No more, no less. Lodder enjoys it too much.'

Hands took hold of Lebasi's arms. He glanced to right and left – Bennek on one side, on the other Lodder, who looked disappointed.

'Come on, lad, let's get it over with,' muttered Bennek, who seemed more sympathetic than his colleague. He pulled Lebasi around towards the door.

'No!' Xela's shout came from behind them. 'We will do it here.' Bennek and Lodder turned Lebasi round again.

Sendra objected: 'Magistrate, a punishment must be public.'

The pulse throbbing in Lebasi's ears drowned out what Xela replied. The men led him to the side of the room. Bennek gestured to him to raise his arms, and Lodder pulled his shirt over his head. Lebasi shivered: the courtroom suddenly seemed colder than the cell. Bennek pointed to a pair of iron rings hanging down the wall on chains, almost as high as he could reach. Lebasi took hold of one in each hand and closed his eyes. A rough rope was being wound around his fingers so he couldn't let go. The bones in his legs seemed to have dissolved. He had to concentrate on standing up – he couldn't fall, but he didn't want to hang there by his arms. He tried to think of a story, a legend that would help him: Xessus the hero had suffered worse than this and come out victorious in the end. 'In a year without a number,' he recited in his head, as all the Xessus legends began. But the details were playing hide-and-seek, as they had in the cell. He opened his eyes and saw his father's dusty boots stop beside him.

'I am truly sorry for this, Lebasi. I will try to explain to you why it must be done. Later.'

Someone out of sight handed Xela the stick. The thickness of a man's thumb, two-thirds of a man's height, with a carved grip. Xela examined it. He roared at the guard, 'Fire and ice, man, take it away and clean it.'

That will be blood, thought Lebasi. *That's why they've made me take my shirt off.* Marrak would be cross at the extra laundry. The ridiculous thought almost made him laugh. He could feel a fit of giggles coming on, as if someone was tickling him – that was absurd...

The stick was back. Xela nodded. Bennek put his head beside Lebasi's. 'You'll want this to bite on, lad,' he whispered, and offered him a length of rope. Lebasi nodded, opened his mouth and clamped his teeth on it. It reminded him of the gag.

'One,' came his father's voice, and he screwed up his eyes. Sparks and lightning flashed in the dark. He realised he had shouted something, but he didn't know what. The rope had dropped onto the floor. It felt as if his back had been cut in half. Nineteen more? And Lodder was worse? Someone put the rope back in his mouth. He braced himself for the second. He wasn't going to cry out again.

'Two.' Just below the first. Just the same force, the same pain. Lebasi bit down hard.

'Three.' He sagged forward, then pulled himself upright again.

There was a hammering noise. At first Lebasi thought it was only the pain in his head, but it seemed the others could hear it too. Xela stopped. The elders were muttering again. Someone was shouting something from the other side of the door. Lebasi heard the sound of bolts, then the door crashing open.

'Magistrate, stop!' Perra's voice.

Lebasi's knees buckled. He hung suspended from his hands, his face pressed against the cold stone wall. He had been ready for the next blow, but not for the relief that maybe, just maybe, it wouldn't be coming. He listened to the voices behind his back.

Bennek first, his reedy voice filled with fear: 'I'm sorry, magistrate, he said it was really important, and when I opened up he pushed past me.'

Sendra, shouting: 'That's what a bolted door is for, you idiot. No one is allowed to come in here. Get him out.'

Perra's even tone: 'I'm not leaving.'

Sendra again: 'Bennek, get some watchmen in here.'

He heard feet retreating, the door closing. The pain in his back was no longer shattering. He opened his eyes and twisted his neck to see what was happening.

Lodder had hold of Perra's arms. He was surely strong enough to struggle free, but he didn't seem to want to. Xela walked slowly across to face Perra, holding the stick horizontal in his two hands. The elders all gathered behind him as if needing a barrier against the intruder.

Perra stood very straight, making himself a little taller than the magistrate. His voice was quiet but even. 'You can't punish Lebasi. It was my fault, not his.'

Lebasi took a gulp of air.

Sendra's voice again: 'Sentence has been passed. It is too late.'

Lebasi breathed out again.

Tannaka stepped forward and put his finger so close to her nose Lebasi thought he might poke her. 'In Xessus' name, woman, have you no heart? Hear him, and if it's true, we cannot carry out an unjust punishment.'

Xela sounded more in control of himself than he had throughout the hearing. 'I will hear him. But Perra, how can this be? There seems to be no doubt that it was Lebasi who stepped across the border, not you.'

Lebasi saw Perra glance towards him, then shake his arms to loosen the grip of the guard. He stuck out his chin and his chest. 'I pushed him.'

The memory spun around Lebasi's head. The pain, the lack of sleep, Bennek's drink all confused him – but surely that wasn't what had happened? Perra had been lying on the grass...

Xela was asking, 'Why would you do that?'

'For a joke.' The elders burst into an angry hubbub.

'Silence!' roared Xela. To Lebasi's surprise, they instantly obeyed. Xela took two steps towards Perra, tapping the stick against his palm. He spoke very evenly and slowly – Lebasi knew that tone: it meant that he was holding down a barely controllable rage. 'For a joke, you decided to break Riadsala's Mercy? No, not you – for a joke, you decided to make it seem that someone else, that my son had done so?'

'All right,' Perra replied, without any sign that he was afraid of or even noticed the magistrate's fury. 'I wanted your son – the magistrate's son – to see that the law was nonsense. I wanted to show him so that maybe he could show you. And if you're going to beat someone for that nonsense, it ought to be me, not him.'

Lebasi wasn't sure why Perra was doing this – he had certainly told Lebasi that the border was only a line in their heads, but as for pushing him over it... true or not, he felt a rush of gratitude. For whatever reason, he was offering to take Lebasi's punishment. But he couldn't let that happen. He had to tell his da.

Xela seemed to be thinking about it. He took another step towards Perra and leaned forward, studying his face. 'And what did you hope to gain by getting Lebasi to show me that the border is nonsense?'

'I hoped you would change the law, because it's meaningless.'

Xela swung the stick in front of him and leant on it like a staff. He tapped his thumb against his mouth. 'Perra, you are either very stupid, or very clever. From what I know of you – and have no illusions, I know a great deal about you – I am inclined to think you are not stupid. You know quite well that I cannot change the law. You know quite well that the effect of breaking the Mercy is that the soldiers might return. For some reason of your own, you want that to happen. I cannot tell why.'

Cattonna, one of the other female elders, protested. 'He cannot want the soldiers back. It was terrible when –'

Tannaka interrupted. 'He cannot remember how it was. He was only a boy when they were here. He's only a boy still, if he wants to see them return. For what – the excitement?'

Perra shook his head. 'I don't want the soldiers back. But why do we have to follow all these rules? I want to be able to greet the donkeymen from the next town properly, not just pass things to them over the border, never touching so much as a finger. I want to invite them back to see my house, maybe go to visit them. Is that too much to ask?'

Xela sighed. 'You know that you would have to put that to the king, not to me. And yes, the king would say it is too much. Even asking it might bring the end of the Mercy, or bring the soldiers back.' He nodded to Lodder. 'Bind him.'

Lebasi was surprised that Perra allowed Lodder to tie his hands behind his back. Xela pointed, and Lodder led him to the chair Lebasi had occupied earlier.

'Please free my son, and sit him by Perra.' Bennek untied Lebasi's hands from the rings and brought him another chair from the back of the room. Lebasi shivered again, and Lodder handed him his shirt. He pulled it over his head and sat down gingerly, careful not to lean his back against the wood. His tunic sticking and unsticking from his skin was painful enough.

Xela waved the elders back to their benches and marched to the dais. He sat in the same posture as before, with his elbows on his knees and his chin on his hands.

Lebasi leaned to his left and whispered, 'Thank you. But you didn't...'

Perra muttered back, 'It's the least I could do. Keep quiet and trust me.'

Xela clapped his hands together for quiet. He stared hard at Perra, then turned to Lebasi. 'Son, is what Perra says true? Did he push you?'

Lebasi hesitated. It would save his skin – literally – but... 'No. He was sitting on the grass. I was nowhere near him.'

Perra started to speak, but Xela held out his hand to stop him. 'Even though you have heard – and felt – what the punishment is, and know that the punishment may shift to Perra if what he says is accepted by the court?'

Lebasi sat on his hands. He did not trust his voice, so he nodded.

Xela stood up. 'Perra, do you hold to your version?'

'I do.'

'Very well. This court of elders has already stated the sentence for an adult – six moons in the cells, or fifty strokes. The court must now decide if that punishment is to be given to Perra, or if Lebasi will receive the remaining seventeen. I cannot pass that judgment.'

He sat down again and rubbed his eyes with both hands.

The elders huddled together. Lebasi clenched his teeth. It wasn't right, but he didn't have the strength to beg them to come to the correct decision. He felt his heart pounding, and each beat throbbed in the bruises on his back.

Tannaka's voice interrupted his thoughts. 'Magistrate, Perra has come forward unbidden. His testimony is not forced. We can only accept it as the truth.'

Perra stood up, stumbling because his hands were tied. 'I choose the stick.'

Xela shook his head. 'You do not get a choice. Bennek, take him down. We will see you again when summer ends.'

Lebasi looked round to find that the keeper had returned with several watchmen, dressed in their dark grey uniforms. Some of them were flicking their eyes towards him awkwardly and quickly looking away – had they been the ones wearing cloaks and masks in the night? They surrounded Perra and led him away to the spiral staircase. Lebasi followed them with his eyes, wishing he could do something for the man who had saved him. Beyond them, he saw that Bennek had left the outer door ajar. He glanced back at his father, who would have given him another seventeen strokes. He scanned the faces of the elders, none of whom would meet his eye. The guards had gone, Xela was ten paces away, the elders would be slow. He jumped to his feet and ran. He didn't know if he was now free to go, and he didn't care. He wanted to be anywhere but in a room with his father.

He didn't look back. He didn't try to pull the door closed behind him – it looked heavy and would slow him down. He slipped through the opening and kept running. Outside, the sun was shining, the sky was blue, a hundred paces away in the centre of the Space the children were gathering for their lessons.

A normal day.

7
AMBUSH

Lebasi sprinted along the avenue to the southern downstreet. As he rounded the corner he allowed himself a quick glance over his shoulder. Xela himself, and only Xela, fifty paces behind. He was faster than his da, he was sure – but the first steps on the cobblestones reminded him that his feet were bare. He didn't care about the pain – he had already coped with more than that – but he would slip. There was an alleyway between two buildings on the right. After years of exploring on his own on freedays when there was nothing else to do, he knew every twist and turn, every doorway and what was behind it. He reckoned he could lose his da. He ran straight across the street and through the opening.

'Lebasi, stop!' Xela's shout was cut off by the stone walls. In thirty paces there was a fork. He turned left. In twenty paces, another: right. Right again, left, left. His da was still calling for him, and Lebasi wasn't far enough ahead – Xela was a better runner than he had thought. He was getting a stitch, he was going to have to stop. He dodged sideways through a doorway into the overgrown garden of an empty house. The weeds had taken over, but the stone-flagged path around the border was still fairly clear. He ducked down and scuttled to the back of the building, keeping his head below the level of the greenery.

He heard the sound of his father's boots, growing louder,

stopping just outside. Xela was gasping, coughing. Lebasi took soft, silent steps, trying to judge which way he would start around the garden. This was another childhood game. He strained his ears for clues.

'Lebasi, I need to talk to you. Come out.'

He kept low and quiet.

'I'm sorry. I need to explain.'

Lebasi didn't want to hear anything Xela had to say.

There was that whip-cracking noise of Xela banging his hands together. 'I'm not going to play hide-and-seek with you, son. I'll see you later at home.'

Lebasi listened to the footsteps fading away. He waited, trying to think of a way to prove Xela wrong. He was good at telling himself stories to pass the time – often stories about leaving the town, going far away – but he knew they weren't real. In the end he would have to go home. He could hide for a while, but he'd have to hide from everyone. There was no one who would help him to escape the town walls. He might steal some food, but if he was caught he'd get the stick again for that, and no Perra to step in.

Why had Perra done that? Lebasi imagined sitting in that dark, cold cell where he had spent half a night, just starting half a year. The unfairness of it nagged at him. He realised that feeling would only get worse. It would be in his mind when he woke up and when he went to bed and all the time between, every day for the next one hundred and sixty-eight days. And afterwards. He decided he had to do something about it. Another seventeen strokes would be better than telling himself forever that he was a coward. Better than knowing it.

He heard more footsteps out in the alleyway. Perhaps Xela had changed his mind and come back. He ran to the doorway and stepped out – to find himself face to face with Sammas. The boy seemed more surprised than he was. He opened his mouth as if to say something, but no words came out. Lebasi was sure that being within an arm's length of Sammas was a bad idea, and didn't want to hear anything he had to say, so he turned and ran. Sammas didn't make a grab – at the corner Lebasi glanced back and saw him only jogging in pursuit – he turned his head and ran straight into Ruffur. It was like hitting a tree. He rocked back on his heels, winded, and felt Ruffur's hands close around his elbows.

Sammas put his hand on Lebasi's shoulder and said, 'Let's go somewhere private to talk.'

Lebasi found himself once more being forcibly marched along. At least he could see where he was going this time. They turned into a deserted back yard, smaller and not as overgrown as the one he had hidden in before. Ruffur spun him around and shoved him against the wall. In spite of himself, he cried out as his back hit the rough stonework. His eyes watered. Ruffur lifted Lebasi up to bring their faces level, then leaned his arm against Lebasi's chest to hold

him there, crushing the breath out of him.

Sammas poked his head beside Ruffur's. His breath stank. Lebasi tried to turn his head away but Sammas grabbed his chin. He flicked his eyes from one to the other. He was surprised to see how red their faces were, their eyes wide, their nostrils flaring. This wasn't teasing, like yesterday at the border. They weren't having fun, they were furiously angry.

Sammas was breathing harder than the short jog along the alleyway required. He was grinding his teeth. 'Rabor's our uncle, Basi. He's not happy with you. He reckons he's going to get grief from your da. Might have the guild taken away from him. He said you'd be sorry if you told.'

Lebasi opened his eyes wide. 'Me?' It was almost funny. But how could he explain that he'd said nothing and still been taken by

the snatchers and beaten by his father, before they either knocked him out or he fainted?

Ruffur pressed harder on his chest. He spoke very slowly, his voice lower than ever. 'You – broke – the – law.'

Lebasi managed to gasp out, 'That was your idea, or Faya's –'

Sammas reached up to slap him on the face. 'Not that law, idiot. You told. We hate reporters. You're going to pay for it.'

Lebasi could hardly make a sound. He shook his head. There was a whooshing sound in his ears.

Sammas sneered at him. 'Not so high and mighty now, are you? Your big important dada can't help you here. And if you go running to him again, telling tales –'

Ruffur barked a laugh. 'But Sammie, we're in school, Ivar saw us. And you know how he can't keep track of who's there and who isn't. So if little Basi gets hurt, he must've slipped on the cobblestones, poor darling.' Sammas started to pat his face with the palm of his hand, again and again, each time a little harder. Lebasi felt sick. He had no idea how to stop them, and there was no way out of Ruffur's grip.

Spots danced in front of Lebasi's eyes. 'It wasn't me. I don't know who – *oooff!*'

Ruffur punched him in the stomach. 'Liar! Who else would it be? It wasn't us, and it wasn't Faya. And how else did Xela know so fast?'

'Maybe the men from the other town...'

Ruffur leaned forward again so their noses were almost touching. He opened his mouth to say something. Lebasi could almost see his brain working through his eyes.

There was a loud *crack:* Sammas fell forwards, shouting, holding his head. A moment later, *thwack:* Ruffur lurched sideways, letting go of Lebasi, who collapsed in a heap on the floor. He looked up at... an old woman, bent, grey-haired, waving a walking stick at the big boys – either of them could've picked her up and thrown her over the wall. Her eyes glittered in her wrinkled face. She sprayed spit as she roared. Lebasi could see she only had half her teeth.

'You little bullies' – not true, they were bigger than her – 'how dare you pick on someone smaller, two to one, you're a disgrace' – *thwack*, hitting Sammas across the back – 'and I know who you are, I'll be telling' – *tokkk*, bringing the cane down on Ruffur's head – 'your fathers and mothers' – *ooofff*, as she prodded Sammas in the stomach – 'and they'll be right ashamed of you.' She faced them, brandishing the stick like a sword. The boys picked themselves up, uncertain, looking at her, looking at each other, wondering. Surely they wouldn't hurt an old woman, but they could, they might... then she stepped forward and growled. They turned and ran out of the gate. Their footsteps echoed between the stone walls and faded away. The woman put her hands on her waist, leaned back – which, bent as she was, almost made her fall over – and laughed loudly.

'Ha! Bullies is cowards, always is.' She looked down at Lebasi and winked. 'No match for me.' He stood up too quickly, felt dizzy, and sat back down. He took a deep breath before trying again. He started to thank her, but she waved a hand and chuckled. 'Oh, I haven't had such fun in years.' She peered at him closely. 'I'm Nomara. You're Lebasi of Xela, aren't you?' He nodded. She put a hand on his shoulder and directed him across the alleyway, through another gateway into a small garden. 'My house,' she explained. 'I was watering my flowers and I couldn't help hearing. Now rest a moment and get your breath back.'

Lebasi sat on a chair by her garden table and let his heart slow down. She leaned on her stick, studying him piercingly through bright blue eyes which seemed younger than her face. After a long pause, she scratched her head and shook it sadly. 'Your poor mother. I was very fond of your mother, you know. Lovely little girl. To be taken away like that...' She looked over Lebasi's head, her eyes distant.

He frowned. Nomara had jumped to a completely different subject. He knew old people sometimes carried on a conversation in their heads and forgot to share it all.

For a moment, the pain in his back, Perra sitting in the cells, Ruffur and Sammas all disappeared from his mind. 'My mother?' he prompted, hoping Nomara would tell him more.

She sighed. 'What's gone is gone, lad. No use mourning the sunset, as they say. Sun'll come up tomorrow, whether you cry or smile.'

'But you remember her, you could...'

She held up a finger. 'I'm sorry, dear, it's in the past. We don't dwell on the past, you know that. Speak to your da. If it's right for you to hear, Xela will tell you.'

Lebasi shook his head. That didn't seem likely.

She brushed her hands together as if to get rid of the subject. 'Greet your da for me. Nice lad, Xela. I've always said so.' She leaned forward and spoke quietly. 'Tell him people are complaining, in private. I'm not one of his eyes and ears, but I hear things. The king wants too much. Xela mayn't be as well informed as he thinks. Tell him to watch for storms out of season. There's foolish talk about something happening, midsummertime.' She nodded twice for emphasis, then went into the house without another word. Lebasi decided there was no point asking for more explanation of any of the surprising things she had said. He called a thankyou to her retreating back and put his head out into the alley. He found no sign of the bullies, and started for home, stopping at each corner to check.

He worked his way back to the eastern downstreet, dodging quickly across the avenues as he descended the hill. A couple of people shouted after him, but no one gave chase. No one seemed to pay special attention – they probably thought he was just an ordinary truant. In the alley that ran alongside his own garden, he stopped to think.

He'd have to face his da. He'd have to tell him Perra had been lying and take the consequences. But now it seemed that wouldn't be the end of it. He'd been in a few fights with Ruffur and Sammas before, always in one of the general battles that sometimes happened on a freeday. He knew they didn't like him because he was clever in school and they weren't. He'd thought they were mean to everybody. But this was much more than that: they were angry, and they thought they were in the right. Surely they wouldn't let it drop? It didn't seem likely that they would listen long enough for him to persuade them that he wasn't the cause of any trouble that might be coming to Rabor.

He tossed a stone across the street, shaking his head. They'd been right about one thing – he couldn't tell on them to Xela. 'Some boys attacked me, Da, but I was rescued by an old woman who could be my granma, if I had a granma. And she suggested I ask you to explain why I haven't got any family, and what happened to my ma?' It was almost funny.

He wondered if he should have stayed the other side of the line.

8
FAYA

He realised he was hungry. He hoped Xela was out, maybe Marrak too – then he could sneak something from the kitchen and go to his room. That thought brought back the last time he had been there, and he shivered. Would he get to sleep so easily tonight? Still, he had no choice. He turned the last corner in the alleyway. Someone was crouching by the opening onto the downstreet, looking out. Someone clearly waiting – surely for him. But it wasn't a watchman, and it wasn't Ruffur or Sammas. He padded closer, making no sound.

'Faya?'

Two days ago, he would have been pleased to see her. Now, he found his hands had clenched into fists, and his mouth set in a hard line. What was she doing here? She was as bad as the bullies – worse, because she wasn't as stupid as them. She was the reason for the bruises on his back. She must have known what she was talking him into. Her ma and da would have told her about the Mercy.

But as she turned around, there was another feeling close behind – maybe she had come to say sorry. Maybe she had been impressed by what he'd done. Maybe...

She jumped to her feet and ran towards him, but she wasn't smiling. She glanced over her shoulder. Lebasi wondered if she was checking that no one would see her talking to him.

'What happened? Where's Perra?'

He asked at the same time, 'What are you doing here?'

'Perra's my cousin,' she told him. 'He lives next door. He woke me up before first light to say you'd been taken by the snatchers and he had to get you out. I played truant to see if you came home.'

'You know about the snatchers?'

She stared at him. 'You don't?'

'Not before last night.' Something about what she'd said puzzled him, but he couldn't quite grasp what it was.

'I've never seen them, but everyone knows about them. Not who they are, though. They could be anyone, your neighbour, your friend's da. They wear masks.'

Above ground, Lebasi found he could smile at the memory of the skull under the hood. Out in the daylight, it was ridiculous. 'They try not to say anything, either. One of them has a name beginning with Dem. Any idea who that might be?'

Faya hesitated for a moment before shaking her head – just long enough for Lebasi to guess that she thought she knew, but wasn't going to say.

'They took me to the cells. I suppose you know about them, too?'

She stared at him. 'Your da's the magistrate. How do you not know anything about anything?'

Lebasi found he had banged his hands together in just the same way Xela did. 'Because no one tells me anything about anything, that's how. Not my da, not the teachers, not anyone else. How am I expected to guess?'

Faya whistled softly, shaking her head. 'How did you get out? Perra reckoned you might be down there for a while.'

Lebasi realised what had been bothering him. 'How did Perra know about the snatchers? It was the middle of the night.'

Faya opened her mouth to answer, then closed it again. She

frowned, tapped her fingers on her chin, and shook her head. 'I don't know. But Perra's got a lot of friends who tell him things. Maybe someone saw the snatchers taking you and let him know.'

Lebasi remembered how he had climbed the downstreet hoping someone would send for Marrak or his da. Maybe she was right, maybe someone had sent for Perra instead.

Faya interrupted his thoughts. 'So... how did you get out?'

Lebasi guessed no apology was coming. His anger bubbled up again. He wanted her to understand what she had done, what she had put him through. After all, if Perra was going to be punished for making him cross the line – when he hadn't done so – then Faya should be in trouble too.

'They had a hearing. All the elders were there. They gave me a choice of two moons or twenty strokes.' He was pleased with her reaction. He put it in his memory with the look on her face as she caught the stone.

'I chose the stick. And I'd had three strokes when Perra burst into the courtroom and told them he pushed me over the line. I don't know why he said that. But my da said if that was true, it was him that had to be punished, not me. The elders gave him six moons in the cells.'

Faya stamped her foot. 'That's outrageous! Half a year underground – they can't...' Her voice faded. She gave him a scornful look. 'And you just sat there and let him do that?'

Lebasi protested, 'I tried, but he told me to shut up. Said it was the least he could do. I wasn't in any shape to argue then. But I'm on my way to tell my da I'll have the other seventeen, and he should let Perra go.'

He enjoyed hearing her gasp. 'Really? You'd do that?'

He was glad he had told her. Now he'd have to go through with it. He had been worried he'd lose his nerve when face to face

with his da.

'Yes, now that I've thought about it. The cells are horrible – I couldn't stand him being stuck down there.'

She was silent for a moment. Her eyes flicked towards his back. Lebasi considered whether to take his shirt off to show her what she'd brought on him, but decided against it. With any luck, her imagination would be worse.

'So your da didn't defend you? He wouldn't make an exception for his own son?'

Lebasi laughed scornfully. 'My da hit me with the stick. And it didn't feel like he was doing me any favours.'

She whistled. 'Maybe we've got something in common, then.'

'What?'

'We both hate your da.'

Lebasi raised his eyebrows. 'What's he ever done to you?'

'You remember my brother Lakim?'

Lebasi nodded. 'Yes, from school. I haven't seen him – he's not in the cells, is he?'

'No. Worse. He's gone to join the army.'

'The army? Where?'

'Away. Beyond the borders.'

Lebasi thought that didn't sound so bad. Away from here might be better, for him at least. Perhaps he could join the army. Faya was still speaking.

'The bravest and the best, they call them, the ones who go to be the king's soldiers. When they turn eighteen. At the beginning of this year, Lakim went.'

'How long – when will he come back?'

'Never. You really don't know anything, do you? When someone's gone to the army, they've gone. Haven't you noticed people who aren't around any more?'

Lebasi started to shake his head. But as he thought about it, names and faces came into his head: boys who were the fastest runners, the best fighters, boys he looked up to when he was small. It was hard to notice someone not being there until Faya made him remember. He changed the shake into a nod. 'I suppose so.' He shrugged. 'Anyway, what's that got to do with my da?'

The answer flashed into his mind a moment before she said the words. He closed his eyes and covered his face with his hands.

'Xela chooses the best and bravest.'

9
XELA

Xela was still out. Marrak said nothing when Lebasi put his head around the kitchen door: he raised his head, nodded, and carried on chopping onions. He seemed no more surprised by a brief explanation of the reason Lebasi was not at school. Lebasi realised Marrak must have known something was wrong when there was no one to eat breakfast – but the news that the snatchers had been in the house while he slept did not appear to alarm him, nor the fact that Lebasi had been held in the cells and brought before the court of elders. The agent said nothing at all – he barely seemed interested – so Lebasi skipped over his punishment and his escape, and asked for the meal he had missed. He took the plate of bread, ham, cheese and dried fruit up to his room. He paused in the doorway, taking in the brightness of the plastered walls, the clean white mattress on the bed, the plain table and chair by the window, the blue sky outside. He tried to fix that picture over the memory of how it had been in the night.

When he had finished eating, Lebasi lay face down on his bed and counted his heartbeats. He could feel each one, distinct and strong, as it pulsed through the bruises on his back. He was trying to blot out everything else – the pain, and the knowledge of what his father did. Xela never liked to answer questions: now Lebasi knew why. He meant to sort out the order of things to say to Xela when he returned. Instead, he fell into an exhausted sleep.

He was woken by the tread of feet on the stairs. One man on the landing made more noise than six men had done in the night. The steps halted outside his door. He kept his eyes closed, his head turned towards the window. He knew he had to talk to Xela. He'd told Faya he would, but he wasn't ready.

'Son, I –'

'Leave me alone.'

There was a pause. Lebasi normally tried not to aggravate his father's temper, but today he didn't care. What more could Xela do to him?

'All right, I understand. But I've brought something for your back.'

Xela's voice sounded different but familiar: level, without a trace of temper, full of patience and understanding. How he used to be...

But it was all a mask, a lie. Lebasi snapped, 'Go away.'

'Come on, I know it hurts. This will take the pain away and make sure it doesn't get worse. I was a doctor before I was a magistrate, you know.'

Lebasi was so surprised he forgot himself and looked round. 'You never told me that.'

Xela was standing in the doorway in the light tunic he wore around the house, holding a tray with two bowls and a cloth. He raised his eyebrows. 'No? It seems there are too many things I never told you. If you let me clean your bruises I'll explain some of them.' He took a step forward. 'And if you don't want to talk to me, you don't have to. Just take your shirt off.'

Curiosity overcame the worst of Lebasi's anger. Xela never explained anything. He didn't trust himself to speak, so he bared his back and put his head on the pillow, his eyes closed. He waited for the pain of something touching his skin, and grasped the sides of the bed in preparation. The stick had been more than he could bear in silence, but this time he was determined not to cry out.

He heard Xela putting the tray down and moving the chair. A clean smell of herbs rose from one of the bowls. He felt the light pressure of a damp cloth, warm and soothing, which was... not painful. He relaxed his grip. Xela worked in silence, and Lebasi wondered if he had changed his mind about explaining. After the cloth came something cool which Xela put on with his fingers. Lebasi was surprised by the gentleness of his hands.

'There. Now you have to lie still, if you can, for a little while to let it dry.' Lebasi heard Xela shift his weight in the chair and drum his fingers on his chin. He could picture him doing it: he was choosing a legend of Xessus the hero to tell Lebasi at bedtime. He would start at any moment.

'In a year *with* a number,' Xela began. He must have been having the same memory. The unusual opening made Lebasi raise his head. Xela gently pushed him back onto the pillow. 'Don't move, you'll disturb the balm.' He put his hand on Lebasi's shoulder. 'Yes, this isn't a story of the hero, it's a piece of history. We aren't allowed to tell it, but it seems that everyone else does.'

'And why didn't you?'

Xela sighed. 'Plenty of reasons. Not because it was against the law. Mainly because my own da told me the story, and it was clear to me that it filled him with nothing but hatred. History – real stories about what happened in the past – they can do that, you know. History is dangerous. It's why it's banned.'

Lebasi lifted his head again. 'Your da?' He was sure that Xela had never mentioned any other member of his family before. It was as Sammas had said – Xela and Lebasi were alone, as if they had grown from seeds.

Xela took no notice of his interest, or deliberately ignored it. 'Two things you are allowed to know: the name of the king and the number of the year. This year is –'

'Eight hundred and seventy-seven.'

Xela nodded. 'That many years since the crowning of the first king. The stories of the hero start without a number to signify that they are even older than that. But this story is from around seven hundred and forty, nearly a hundred and forty years ago.'

Lebasi tried to imagine why that could matter. Tannaka was eighty. If there had been someone Tannaka's age when Tannaka was born... but Xela was speaking.

'There was a rebellion against the king, starting here in this town and spreading across the whole of Xessus. The king then had the same name as the king now – Rednaxela. Third king of that name. He was a great general in his time, but he'd been injured in wars away to the south, so he sent others to try to deal with the rebellion. The Xessans had a leader, Dennara, who was lucky and clever in equal measure, and they beat off two of the king's armies. Rednaxela was furious. He sent his eighteen-year old son Riadsala with an order to burn Xessus to the ground, leave not a stone standing on a stone, not a man, woman, child or beast alive. If he wanted to be king, he had to put the rebels down, destroy them.'

'And he won.'

'He did.'

'But he didn't do what the king ordered.'

'No. He was young, he wasn't twisted by old war wounds, he saw the beaten army as people, not enemies. It was a brave thing, to defy his father, even if Rednaxela was three eightnights hard march away to the south. Dennara asked for mercy, and mercy he got.'

'The Mercy –' breathed Lebasi.

'Of Riadsala,' Xela completed. 'To give it its proper name. He made Dennara swear to it on behalf of his people. He said that a breach of the Mercy would bring down the wrath of Rednaxela: Xessus would burn.'

'What did he promise?'

'Dennara and those who wanted to go with him were granted the freedom of the wilderness. At the edge of Xessus, the edge of the kingdom, there is a wall – you've heard of it in stories: it's the Westwall that the hero built in a year without a number. The legends may be true or not, but the wall is real enough. Dennara and about five hundred men, women and children went out through the gate. Nothing and no one has come back through it since. The Mercy for those who chose to stay was this: they were to pay heavy taxes every year to the king. A governor and an army from the south would stay here to make sure they did. Xessans would no longer be allowed to travel from town to town, so it would be impossible to gather an army. They could have no weapons, they could learn no fighting skills, they couldn't be taught history, or anything else that might be used against the king. We are not allowed to read or write – you've probably never heard those words, have you? People aren't even supposed to know the names of the other towns in the district, let alone the lie of the land between them. From then, Xessans learned to say that we do not dwell on the past. We were to forget the idea of rebellion; we were to forget Dennara. We could have life, but we could not have freedom, because we had used our freedom to defy the king. That is what Dennara accepted. That is what we live under now.'

Lebasi's hunger to hear the story had overcome his anger, but now it returned. 'But you didn't think that me walking over the border would make the king burn Xessus, did you? And if it would, how would hitting me with a stick stop him?'

Xela's voice became dangerously slow and even. 'No, it was not to keep away Rednaxela's fury. For over a hundred years, the king's soldiers enforced the law, and they were brutal and bloody. When I became the magistrate they were withdrawn to the edge of Xessus. I made a deal with the king: we keep Riadsala's laws and the soldiers stay away. If anyone breaks the Mercy, they have to be punished, to show that we are serious. If we do not keep our side of the bargain, then the army will return, and life will be worse for everyone.' He took several deep breaths. 'And who knows, if people got used to the idea of breaking the Mercy, then the army might just carry out the threat. Over a small area. Burn a few farms, hang a few Xessans in the trees.'

'So you made a deal like Dennara made a deal? Xela's Mercy?'

Xela stood up as if he had been stung. He jabbed a finger at Lebasi. 'You have no idea how much that hurts. I have no choice, no choice at all. I keep the law to stop the soldiers coming back. You heard the elders. It was worse before. They lived most of their lives under the Westwall Guard. They put Perra in the cells, it wasn't just me.'

This was the moment to speak. Lebasi pushed himself up and swung his legs around so he was sitting on the edge of the bed. As he stood up, Xela leaned forward and touched his arm where Ruffur's fingernails had left their mark.

'Who did this?'

'It's nothing.'

'It's not nothing, someone had a go at you –'

Lebasi's anger boiled over. 'Are you joking? You had a go at me. This is a little scratch on my arm. It hardly hurts at all. And you're asking me to tell on someone? What are you going to do, put them in the cells for half a year? And then I have to go back to school with their friends –'

Xela held up his hands. 'All right. I understand. I get it all the time. No one wants to be the one who puts the finger on a bully. But you're not being noble, you know. You're letting them get away with it so they'll carry on hurting someone else. It's not just you, it's all the other children they knock about. Are you going to let them do that? If you tell me what happened, I can do something about it. That's part of my job.'

Lebasi shook his head. A dozen different replies were spinning around it. A part of him understood the anger Ruffur and Sammas felt – the idea of telling tales to his father boiled his blood, too. He wasn't going to try to explain that. What came out was, 'Perra was lying. He didn't do anything. He was resting on the ground when I walked over the line, nowhere near me. You should let him go and give me the other seventeen.'

Xela took a pace backward. He folded his arms across his chest and studied Lebasi's face. Lebasi could feel his own pulse racing. The throbbing had returned to his bruises, reminding him that the rest of the punishment would be much worse.

To his surprise, Xela smiled. 'Is that the truth?'

Lebasi didn't trust himself to speak again. He nodded.

'Well, I am proud of you. You have obviously listened well to the stories of Xessus and learned what's right. You will certainly have to be punished.'

Lebasi stood up straighter, trying not to blink. His eyes were watering, and he didn't want to make it seem that he was crying.

Xela stepped across to the window, giving Lebasi a chance to wipe his sleeve across his face. He leaned on the sill and looked uphill, as if he could see through the ground into the cells. He sighed and shook his head. 'But don't imagine that Perra is innocent. He does things for a reason, that one. I don't know what his reason is, yet, but until I find out, I'm happy that he's somewhere he can do no harm –'

Lebasi protested, 'But you can't –'

Xela turned sharply, making a chopping motion with his hand. 'Yes, I can. Within the bounds of Riadsala's Mercy, I can do what I want. And that means for you – no more stick. Enough of that brutality. But I need people to see that you are not getting away with a breach of the law, magistrate's son and all. You will be apprenticed to the waterworkers, not just on workdays but every day until I decide you're done. A watchman will take you to meet the guildmaster tomorrow at daybreak and will bring you back at the end of the day. In between you will be confined to the house. I hope that will make you feel less guilty about Perra sitting in a cell on your behalf, and reflect that whatever led you to take a walk across the borderline, it was a fool's idea.'

Xela turned and marched out of the room. Lebasi sat down heavily on the bed. He wouldn't even get the chance to tell Faya that he'd tried.

10
WATERWORKER

A hand on his shoulder – Lebasi woke from a deep sleep and sat up in a hurry, his heart racing, but it was only Marrak. He held a lantern in one hand and those boots in the other. It was as if the last two days had been a dream, but the pain in Lebasi's back told him that it had all really happened. This time Marrak left him to lace the boots on his own by the light of a candle.

As he ate a hurried breakfast, Lebasi asked the agent, 'Where's my da?'

He didn't look up from the onions he was chopping. 'Gone away early. Two days, maybe three.' Lebasi wouldn't miss him. The only thing he was interested in hearing from Xela now was the end of his sentence. Still, he reflected, he wouldn't run into Ruffur and Sammas again anytime soon. Maybe they would have moved on to someone else by the time he was back in school. Not likely, but at least possible.

The watchman knocked on the door to summon him into the half-light before dawn. Three days in a row, now – and for every day of his punishment to come. He decided to make the most of the empty street, the quiet, the cool freshness of the morning. He had looked forward to the trip to the border as a break in the sameness of schoolday, workday, freeday, round and round, and it had certainly provided that.

The waterworkers' guildhouse stood on the second avenue just north of the eastern downstreet. The watchman held the door open and waved Lebasi inside. 'Wait for Anibor,' he said, and left. Lebasi wondered whether Xela or the watchman had considered whether he might run away – but where could he go? Anyone who wanted to avoid trouble would turn him back in. He began to see the strength of Riadsala's Mercy and the deal that Xela had made with the king. What choice did he have but to comply?

He looked around the room. The first rays of the rising sun were shining in through the upper windows. In the warm red light, Lebasi took in the neat racks of equipment, pickaxes, shovels, gloves, lanterns, wooden hats. On the back wall, a line of thick woollen jackets hung on pegs. He walked over and felt the material. He couldn't imagine anywhere in the town a worker would need

something like that – apart from Bennek and Lodder when they were taking Perra his meals –

'Lebasi of Xela.' It was a statement, not a question. He turned to find Anibor standing in the doorway. He recognised him, of course – all the guildmasters were well-known in town – but he had never spoken to him before and didn't know what to expect. All he knew was that people didn't seem to like being apprenticed to the waterworkers.

Anibor looked him up and down. 'All right. Not too tall, that's a relief. Won't be forever bumping your head.' Lebasi noticed that Anibor himself was almost square – about the same height as himself but much wider, with arms and legs that even Ruffur would envy. His bald scalp was criss-crossed with old scars. He sensed Lebasi's gaze and ran his hand over his head. 'I'm used to it.

You'd better take a hat, in case. Find one that fits you.' He pointed to the rack.

Anibor gave Lebasi a pair of overboots that wrapped around his own and fastened all the way up to his thighs. He added a shovel and a pack to carry over his shoulders. Lebasi gritted his teeth as it rubbed against his bruises. Anibor lit a lantern for each of them and stood back to inspect his apprentice.

'Xela has made it clear to me that this is a punishment for you. I don't take that kindly. To me, being a waterworker is an honour, and I expect you to remember that.' Lebasi nodded. 'Some of what we do isn't nice, but the town can't live without us. You treat it as a punishment or a privilege, that's up to you.'

He put his hand on a heavy door in the back wall of the room. 'To start with, you might not recognise the privilege. It's the sewers for us today.' He pulled open the door and the stench almost knocked Lebasi over. He gagged and turned his face away. Anibor laughed and stepped inside. Lebasi knew there was no choice: he took a last breath of fresh air, and followed the guildmaster into the opening.

✳ ✳ ✳ ✳

Over the next four eightnights, Lebasi worked through all the guild's tasks, sometimes with Anibor and sometimes with other waterworkers. Six straight days in the sewers were horrible. They had to clear blockages of stinking filth and repair damage in the tunnels. And trap rats. And finish off rats that hadn't been killed by the trap. And carry dead rats back to daylight to be burned. At the end of their shift, the men washed under an artificial waterfall – they wouldn't want to sit in a bath with what they had to clean off themselves. The overboots were taken away to be scrubbed by the guild of launderers overnight. Lebasi was escorted home each evening by a watchman who didn't get too close. He tried to rinse the smell out of his throat so he could face dinner. Marrak's expression suggested that he might not have got rid of all of it from his clothes.

On the seventh day, things improved. No overboots, but a warm coat, and a different door leading into a tunnel without a smell. Lebasi tried to work out how they could start next to each other but not intersect – one went down and right, the other up and left. After fifty paces he could sense the tunnel opening out into an echoing space – echoing with the drip and slop of water. Anibor held up the lantern to show a cavern containing a lake. Regular columns held up the roof. Lebasi worked out that they must be underneath –

'The Space,' Anibor confirmed. 'Too thick to fall through, I'm glad to say. And down here, enough fresh water for the whole town to live on for three moons.'

Lebasi ran his hand over the base of one of the columns. 'How long has this been here? Who built it?'

Anibor laughed. 'Since a year without a number, boy. I reckon Xessus the hero made it. No one else could have done. But we don't dwell on the past. We just make sure it all works for the present, and will be here for the future. That's our job.' He pointed at something moving in the water on the edge of the lamplight. 'And to kill the menking rats. We've got a few traps to clear. Let's get to it.'

On another day, Anibor took him to the corner of the northern downstreet and the second avenue. 'This is how we get the water up from a canal outside the walls,' the guildmaster explained. 'There's another pumping station on each avenue all the way down to the gate.'

Lebasi was fascinated by the interlocking cogs of the pumping machinery. He spent several days working with the oxen which turned the great wheel, lifting water out of a cistern which was being filled by the next station down. He led the animals on their endless round. The wooden teeth of the wheels and the beasts' hooves made a gentle, soothing sound: click, click, trudge, trudge, as the buckets rose one by one.

As the days passed, Anibor thawed and seemed pleased with his help. Lebasi's back became less stiff and sore. Meanwhile, Xela went away on business regularly. When he returned, he often ate before or after Lebasi. They hardly spoke, which suited Lebasi fine. There was no indication of when his sentence would end and he would have to rejoin school. He had almost stopped caring. He had forgotten that this was a punishment. The watchman had given up escorting him to work long ago. He didn't even mind the occasional day back in the sewers.

11
DRAINS

On the third Firesday before Midsummer, Lebasi arrived for work as usual as the sun was rising. To his surprise, Anibor was already in the equipment room, sipping a cup of hot tea. He rose to acknowledge the boy's respect, stretched his arms and smiled. 'Morning, lad. We're underground again today.'

Lebasi glanced across at the rack of overboots and couldn't help touching his nose. Anibor laughed. 'No, this is different. I've a special treat for you. We're going down the rainwater drains.'

That brought an image to Lebasi's mind. 'I know. One comes out opposite our garden. But there's hardly ever any water in it.'

'You've good eyes. I thought it was well hidden.'

Lebasi pictured the smooth rockface, the dark shadow in the middle, a small bush growing precariously. 'I've seen the waterfall sometimes in winter. It has to come from somewhere – it couldn't just be a crack in the rock.'

Anibor nodded. 'Aye, it flows in a storm. But that's not common these days. Must have been once, or they wouldn't have bothered to build a system that'll deal with a flood.'

'When do you think they built the tunnels, Anibor? Does anyone remember a time when there was more rain?'

Anibor smiled. 'It's always sunny in the past, lad. It only ever rains in Xessus in winter, and my da told me that his da told him it's been the same way ever...' His voice died, and he stared at Lebasi with something close to fear in his face. His tone changed. 'We don't dwell on the past. The tunnels are there and we look after them now so they'll be there in the future. Don't you worry your head about how or when. And don't you tell your da what I just said.' He turned away and started talking about something else. It was clear the subject was closed. Lebasi stared at Anibor's back. Not dwelling on the past was one thing, but to be afraid that the magistrate would find out that you remembered... that your apprentice would tell him... Lebasi felt a surge of anger again, that Anibor could think he would break the law of silence and make a report.

He could remember only three proper downpours in his whole lifetime. Water had gushed out of the hole and fallen in a cascade down steep rocks into the deep pit which dropped away beside the garden wall. He'd spent days investigating where it went from there: another tunnel ran out under the ninth avenue to the town walls and the fields beyond. The garden had a tall, strong parapet to stop their goats falling into the drain. Lebasi often climbed up onto it and looked down, enjoying the dizzy feeling that challenged him to fly.

He wondered if he'd remember those rainstorms when he grew up, and whether he wouldn't be supposed to.

Anibor handed Lebasi a coat and a pack, and led him to a door they had not yet tried on the far left of the back wall.

'Aren't we going to take a lantern? Or any tools?'

Anibor patted his shoulder. 'No, this is by way of being a holiday. You've worked for me five eightnights without a break, Sunsdays and Moonsdays while your friends are all out there playing tag, never a complaint.' Lebasi knew they wouldn't let him join in, so he wasn't missing much, but he didn't point that out. 'So today we're just going exploring. No work. There aren't even any rats in the rainwater drains – nothing for them to live on.'

Behind the door, the passageway sloped evenly downhill, with a rope attached to the wall at waist level on the left. Lebasi could see that it turned left after ten paces. Anibor pointed to the rope. 'Hold that as you go along and you know you're in the middle of the tunnel where it's high enough not to bump your head. And put your other hand on my belt. We'll save on lanterns and you'll get an idea of what it's like to be a proper waterworker. Find out how you like it in the dark.'

Anibor closed the door behind them. Immediately they could see nothing. Lebasi felt the guildmaster step past and set off after him, guided only by the rope and the belt in his fingers. As they turned the corner and went further underground, he took in the different atmosphere. The sewers had been warm, moist and smelly. Down here it was colder than anywhere he'd ever been, and he appreciated the jacket. He missed the gentle burbling of the muck and water flowing slowly past. The dry air caught at his throat and made him want to cough. He sniffed, but there was nothing to smell.

Anibor's voice echoed all around him. 'Watch your feet. Well, you can't watch them, but just be aware of what you're standing on before you put your weight down. There are a few uneven bits. You could break an ankle down here, and I don't want to have to carry you back up again.' He patted Lebasi on the shoulder, somehow knowing exactly where he was in spite of the complete darkness. 'I would, though. That's the rule. A waterworker never leaves a man underground. So if you're going to hurt yourself, I'd be grateful if you'd do it soon, before we've gone far.' Lebasi wasn't sure if he was joking. He laughed nervously and said he'd take care.

After fifty paces Lebasi's hand struck a knot in the rope. Anibor said, 'The tunnels aren't steep, so to get up and down the hill there are ladders cut into the solid rock, and there's a knot in the rope two paces before them going up and going down. The ladders are about the height of five men, so pay attention to the knots, if you don't want to break your nose going up or your neck going down.'

Lebasi wanted Anibor to keep talking. His imagination created shadowy pictures of what might live underground, things with many teeth or sharp claws waiting for a two-legged meal to stray into their grasp. He needed to be sure the belt in his right hand still belonged to the guildmaster. The way their voices bounced around the walls was unnerving, but better than footsteps alone. The echoes sounded like unseen company or pursuit... he shivered.

Anibor's voice cut across his nightmares. 'You wouldn't believe the work that went into making these tunnels. It's a shame we don't get enough rain to make it worth the effort.'

'Why do you come down here, if the tunnels don't do anything?'

'Oh, we have to check them over from time to time. But I've brought you down here to show you something. We're almost there.'

Lebasi realised he could make out Anibor's outline. There was a faint light from somewhere – not flickering like a candle, but steady as daylight. That seemed impossible: they'd been going deeper and deeper underground – fifteen ladders. He glanced to the side, and could imagine there were walls instead of darkness. He blinked, and was sure of it. They kept walking. The light grew stronger, although its source was hidden from Lebasi by Anibor's body.

As the guildmaster's silhouette became more distinct, Lebasi saw the tunnel was just the right size for a full-grown adult of Anibor's shape – if he'd been taller he'd need to stoop, and he had to walk in the centre with his hand on the rope or he'd brush his shoulders against the sides. There was more room for Lebasi, but if he didn't keep his left arm extended he'd bang something somewhere.

Anibor stepped aside. 'There!' he exclaimed, sweeping his hand around. Lebasi's eyes had grown used to the glimmer, so he wasn't completely dazzled by the stronger light. He took in every detail – his eyes were hungry for something to look at. The last twenty paces of the tunnel widened out into a room. Ahead, an opening to the air, half obscured by a bush. Stone benches carved into the walls. Neat stacks of equipment – chisels, hammers; lengths of rope, coiled and tied; piles of small wooden torches.

'This is the end of the branch,' Anibor went on. 'I brought you here for a treat.' He smiled at Lebasi's puzzled expression. 'Come here, look out the door. But don't let go of me or the rope – it's a long way down.'

Lebasi approached the opening cautiously, holding on as instructed, trying to get used to full sunlight. As he screwed up his eyes, he realised he knew this view in every detail – the red tiles of nearby roofs, the pattern of the town fields beyond the walls, the shape of hills on the horizon – it was as if he was looking out of his bedroom window. He started to ask, 'Where...?'

The guildmaster crouched down and put his arm across to make a barrier. He pointed to the left and grinned. 'Look over there.'

Lebasi followed Anibor's hand: a steep rocky face topped by a rough stone wall, and beyond it – his own house and garden. The wall was only about ten paces away, on the same level as the opening. He laughed, and looked up, right, left. He knew what he'd see. He'd stared at this hole in the cliff from the top of the garden wall many times. It was right in the centre of a blank rock face, ten paces from either side. Directly overhead, the rock rose another ten paces – the height of five men – to where a twisted tree grew out of the foundations of the alley wall. He glanced down. He wasn't bad with heights, but the drop into the pit was alarming, three times as deep as the height to the tree. He gulped and leaned back from the doorway.

Anibor rested a heavy hand on his shoulder. 'Now then lad, if

you'll just let me throw you across the gap, you can go home early.'

Lebasi took a step backward. The man burst out laughing. 'Of course, if you prefer to walk all the way back up to where we came in, I don't mind. You should see your face!' Lebasi grinned, and pummelled Anibor's side with his fists.

They sat on a stone bench to eat their lunch. Anibor was unusually quiet, staring at the floor as he chewed. At last he brushed the crumbs off his hands and turned to Lebasi.

'This is our last day together.'

Lebasi looked up sharply. 'Really? My da hasn't said anything.'

'He has to me. Tomorrow is Airsday, and you'll be back at school.'

Lebasi's mouth turned down. Anibor smiled. 'I'll take that as a thankyou. For someone on punishment drill, you've been a good worker. So thanks to you as well.'

He rubbed his hands together, then clapped them. Lebasi guessed there was something else he wanted to say.

'You're not like your da, then.'

'What?'

'Promise not to say I told you.' Lebasi nodded. 'He came down in the tunnels just once, when he was first magistrate. Never been apprenticed to the guild. Wanted to see everything in the town. Couldn't stand it, couldn't breathe. Happens to some people. We had to lead him straight out again.'

Lebasi smiled. Bennek had said the same. It was funny that Xela had sent him to the one place in town he would never come to find him.

Anibor was still speaking. 'You're not like that, though. I can tell. You've a touch of the burrower about you.' This was clearly meant as a compliment.

Anibor was silent again, tapping a finger against his lips. He turned to Lebasi with a solemn expression. 'Now then, lad. There's something I'd like you to tell your father. I can't tell him straight, and I can't tell you why. But there's trouble brewing. People are saying things I've never heard before. I don't know where it's coming from.'

'What sort of things?'

Anibor scratched his chin. 'I don't know how much you know about life after school. We have to work to feed ourselves, and we have to send taxes to the king. Xela's the king's magistrate, he has to tell us how much the king wants. I don't hold it against him, it's his job. He does it better than anyone else would, I reckon. That's why people voted for him, years ago, when you were just a baby. But when you have to pass on bad news, some of it sticks to you. This year the king's asking for more than last year, and last year was more than the year before. People think there won't be enough left for us.'

Lebasi protested, 'Surely you can tell him? Don't people say things like that all the time?'

'No, that's not what I want you to say. There's something new. There's talk of a big change coming. Midsummer, people say.'

Lebasi suddenly remembered Nomara. She had told him the same thing, five eightnights ago, and he had completely forgotten to pass it on to Xela. He shook his head. 'He hardly speaks to me, and I don't think he listens to me at all.' Even though he liked Anibor, he didn't want to run messages to Xela for him.

Anibor nodded. 'All right, I tried. Maybe I'll find some other way. Maybe his eyes and ears will pick it up. But I think the ones who are in on it are keeping it very close.' He stood up and stretched. 'Time to go. We'll light torches and inspect some of the side-passages on the way back so we can say we've done our job. Then you can have the rest of the afternoon off.'

Lebasi took a last look at his house across the pit, then turned to follow Anibor into the black mouth of the tunnel. The guildmaster walked fast and climbed fast, and complimented Lebasi on how he kept up. 'Good lad. This would be a short cut for you to school, you know – if only you could fly that little distance.'

Lebasi gasped. If he could fly that little distance! He would have a place where Xela never went, a refuge where Ruffur and Sammas couldn't find him. A way around the town beyond the reach of those eyes and ears. He concentrated on the steps, the turns, the ladders, the branches in the tunnel. He ran the route forwards and backwards in his mind as they climbed. His memory was very sharp. By the time Anibor opened the door into the equipment room, blinking in the brightness, he was sure he could find the way again, even in the dark.

And he had an idea about how he might learn to fly.

12
UNDERGROUND

By the end of the next day Lebasi was convinced that a refuge would be a good idea. His reappearance in class caused an outbreak of suppressed muttering from all sides, although whenever he looked at anyone they stopped talking and avoided his eyes. Ivar nodded to him at the beginning of lessons but then behaved as if he had never been away, as if there was nothing abnormal. He even rebuked Lebasi for not knowing the answer to something that he had only talked about last Mindsday, and changed the subject quickly when Lebasi pointed out that he had missed that lesson. He wondered if this is how it was for everyone else, just as it had been with him and Faya's brother. If someone isn't there, forget them. If they reappear, ask no questions. He glanced across the Space to the door behind which Perra was sitting in the dark. Did anyone apart from Lebasi remember he was there?

At morning break, Faya sought him out to prove that one person had not forgotten. She at least seemed to have noticed that Lebasi had gone, but she didn't welcome him back. Without a 'hello,' she went straight to 'I haven't seen my cousin lately.'

Lebasi was in no mood to apologise. 'I tried. I told my da Perra was lying, I offered to take the punishment. He said he wanted Perra out of the way for a while so he left him there and sent me to work in the stinking sewers, so it's not been a holiday for me either.'

Faya turned her nose up as if some of the odour still clung to him. He decided there was no point trying to please her, shrugged and walked away. Then he spotted Ruffur and Sammas eying him up from across the Space. He'd asked his father about Rabor, and been told bluntly that it was hard to replace a guildmaster and his deputy both at once, so he hadn't received the punishment Xela seemed to think he deserved – but the fact that their uncle had kept his status didn't appear to have made any difference to his nephews. Lebasi made sure he was as far from them as possible for the rest of the day. At the end of lessons, he checked where they were and ran to an alleyway in the opposite direction. He kept going until he was sure he must have lost them, but when he reached a corner from which he could see his front door he spotted Ruffur lurking in a doorway between him and safety. Sammas was further down the street cutting off the route from the ninth avenue.

Lebasi hoped they might get hungry for their suppers and leave. He was hungry for his own now. He worked his way back up and around the alleyways to come to where he had met Faya. It wasn't easy to climb the wall and jump down into the garden, but he'd done it before with less incentive. He opened the front door and waved to each of them in turn before slipping back inside. It might have been better to leave them waiting there all night, but he couldn't resist seeing their expressions.

Still, the ferocity of those expressions confirmed that he needed a safe place.

Watersday passed in much the same way as Airsday. He worked out that as long as there were only two of Ruffur and Sammas, and three ways back into his house, he could survive for a while. But it was just a matter of time before they caught up with him somewhere. The last thing he wanted was to have to go to Xela for protection, and the second-to-last was to have to explain another beating to Xela. Xela himself was out of town again, anyway. So on Moonsday, when everyone else would be having a freeday, he packed a small lunch in a big bag and set off for the waterworkers' guildhouse. He reckoned he could make an excuse if anyone was there – he was looking for Anibor with a message from Xela, or he wondered if he'd left something behind on his last apprentice day – but the building was deserted. He hurried straight to the leftmost door, pulled it open and slipped inside. He took a deep breath, shut out the light, felt for the rope with his left hand, and set off.

He'd run the directions over in his mind again and again during the two schooldays. He was absolutely confident he wouldn't get lost. He was also sure he wouldn't meet anyone, because Anibor hardly ever came down here, and they had just carried out an inspection. So he was safe.

It didn't take long for confidence to disappear into darkness, silence and cold. In his hurry to get into the tunnel he hadn't bothered to grab a jacket or a hat. He was shivering, not only with the temperature: he kept telling himself he knew the way, and the ladders kept appearing where he expected them, but the thought came to him – and wouldn't go away – that if he took a wrong turning and got lost, no one would ever find him. Nonsense! He could turn round and go straight back to the exit into the equipment room. But there were side-tunnels that he might go into by mistake in the dark – what if he couldn't find the way back? Of course he could...

Then there were the footsteps. Were they just his own, reverberating, or was there someone else? If he stopped suddenly, there was a pit-a-pat before silence drew in. Was that just the echo dying, or was there someone – something – keeping pace with him, stopping just after he did? His imaginings before, with his hand on Anibor's belt, had only lurked in the background. Now

they were taking clearer shapes. His mind's eye could still see in the dark. He knew all the stories about beasts that lived underground, dragons – no, they wouldn't fit in here – and giant snakes – no, they wouldn't have feet – and giant rats and... surely they were just stories. He took a gulp of air that tasted dry and stale, and carried on.

After the fifteenth ladder he felt the air change. His spirits rose. He tried walking quicker, just to see how fast he could go – or maybe to get to daylight sooner. He could certainly manage double speed. The tunnel bent a little to the left, and there was the small round light ahead of him, the doorway in the distance. He laughed with relief and broke into a run. He promptly bumped his head and fell over. He picked himself up, rubbed his bruised scalp and scraped knees, felt for the rope and carried on at a more sensible rate.

He ate his lunch by the opening, peering out cautiously at the view. He sat as close as he dared to the sunlight which caught the edges of the opening, trying to pick up some warmth. He didn't suppose anyone would look in this direction, but if they happened to do so at exactly the wrong moment they'd certainly report seeing a boy's head appearing beside the bush. They might recognise his face and tell his father; it might be Marrak, working in the garden, who saw him. Even if the news didn't reach Xela, it would surely go to the guild of waterworkers, and Anibor would guess that it was him. He didn't know what Anibor would do about it. He might be impressed that Lebasi could find his way back, but he wouldn't be happy to have unsupervised intruders in his tunnels. Particularly intruders who borrowed things.

Lebasi measured one of the ropes by holding it across his chest. He reckoned it must be twenty or thirty paces long, and strong enough to hold his weight. He coiled it up again and opened his bag. He stared at it for a moment before putting it in. The penalty for stealing was ten strokes. But surely even Xela's mysterious eyes and ears couldn't reach this place. He told himself this was only borrowing, not stealing. He wasn't taking it far away. And the penalty for getting caught on the streets by Ruffur and Sammas might be as bad as the stick.

The journey back to the third avenue wasn't as eerie as the descent, because Lebasi reckoned the dragons, snakes and giant rats would have eaten him on the way down if they were going to. He experimented with moving quicker, trying to balance speed against safety, and still being able to count his steps and spot the knots in the rope. He found that he could, with practice, run uphill in the tunnels, and still climb the ladders at a good rate. He paused at the top of the fifteenth ladder to catch his breath. From here, he knew it was about fifty paces of gently rising ground to the door.

He heard voices. He gripped the rope and turned his head from side to side, trying to judge where they were coming from. Not from below. Not, as far as he could tell, from the tunnel up to the door, which he knew ran a little to the right. Anibor had lit the lantern for some of the ascent, so they could inspect some of the side tunnels, but he had put it out several levels below this. Lebasi took a step forward, and the voices suddenly became clearer. They were still faint, but much more distinct, and from the left. Lebasi lowered himself onto the floor and lay across the tunnel, keeping his feet against the wall to which he knew the guide rope was attached. With his hands he could make out an opening in the wall, about a pace and a half wide. There was no light and no breath of air to indicate that it went anywhere, but he could just pick out one word, then the closing of a door, and the scraping of bolts.

The word was 'Perra'.

13
A PLAN

Lebasi sat in the dark for some time, trying to draw a picture in his head of the top of the town. The entry to the drains ran roughly south from the guildhouse. This top ladder was probably under the eastern downstreet – that opening must lead west. The levels were about right. Sound couldn't lie: that corridor under the courtroom was connected to this tunnel.

He risked crawling across and gingerly standing up to examine the opening more closely. As long as he remembered which wall he was touching, he should be able to turn round and know which way to go. He moved slowly, conscious of the invisible drop close by. He ran his hands up and down both sides of the side-passage, but there was nothing to feel. There hadn't been a guide rope on any of the branches he had inspected with Anibor, either. He didn't fancy going into an unknown passageway with no idea if there could be further turnings and junctions, or drops. Could he risk a lantern? What if Bennek or Lodder saw the light? He thought of the rope in the bag on his back. That would help, but it surely wouldn't be long enough.

By the time he had been all the way to the bottom of the tunnel, collected another two ropes and come back again, he reckoned it would be too late to explore that day. If he was late for dinner, Marrak might ask questions. He certainly didn't want anyone to look in the bag. He listened for some time at the door before he was sure there was no one in the equipment store. He checked at the window before slipping out onto the avenue. The bell rang as he turned into the downstreet; from the position of the sun, he reckoned that must be the gate warning. Anyone outside the walls would be turning their eyes to home, and Marrak would be laying the table.

He had forgotten about Ruffur and Sammas until just below the seventh avenue. Fortunately Ruffur was stupid enough to shout before starting the chase; as his pursuer was running uphill, Lebasi was able to slip quickly into a side alley and find a hiding place in an empty house. He knew there was another way out, but he didn't need it – he watched both boys running past the front door, Sammas swearing at Ruffur's back. He hoped his plan for getting into the drains would work.

He climbed the garden wall again. Sitting on the top, he checked for any sign of Marrak, then dropped the bag behind a gooseberry bush. He could collect it later when he knew where the agent was. He was glad he had left it behind, as Marrak was standing in the hall when he came in by the back door. The agent raised an eyebrow.

'I did not see you returning, Lebasi. Have you been home long?'

Lebasi decided that the truth – or part of it – was safest. 'I climbed in over the wall. There are a couple of boys I need not to run into, and they were probably waiting for me in the street.'

A hint of a smile crossed Marrak's face. He folded his arms and studied Lebasi as if judging whether this was a reasonable explanation. After a pause, he said, 'If you give me their names, I can make sure that they do not wait tomorrow.'

Lebasi shook his head. 'Thanks, but no. I can deal with it.'

Marrak nodded. 'If you find that you cannot, let me know. It does not have to go to your father.' He seemed to realise that he had said more to Lebasi in this conversation than in the previous eightnight altogether, pointed towards the eating room with the single word 'Dinner', and went to serve Lebasi's plate.

Lebasi ate alone, hardly seeing the familiar view from the eating-room window. If he could find Perra's cell, what would he do? Let him out? But where could he go, where could he hide? Maybe he should just tell him he wasn't forgotten. Or ask him what he wanted to do. Should he take him some food? He had no idea how well fed a prisoner would be.

He decided to discuss it with Faya. At the very least, it would give him a reason to talk to her.

✷ ✷ ✷ ✷ ✷

At school the following morning, he managed to catch her eye. He tugged his earlobe, the sign for a secret. She scowled at him, but still found him at break.

'What?' Her expression was so stony he almost abandoned the whole idea, but if he did, nothing would change. It was worth a try.

'I think I can find a way to talk to Perra. Maybe get him out of the cells.'

'What?!' It was the same word, but her tone was completely different. She glanced quickly around to make sure no one was nearby, and put her head much closer to Lebasi's. Her hair smelled of apples.

'I've been exploring the rainwater drains. I heard the guards talking to him. There must be a way through. I'm going to look for it on Sunday.'

Lebasi nearly laughed at the way her face seemed to reflect her thoughts. The set of her eyes, her brows, her mouth had been a picture of anger, like an actor playing one of Xessus' enemies. He watched as confusion, joy, doubt, and possibly a little fear ran across her features. He was pleased that she seemed to finish with something that looked like admiration.

'What'll happen when your da finds out he's missing? What if your da finds out it was you?'

Lebasi had asked himself this question, but had tried to avoid thinking about it. Now he needed an answer, the first thing that came into his head was, 'I might run away. Beyond the borders. Where he can't find me.'

Faya's expression matched her astonishment when he had tossed her the black stone.

'But first I'll ask Perra what he wants to do. He might think it's best just to stay where he is, come out at the end of six moons, get on with his life. That won't happen if he escapes.'

Faya's face had settled down. She put her forehead against his and fixed him with her green eyes. 'Are you really going to do this, Lebasi of Xela?'

Once again, saying it to Faya made it certain. 'Yes. On Sunday, I'm going to find the way from the drains to Perra's cell, and if he wants, I'll let him out.'

She smiled. 'I'm sorry for what I said up at the border. I'd got you completely wrong. You really aren't your da's boy.'

Lebasi was surprised by a pain in his chest. It could only be from what she said. Surely, he thought, he wanted more than anything to be someone other than his father's son – but his heart told him otherwise. Maybe, he reflected, if he didn't have Xela he didn't have anyone at all – grown from a seed, like a vegetable.

Faya was saying something else. He tried to pay attention. She repeated, 'Is there anything I can do to help?'

He was about to say no when he caught sight of Ruffur lurking behind a tree fifty paces away. Faya turned and followed his gaze.

'Do you know they're out to get me?'

She laughed. 'I heard. I also heard they're not getting very close.'

'Close enough. Dodging them might make it difficult to get into the drains on Sunday.'

She held up her left palm. 'Consider it done.' He placed his right palm against her left and let her link her fingers with his. No one had made a deal with him since he was six. He grinned stupidly as she walked away.

14
SHELBA

Lebasi didn't know how Faya managed it, but at the end of the day he watched Ruffur and Sammas leave the Space in the direction of their homes, north and west, and his careful reconnoitring of the eastern downstreet told him it wasn't a trick. He was able to walk straight to the front door for the first time since he had returned to school.

Just inside were his father's boots, still dusty from the road. He felt that pain in his chest again. He told himself that everything Xela did was wrong: enforcing the Mercy, tearing families apart, imprisoning Perra for nothing. Using the threat of the snatchers, the cells and the stick to terrify people into obeying the law. But Lebasi could not disentangle that Xela from the da who played games and spoke the special language. He was surely still there, somewhere underneath.

Lebasi took a deep breath and went through to the eating-room. As soon as he saw his father, sitting at the table with a mug of beer in his hand, Lebasi was certain he knew everything or would guess it immediately. How could he think that he could hide something so big from Xela? But he and Faya had linked hands on it, he couldn't go back on that. All he had to do was to behave as if everything was normal, after all. Maybe his da was now so used to ignoring him that he wouldn't notice anything he did – in spite of the eyes and ears. But suddenly he couldn't remember what was normal. Everything that came into his mind to do or say seemed artificial, an admission of guilt. How did he usually stand, how did he sit? He wondered if everyone who came before Xela in court felt the same way, or if it was just him.

He made the sign of respect – surely he hadn't done that recently? He said, 'Good evening, Da, I hope you are well.'

Xela looked up from his beer and smiled. It was a sudden reminder of the old Xela, a face out of the past. 'Thank you, son, I am. I've spent four days listening to people arguing with each other about nothing, knocking their heads together, and I've had a long walk today to get here, but this is Marrak's best beer and I don't have to see anyone until later this evening. Sit down and tell me what nonsense Ivar is filling your head with at the moment.'

There was nothing for it but to join Xela at the table and discuss his lessons. 'He's never still telling stories of spellmakers to the oldest class? I'll have to have a word with him.' Xela tapped his finger on the table. 'It's time you all realised there's no magic in the world, Basi. It's just us, and we've got to get on with it.'

Marrak's bald head appeared around the kitchen door, shiny with the heat of cooking. As usual, he said nothing: he nodded to Lebasi, who raised his right hand to his heart in respect, and disappeared again. A few moments later he marched in with two plates of chicken and rice. He placed them precisely on the table and produced knives and forks from his apron pocket. He made the sign of respect to Xela and went back to work without a word.

Lebasi couldn't remember the last time Xela had talked so much, or seemed so interested in what he was doing. He felt more and more awkward as they discussed arithmetic, medicine, Xessus stories and sport. His determination to help Perra was fading. He needed to make his father unreasonable again. Or take advantage of his good mood.

He decided to test Xela's reaction to talking about the past, to see if he might forget the law for once. He had been calling back the special language, word by word, ever since the hearing. 'Da, do you remember how we used to speak?'

Xela's eyes opened wide. 'What did you just say?'

Lebasi was disappointed. Perhaps he no longer understood it. 'I said, "Da, do you remember how we used to speak?"'

'No you didn't, you... how can you possibly remember that? It was years ago, you were tiny.'

'I've been trying to get it back.'

Xela glanced towards the kitchen door. He rubbed his hand across his forehead. 'It's a childhood game, Basi. Not something for here and now. Forget it. Don't use those words again.'

Lebasi wondered why Xela should be concerned that Marrak would overhear a game. Perhaps he was embarrassed. Maybe the surprise would shake him into letting something slip. Lebasi leaned forward and spoke quickly. 'Will you tell me about my mother?'

Xela had just swallowed a mouthful of beer. He sat frozen, staring at the mug in his hand, his eyebrows slightly raised, as if his thoughts were a long way away.

'Da, please. I don't even know her name.'

Xela lowered the mug slowly to the table, but his eyes remained fixed on it. 'Really? Have I never told you that?'

'No.' Lebasi waited. 'Please. Something.'

Xela took a deep breath and let it out. His mouth moved as if in a private conversation. He rubbed his hand over his beard, then shook his head. Lebasi started to protest again, but Xela began to speak, still apparently addressing his drink. His voice had become flat. 'Your mother was called Shelba. What can I say about her? She was the same age as me. She was beautiful, or at least I thought so. She wasn't tall, but she was strong, she'd brown curly hair and brown eyes.' He turned towards Lebasi, but he still seemed to be seeing a different time and place. 'The exact same colour as yours. And a dimple in her right cheek when she laughed. She was funny, she laughed a lot. She was kind. Her house was a place where I seemed to be welcome. So I called often and stayed long, as they say. Well, time passed and I married her and we had a house of our own.'

His voice faded away. He turned and stared out of the window.

'What happened to her?'

Xela shook his head, and this time it clearly meant that there would be no more. Lebasi was surprised to see him wipe his sleeve across his eyes.

'Da, I need to know. Tell me.'

'I cannot.'

'That's not fair –'

Xela banged his fist on the table. His jaw was working as if he was chewing gristle. 'Fair! You have no idea how unfair, or how much pain it causes me to even think about it. It's something you cannot understand.'

'I can't understand because you never –'

'No, you listen to me. I tell you that you cannot understand because you didn't know her, you didn't love her like I did. You don't know what it's like to miss her every moment of every day,

to have to carry on doing my job with a great empty space inside of me, dealing with idiots arguing about things that don't matter. If I had an eightnight and a clear head, I couldn't put all that into words so you would feel it like I do. But my head's not clear, with you springing this on me suddenly. If I say anything at all, it'll come out all wrong. I'm not going to start unless I can get it right.'

Lebasi stood up. 'Springing it on you? It's only been, what, sixteen years?'

Xela's anger seemed to have passed. He was staring out into the twilight again. 'Sixteen years, one eightnight and four days,' he said softly.

Lebasi was angry, but it wasn't the pure rage he'd wanted to feel. The thought of his father's grief, his tears, nagged at him as he lay on his bed and stared at the ceiling. At least he had a name now: Shelba. Maybe he could persuade Xela to tell him more. But he was worried that his resolve to rescue Perra might slip by Sunday.

It would have to be tonight.

15
INTO THE PIT

Lebasi stayed in his room and waited for Xela to leave. He was pleased to hear Marrak going with him out of the front door. He knew that one of them would look in on him before they went to bed. He thought of some helpful ideas from the Xessus stories – he could make a body-shape under the sheet with clothes and cushions from downstairs. Close up it wouldn't convince anyone, but after some adjustments he reckoned that it would be all right – at least by lantern-light from the landing. They wouldn't come in. He found a black tunic that wouldn't show up in the shadows, and he put on those boots again. Finally he retrieved the bag from the garden. He had hidden it in a better place outside, as he didn't believe anywhere in the house was safe from Marrak's eyes. He measured out the three ropes – thirty paces each – and tied them together. He hoped they would reach.

He took some apples and a piece of bread from the kitchen. He would have liked to take a water-skin, but he couldn't fit it in the bag with the rope. Perra would have to last the day. If he decided to come out. Lebasi wondered again and again whether he would simply choose to serve his sentence, and this was a mad and dangerous undertaking for nothing. But Perra's words – 'the least I could do' – echoed in his head. And, of course, he had told Faya.

The curfew bell rang. The stars were already bright, but the moon hadn't risen yet. Lebasi was stiff and cold, crouching behind a row of tomato plants in the upper garden. He wanted to know that his trick had worked and they wouldn't be looking for him until morning. At last he heard the sound of the door. A lantern appeared in the eating-room. Xela and Marrak were silhouetted in the window. From their gestures, they appeared to be having an argument. Lebasi decided that it could be useful to know what they were saying. They were keeping their voices down so the words wouldn't carry upstairs, but he could crawl unnoticed to lie under the window-sill.

Marrak's speech still sounded different from everyone else's, even after living in the town for sixteen years. 'I also am hearing these rumours. I am thinking we should call for the Guard.'

Xela's tone was one Lebasi knew well. He could imagine his lowered brow, his clenched teeth. 'Marrak, in all my years as magistrate I have kept the Westwall Guard out of my district. I will not call for the soldiers now, I will not call for them ever.'

Lebasi was surprised to hear Marrak arguing back against his master. 'There may come a time when unwelcome things are necessary. It is said where I come from, "mend your roof while the sun is shining". That is what I am saying.'

Lebasi could hear a deep breath drawn in, as if Xela was about to lose his temper and shout. There was a pause, then a sigh. His father's voice was calmer. 'I hear you, Marrak. But I don't think it's raining yet. I'll get reports, I'll speak to people, I'll put a lid on this. As I always have before.' There was the sound of him banging his hands together, but much softer. 'Without the help of the king's army.'

Footsteps. Lebasi rolled against the wall. Xela's fingers were on the sill. His head appeared. All he had to do was look down... but he was staring into the distance, to the south.

Lebasi thought that Marrak must have gone, but his voice came

again. 'Very well. I will wait until Midsummer. But then there must be a decision, a proper decision.'

Xela's hands vanished as he turned away. He was saying something, but Lebasi couldn't focus on it. Two thoughts were fighting for attention in his head: Nomara and Anibor – storms out of season, a big change coming at Midsummer – and Marrak talking to Xela as if they were almost equals. He waited to hear them walk away from the window, then crept back to the tomato plants. He watched the light glow briefly from his own bedroom window – there was no shout, no discovery – and ran to the corner of the garden where only someone leaning their head right out could see him climb the wall.

Out in the alleyway, he had too much on his mind to worry about what he'd heard or what he was going to do. He had to make sure no watchman saw him, let alone caught him. He hoped that they stuck to the main thoroughfares, but he couldn't be sure – and he still had to cross seven avenues and one downstreet to get to the guildhouse, with the moon on the point of rising. He would keep to the back lanes and... he stopped at the corner where the gnarled rowan tree grew out of the wall over the drain pit. He stifled a laugh. This was the whole point, after all. To get into the tunnels from here. He looked over the edge. In the starlight it was hard to judge the drop, but the moonglow in the east was enough to pick out the familiar crack in the rockface running down from the tree to the opening. He put his weight against the tree to test it. He would need to be able to pull the rope down after him. He dropped half the rope on each side of the tree, checked the knot carefully, wrapped one line around each arm and climbed over. He clamped his legs around the trailing ends and started to lower himself down.

He had to tell himself that he had done this in class, up and down ropes tied to trees on the Space. It was easy. He had never fallen. But some people did fall, half a manheight onto flat ground. He didn't like to think how far it was to the bottom of the pit. The rope stuck on his sleeves, but he couldn't grip it with his legs – it was all wrong – his heart pounded and his hands sweated. He was bathed in white light as the moon cleared the eastern horizon. He glanced to his right. If Marrak or Xela decided to look out of their windows now... he loosened his grip and slid quicker, too quickly! He grabbed hold again and stopped. He risked a peek down. The pit was still in shadow and seemed to have no bottom. But the bush that grew out of the doorway was only just below him. His feet cleared the top edge and he swore as his shins banged on the rock. His stomach scraped past and his toes touched a flat surface, but his heels were still out in the air. He grabbed at the bush with his right hand and pulled himself in.

He dried his palms on his tunic and sat on the floor until his heart stopped thumping. He wondered if it would have been easier to dodge the watchmen. But he had proved the route into the tunnel was possible. He would think of a better way to do it next time, now he knew it worked. He pulled one end of the rope until the other end came over the trunk and whipped down past him into the void. He hauled it back in, coiled it up and put it in his pack. He took one last deep breath of fresh air, one last eyeful of moon and starlight, and felt for the guide-rope.

16
BURROWER

Lebasi felt strangely at home in the tunnels on this third climb. He didn't mind the dark. He no longer imagined that he would meet anyone or anything. The echo of his footsteps was companionable instead of sinister. He counted the steps and the ladders. At the top of the fifteenth, he took another four paces and knew he was standing opposite the opening that somehow, somewhere led to Perra's cell.

He sat with his legs across the tunnel and opened his pack. He took out the coiled rope and placed it carefully on the floor beside him, making sure that it would run freely. After a moment's thought he put the pack uphill beyond it. There was no point in carrying a bag up the side tunnel and back again. If he returned with Perra, he could have his apples then.

He felt above his head and tied one end of the line to the guide-rope. He fastened the other end around his waist, and stood up. He took a cautious pace forward and reached out with his hand. There was the opening. He'd thought carefully about the best way to proceed: his left hand touching the wall, his right hand in front of his forehead, small steps, counting all the way. He'd practised so that he reckoned he could keep the length of those small steps roughly equal – three to a full pace. And he'd measured out the distance from the guildhouse to the courtroom door as best he could – more than a hundred paces, to be sure, but he hoped that the corridor with the cells ran east from the bottom of the spiral staircase. If it ran west, it wouldn't be so good. He didn't want to run out of rope.

He had counted to two hundred and seventeen without his left hand finding a gap or his right hand finding an obstacle. He realised he was whispering the numbers out loud. Something about the sound of his voice, or a growing sense of being a burrower, told him that the tunnel was changing shape. He reached his right hand forward and felt solid rock. He lowered his arm. There was a wall in the way. But he had heard voices. He certainly hadn't gone far enough to have passed the cells. Had there been an opening on the right that he had missed? He could turn and go back.

A draught touched his knee below the hem of his tunic. He lowered his hand to waist height – still solid rock – then below waist height. He crouched down and groped around with both hands. There was a hole in the wall, narrower than the main passage, a pace across and a pace high. He sniffed the air: it smelled different. Damp, musty – it took him straight back to his night in the cell. This must be the way through. But he would have to crawl.

He sat with his back to the cold stone wall and breathed slowly. Was it so different from walking in the dark? Yes, it was. He had an inkling of what Xela must feel in the tunnels. He could turn round and go back, but he had come so far. He owed it to Perra to try. He had told Faya that he would, but she only thought he would try on Sunday. He banged his hands together. The sound echoed around him. He put his head down again and listened for any sign that this hole really led to Perra's cell. There was only silence, and that smell.

He put his hand on the rope. It was his connection to the way back. There was still some slack in it. He half-turned backwards, then shook himself. He had to go through with it.

He lay down and started forward on his stomach. He had to keep his arms in front and worm his way along. Even in the darkness, he felt the walls and ceiling closing in around him – there was a change in the sound his movements made. It was one thing to be able to stand up, turn around, and reach his hands out in either direction, but now he sensed the weight of the earth above him pressing down. What if the tunnel narrowed and he got stuck? No one would ever find him. Yes they would – the next time Anibor went down the drain he would find Lebasi's rope and follow it. But when would that be? He moved his arms and legs, still counting, trying not to think about it. It occurred to him that he didn't know how many of his crawls made up a pace, but he counted anyway.

Faya. Faya might guess where he was, if he didn't turn up at school tomorrow. But she didn't think he was doing this until Sunday. And would she tell, or would she think that was breaking the law? And would they find him soon enough?

He tried crawling backwards, to make sure that it was possible, taking numbers away. Ivar was always telling them that adding and subtracting were useful skills in life. The slow ones like Ruffur and Sammas couldn't see the point – but then the thought of Ruffur wedged in this hole struck him and he laughed out loud. The

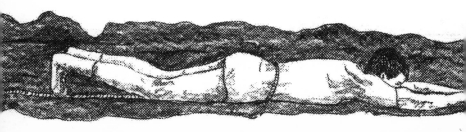

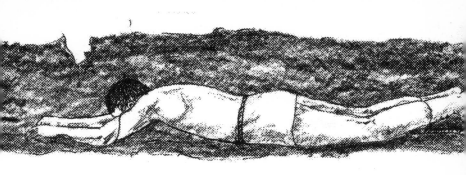

echoes in the confined space sounded like a mad person. This whole scheme was crazy. He edged forward, adding to the count again.

The sound changed. Afraid of what he might find, he reached his arm above his head. There was nothing. He felt around on either side. The passage had opened out again. It was still completely dark. He stood up slowly, wary of banging something on a wall or a ceiling, but he was in the clear. His hands told him that this space was a pace and a half wide and a couple of spans higher than his head. His heart raced – it was the right size for the corridor, and it certainly had the right smell. He put his left hand on the wall and his right in front of his face again and took a pace forward. The rope tugged at his waist. He turned and pulled on it. It was taut. One hundred paces from the drain.

There was nothing for it but to untie himself. He laid the end across the tunnel. It would tell him where the crawl began, at least. Now it was important to know which way he was facing. If the spiral stairs were at the far end, the doors would be on the right. He changed his hands over and walked forward. Yes! He had to stop himself shouting as he felt the stone change to wood. He tapped gently and whispered, 'Perra?' There was no reply.

He took another four paces and found another door. 'Perra?'

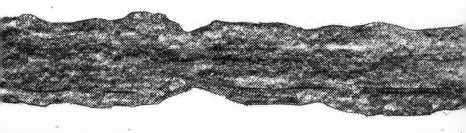

Still silence. What if he was asleep, and needed a loud noise to wake him? What if there were other people in the cells, thieves, maybe murderers? Lebasi told himself that they were behind bolted doors, and he would only open the right one. But which was it?

At the fourth door, his whisper was answered by a dry croak. 'What?'

'Perra, is that you?'

'Who do you expect, Xessus himself? King Rednaxela?'

'It's me, Lebasi.'

'WHAT?' Perra's voice changed. It was hardly any louder, but life had returned to it. Lebasi heard movement, the sound of hands finding the door.

'I've come to get you out. Unless you want to stay there for the rest of your sentence and come out when my da says you can.'

There was a pause. Perra chuckled under his breath. Lebasi felt a shiver run down his back – the madness of his own laughter didn't seem far away.

'Tell me you're not just a dream, Lebasi. Talk to me. Tell me what day it is.'

'It's the middle of the night. Tomorrow is the third Mindsday before Midsummer. And I'm really here.'

'Before Midsummer? Three eightnights?'

'Two and a bit.'

'How are you going to get out past the guards? How did you get in?'

'There's another way. From the drains. There's a place you can hide, until you can find a way to get out of town.'

'Lebasi, you are a hero. Can you open this door? There are bolts top and bottom. Try to do it quietly. I don't know how far away those menkers Bennek and Lodder are.'

'They ought to be asleep. But I'll be careful.'

He found the upper bolt and used both hands – one pulling, one holding it back – to open it gently. It squeaked in protest, seemingly deafening in the surrounding silence. He stood still, listening. After a moment he started on the bottom one. It was stiff. He twisted it back and forth, but he couldn't shift it. He changed his hands so both were pulling. The bolt shot back with a sound like a whip cracking and he fell over, banging his head on the wall. He heard the door creak open and felt a hand on his outstretched leg.

Perra whispered, 'Are you all right?'

'Yes, but...'

They both fell silent. They could hear voices, faint and distant, but they were surely responding to the noise. Lebasi felt for the wall and checked he knew which way he was facing. He whispered, 'Quick, put your hand on my belt and follow me.'

Perra murmured back, 'Just a moment. Keep your hands clear, I'm going to close the door.' He pulled it shut and worked the bolts. The voices were louder now.

'Come on.' He found Perra's hand in the dark and guided it to hold on to his belt.

'Go.'

Lebasi walked as fast as he could, following the wall with his left hand. He counted three doors, then another four paces. He glanced back. There was a glimmer of light – a lantern coming down the stairs.

'We have to crawl,' he whispered.

'What?'

'Small tunnel. Nasty. But it doesn't get any narrower, I promise.' He found the end of the rope and put it in Perra's hand. 'Hold onto this. I'll go first. Keep crawling, and I'll let you know when you can stand up.'

He hoped Perra was a burrower like him. If he panicked, they might both get stuck. But the light was brighter, so there was nothing for it but to get down on his stomach, take hold of the rope and grovel into the unseen opening.

To Lebasi's surprise, it was a great deal easier the second time. He knew where it went, and he knew he wouldn't get stuck. His main fear now was that he would get caught. He counted in his head again, but he sensed the tunnel opening out around him before he had reached the same number. He pulled himself up into a crouch and listened. To his relief, there was the sound of limbs moving just behind him. He found Perra's arm and helped him out.

Perra was breathing heavily. He put a shaky hand on Lebasi's shoulder. He muttered, 'Fire and ice, Lebasi, you are more than a hero. You went through there not knowing where it went?' Lebasi felt his chest swelling.

He hissed, 'Shhh.' Now the tunnel was clear they could hear Lodder and Bennek again. Lebasi put his head down by the opening and was shocked by how clear and loud they were. He thought for a moment that they must be crawling in pursuit, but that couldn't be right.

Bennek's whiny voice: 'He has to be there.'

Lodder's lower tone: 'He's not.'

'You've got the wrong cell.'

'Help yourself, bonehead, look in all of them.'

There followed the sound of bolts being drawn and doors opening. Swearing. Doors slamming again. Lebasi and Perra stood in the darkness, straining their ears.

Bennek again: 'He can't have disappeared into the rock.'

'You must have left the door unbolted.'

'Don't be an idiot. Anyway, where could he go if I did? Unless you let him walk out the front door.'

'What about that way?'

Lebasi remembered the rope. He put his hand on it and pulled, as smoothly as he could. With his head almost at floor level, he could see the glow of the lantern at the far end. He dropped the line and held his breath, realising how sound travelled up and down.

Lodder's voice was suddenly much clearer – he must be looking down the tunnel. 'Do you think he could've...'

'If he's gone down there, we'll not see him again.'

'That's not going to help us, is it?'

'There's one way to tell if he's in there. He'll block the flow, won't he?'

There was a pause. 'How do we explain it to Xela? That line comes out right by his house.'

'We needed to do a bit of a clean. Maybe opened the screw a bit far, took a while to put it back. Anyway, he's not going to come down here and look, is he?'

'All right then.'

Lebasi stood up and felt for Perra's head in the dark. He put his lips close to his ear and whispered, 'I think they're going to put water down the tunnel. We need to go as quick as we can. Hold my belt and bring the end of the rope.'

He put his right hand on the wall now and ran the rope through the other. No small steps: after fifty-seven full paces, he heard a splashing, gurgling sound behind them. 'Not far now,' he called, knowing that no one could hear them through a tunnel full of water. The sound grew closer – sixty, sixty-five – it was on them, water around their ankles, then with a roar it was around their knees, pushing them forward. 'Hold on,' Lebasi shouted, taking hold of the rope with both hands and pulling. Perra stumbled into his back, they were both staggering. If they fell they would be washed over the drop.

He felt the pressure of the water and the sound change at the same moment. He lurched to the left, sure he was back in the main tunnel. He fell over on dry stone, his hand striking the bag he had left behind. Perra landed on top of his legs. They held onto each other and laughed with relief as the flood churned invisibly over the ladder below.

As quickly as it had come, it stopped. The roar was replaced by the sound of trickling and dripping.

Then voices again, faint now. Lodder's voice, as distant as when Lebasi had heard that single word on Moonsday: 'He can't have been down there. Water'd have backed up if he was. Stands to reason, he'd block the drain.'

'All right, he's not down there, and he's not up here. Are you going to report it, or am I?'

17
MESSAGES

Lebasi wondered if they would tell Xela immediately, or if they would wait until morning. If immediately, then there was nothing he could do. There would be noise in the house and he would be expected to get up. When he didn't they would check, and his absence would be discovered. But even if he left Perra here and went home as quickly as he could, he wouldn't make it before the guards. He had to hope they would tell Xela in the morning, by which time he could – if he was lucky – be back in his bed.

Perra interrupted his thoughts. 'What now, Basi?'

'The place I think you can hide is at the bottom of this tunnel. It comes out just by our house, but you can't get into it – well, you can, but only with a rope. I was apprenticed to Anibor and he said he hardly ever goes there. And I can use this rope to lower you down food and water, after dark of course.'

Perra considered. 'All right. It's probably the best thing until I can find out what's going on. I haven't had any news. How long has it been?'

Lebasi had always been able to work out dates. 'Eight and a half eightnights. Two and a half of your six moons.'

'And has there been any trouble? Has your da noticed anything unusual going on?'

'I heard him and Marrak talking about rumours tonight when

I was about to come for you. Marrak wanted to send for the Westwall Guard, but my da was dead against it. Said he'd never ask for them.'

'Good. Let's go and find your hiding-place, then.'

By the time they reached the room behind the doorway, Lebasi had realised what two and a half moons in a small room underground must be like. Perra had been fit and strong, but he needed frequent rests and struggled to hold on to the ladders, which were wet and slippery. In the dim light, Lebasi could see his hair and beard had grown long and straggly.

He lay down on one of the benches and breathed heavily. At last, he turned his head and said faintly, 'I'm glad your refuge was downhill and not uphill. I don't think I'd have made it.'

Lebasi apologised that he had so little food and no water. The drain was so well-built that there were no puddles – the flood had all gone into the pit.

'It doesn't matter. Fresh air and freedom is nourishing on its own, believe me. I hope you can get me something more solid soon, though.' He got up and walked to the opening. 'No lights in the magistrate's house. Looks like Bennek and Lodder haven't raised the courage yet to tell your da.' He stood staring out over the moonlit rooftops for a few moments, then turned back to Lebasi. 'I need you to do something else for me as well as food.'

'I'll do what I can.'

'I need you to pass some messages. I think it's best if no one knows where I am except you, and as few people as possible know that you've got anything to do with me. It's hard to be sure of people in this town. Who do you trust?'

Lebasi thought for a moment. 'You and Faya. No one else.'

Perra laughed. 'Good choice, if you're only having two. How's your memory?'

'Good.'

'Let's test it. You need to give these messages to Faya. She'll know who they're for.'

Perra reeled off some lists of words that made no particular sense. Lebasi concentrated on remembering them – it was one of the school exercises that he was best at – while wondering what they meant. They were clearly in a code of some sort. Years ago, when he had been allowed to join in more games, the children had often used secret messages like this.

'Repeat them back to me,' Perra ordered. Lebasi did so perfectly. 'Good lad,' Perra said, patting him on the shoulder. 'You could tell Rabor what was in every donkey's load that day, first time, and no one else could. Seems like I've got the best possible person to help me.'

✳ ✳ ✳ ✳ ✳

Lebasi left one rope behind and took the other with him. After everything else that night, the journey home was enjoyably dull. There was no one in the equipment store. He slipped outside into the shadows of the guildhouse's veranda. Thirty paces away, a watchman was patrolling the second avenue – but he was going north, and there surely wouldn't be two close together. Lebasi flitted from doorway to doorway, gained the cover of an alleyway, and made his way back to the wall of his own garden. As he passed the rowan tree, he pictured Perra, relatively free, five manheights below his feet.

He hid the pack with the rope in the garden again, and decided that the safest way back to bed was through his window. It would be a shame to be caught on the landing creeping past his father's room. He had climbed the wall before, only in daylight, but after the blackness of the tunnels it seemed like nothing. He felt as if his eyes could distinguish a hundred grades of shadow. He hauled himself over the windowsill, silently distributed the fake body to different parts of the room, and fell into a grateful sleep.

❊ ❊ ❊ ❊ ❊

The rising bell came too early, but he needed to be up for breakfast and raise no suspicions. Xela nodded in response to his respect. He had a sudden inspiration to show that he had slept at home.

'Did you hear the water running last night, da?'

Xela glanced out of the window. 'Yes. Strange. There wasn't any rain, certainly nothing that would make the drains flow. I'll have to ask Anibor about it.'

Marrak brought in two bowls of cut fruit and went back to the kitchen. There was no more conversation.

He had managed a normal start to the day.

❊ ❊ ❊ ❊ ❊

Faya spotted him tugging his ear and found him during break. She looked around for Ruffur and Sammas. 'They aren't bothering you, are they?'

'No.' He grinned, and leaned his head close to hers. 'I've got some messages from Perra for you to pass on.'

He was beginning to enjoy her astonished expression. 'You haven't... you didn't... you said you were going to try on Sunday!'

'I decided to do it quickly so I couldn't change my mind.' He blushed. That had come out more honestly than he intended. But she smiled at him, a wholehearted, admiring smile, and he blushed some more.

'Where is he?'

'He said it was better if only I know that.' He held up a hand as she started to protest. 'And he gave me messages to pass on through you to other people, and he said it's best if I don't know who they are – so we're equal, aren't we?'

She nodded, grudgingly. He relayed the messages one by one, asking her if she knew who each was intended for, and getting her to repeat them in turn. Her memory was as good as his. She held up her palm again, and this time held on to his fingers for a moment more than was necessary. 'Well done, Basi,' she said, as Ivar called for the class to return.

That evening, Lebasi waited for questions, comments, any indication that Xela and Marrak were organising a search for the missing prisoner. There was none. Xela remained in the same bad mood that Lebasi had put him in the previous evening. Marrak came and went with food and without speaking. Lebasi found himself on the point of asking a question that would give everything away. Gradually it dawned on him that Bennek and Lodder had decided that neither of them would make that report. If Xela never went underground, there was a possibility that Perra would not be missed for three and a half moons. They could just be stupid enough to prefer to wait and see if something came along to save them, rather than facing the certain wrath of the magistrate now. After all, how much worse could it get?

'What's so funny?' Xela caught him grinning to himself.

'Oh, just something Ivar said in class.' He guessed that Xela wouldn't be sufficiently interested in his day to ask what it was.

He was right.

He realised that getting food and drink for Perra was going to be difficult. In his haste to carry out the rescue, he had not thought about what came next in any detail. The kitchen was Marrak's kingdom: he knew where everything was, and how much of it there was. He provided good meals that were obviously enough; how could Lebasi need anything else? If Marrak went out for the evening he could raid the larder and find an excuse later, but Marrak seemed to have settled at the eating table after Xela and Lebasi finished dinner and showed no sign of leaving. Hanging around the house checking where he was would be suspicious, so Lebasi went for a walk up to the rowan tree.

As he reached it, he felt a hand on his elbow. He turned, his heart jumping, wondering if it would be Xela, or maybe Ruffur and Sammas.

'Faya! You startled me.'

'Sorry. But there were replies to some of the messages, and they said I should get them to you tonight.' She leaned in close. 'Everyone's bursting with excitement.'

'You didn't tell them I...'

'Of course not. They're all dying to know what's going on, but I told them Perra said it was better not to know, and they accepted that. As far as they know, he's still in his cell – I just said that someone had got a message out.'

Lebasi grinned. 'I think that my da doesn't know any different, either. He and Marrak haven't said anything. The guards must be too scared to say.'

Faya laughed. 'Perfect.' She held up a bag. 'I guessed you might find it difficult to get supplies without being noticed. It's easy in my house. Here's fruit, bread, some dried meat, and a flask of water.'

He nearly hugged her. 'That's great. I'll get it to him as soon as it's dark.' He tucked it out of sight among the tree's roots. She wasn't to know how convenient this would be. 'I'll pick it up later – I don't want to risk taking it into the house.'

She gave him the replies – they repeated them back and forth, to check – as they walked together down the alleyway to the corner.

Marrak was standing on the doorstep, looking in their direction. Faya put her arm around Lebasi's neck and kissed him, then sauntered away up the street, waving over her shoulder. Lebasi stared after her, a silly grin on his face. He guessed it was an act for the agent's benefit, but he hoped it wasn't.

Marrak raised an eyebrow as Lebasi went into the house, but said nothing.

18
PERRA'S REPLY

Lebasi waited until Xela had looked in with his lantern before recreating the body in his bed and climbing out of the window. His eyes weren't as sensitive tonight, but it was easy enough to get to the ground, retrieve the bag with the rope and climb into the alley. He managed the descent from the rowan better, too – he was getting the knack of feeding the rope through his hands, alternately gripping and relaxing.

He stood by the bush and listened. The room was silent, and the stars didn't penetrate the shadows. He took a step inside. He whispered, 'Are you there?'

He jumped as Perra took hold of his right arm. He felt the cold metal of a blade pressed against his neck.

'It's me, Lebasi,' he croaked, trying not to move.

The hands relaxed. 'Sorry.' Perra turned him around and put his hands on his shoulders. 'I've been a bit on edge all day. Trying to get used to daylight and all this space. Waiting for someone to come out of that tunnel or through the window. Missing the lovely meals Lodder and Bennek used to bring.'

Lebasi rubbed his throat. 'Where'd you get the knife?'

Perra waved a hand around the room. 'I've had nothing to do all day but look through the gear. There are some things here that I could use in a fight.'

Lebasi quickly reassured Perra that it didn't seem that anyone was looking for him. He handed over the food and drink, explaining that Faya had brought it. The moon had risen outside and Lebasi's eyes had adjusted to the dim light: he was shocked at the way Perra's eyes had sunk into his face. Maybe it was a trick of the shadows, or maybe Perra was joking about the meals. Together with the long, lank hair and beard, his thinness made him look old and fragile. He stuffed the food into his mouth in handfuls.

While Perra ate he passed on the messages. He was so hungry that he hardly seemed to be listening, but he checked a couple of words when Lebasi had finished, and wanted to be sure that Faya didn't know where he was. At last he seemed satisfied.

'Good work, Lebasi. I think I'll appoint you and Faya as first scouts of the revolution.'

'What do you mean by that?'

'Big change coming – that's a revolution. Xessans are going to stand on their own again. We're going to tell the king what to do with Riadsala's Mercy.'

'But what about the Westwall Guard?'

Perra touched his ear. 'We've got help coming. Don't you worry about the Guard. We've just got to get things going, make the people realise that they've got a choice.'

'Right...' Lebasi wondered what would happen to Marrak and Xela, but he didn't want to ask. He had a queasy feeling in his stomach that he wouldn't like the answer, but as long as he didn't confirm it he could look the other way.

Perra gave him some more messages to remember. 'I won't be able to see Faya until later on tomorrow,' Lebasi said. 'It's an apprentice day. I'll be working in a refreshment house on the northern downstreet. I don't know where she'll be.'

Perra laughed. 'Those messages you took today should sort that out. I think you'll find she's working with you, and she'll be able to pass them on at lunchtime. And you can bring me replies tomorrow night. Tell Faya I'll need more water – that flask isn't much for a whole day. I could use some for washing, too, but maybe that's going to be too difficult.'

Something awkward occurred to Lebasi. 'What are you doing about...' He glanced around the room.

Perra laughed. 'Don't put on any of the wooden hats in here unless you've checked the contents. I'll tip it out when the moon's set.'

Lebasi turned back to the opening. 'Shall I pull the rope down now?'

Perra stood by the bush and tugged the two ends. 'I think we can leave it there. See, it lies in a crack in the rock. Does it show at the top?' Lebasi shook his head. 'Then I'm a bit happier if I've got a way out – of sorts.' He glanced across at the house, then drew his head in sharply. 'There's a light on in one of the bedrooms.'

Lebasi peered around the edge of the bush. 'My da's room,' he whispered. Moonlight flooded the garden and the rockwall with its silvery glow, transforming the familiar objects into something out of a Xessus story. He sat back down. 'I can't risk climbing the rope in this light, especially if he's awake.'

'It's probably safer to go up the tunnel. If you get caught by a watchman in the street, it won't come straight back to me – if you don't tell.'

'Of course I won't tell.'

'Even if your da uses the stick?'

Lebasi found himself getting cross with Perra. 'What are you talking about? I've had the stick already. It doesn't scare me. I won't say a word. I swear.'

Perra clapped him on the shoulders. 'Good lad. Sorry, I was just testing you. I have to be sure.'

Lebasi's anger passed. He was thinking about how most of the

children in the town would finish that promise. 'I swear on my mother's life,' it went.

'Perra, what happened to your ma?'

'What? Where did that come from?'

'When we were on the way to the border that day, you said your ma died when you were six, so you could understand how I felt about not having one. How did she die?'

Perra sat on one of the benches. He stared at the ground, but he seemed to be seeing something else. 'There was an accident. We were walking on the western downstreet when an ox-cart got loose uphill of us. Some soldiers were picking on the old man whose cart it was, and we were watching, my sister and me. The soldiers used to bully people, steal stuff, just throw their weight around, back then. Tannaka said I wouldn't remember how it was, but I do. We were so busy watching them, just kids thinking it was exciting, wanting to see some action, that we didn't notice the ox wasn't hitched to the cart. Didn't see the wheels starting to move. Just stood there looking the wrong way, like kids do. Our ma had been calling us to come, stay away from trouble. But we didn't. Then she was really shouting and we looked round, but we were too frightened to move. She ran up and knocked us left and right, and then it hit her.' He put his elbows on his knees and rested his chin on his clenched fists.

Lebasi whispered, 'I'm sorry. It must have been horrible.'

'It was. She didn't die straight away. She was badly cut. The doctor tried to mend it and he couldn't, and then it turned black and she got a fever and she died of it. It took her twelve days to go.'

Lebasi stared at the floor. He didn't want to stir up bad memories for Perra, but surely here was the only person in town who might answer his question.

'Do you know how my ma died?'

Perra didn't say anything.

'Come on, tell me. You're not my da, you're not someone who's going to say we don't dwell on the past. I want to know what happened.'

Perra sighed. 'I don't know. No, really, I don't. I was only about nine myself – sixteen years ago, right? But I'll tell you what I do know. And that is that no one's sure what happened to her. They say she was around when Xela was appointed magistrate, then she wasn't around, and Xela was wearing mourning clothes. I can tell you she's not buried in the main cemetery outside the eastgate – I worked there for a spell, and I had to memorise every grave. There's another burying place further out – maybe she's there. That's for people the elders think will bring bad luck on the town.'

'Bad luck? How?'

'People who've died of a disease. People who've killed themselves. People who've been murdered. Bits of the past that the magistrate and the agent would like no one to dwell on. My own da had to fight to get my ma put in the normal cemetery. He persuaded the elders that the accident caused her death, not the fever.'

Lebasi stared into the dark mouth of the tunnel. His voice had become flat. It sounded strange and distant as he formed his words. 'What are you saying?'

'I'm not saying anything. But nor is Xela. And you know what a temper he has.'

✻ ✻ ✻ ✻ ✻

Lebasi turned the idea over and over as he climbed back up to the equipment store. It was impossible. Xela was so sad at the memory of Shelba. But could that sadness be guilt? It would certainly be a reason never to talk about her. What else would make him refuse to explain? Maybe he hadn't intended it, maybe it was an accident – or maybe his temper had run away...

Whatever had happened, one thing was certain. In this town the magistrate, and only the magistrate, could get away with murder.

19
EAVESDROPPING

Lebasi was glad that Xela went away and didn't return for five days. He felt the suspicion, the accusation, burning in his eyes whenever he thought about his father. How could Xela not see it in his face? And if he saw it, and understood, what then?

Marrak spoke even less than usual. Meals were simple and hurried, and the agent spent most of his time out of the house. Lebasi even risked taking some food for Perra from his kitchen, and nothing was said. Most days there were messages to relay backward and forward. Some days he just lowered the bag of food down the rockface, some days he climbed down himself. He tried climbing back up the rope one night, when there was no moon, but found it was too steep. He could feel his arms tiring too quickly to make it all the way to the tree, so he slid back down. If his arms weren't strong enough, at least his legs were getting fitter than they had ever been. The regular journey up the tunnel was taking less and less time each night.

By the time Xela came back from his journey, Lebasi had controlled his expression. They spoke little, which seemed to suit Xela as much as it did Lebasi.

Perra asked him to listen to Xela and Marrak's conversations whenever he could. He particularly wanted to know where Xela would be over Midsummer, the three special days that fell outside the normal run of the eightnights. He learned to lurk in the hallway and to look as if he was just passing in or out if they noticed him.

On the Sunday before Midsummer – one eightnight before the first of the special days – he found out what Perra wanted to know. He had met Faya to exchange the latest messages, and came home some time before the lunchtime bell. He opened and closed the front door silently, and heard voices from the eating room.

Xela's growl was full of suppressed rage: '... my decision. It is not for you to question it.'

Marrak sounded equally angry. 'If not now, then when? We need them here before there is real trouble.' Lebasi held his breath. No one spoke to the magistrate like that. What was Marrak thinking?

Xela hissed back. 'We have an agreement. I have a deal with the elders and with Captain Semaja. The Guard don't enter the Westwall District, we stick to the threbbing laws and we get to pretend we're free. That is how it has been these sixteen years and it's how I intend it to stay.'

'But these injuries change everything.' Lebasi took two silent paces nearer to the doorway. Injuries?

'It could be a coincidence.'

'You know it is not. We have not had more than one, two such accidents each year in this town, and now four in an eightnight? And all of them to our men?'

'Even they reckoned it was bad luck.'

'Then you should be even more wary. The people who are doing this are very clever. Or your own watchmen are too frightened to tell the truth to you. So far they have all at least been able to give you a story. Will you wait until someone is killed?'

There was an angry grunt. Then Xela sighed and spoke softly. 'Oh, Marrak, let's not argue about this. Something's going on, and we need to deal with it together. I can't fight with you as well as

keeping control of everyone else.'

Marrak snorted. 'Then do your obvious duty.' Lebasi bit his knuckle. Xela would burst.

Instead of fury, there was a note of desperation in Xela's reply. 'Look, give me a few days to find out what's going on, all right? I've got to go to the Westwall, you know that. I'll get to talk to Romesh at Nampetch and Alfas at Marstor on the way and see what they think. I'll get a chance to see if this is something or nothing. But people seem to be jumpy, stirred up. Honestly, if you bring the Guard here now, I can't answer for what will happen.'

The names meant nothing to Lebasi. He memorised them to pass on to Perra.

There was a sound of a finger tapping on wood. Lebasi pictured Marrak emphasising his point. 'That is exactly why we should send for them. To stop anything happening.'

There was that impatient clicking of the tongue again. 'Marrak, you know the law. If there's trouble, they're supposed to carry out Rednaxela's bloody command. Burn the place. Right now, I think there might be enough trouble to set them off. Give me a few days to calm people down.'

Marrak sounded surprised. 'You don't think they would really do that? That is what you believe? Surely –'

'Oh yes. I believe it exactly. And I believe it more than ever right now. Three days ago I was talking to Cretor down at Gattras. There's a new captain at Enola, someone fresh up from Egator, young and keen. Some sort of nobleman, they say. He's been rousing up the troops, taking them out on exercises. Story is Semaja's not best pleased about it. He's happy with his quiet life.'

'Well?'

'Don't you see? New captain, wants to be a big noise. Brings the troops to put down some trouble. Anyone looks at him the wrong way, he'll make an example of them. The way people are at the moment, I think they'd fight back. And then...' Xela's voice faded away. Lebasi heard his footsteps receding and pictured him walking across to look out of the window. He went on: 'I bet it would suit him, you know. A young captain wants to make a name for himself, but he gets dispatched north instead of going to the proper war. He sees the chance to stir up the locals a bit so he can look like he's put down a rebellion. Province pacified, king's grateful, captain gets promoted. Who cares if a few hundred Xessans get killed on the way? A few thousand?'

There was a long pause. Lebasi found he was holding his breath. He wondered if Perra could really organise the Xessans to fight the soldiers. Lebasi wanted the end of the Mercy, but what would the price be? How many Xessans would be left afterwards?

Marrak spoke in his usual slow, deliberate way. 'All right. I will not send for the Guard yet. But I will have to make a report of all this.'

'Fine. You write what you want. But give me time.'

Lebasi could hear the movement of feet. He stepped quietly back to the front door so he could pretend he had just come in, but it seemed they'd gone into the kitchen. *You write* – that was one of the things Xessans weren't allowed to do, he remembered. But southerners like Marrak could. What did it mean?

The voices started up again as they returned. Marrak was changing the subject. 'What about the other matter? You will still visit those awkward farmers?'

'Of course. My annual call to spread joy and happiness.'

Marrak sounded doubtful. 'You don't think they could be more trouble than usual?'

Xela snorted. 'Marrak, you're always the pessimist. I know them better than you ever could. They're all talk and bluster, trust me. They argue, they strut around a bit, they give in. They've never done anything, and they never will.'

'Very well, magistrate. How long will you be away?'

'I'll go on Kingsday. That gets me to the Westwall on Midsummer itself, which is when Gortan will be expecting me. And back on the following Airsday. I'll send you signals along the way, so if I need you to take any action before I get back, you'll know. And you can keep me informed about anything happening here, and ask – ask me, mind you, not tell me – what's to be done about it.'

※ ※ ※ ※ ※

Perra was delighted with this report. He shook his head when Lebasi asked about the accidents, but he was able to tell Lebasi who all the names referred to: Nampetch, the town Lebasi had seen from the border, and Romesh its mayor, in charge of local law but subject to the magistrate; Marstor and Gattras, other towns, with Alfas and Cretor as mayors; and Enola, the army camp two or three days' march away on the edge of Xessus, where Captain Semaja commanded thousands of the king's soldiers – the Westwall Guard.

'How do you know all this? We aren't supposed to learn anything about other places.'

Perra tapped his ear. 'A donkeyman gets to talk to people at the borders, other donkeymen, who go to other borders. You get to recognise who will tell you things that are useful.'

'Do you know why Xela has to go to the Westwall? He said that's the end of the kingdom, where Dennara was exiled into the wilderness after the rebellion.'

'He told you that?'

'Only to explain why he'd had to hit me with the stick.'

Perra shook his head. 'I've no idea why he's going there. But if

Marrak thinks this Gortan is trouble, he might be a friend of ours.'
He laughed. 'He's off to the end of the kingdom – that's what's
coming here while he's gone. The time for watching and waiting
is almost up.'

As he committed an unusually long string of messages to his
memory, Lebasi wondered what came after watching and waiting.
More accidents? At least, by the sound of it, he wouldn't have to
worry about what Perra intended to do to Xela. He would be
somewhere else when the revolution started.

20
DOCTOR

On Moonsday afternoon, Lebasi was lying on the landing surreptitiously listening to Xela discussing his journey with Elmass, the master of the guild of woodworkers. Elmass was arranging to deliver something for Xela to take with him. It would be carried on an ox, and Elmass was assuring Xela that the quality would be good, but both men seemed to be deliberately avoiding describing the load. It was almost as if they knew someone was eavesdropping.

They were interrupted by a hammering on the front door. Lebasi stood up and looked over – there would be nothing suspicious about responding to the noise. Marrak appeared in the doorway of the eating-room. Before Xela could reach the door, it burst open and a man rushed in, out of breath, red faced. He gripped Xela by the shoulders. Lebasi felt a lurch in his stomach. It was Faya's father.

'Xela, you have to come to my daughter.'

'Hoban, sit down, what are you talking about?'

He didn't sit. He half-turned and pointed towards the street. He seemed to be trying to pull Xela with him. 'My daughter. She's dying.' His face was wet with tears and his words were slurred.

Lebasi found himself beside his father. 'What's happened to Faya?'

Hoban glanced down at him. 'Faya?' His face was blank. Then he shook his head. 'No, not Faya, her little sister Kara. She was climbing a tree, she fell into a thorn bush. An eightnight ago. Cut herself. It's gone bad.' He pulled at Xela's arm. 'Come on.'

Xela removed Hoban's hand. 'I'm sorry to hear this. But it's a job for the doctor, not the magistrate.'

To Lebasi's surprise, Hoban burst into tears, his shoulders shaking. Xela took hold of the man's upper arms and leaned forward, fixing his distracted eyes. His voice was gentle, but firm, as if he was dealing with a child frightened by a nightmare. Lebasi remembered that tone.

'Calm down, man. You need to get Abarron. Why have you come here?'

Hoban swore. 'Abarron treated her when she did it. Bandaged it all up, said it would be fine. But it's not fine. She's got a fever, she's drifting in and out of sleep, the arm smells.' He wiped his hand across his face. 'Like my sister's leg.'

Pieces fell into place in Lebasi's brain. Perra and Faya, cousins. Perra's mother, Hoban's sister...

Xela lowered his head. 'I was Abarron's assistant. We couldn't save her.'

'But you could have, Xela. You argued with Abarron. It was you who told the elders the fever came from the cut, that treating it differently would have –'

Xela cut him off. 'I was young and hot-headed. I thought I knew everything back then. And even if I was right, I don't know that I could have made her well. Abarron is –'

'An old fool. He's come back and looked at her this morning and he says she'll get better. But she's going to die, Xela, unless you do something.'

Xela shook his head. 'How can I? It's the doctor's job. I haven't looked at a patient in sixteen years. I wouldn't know what to do.'

Hoban shook off Xela's hands and grabbed him by the shoulders.

His eyes were wide, wild. He glanced at Lebasi, then put his face right against Xela's. 'In the name of Xessus, man, you owe me a child. Abarron's going to leave her to die. You have to try, at least.'

Xela took a pace backwards. He turned his head to the side as if Hoban had slapped him. His jaw muscles were working. Lebasi was surprised to see a glint of water in his eyes. Maybe choosing Lakim had not been easy.

Lebasi noticed for the first time that Elmass was still there. He was shaking his head, his knuckles pressed against his lips. Marrak pushed him aside and stepped between Xela and Hoban. He spoke quickly, in the same tone that Lebasi had heard through the eating-room window. 'Magistrate, you are not the doctor. You cannot –'

Xela made the chopping motion with his hand that showed he would not tolerate contradiction. 'Marrak, you do not stop being a doctor just because you have another job. Hoban is right.'

Hoban's face changed instantly. His shoulders rose. He let go of Xela and stepped back, repeating 'Thank you, thank you.'

Xela shook his head. 'Don't thank me yet. You need luck as well as skill. You also need practice, which I do not have. But I will come and look at her, and talk to Abarron about her. Is he at your house?'

Hoban flopped backwards onto the hall bench-seat. 'When he said she would recover, I sent him away. To be honest, I chased him out. I had been drinking. He may not be keen to come back.'

Lebasi expected Xela to be angry, but he simply nodded. 'Very well. I will see what I can do on my own. Lebasi, you'll have to help me. I need boiling water. Run ahead and tell Hoban's wife to put as many pans on her fire as she can. You know where?'

'Yes.'

'And then I will need ice, to cool the water down again.'

Lebasi stared at him. 'Where can I get ice at this time of year?'

'The waterworkers collect it in winter and keep it underground.

You know their guildhouse?' *Better than you might guess,* thought Lebasi, nodding. 'If there's anyone there, tell them you need as much as you can carry. If there's no one, take the far right-hand door. You'll need a lantern. Go down the passage. You ought to find it easily enough. Get a sackful and bring it to Hoban's house.'

Xela turned to say something to Elmass. Lebasi ran out into the street and set off uphill as if Ruffur and Sammas were after him.

Faya's home was on the seventh avenue just beyond the southern downstreet. The front door was open. Lebasi had never been inside. It was smaller than his own house, even though a family of five lived there – or had done, Lebasi reminded himself, until Lakim was taken for a soldier. The ground floor was a single room divided only by posts holding up the upper storey.

He called out, 'Hello? Faya?'

Her mother Rennia appeared at the top of the stairs. 'She's not here – oh, Lebasi – is your father coming?'

Lebasi passed on the instruction. The news had the same effect on her as it had on Hoban – she stood straighter, her eyes seemed to brighten. She glanced behind her at something – it must be Kara – distractedly ran her fingers through her hair, and hurried downstairs.

After all his running and climbing in the tunnels, Lebasi hardly felt his feet touch the ground on the way to the guildhouse. It was strange opening the door and hoping that someone would be inside. On a freeday, it seemed unlikely, but two men he recognised from his time as an apprentice were tidying the piles of equipment.

'Ice,' he panted. 'Xela needs a big bag of ice. For doctoring.'

One of them started to ask questions, but the other ran straight to the right hand door, grabbing a cloth sack as he went. Lebasi had hardly recovered his breath by the time he returned. He gasped as the man put the shoulder straps on him.

The other laughed. 'Bit cold, isn't it? Now get to your da

before your sweaty back melts it all.'

Lebasi sprinted again, around the second avenue to the southern downstreet, then downhill in leaps, dodging people and donkeys, feeling the chill spreading up and down his spine. If Xela failed... if Kara died... what would Faya think of him then?

As he came through the door, Xela was carrying Kara down the stairs. Her eyes were closed, but she wasn't asleep. Her forehead glistened. She was wearing a sleeveless tunic, and her right arm – gently supported by Xela's hand – was tightly wrapped in bandages. He smiled at Lebasi.

'Well done, Basi. Take it to Rennia.'

Faya's mother was tending a roaring fire over which four large pans were hanging. She opened a cupboard and dragged out four wooden buckets. Hoban took the ice and started to break it up into small chunks with the hatchet he had been using to break up firewood.

Lebasi turned to see Xela lay Kara on a table by the window. He whispered something in her ear and listened to her reply, then picked up a bag from under the table and walked across to the fire. 'Rennia, Hoban, I need you to stay here and deal with the water. I am going to have to cut her, and I do not want you suddenly to change your mind about whether this is a good idea. Lebasi will help me.'

Lebasi gulped. Xela said he was out of practice, but Lebasi knew nothing about doctoring at all.

Xela glanced into the pans. He took some metal tools out of his bag and lowered them gently into the one that was steaming most vigorously. 'Let them boil properly. Count to fifty once they're boiling, then stand the pan on the ice so I'll be able to put my hand in to get the instruments out again.' He suddenly smiled at Hoban and Rennia and reached out to grip each of them on the shoulder.

'She's a strong girl. I assure you, she's not as bad as your sister was, Hoban, nor as far gone. But you're right, it will be serious, if the wound is not cleaned properly. Come with me, Basi.'

Lebasi followed him back to the table. Kara opened her eyes. There were shadows under them, and there was a sickly yellow tinge where they should be white. Xela smiled down at her. Lebasi remembered that look, and the feeling that everything would be fine, because his da could do anything. Had Xela changed his mind, or was he very good at covering up his doubts? She smiled back with such a look of trust that Lebasi's chest hurt. What if –

'Where's Kara?' Faya's voice at the door was high and trembling, then angry: 'What's he doing here?'

Hoban started to speak, but she rushed across the room and threw herself at Xela. 'Go away! I shan't let you touch her, you mustn't hurt her, you...' She threw a string of swear-words at him.

Xela caught her by the arms and held her as she beat against his chest with her fists. He didn't try to stop her. Faya seemed suddenly to run out of energy. Her hands dropped to her side and her head drooped. Xela crouched down so he was looking up into her face.

'Faya, I know you don't like me, and I understand why. But right now, Kara needs my help, and she needs your help. We have to put our differences aside. Can you do that, not for me, but for Kara?'

Faya turned her head away.

Xela's voice was hardly more than a whisper. 'You may not remember, because you were small yourself, that Kara was the first baby of spring, the year she was born. I carried her round the walls of the town in my arms when she was an eightnight old, presented her to the townspeople. She is dear to me. I can't promise to heal her, but I promise to do my very best for her.'

Reluctantly Faya looked into his eyes. 'Will you hurt her?'

Xela nodded. 'I have to clean her wound, and that will be

painful. I don't think your ma and da can watch it. That's why she needs her big sister, and why I need you. I want you to hold her other hand, to talk to her, to reassure her. Please?'

'All right.'

'Thank you.' Xela patted her shoulder.

He rummaged in the bag again and gave each of them cloths to tie over their faces and their hair. 'She's probably sick because something has got into her cut. I'm going to clean it out. We don't want anything else to fall off us and replace whatever we get rid of.'

He washed his hands in a basin of water so hot that steam came off them as he lifted them out. Lebasi did the same, scrubbing at his nails, shaking the scalding pain out of his fingers afterwards. Rennia gave him a clean plate on which he laid the boiled tools – three small knives with tiny blades, four blunt metal rods, two small pairs of tongs. He placed it on the table next to Kara.

'Let's have a look, shall we?' Xela started to unwind the bandage. In the centre, it was stained brown and yellow. As Xela finished peeling it away, Lebasi had to turn his head. Kara's upper arm was red and badly swollen, but most of all it smelled of something rotting. Xela seemed hardly to notice. He pointed to four puncture marks, peering closely at each one in turn. 'Those thorn bushes are vicious. But see, these aren't the problem. They're healing. This one, though...' He bent forward and looked intently at the centre of the swelling.

'Now's the time for us all to be brave. Are you ready, Kara? Lebasi, stand here and press down with this clean cloth.' Xela picked up one of the knives. 'And I need you to watch, all right? I'm sorry, it's not pretty, but if I tell you to do something, you must do it straight away. Keep your eyes on what I'm doing.'

Xela placed the blade against the scarlet, distended skin. He hardly seemed to move it, but it must have been very sharp: a thin line of blood appeared. Lebasi placed a bowl underneath her arm to catch it. Xela used the blunt sticks to separate the skin and made more careful cuts. Something yellow and sticky oozed out of the new wound. Xela picked up a jug of cooled water and washed it away.

Lebasi glanced at Kara's head. She had turned her face away and was staring into Faya's eyes. Faya was singing a lullaby. He felt a stab of jealousy. She had the easy job. She didn't have to look at that disgusting –

'Basi! More pressure, please.'

He snapped his attention back. 'Sorry.'

Lebasi remembered the pain of the stick on his back. Was this any less than that? That had felt like a cut, but this was a real cut with a sharp knife. Kara made no sound.

'Good girl,' Xela murmured. He cut and probed and cleaned while Lebasi pressed down as directed, then brought more water and took the dirty instruments to be boiled again. Hoban and Rennia sat by the fire, facing away.

Xela clicked his tongue under his mask. 'Here we are. Basi, I need to keep my hands where they are. Can you use those tongs? Can you see that piece of thorn?'

Lebasi forced himself to look into the red, raw muscle under Kara's skin. Xela had pushed the flesh back to reveal something black and pointed. 'Steady hands, now. Get a good grip and pull gently.'

Lebasi held up the fragment of plant in the sunlight and stared at it. 'Would that really have killed her?'

'Not that, son, but what's on it. Dirt of some sort gets into a wound and makes it go bad like this. Now we've got it out, it should get better. I'll just check there's nothing else, and we'll clean everything up.'

By the time Xela pressed the skin back together and started to wrap Kara's arm in fresh bandages, Lebasi had recovered from the nausea he had felt to begin with. He glanced for the first time at his father's face – or the little of it visible between the mask and the hat. His eyes seemed different, calmer and more peaceful than normal. There were the wrinkles of a smile in their corners. He noticed Lebasi looking at him and leaned across to whisper, 'This is a better job than being magistrate.'

✻ ✻ ✻ ✻ ✻

Lebasi sat on the floor with his back against a post, his mind worn out by the concentration, his body drained by the activity. He half-listened as Xela explained to Hoban, Rennia and Faya how to look after Kara's arm. 'She needs rest, and a handful of these herbs brewed in hot water four times a day. I'll come back later to change the dressings and show you how to keep everything clean.'

Hoban had sobered up. Even so, he flung his arms around Xela and cried on his shoulder. 'Thank you so much, Xela. I knew you could do it.'

Xela stepped back and placed his hands on the man's shoulders. 'No, Hoban, it is I who should thank you, for your faith. It is good to do something useful, once in a while.'

Lebasi started. He had almost fallen asleep. He stared out of the window: the sun was low to the horizon. He realised that he had not had a chance to speak to Faya alone, to exchange messages. It was only six days to Midsummer, and Perra would be wondering what was going on.

He watched Faya saying something to Xela. Her face had changed: she seemed puzzled, as if she couldn't work out the answer to a question in class. It was an expression he was used to seeing on the likes of Sammas and Ruffur, but not on her. He wondered if she would be able to remember whatever she was supposed to pass on to him for Perra.

21
CLOSE CALL

Marrak was waiting for them at the front door. His expression was even sterner than usual. He didn't ask about Kara, but simply said, 'Magistrate, there is something I must show you.' Lebasi followed them out into the garden and across to the wall overlooking the pit, the happiness of the successful operation seeping away into a sense of dread at what the agent might have seen. He pointed downward.

'Someone is throwing food waste and excrement into the drain pit.'

Xela peered into the shadows. On another day, Lebasi thought, he would be angry. He laughed. 'Someone doesn't like us, Marrak. See if you can guess who it is. Shouldn't be too hard to narrow it down to five or six hundred.'

Lebasi watched the agent stare intently at the bush growing out of the rock face. It was just as well that the rope was well hidden, lying in the crack. But if he chose to go up to examine the rowan tree...

'I wonder, magistrate, if some of the waterworkers are using the drain for purposes for which it was not intended. I will speak to Anibor.'

Xela shrugged. 'If you must, Marrak. But can you give us some dinner first? I'm starving.'

Lebasi struggled to eat his meal. Marrak kept glancing out of the window every time he brought something in or cleared plates away. Xela told him not to worry about it, but he was clearly not going to let the matter rest. Once Xela was supplied with a mug of beer, Marrak declared that he was going to call on the guildmaster.

Xela raised his eyebrows. 'Tonight? He won't thank you for that. Are you planning to go and look?' Marrak nodded. 'Well, if you really think it's necessary. I'm going to finish my drink and then I'll get back to Hoban's to change the dressing and see how the girl is.'

Lebasi listened to his father thinking aloud about Kara's treatment, counting steps in his mind – Marrak would be at Anibor's house; he would be persuading Anibor to come out; they would be approaching the guildhouse.

'I said, do you want to come and visit our patient?'

Lebasi realised Xela had asked him twice. 'Sorry. No, thank you. But I enjoyed it – well, maybe not enjoyed. I was glad to help you earlier, but I've had enough doctoring for today.'

Xela rested his hand on Lebasi's shoulder. 'It was good to have you. You did well. I won't be long.'

Lebasi came to the door and watched him set off up the street. He felt an ache in his stomach. Now it seemed all wrong to be helping Perra. But he couldn't abandon him to be discovered by Marrak without trying to give him a warning. As soon as Xela was out of sight, he ran up the alleyway to the rowan tree, looked all around to check that no one was watching, and slid down the ropes faster than ever before.

Perra got up from a bench. 'You're early. It's still daylight. Has something happened?'

'Not yet, but Marrak's spotted what you've been throwing in the pit. I think he's coming here now, with Anibor.'

Together they scurried around the cave, covering up every visible sign that someone had been living there. They were still checking the corners in the half-light when a faint voice came from the tunnel. Perra strode over to the bush and put his hand on the rope, ready to climb up or down. Lebasi shook his head. 'Too risky. There's a side passage just uphill, before the first ladder. Better to hide in there. Quick, though.'

Lebasi led the way into the darkness, Perra holding his belt again. He measured thirty paces and put his hand out to the left – yes, there was the opening.

Ahead, a light appeared, growing brighter. He could make out the bottom of the first ladder. A pair of feet came into view, climbing down. He ducked into the hole and sensed Perra following close behind him. If they were carrying torches or lanterns, they might cast enough light to see down the tunnel – was it straight, or did it have a bend they could hide around? He walked as quickly as he dared, one hand on the wall and one in front of his head.

Anibor's voice came, faint and echoing. 'I'm telling you this is a fool's errand, Marrak.'

Marrak's reply was suddenly loud and clear, as if he was standing right beside them. 'I will be the judge of that.'

Lebasi could see the wall. He pressed himself against it and closed his eyes. He remembered how a flaming torch made the rats' eyes glitter in the darkness. The light disappeared, and Anibor's voice came more faintly from around the corner.

Perra whispered in his ear, 'Let's put the stuff down and go back so we can hear what they say.'

Lebasi would have preferred to keep going further up the tunnel, but he didn't want to risk the noise of protesting. He followed Perra back to the junction.

Marrak was asking questions. 'Do you notice anything different from when you were last here?'

Lebasi held his breath. He remembered how Anibor had

counted the equipment almost without thinking. He knew what ought to be there and where it ought to be lying. Some of it had certainly moved, and some of it had gone.

There was a pause. 'It all seems the same to me.'

'You do not seem so sure.'

Anibor's voice was more confident the second time. 'Everything's here, Marrak. I should know.' Something about the way he said it made Lebasi certain he knew things were missing or in the wrong place, but for some reason he wasn't going to tell the agent.

'It is smelly in here. Surely it should not smell so much.'

'Oh, that's normal in the drains.' Lebasi knew that it was not. Anibor had wanted to warn Xela about something happening at Midsummer – now he was ignoring the clearest signs that something was amiss in his own domain. What had changed his mind?

There was silence. Perra leaned forwards. Lebasi wanted to warn him about reflecting the light, but dared not speak. Suddenly Perra turned and put a hand on his arm. Lebasi led the way quietly back into the tunnel. Glancing behind him, he saw torchlight on the far wall.

'What is in these turnings, Anibor?'

'Oh, for goodness sake, man, if you want me to look in all the branches we'll be here all night. I was in the middle of my dinner.'

'I will look in this one. Give me the torch.'

Lebasi and Perra crouched against the wall.

Marrak swore. 'You clumsy fool! Now it has gone out.'

Lebasi opened his eyes and risked a quick glance. There was only blackness. Anibor must have dropped the torch. There was the sound of flint striking steel.

Anibor's voice came clear and close: he had to be exactly at the junction. 'There's not enough left on it to burn.'

'Light another.'

'The other torch is for emergencies only. If you sprain an ankle halfway up to the exit, we'll want it then.'

'If someone is hiding down here, that is an emergency. Light the torch.'

'Marrak, you're chasing ghosts. And let me tell you, you may be second only to the king up top, but down here I'm in charge. And I'm not using up the reserve torch.'

Marrak swore some more. Lebasi had never heard him so angry.

Anibor sounded equally furious. 'You mind your tongue, put your hand on my belt and we'll go home. Count yourself lucky that a waterworker never leaves a man underground.'

Their footsteps receded. Anibor's words ran around Lebasi's head. *Second only to the king. Second only to the king.* It was like a torch in the darkness: Marrak was the king's man, not Xela's. How could he not have seen it before? He had so strongly believed in his father's power that he had ignored all the evidence. Perra must know – everyone must know. Lebasi felt his face grow hot as he realised, once again, that he was the only one in town who didn't understand anything about anything.

Anibor must have guessed that there was an intruder, and exactly where the intruder was – did he also know who? And why was he protecting them? Could he be one of the people to whom Faya passed messages?

22
BETRAYAL

They retrieved the things they had hidden in the tunnel and returned to the room by the door. Lebasi explained that he had no food and no messages because he and Faya had been too busy with Kara.

'Don't worry about it. What I need from you this evening is to take me up to the way out. I've got somewhere else to stay. Somewhere a bit more comfortable.'

'Are you sure it's safe?'

Lebasi could see Perra's grin in the half-light. 'Looks like it might be safer than here. Earthsday, Mindsday, Kingsday – just three days left until the start of the Midsummer special days.' He rubbed his hands together. 'It's all about to begin.'

'What's going to happen?'

Perra put a hand on his shoulder. 'It's still best that you don't know. I trust you absolutely – you've been through a lot for me, and again just now – but the fewer people who have that information, the less likely it is to get out.'

Perra gathered up a few things into a bag – his knife, a blanket, a water-flask. He scanned the room. 'I shan't miss this place. But believe me, it's a palace compared to my cell.' He clapped Lebasi on the back. 'Lead the way, scout. Marrak's right. I could really use a proper wash.' He stroked his beard, which had grown long.

'And a shave.'

Lebasi listened carefully at the equipment room door before opening it a fraction. The guildhouse was empty. He caught the echoes of the bell reverberating in the air.

'That's the curfew warning – I'd better run. Are you all right from here?'

'Someone is coming to meet me. We'll stay safe by keeping you separate – he won't see you and you won't see him. Don't worry, we'll meet again on the first special day.'

'When? Where?'

Perra smiled. 'You'll know.'

✳ ✳ ✳ ✳ ✳

Lebasi slipped in from the street as the curfew itself sounded. As he took off his sandals he realised that Marrak was standing in the doorway to the eating-room, his arms folded, studying him closely. He stood up sharply.

'Marrak! You startled me.'

'Where have you been?'

Lebasi tried to think of something without appearing to pause. 'I wanted to find out how Kara was doing.'

Marrak's mouth twitched. 'And how is she doing?'

Lebasi glanced down. Xela's boots weren't there. He must still be at Faya's house, and he would know that Lebasi had never called. 'I didn't realise how late it was. I started out, then the bell rang so I came straight back. I'll have to wait for my da to tell me.'

'You could have gone on and come back with Xela. He does not have to worry about the curfew.'

Once again, Lebasi had the feeling that the truth must be plain in his face for the agent to see. He wondered if he had picked up the smell of the tunnel room, and in a moment Marrak would notice it. 'I suppose I could. But he might have left already, and then I'd be stuck.'

Marrak took a step towards him. Lebasi was rescued by the door behind him opening. Xela stepped inside, started to take off his boots, then stood up and stared at each of them in turn. 'What's going on? A meeting in the hall?'

'Lebasi says he came to see how Kara is, but he did not arrive before the curfew bell.'

Marrak's voice was full of suspicion, but Xela raised no objection. He seemed to have forgotten that Lebasi had turned down the invitation to join him for his house call. He put an arm round Lebasi's shoulders and led him past the agent into the eating-room. 'She's doing fine. Fever's down, swelling's down, wound looks clean. I changed her dressings and washed it again. I think she'll get better now.'

Marrak said that he wanted to discuss his investigation of the tunnels with Xela, so Lebasi gratefully left them to it and went to wash. Whatever Marrak had seen or suspected, this was one conversation he didn't need to overhear – he had been there, after all, and Perra was safely gone.

* * * * *

The next day, Faya was not in class. Lebasi guessed that she had stayed at home to help look after Kara. To his surprise, several of the younger children – five girls, two boys – came to speak to him at morning break. They formed an awkward group around him, looking up with their hands behind their backs as if they were addressing a teacher.

The tallest stepped forward. 'We're Kara's friends. We heard you saved Kara's life.'

Lebasi smiled at her. 'I didn't, my da did. I just did whatever he told me to do.'

She smiled back. 'Thank you.' She solemnly made the sign of respect, followed by each of the others. Lebasi had never received respect before. He hastily touched his fingers to his forehead in acknowledgement, and stared after them as they ran away. His own class ignored him as they usually did, but he cared less than he had before. He smiled to himself, watching them playing their everyday games. He knew things they didn't.

The next day was Mindsday before Midsummer: Lebasi knew that Ivar would abandon lessons early, because he did so every year. Everyone, from the smallest to the oldest, was too concerned with the Midsummer feast. The teachers organised games and races in the morning to try to use up some of the children's extra energy, then had them act out some Xessus stories in the afternoon. Lebasi recognised his new young friends among a horde of locusts sent by the goddess Artay to destroy the crops. He was one of the farmers trying to fend them off. The action was threatening to result in some squashed insects when Xessus arrived to negotiate with Artay and call off the plague.

Lebasi watched Nomis act the part of the hero. He fitted it well – tall, strong, handsome. The bravest and the best, Lebasi thought. Anibor's son. Had the guildmaster realised that he would lose his boy to the army, if nothing changed? Had Xela told him so? That would explain –

'Basi!' He turned to see Faya on the edge of the Space, beckoning to him. The story was almost over. The locusts were swarming back to their own class. Some of the farmers had decided to go home early – Sammas and Ruffur were nowhere in sight – and Ivar himself was hardly paying attention. Lebasi jogged across to meet her. She linked her arm with his and started walking with him around the Space.

'How's Kara?'

'Much better. She's awake properly now, and she's eating. My ma and da are so happy.'

He nodded. One child lost, one child saved.

Faya lowered her voice. 'What's happened with Perra? I couldn't get away to find you any food, and there were some messages I didn't –'

He cut her short. 'It's fine. He came out of his hiding place that evening. I don't know where he is now, but he said someone was going to put him up until... until it starts.'

She let go of his arm and stopped. She fiddled with her hair. 'I'm confused. I still want the Mercy to end, but I don't hate your da any more.'

He nodded. 'I know what you mean. My da's leaving town tomorrow morning, so whatever Perra's got planned won't affect him, at least not straight away.'

She studied her feet. 'I want to say sorry. I knew Lakim going wasn't your fault, but I so wanted to get even with Xela that when Perra suggested it, I said I'd do it. I knew you'd get into trouble, but –'

'What? Perra suggested what?'

She looked up. 'Talking you into crossing the line. Those other idiots were dead keen, of course, though they didn't think you would. And you wouldn't, if it had just been them. They'd have had to pick you up and throw you over.'

Lebasi took a step backwards. 'Perra suggested it? When?'

'The day before. It was a freeday, he explained the whole idea. Asked me to take someone's place on the donkey team. Said he could arrange for Ruffur and Sammas to come and help.' She frowned. 'I hadn't realised you didn't know.'

Lebasi felt anger rising in his chest, just as when he had seen Faya waiting for him outside his house that day. He scanned the Space, wondering where in the town Perra was staying. 'So what was the whole idea? Or was the whole idea just to get me beaten?'

Faya tapped her knuckles together nervously, glancing left and right to avoid looking in his eyes. Her voice was unsteady. 'I'm sorry, all right? I was only thinking about Lakim, to make things fair. Perra said he had an idea to force people to really see Xela for what he is. He'd send off other people's children to the king's army, he said, but he surely would let off his own son if he did something bad. And then people would see how unfair it all was, and they'd make a big protest.'

'But my da didn't let me off.'

'No. That was why Perra —'

Another thought hit Lebasi with such force that he grabbed Faya's arm. 'Who told my da? If I was supposed to get into trouble, that would only work if my da knew, wouldn't it?'

The tears in her eyes gave Lebasi his answer. He flung her arm away and turned his back.

He had heard her angry, but he had never heard her being miserable. It occurred to him that it didn't suit her. 'He told me how to do it so it wouldn't look obvious. I had to be talking to someone about it where Demmor couldn't help but hear. He's a watchman, so —'

'And he's a snatcher.'

'I suppose so.'

'You know so. That day, I told you the leader's name began with Dem. You looked like you knew who it was.'

The pleading look in Faya's eyes might have blunted his anger, but something else occurred to him. 'Ruffur and Sammas – they were going to beat me up because they thought it was me that told. They probably still do.'

Faya nodded. 'Perra didn't trust them with the whole thing. They thought it was just about getting you to cross the line. They didn't know the rest of it.'

'So you were happy for them to think I'm a reporter, and get a battering from them as well as the stick from my father?'

'I've said I'm sorry. What else can I do?' She put a hand on his arm. He let it stay. 'You won't tell Xela about Perra because of this, will you?'

'WHAT?' He jumped round, feeling his face go bright red. She took a step back, but he followed her. She put up her hands to try to get him to lower his voice, but he was too angry to care. People were looking their way.

'What do you think I am? That day you said I was my da's little boy, and you were wrong. Now you're saying that I'll go running with tales, and you're wrong again. I thought you knew something about me.' He realised that his finger was almost touching Faya's nose. He pulled it back, clenched his fists, let out a roar, and stomped away from her. He strode off the Space into the western downstreet without looking back.

23
PARTING

Lebasi sat on the roof of an empty house on the third avenue and watched the sun go down. He heard the curfew warning bell, but he didn't take any notice. What did it matter? Perra had asked him, 'Who do you trust?' He had had only two names to give. Now he had none.

Did it change anything, though? He didn't trust his father, either. He might be a good doctor – he might wish he was the doctor instead of the magistrate – but he was the magistrate first, and he carried out the duties of his office. Riadsala's Mercy was wrong. Perra was right to try to start his revolution, and Lebasi wasn't going to go running to Xela any more than he would have told him about Ruffur and Sammas.

And there was still the question of what happened to Shelba. Xela was going away. He was supposed to come back on Airsday after Midsummer – but by then, everything might have changed, and he might not be able to return. The suspicion of murder Perra had planted still nagged away at him. He needed to know. What more could Xela do to him if he asked? There was nothing left that would hurt.

He climbed down from the roof and walked home down the middle of the deserted avenue, then the middle of the deserted street. All the houses were shuttered and quiet. No one challenged him. He remembered the injuries that Marrak had spoken of. Maybe there were no watchmen left.

He was surprised to find the eating room empty. Marrak put his head out of the kitchen. 'You are out after curfew.'

Lebasi was in no mood to give excuses or to explain. 'Where's my da?'

Marrak folded his arms and studied him. 'You have argued with the girl, Faya.'

'How do you know about that? What's it got to do with you?'

Marrak smiled. 'It is reported. And I was once a young man, you know. I will get your dinner.' He turned back to the kitchen, apparently satisfied that a squabble with a girl was a good enough reason to miss the curfew bell.

'Where's my da?'

'He has gone to bed. He has to leave very early in the morning.'

Lebasi stared out of the window as he ate his food. He decided to catch Xela just before he set out. He'd be distracted by the journey, and he'd have to go straight afterwards. If there was going to be an argument, it would be shorter than if he woke him now and gave him the whole night to be angry about it.

✳ ✳ ✳ ✳ ✳

Lebasi slept lightly, listening for his father getting ready to leave. He woke from a doze and heard soft voices downstairs. The stars were still bright in the sky. As it was almost Midsummer, that meant it must be very early indeed.

Xela was sitting at the table with a plate of dried fruit. His face looked lined and tired in the lamplight, but he smiled at Lebasi and pulled out a chair. Marrak poked his head around the door, disappeared, then returned with two mugs of tea and another plate. He didn't speak.

As they finished breakfast, a low voice came from the front door. 'Xela! Are you there? It's Elmass.' Xela signed with his hand for Lebasi to stand behind the door, tapped his finger against his lips and then his ears. Permission to listen in. That was unusual. Xela stepped out into the hall.

Lebasi could see a little through the crack between the door and its frame. Elmass made the sign of respect, and Xela touched his forehead.

'The ox is tied to your front door post. As required, five javelins, forty arrows, two longbows, six helmets from the woodworkers of this town. Plus another forty arrows from the outlying villages. That's our quota for the year.'

'Thank you, Elmass. I'm sure they're good quality?'

Elmass tutted. 'You know I wouldn't settle for anything less. I've looked them all over myself, and they're all sound and straight. But it breaks my heart to spend so much time and effort making something that will never be used. How much is there now?'

Xela leaned close to Elmass, but he half-turned so his voice carried to Lebasi. 'You know I can't tell you anything about the storeroom where there are a hundred years' worth of arrows and javelins and helmets and longbows from all the towns and villages of the district.' He tugged his earlobe, just like a child in class with a secret. 'So you wouldn't be able to work out that there must be about ten thousand arrows in there by now, because I wouldn't have told you anything of the sort.'

Elmass chuckled. 'Of course. Almost makes you want to have a battle, doesn't it?'

Xela hardly moved, but Lebasi could see the sudden tension in his face. 'A battle, Elmass? What do you have in mind?'

Elmass took half a step back and spread his hands. 'Honestly, Xela, it was just a joke. I didn't mean anything by it. Just all those bits and pieces sitting in that store never being used.'

Xela relaxed again, and Elmass coughed nervously. He shifted from one foot to the other. Xela studied his face. His voice was gentler. 'If you have something to say, friend, then say it.'

'I've been hearing strange talk around some of the inns. Mostly beery nonsense. Nothing worth reporting with names. But who knows what it leads to? If some people are saying things in public, others will be talking in quiet places, with no beer, and some may have ideas they wouldn't normally have. May share them, find that more people have the same ideas. I don't know.'

Xela put a hand on the man's arm. 'I'm aware of it. I think it's nothing, at least for the moment. If you get a chance, just say loose talk is unwise. Don't get upset, don't provoke anyone. I'll be back on Airsday, that's six days. Keep Marrak informed. I'm sure this will pass.'

Elmass didn't look convinced, but he made the sign of respect and left. Lebasi stepped out and watched Xela putting his boots on. Nomara was right: he was much less well-informed than he thought. Lebasi was on the point of telling him everything – but let him first answer a question.

Marrak appeared from the kitchen with a leather food-pack and a water skin. They all went out to the street and found the ox tethered. The bundles tied to its back were wrapped in sackcloth. Lebasi assumed this was to hide the fact that everything underneath was against the law.

He put his hand on a long package that might have contained javelins. 'I thought we aren't supposed to have weapons.'

Xela turned from inspecting the loads. 'These aren't for us. They go in a big store-room, as I said to Elmass. There they wait for a time that the king's army needs them. And if I don't take them every year, the king will be angry.'

Marrak sniffed. 'It is a waste of time.'

'You tell his majesty, then. Until he orders me to stop, I'm going to stick with it. Anyway, it gives me a reason to see the mayors and get a feeling for what's going on in that part of the district.'

Marrak made the sign of respect and went back inside. It was clear that Xela was about to leave. Lebasi had not worked out how to ask about Shelba. He tried for more time: 'Can I come with you as far as the gate?'

Xela ran his hand through his hair. 'I don't see why not. I don't think we'll meet any watchmen. They're a bit short-handed at the moment.' He handed Lebasi a cloak from the rack by the door. 'Here, it's cool at this time of the night.'

It was the same route that Lebasi had followed to the donkey stables for his apprentice day. The sky was beginning to lighten, and there were noises of stirring in the houses as they passed. The ox was big and black and slow-moving and a little smelly. Its curving horns looked vicious to Lebasi, but Xela assured him he could lead it all day by the rope attached to the ring in its nose and it wouldn't complain. 'He won't cause any trouble. Same as everyone else in Xessus.'

Lebasi could not believe that Xela, who knew everything, could be so blind. 'Why do you think that?'

'I told you about Dennara being sent into the wilderness with the men and women who agreed to follow him. All the guts and backbone of Xessus walked out through the Westgate that day. They left behind the people who were afraid, and they taught their children to be afraid, and that's how it has been for generations.' Lebasi thought that sending away the best and bravest children every year would have the same effect, but he had never challenged Xela about that. His da was still speaking. 'You saw the elders at the hearing. Only Tannaka spoke up for justice. The rest of them were all in favour of enforcing Riadsala's Mercy.'

'The rest of them and you.'

Lebasi took a step away, expecting a sharp reaction. Xela only shook his head, keeping pace with the ox. 'I told you. I am bound by the law and by the decision of the elders. I cannot let my own son go unpunished just because he is my son. If I did that, there would be –'

'Trouble? From the people who have no guts and backbone?'

Xela opened his mouth, closed it again, glanced at Lebasi, then chuckled. 'I can see that Ivar is teaching you something, at least. How to argue. Yes, maybe, even from them.'

Lebasi thought hard. Xela and Perra agreed on that, at least – it had been Perra's hope to cause trouble when Xela failed to apply the law to Lebasi. He could not bring himself to tell Xela he was mistaken in thinking every Xessan was a coward, but equally he could not let him walk away without some sort of

warning. He stood as tall as he could, not quite up to Xela's eye-level. 'Has anyone ever fought back since Dennara? A hundred and forty years is a long time to give in.'

Xela's smile disappeared. 'We have no choice. You don't understand –'

'No, I don't understand, because you never explain. You're the one who told me I should stand up to the bullies, you –'

Xela interrupted. 'I did no such thing. You're like me, you remember every word anyone ever says to you. Think. What did I say, exactly?'

Lebasi pictured Xela sitting beside his bed in the lantern-light.

'You told me to put the finger on them. You told me not to let them get away with it. Not to let them do it to anyone else.'

'And did that mean standing up to them? Fighting them, when they're stronger and meaner than you?'

Lebasi remembered how it felt when he tried to struggle against Ruffur's arm. Pointless. But Nomara had attacked them, driven them off...

Xela spoke slowly and evenly, as if holding himself in. 'I wanted you to tell me their names so I could do something about it. If the bully's bigger than you, you need someone to frighten them. The bullies here are frightened of me, but who frightens the Westwall Guard? Who do we tell? Who's going to do something about the king for the people of Xessus?'

'We could try, instead of just rolling over.'

Xela stopped and pressed his forehead against Lebasi's. He gripped Lebasi's shoulders hard, then let go, turned aside and banged his fists together, growling something incomprehensible. The ox halted and turned its great head, as if to see what the matter was.

'I don't want to part like this, but I'm not discussing this with you here, now. You know nothing of the Westwall Guard, of what it was like when they were posted all through the countryside. We keep them out, we live like free people.'

Lebasi glanced down the avenue. The gate was fifty paces away. It was now or not at all. One last chance for Xela to find out. 'Tell me about Shelba. Now, before you go. You said you'd need an eightnight to get the words straight. You've had more than two.'

Xela seemed to swell, to grow taller. He held his arms out, fists clenched, trembling, as if he was holding up a great weight. Even in the dim light, Lebasi could see the muscles in his neck standing out.

'Da, I need to know. People say terrible things.'

'I don't care what they say. They don't know.'

'What about me, though? You ought to care about what I think. All I get are the things other people say.'

Lebasi could hear Xela's teeth grinding. The thought crossed his mind that Perra might be right, Xela's temper could have run out of control. He took half a step back, ready to jump.

'I can't bear –'

'Tell me!'

'I can't bear for you to think badly of her.'

'Why would I...?' Lebasi's voice trailed away without finishing the question.

'It was her choice. You, a baby, me, a young father. She decided we could manage without her. Abandoned me to bring you up alone. What she chose to do still makes me more angry than I can stand, and I knew her, I loved her. You were too small to even remember her. How could you forgive her for that?'

Abandoned? What could that mean, when the people of the town weren't allowed to spend a single night outside the gates? Impossible. Xela could only mean... Perra had talked about the burial ground for people who brought bad luck. Diseases, murder victims – and people who killed themselves. Xela had appeared in mourning clothes. His grief wasn't guilt – unless maybe he had driven her to do it with his temper.

He breathed, 'Why did she do that?'

Xela's hand cut him off. 'No more. Go home, keep out of trouble. I'll talk to you when I get back.' He wiped his sleeve across his eyes and turned, pulling the ox's rope.

Lebasi watched man and beast amble away until they disappeared around the corner of the street that led to the gate. He pressed his knuckles into his temples. His head seemed too full. He wanted not to have to think. He was almost too tired to walk back up the hill to his bed.

24
FLAG

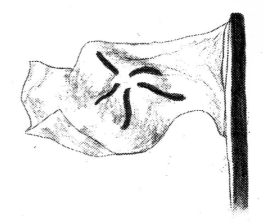

Lebasi lay on his bed with his shoes on. He heard the rising bell, but took no notice. He was supposed to be helping to set up the Space for the Midsummer feast, but he didn't care. Marrak didn't come to get him. He closed his eyes and tried to doze, wanting to forget everything.

At the mid-morning break bell, he gave up and admitted that he was wide awake. Too many thoughts were running around his head. In particular, he wanted to find Perra and shout at him. He ate the food that Marrak had left on the eating-table and set off for the Space.

Everything was as he expected. There was no sign of a revolution. Workers and apprentices were arranging tables and chairs. The stage for the singing and dancing was taking shape on the left. He scanned the Space. He had no idea where in the whole town Perra might be.

'Lebasi! About time. If it wasn't Midsummer I'd give you a good hiding.' The manager of the refreshment house grabbed his arm and pulled him towards the other workers. Lebasi didn't argue. He could watch and wait here as well as anywhere. He picked up a stack of chairs and fell in behind some other apprentices carrying a table.

'Basi!' He turned round, wondering who sounded so pleased to see him. Kara's friends, all seven of them, lined up to give him respect again.

'Would you like some water? We're supposed to bring food and drink to everyone.'

Lebasi couldn't help smiling. He watched them running across the Space, pestering people to ask for a mugful, spilling half of it in their hurry to deliver. They brought Lebasi something every time they passed.

'Enough,' he said at last, as they crowded around him again during the lunch break. 'You've been feeding me so much I shan't be able to move.' They laughed as if this was the funniest joke they'd ever heard. Lebasi studied each of them in turn. This never happened: seven people all grinning at him, liking him. They might only be small, but a light, fluttery feeling in his chest was fighting against his anger.

He worked through the afternoon singing along with the entertainers practising on the stage. The work helped him to forget about everything else.

When the afternoon bell rang, the Space had been transformed. Lanterns, ribbons and puppets hung from the trees. Tables and chairs were set for the feast. Pitches and tracks had been marked out for games and competitions. Roasting fires had been built up, waiting to be lit. Under the shade of the trees, four men were guarding a large number of barrels of beer.

Lebasi's boss rested a sweaty hand on his shoulder. He said 'All ready for tomorrow, eh?' Then he winked, as if to say, 'You and I know something about tomorrow that other people don't.' Lebasi started to ask a question, but the man touched his ear and turned away.

Lebasi slept fitfully. He dreamed of his father, somewhere out on the road with the ox, walking into the distance. He dreamed of Faya, pointing at the stone across the borderline. He dreamed of Kara, lying on the table, Xela holding the knife against her arm – but then it wasn't Kara, but a grown woman whose face he couldn't see.

It was a relief when the rising bell roused him. The early morning sky was as clear as usual. The lower reaches of the town, and the countryside beyond, seemed as peaceful as they had on every other day he had looked out of his window.

He had just finished breakfast when someone hammered on the front door. Marrak strode out of the kitchen, drying his hands on his apron before tossing it onto a chair. Lebasi followed him out into the hall. He pulled open the front door to find a man in a dark grey uniform, panting, his hands on his knees. Lebasi recognised him as one of the watchmen who had taken Perra down to the cells. There seemed to be something wrong with him: his eyes were too wide open. Lebasi could see blood on his forehead.

Marrak pulled him inside. 'What has happened, Hamon? Calm yourself.'

Hamon flopped onto the bench and raised his arm. 'Look at the bell tower.'

Lebasi joined Marrak on the front step. They could only see the very top of the tower over the rooftops, but it was clear that something was hanging from it – a large piece of cloth.

Marrak began to ask, 'What is it?' But then the morning breeze caught it and blew it out straight. Marrak put his hand to his mouth.

Lebasi had never seen anything like it before. It appeared to be a bedsheet or tablecloth on which someone had drawn a figure in charcoal: five lines, one straight up at the top, two just above the horizontal, two diagonally downwards. If the top line had been replaced by a circle, it would be a crude drawing of a person.

Lebasi turned to the agent. 'Marrak, what does it mean?'

The agent was still staring at the banner. He snapped his attention back to Lebasi, glanced quickly up and down the street, then pushed him and Hamon back into the hall, slamming the door shut behind them. 'I told your father, I told him. Now he is gone, and they have taken the bell tower. I cannot make a signal.'

Lebasi started to ask a question, but Marrak had disappeared into a store-room off the hall. He returned with his arms cradling several iron bars. Lebasi had never seen them before. Working in silence, the agent set them across the inside of the door, resting the ends in slots on each side. Lebasi had often wondered what they were for.

When he had finished, Marrak turned and leaned on the door. 'It is the mark of Dennara. The flag of old Xessus. To show that sign requires a sentence of death, anywhere in the kingdom.'

Hamon groaned. 'Tell him about the brand, Marrak, why don't you?'

Marrak's mouth twitched. 'When Dennara was exiled, those who went with him chose to go. Riadsala made sure they could not come back. That mark was burned into their skin with hot iron before they were sent into the wilderness.'

Marrak hurried around the ground floor, pulling the shutters closed and barring them. Hamon sat with his head in his hands. For something to do, Lebasi fetched a cloth and some water and offered to clean his cut.

'What happened to you?'

'I had the night watch up at the Space. All quiet. Bellman comes and goes up, rings the rising bell, time for me to go home. Then I look up and there's this thing hanging there, bellman must have put it out, I can't see it properly until the wind catches it. And then I set off at a run to come here, and suddenly there's men in masks at the corner of the downstreet, and they give me a bit of a hiding –'

There was a knock at the door. Marrak appeared in the eating-room doorway. Lebasi stared at the tough leather breastplate and the iron helmet he was wearing. He held a small round shield on his left arm and a short sword in his right. Lebasi had never seen such things before. He wondered where Marrak kept them, illegal as they were for anyone in Xessus apart from the king's man. They looked dusty.

He muttered to Lebasi as he walked past, 'I am as in practice with these as your father is with his surgeon's knife. Let us hope I remember as well as he.' He stood behind the door and called out, 'Who is there? What do you want?'

'Good morning, Marrak.' Lebasi recognised the voice, but the agent plainly did not. 'It's Perra.'

'Bennek and Lodder are taking the holiday spirit a little far, are they not?' Lebasi was surprised: he couldn't remember Marrak ever making a joke before, and this seemed a serious time to start. His respect for the man increased.

'Have you got Lebasi in there?'

'Why do you want to know?'

'I've come to take him up to the Space. Guest of honour at our meeting.'

Marrak turned and studied Lebasi's expression. Lebasi spread his hands as if he didn't understand. The agent faced the door, resting one hand on the handle of the sword. Lebasi was surprised at how even his voice remained – it was as if he was saying it was time for dinner. 'Hamon says he was attacked. It seems I would be foolish to open this door.'

Perra sounded equally calm, cheerful rather than threatening. 'Marrak, I give you my word that we will leave you in peace for the time being. It's Midsummer. I have no wish to hurt anyone in this town. Let me have Lebasi, and you and Hamon can keep each other company.' There was a pause. 'But if you don't open the door, I've men out here who will.'

Lebasi stepped forward and whispered in Marrak's ear. 'It's all right, I'll go with them.' Marrak shook his head.

'Perra, if everything is peaceful, can I make my usual morning rounds? I would like to see the view from the bell tower.'

Perra laughed. 'Of course you would. But I'm afraid that won't be possible today, or ever again. You'll stay put while the town decides what to do with you.'

Marrak sighed. 'You know that this is already enough to bring the soldiers back forever. Perhaps Xela is right. Perhaps they will burn the town, maybe they will hang the women and children from the trees as Rednaxela ordered. That is what you have done.'

Perra banged on the door. 'They will have to fight us first. And we will be ready for them. More ready than you and Xela think. Now send out Lebasi, before I break this door down.'

Hamon had put his head between his knees and was rocking gently from side to side. Marrak stood back from the door and levelled his sword. 'You shall not have him, Perra. You would not dare to ask if Xela were here. And as Xela is not here, you will have to get past me.'

Lebasi could have hugged Marrak, if he wasn't carrying a sword and shield. He didn't want Perra to break the door down, and he didn't want Perra to have to explain that he really would be a guest of honour – first scout of the revolution. 'Sorry, Marrak, I can't let you fight them for me,' he muttered, then ran upstairs. He didn't think Marrak would leave the hallway. He climbed out of his bedroom window and halfway down the wall before jumping into the garden. He was up and over into the alleyway and out in the street in the time it took to take ten breaths.

A small crowd had gathered. Some of them wore masks. Several were struggling with a log that they had lined up across the street and were manoeuvring to use as a ram. Lebasi shouted, 'Stop!'

Perra turned from the door and smiled. 'That's all right, Marrak, he's out here already. You can go back to whatever it is you southerners like to do in the morning.'

He started uphill towards Lebasi. Marrak's voice came from inside, but Lebasi could not make out the words.

25
REVOLUTION

After only seeing Perra in the half-light of the cave, it was strange to be able to look at him properly. He was thinner than he had been back in the spring by the border, paler and with a faraway look in his eyes that had not been there before. But he had shaved and cut his hair since Moonsday, and he was bouncing on his feet as they climbed the downstreet.

Lebasi was determined to challenge him about putting the other apprentices up to getting him beaten, but he didn't know how to with a crowd of Perra's supporters following close behind. Perra saved him the trouble. He put an arm round Lebasi's shoulder as they walked, and said, 'Faya tells me you're not best pleased with me.'

'No.' Lebasi couldn't think of anything to add.

'I'm sorry, Basi, but you can't start a fire without striking a spark. That's a bit rough on the flint and the steel, but we need light and heat to live.'

'Why did you pick on me?'

'I needed something to make everyone see how unjust the law was, and how it was enforced. I was sure your father would let you off, and then everyone would get up and riot.'

'You were wrong.'

'Yes, I misjudged him. He's a fair man, fairer than I realised. I had someone listening outside the court. When I realised he was going to beat you, I knew I had to step in. To be frank, I thought for a moment he might do what the law requires and beat you in public, and that would probably have been just as good at starting things off. Next best would be if he'd given me fifty strokes out in the Space.'

'You might have died!'

Perra squeezed his shoulder. 'I suppose I might. But there would have been enough people who'd know that it was wrong. It would make them do something, you see? Until you set the spark, everyone carries on and no one will ever change. We lie down in the street and let the ox-cart wheels roll over us.'

Lebasi almost stopped – was Perra thinking of his mother? He glanced at Perra's face. His grim expression showed he had chosen the image deliberately.

Lebasi tried to turn his mind to the present. 'But he didn't beat you.'

Perra shook his head. 'No. He's clever as well as fair, your da. He knew I was up to something. What he didn't know was how important Midsummer was, and how difficult it would make things if I was locked away. It would have been a lucky guess for him, that I'd need to be on the streets to have another go at setting that spark today, and he'd put me underground for another quarter of a year. But I was lucky too – even if it didn't show everyone what Xela is, it showed you. And you rescued me just in time to put everything in place. So you really are the guest of honour, Lebasi. Marrak thought I was being sarcastic, maybe kidnapping you as a hostage, but I meant it. Without you and your bravery that night in the tunnels, none of this would be happening.'

When Perra said 'what Xela is', the image that came first into Lebasi's mind was his father's eyes focused on Kara's arm, saving her life. He wished he could show that picture to everyone instead of Perra's version.

He glanced around at Perra's followers. Why were they wearing masks? He thought of Hamon, a grown man shaking with fear. Marrak, ready to fight to protect him from the rebels. His da, somewhere out in the countryside with an ox-load of weapons. Were the other towns in revolution too?

People were coming out of houses and following them up towards the Space. The older ones wore frowns and shook their heads. Many of the younger men laughed and danced and shouted. Children scampered around the edges of the crowd. Lebasi and Perra led the way out of the eastern downstreet and found more people emerging from other directions. Arms were raised, pointing at the sign on the flag. Some were singing songs from the legends of Xessus. Lebasi could see a group of young men had gathered round the beer barrels and were passing out mugs. He glanced back to pick out the courtroom door: it stood open, and Bennek and Lodder were kneeling on the avenue with their hands on their heads, surrounded by people jeering at them.

Perra made his way onto the stage. He blew a loud whistle. Lebasi followed him and looked down on the mass of people, seeing more masked men with sticks herding them like sheep at shearing time. Most seemed to be in good humour, but he saw some arguments break out and be settled with a shake of the stick, or sometimes a blow. Gradually the crowd gathered in front of the stage. It seemed that most of the town was there, early for the feast. Lebasi realised that many of them were staring at him, pointing, whispering. He turned red and stepped back, putting himself half behind Perra. He glanced to the left – there were several men of Perra's age, and Faya. She kept her eyes forward and her face stony.

Perra held up his hands for quiet. 'Friends! Today is the first of the special days of Midsummer. It is a very special day: the first day

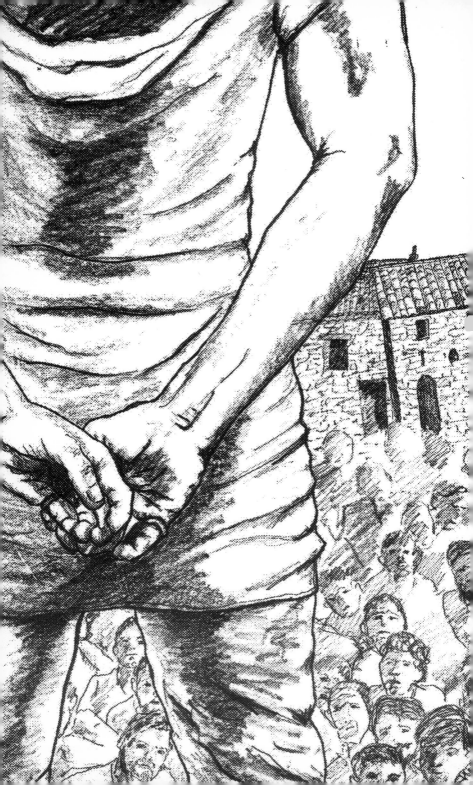

of the new age of Xessus, an age without the king.'

There were some cheers, but in the breadth of the Space they sounded half-hearted.

'From today, you will be able to go out into the fields without waiting for a gatekeeper to say you can go, you will be able to stay with your friends in the villages, you will be able to go to visit the other towns and trade with them.'

Each announcement was met with gasps. Some of the listeners hugged each other. Others shook their heads. A voice shouted, 'You'll bring the Guard on us, you young fool.'

Perra spread out his hands. 'Let them come. We will be ready.'

A white-haired man pushed his way to the front and jabbed his finger up at the stage. 'We can't fight the Guard. You don't remember, you've never seen them. You ask the greybeards, we know.'

A woman in the front row agreed. 'Longbows and swords, they have. And they used to use them. Sometimes for a reason, sometimes for no reason but to show us they could. What have we got? Sticks and stones, and we don't even know how to fight with those.'

Lebasi thought of his father's words: *all the guts and backbone of Xessus...*

Perra tapped his fingers together. 'I know this is strange. I understand it's alarming. But freedom is worth fighting for. I should know, I've been underground these last three moons.'

'How'd you get out, then?' came a voice. Lebasi wanted to sink into the woodwork. He hoped Perra wouldn't say.

'I have friends you would not expect,' he laughed. Lebasi saw people looking at each other, shrugging. 'And we, the people of Xessus, have friends you would not expect. We will not have to fight the Guard alone. And we have swords and longbows too, and we are learning to use them, starting today.'

Lebasi felt a hand on his shoulder. He turned to see the face of a man he did not recognise. He was smiling, but his grey eyes seemed to bore into Lebasi's head. He had a high forehead and a long straight nose, which he was looking down like someone who expected his orders to be obeyed without question. He gave Lebasi's shoulder a squeeze and stepped past him to stand beside Perra. He held his hands loosely behind his back. Lebasi stared at them. There were no tattoos. He took in the man's skin, a little darker than most Xessans. His leather boots, dusty from a long journey, his finely-made cloak, gold rings on his fingers. A southerner. He was certain of it, even though the only other one he'd ever seen was Marrak.

The people in the front row fell silent at the sight of the stranger. Perra turned to him and smiled. 'Here is someone to tell us that we have friends in the south.'

The man's voice was deep and seemed to fill the Space. 'Good morning, people of Xessus. I have come from Egator –' A thousand people breathed in, a thousand breathed out. No one spoke, but there was a sound like a giant sighing.

He waited for silence to return. 'I have come from Egator to find out if you people know your history.' There was a sound of shifting feet. Some stood straighter, some lowered their heads. Lebasi could see they did know, and many thought that history was dangerous.

The stranger pointed up to the flag flapping at the top of the bell tower. 'You know what I am talking about. You are concerned I will say things you dare not speak aloud. Well, how about the name of Dennara Al-Annaram, then? Who is for remembering the greatest Xessan who ever lived, since Xessus himself walked the earth?'

Someone called out, 'We don't dwell on the past.'

The southerner wagged a finger. 'You are telling me what

you have been told to believe. You must know your history. If you do not know where you have come from, you do not know where you are, and you certainly have no control over where you are going.'

He leaned forward, as if sharing a secret with the throng. 'You think the south is all for the king, all against the memory of Dennara. I am here to tell you it is not so. There are some in the south who think well of the people of Xessus, who regret your long suffering under the cruel laws of Riadsala. I want to find out if you are ready to stand up for yourselves, or whether you are content to be ruled by the distant king.'

Full-scale muttering broke out at that. Someone called out, 'What do you mean, then? We can't stand up for ourselves against the Westwall Guard. If we try anything, they'll march in here and cut us to pieces.'

Someone else shouted, 'You say we're going to learn how to use longbow and sword. How d'you know Xela hasn't sent for the Guard already? We'll not learn to use them in two days.'

Perra stepped forward again, holding up his hands for quiet. 'Xela suspects nothing. He has sent no message. Marrak is confined to his house.'

The objector argued back. 'What about when Xela finds out, though? He can pass the news quicker than you can think it.'

Perra folded his arms. 'Do not worry about Xela. He is on a long journey to the Westwall, and when he gets there, he will find a surprise waiting for him.'

Lebasi looked round sharply. He was about to speak, but several voices from the crowd were quicker. 'What sort of surprise?'

Lebasi could only see the side of Perra's face, but the man's smile chilled his stomach. 'We will not be seeing our lord magistrate again.'

'No!' The thought had obviously escaped his mouth. Perra, the stranger, the other men on the stage and Faya all turned towards him. He spoke quietly, not wanting the people in the crowd to notice him. 'What are you going to do to my da?'

Perra shook his head. 'Flint and steel, Basi. The spark is in the tinder, and it has to burn.'

He realised that any protest would be a waste of time. If there was one thing he knew about Perra, it was that the man was sure his way was right. The Mercy was evil, and Xela stood for the king's law – Lebasi could see that. Part of him still ached with the humiliation of the beating, the realisation that his own father wouldn't protect him. But there was a sharper pain in his chest at the thought that Xela was walking into a trap – they were going to kill him – he had helped to make that possible. His lungs filled up with air which he couldn't breathe out.

And there was another thing. Only Xela knew what had happened to Shelba. Perra couldn't tell him. He had to know. He had to see his father again. But how could he interrupt Perra in his moment of glory and explain all that? If he tried, and Perra didn't think his need to find out about his mother was a good reason to spare Xela, even for a little while, then he wouldn't have the chance again.

Those thoughts churned around his head in moments, while Perra fixed him with a steady gaze. He shrugged, as if he accepted that the man was right. Perra turned again towards the crowd. Lebasi could no longer concentrate on what the man was saying. He could only think of Xela, and how they had parted. He ran his eyes across the crowd, every face turned upwards towards Perra and the man from the south. He glanced sideways at Faya, who was staring at the floor. He took a silent step backwards, then ran towards the side of the stage and jumped. He staggered as he landed but kept his feet, and sprinted towards the edge of the Space.

The crowd were gathered in front of the stage. There was no one between him and the nearest downstreet, his own.

Cries of 'Stop him!' came from behind. Some of the men with sticks were moving in the corner of his eye – but he was already between the buildings and running. The street ran straight to the third avenue – he could see people down there, people still coming up from the outer circles, people hearing the shouts from behind him. He reached the second avenue and turned left without a moment's hesitation. He heard something heavy fall behind him – someone had thrown a stick.

There were alleys on the left, but they led straight back up to the Space. There was a long, low building on the right with no gaps – ahead, more men were coming out onto the avenue. He was trapped.

He saw a familiar door on the left, ran to it and dragged it open.

26
MARRAK

The pursuit was at the door while he was still dodging between the piles of equipment. He pulled things over as he passed them, hoping Anibor would forgive him. It wasn't Anibor's fault. As he tugged the drain door open he had to glance back. They were halfway across the room, four or five of them. But he was fast, and he knew the tunnel. Would they dare to follow him into the dark?

He could hear them swearing as he made his way around the corner, counting his steps and feeling for the first knot. He was right. They weren't coming down without a waterworker. But maybe there'd be one in Perra's gang, maybe there'd be one close at hand.

At the top of the first ladder he turned to feel for the topmost rung, and he could see torchlight. He swore, and scampered down faster than was safe. Turning again at the second ladder, he could see nothing – he was quicker than them. He could hear noises, but they were growing fainter. Third ladder, fourth ladder, fifth ladder. Now there was only the familiar echo of his own feet. He wondered how he had ever worried about giant rats.

The room at the end was as he'd left it. He untied the rope from the bush and peered out. There would be no point in going down, there was no way out of the pit. He leaned back and looked up – he'd tried that before, and it had been too steep. Could he do it now, with fear to give him a lift? He glanced across at the garden wall, on the same level as him and just ten paces of steep rock away, and had a different idea. He wrapped three turns of one end of the rope around his right wrist and three turns of the other around his left, and pulled. It was taut, and he knew it would hold him. Was that a noise somewhere behind him in the tunnel? It would have to work. He put his weight on the rope and stepped out onto the face, trying to angle himself so his feet would grip, and started walking.

Ten paces, nine, eight, seven, six... it was getting harder... five, four... the tree was behind him now, and the angle of the line meant that he was trying to walk uphill. It wasn't working... three, two... his foot slipped and he was swinging, spinning on the line. He held tight and hoped he wouldn't fall. As he flew past the opening he strained for an idea. They were coming, and he would just be dangling here.

At the end of his arc he had to use his feet to fend himself off from a jutting rock. He started to swing back again, turning his body round. He passed the doorway, his feet waving uselessly under him until he was able to plant them on the face. He was four paces short this time.

He needed a run-up to make it all the way – and it came to him. He kicked away from his house. Another kick, another, then faster past the cave, spinning on the rope to get a good shove off from the outcrop. Facing the right way now, he put in three more springs on the way back. The wall came closer, closer. He got his feet on it, but lost his balance and swung down again, banging his shoulder. Still, this time he knew it could be done. He righted himself and put more force into his kicks. He clenched his fists, hoping he could shake the rope off quickly when he needed to. Four, three, two, one... feet on the wall... he threw his weight forward, freed his wrists, teetered for a moment, then grabbed a bush with both hands and pulled himself into it. The rope slid over his arms and fell back. Without his weight, it snagged on something higher up and dangled halfway between him and the opening. A head appeared out of the rockface, looking down. Lebasi shrank back among the leaves.

'Well where is he then?'

Lebasi couldn't hear the reply.

'He's not down in the pit.' The man turned from side to side. Lebasi held his breath, wondering if he would spot the rope. 'Unless he can fly, that's where he'd have to be.'

A second head appeared. 'Menk it. Maybe he slipped into one of the side passages. I thought I saw something move against the light, but my eyes must've been playing tricks.'

'Do you know who it was?'

'No. I just heard them shouting "stop him".'

Lebasi let out a slow breath. They wouldn't put it together for a moment that this was where the fugitive wanted to be, exactly. If they didn't know it was the magistrate's son they were chasing, they wouldn't realise that he might have been trying to reach his own house. That would give him a little time.

The heads disappeared. Lebasi ducked behind the wall and ran across the garden. He realised that all the doors were still barred and the ground floor windows shuttered, so he climbed the wall and swung himself through his bedroom window.

'Marrak?' he called out, as he hurried along the landing.

The agent rushed into the hall. He was still wearing his armour and carrying the sword. He stared at Lebasi, then dropped the blade and bounded up the stairs. He gripped Lebasi by the shoulders, looking him up and down.

'You are all right? They have not harmed you?'

Lebasi shook his head. To his great surprise, Marrak put his

arms around him. It was an uncomfortable hug against the hard chest armour, but it was more affection than the agent had ever shown him.

They went together down to the eating-room. Hamon was sitting on a chair muttering to himself. He took no notice of Lebasi's arrival and seemed to have retreated into a private nightmare. Lebasi gave Marrak a quick report on what was happening on the Space. He finished with the threat to Xela. 'We have to warn him, Marrak.' He remembered how he'd parted from his father that morning. He swallowed. He might never see him again.

Marrak drummed his fingers on the table. He turned to the window and looked up at the sun. 'I need to send a signal to the agent at Gattras.'

'How do you do that?'

'There is a machine in the bell tower which reflects the sunlight. There is a man in the hills over there' – he waved out of the window – 'who sees the flashes and passes the message on to Gattras, which is on the other side of that ridge.' Marrak spread his hands and shrugged his shoulders. 'But I cannot go to the bell tower.' He muttered something under his breath, then loud enough for Lebasi to catch the words. 'I told him, but he would not listen. He would not listen. It is raining now.'

Lebasi stared out of the window. 'Where's the man who passes on the messages?'

The agent pointed due south.

'So you can see him from here, or where he is?'

Nod.

'You signal with mirrors?'

Another nod.

Lebasi opened the cupboard where the eating utensils were kept and dug out the one silver plate they possessed. He held it out and raised his eyes towards the ceiling.

Marrak bared his teeth. 'It might work, yes.' He took the plate and strode out of the room. By the time Lebasi reached the upper floor, Marrak's feet were disappearing through the hatch onto the flat roof. Lebasi scrambled up the ladder after him. Poking his head out, he saw the agent crouching by the parapet at the southern corner of the house, his hand shielding his eyes as he scanned the haze on the horizon.

Marrak glanced round. 'I need to concentrate, Lebasi. Please do not disturb me. Do not show yourself to the men below. And do not fall off. That would be the berry on the top of the cake.'

Lebasi climbed out and crawled on all fours to peep down into the street. There were men with sticks standing by the corners of the house, four uphill and four downhill. He scuttled across to the western edge to look down into the upper garden and the path beyond. At first he thought there was no one there, but then a movement caught his eye and he realised two boys were beyond the wall, playing a game on the pathway. On the special day in any other year most children would be enjoying a picnic in the meadows outside the southern walls. On this day nearly everyone would surely be in the crowd up on the Space, listening to Perra and the southerner talking revolution. There was no good reason for anyone to be hanging around the magistrate's house. He wondered if they were the children of the men in the street.

Lebasi reckoned Perra would work out where he had gone in the tunnels. After all, Perra knew where the drain came out, better than anyone. It was only a matter of time before he came looking. That log was still lying in the street ready to break down the front door. But maybe the message would take a little while to get back up the tunnel to the guildhouse, and maybe Perra would still be talking to the crowd. After all, what could Lebasi do to stop his revolution?

He would have a lot on his mind, and he wouldn't be worried.

Turning to watch Marrak, Lebasi's eye was caught by a bright flash in the distance. Marrak shielded his eyes and stared intently in the direction of the blinking light, his lips moving silently. He glanced upwards towards the sun, held the plate so the light reflected on the parapet, then lifted and turned it left and right, brows furrowed with concentration.

Lebasi saw more flashes from afar. Marrak sent another signal, there was another reply. He sat back and wiped his forehead with a handkerchief. 'The man in the hills spotted the light. We are not exactly on the same line as the bell tower, and not as high up, but he saw us all right.'

'Did you send a warning? Can he pass a message to my da?'

Marrak shook his head. 'No. We must think of a different way to do that.' He gazed towards the southern horizon. 'I have told him to send for the Westwall Guard. The time is here, they must come now. It may already be too late.'

Lebasi pictured the men in the street below with their sticks, the swords and longbows Perra said he had. He remembered his father's words: if anyone tries to fight the Guard, they will leave not a stone standing on a stone, not a soul alive. The townspeople knew they could not fight the Guard now, and surely couldn't learn to do so in the two or three days it would take them to get here. Would they even try, when the soldiers arrived? Anyone who had any courage would be in the army facing them. But the fact that they'd dared to start a revolution would surely be enough to bring down Rednaxela's fury. He remembered his father talking about the nobleman from the south, ready to make a name for himself with the blood of Xessans. He stared at Marrak in horror.

He gasped, 'What have you done?'

27
THE RUN

Marrak's face passed through astonishment to fury. 'How dare you, boy?'

Lebasi held up his hands, thinking quickly. 'Sorry, Marrak, I just mean my da needs to know. The Guard are coming here, not going to the Westwall. They won't be able to protect him, will they?'

Marrak's anger evaporated. His shoulders sagged. He sat studying his reflection in the plate. 'No. The towns he is going to, I cannot signal to them from here, and there is a hill that blocks Gattras from them as well. Xela is on his own.'

It was not a time to worry about information gained by eavesdropping. Lebasi said, 'I heard you talking about someone he has to visit, someone who argues with him. Do you think that's where Perra's surprise is going to happen?'

Marrak nodded. 'Yes. He thinks he knows them so well, they will never hurt him. But things have changed. That is where an ambush will be sprung, for sure.'

'I'll go.' Lebasi spoke the words before his brain had fully formed the idea. It was the only way. It was impossible, but there was no other possibility.

Marrak's first glance told him how ridiculous the suggestion was, but then the man's eyes narrowed, his shoulders straightened and he raised a hand to his chin. 'You play the chasing games in the streets, do you not? You are good at them?'

'Yes.'

Marrak nodded vigorously. 'That is what you must do. You can get past these people, get to the gates, go. Yes, yes. That is the answer.'

Now he was thinking about it properly, Lebasi was less sure. 'But I don't know the way to the Westwall.'

Marrak was scrambling to his feet. 'Come, I will draw you a map.' He stopped. 'But you must not take it with you. You could not be caught with such a thing. No, no. You must remember it. Can you do that?' He didn't wait for an answer, but scurried across to the open hatch.

Lebasi followed him down to the landing. Marrak turned into his own bedroom, beckoning Lebasi to follow. That door was always closed; he had only stolen furtive glimpses before. There was a table by the window, and shelves on the walls full of rolls of a thin material. He took one and spread it on the table, weighing down the corners with small stones. He picked up a feather from the shelf, dipped the pointed quill into a pot of black liquid, and started to make markings on the material. Lebasi watched in fascination. He had never seen any of these things before – what more secrets did Marrak keep in the house?

Marrak was speaking as he drew. 'A map is a picture of the land, as if you are a bird, high up, yes?' Lebasi nodded, hoping the meaning would become clear. 'Xessans are not allowed maps. That is why you must carry it in your head.' Lebasi realised the lines along the top of the scroll were shaped like jagged peaks. Marrak tapped them with the feather. 'The way you will know where you are going, it is the mountains. Always on your right, you go west until you reach the end of them. Here, there is a tall peak that local people call the Eagle's Nest. Then there is nothing.' Marrak drew a bird above the last mountain. Lebasi guessed it was supposed to be an eagle. He hoped the rest of the map was more accurate.

He marked three crosses below the ridge. 'You have heard the names of the towns, yes?' Lebasi nodded. Marrak pointed. 'Trengam, here. This is Nampetch. Do not go there. This is Marstor. You cannot see Marstor from Trengam, but you will pass between it and Nampetch. You will be safer in the countryside, in the fields. Not on the roads, not in the towns.'

Lebasi's head was spinning. 'But it's not allowed. I can't just walk over the border, I can't go outside Trengam's land.'

Marrak gave him an unexpected grin. 'The people of Marstor do not have two heads, boy. They look the same as you. You do not have the tattoo yet. Who can tell you are not supposed to be there?'

'But what if someone asks me –'

'Think of something. You have a brain. Tell them a story.' He went back to drawing.

Lebasi felt objections building in his chest, in his head. There were too many. It could never work. He'd be stopped, he'd be caught. What would happen to him then? But he imagined his father, a tiny speck moving somewhere on Marrak's diagram, walking unknowingly towards danger. He thought of the Guard, somewhere off the bottom of the picture, the new captain preparing to lead them to Trengam and end the Mercy. He took a deep breath, and dismissed his doubts. He would do it. There was no choice at all. He started to study the map in earnest.

'So. Your father will have taken the main road from here to Nampetch yesterday, then today he will travel towards Marstor. It is out of his way but he wants to speak to the mayor. Tonight he will camp somewhere along here, it depends whether the mayor will come to meet him or not. Tomorrow he must go on west to the road that is this line, but the ox is slow and he will not drive it hard. He will not be at the farm until the next day, Midsummer, in the

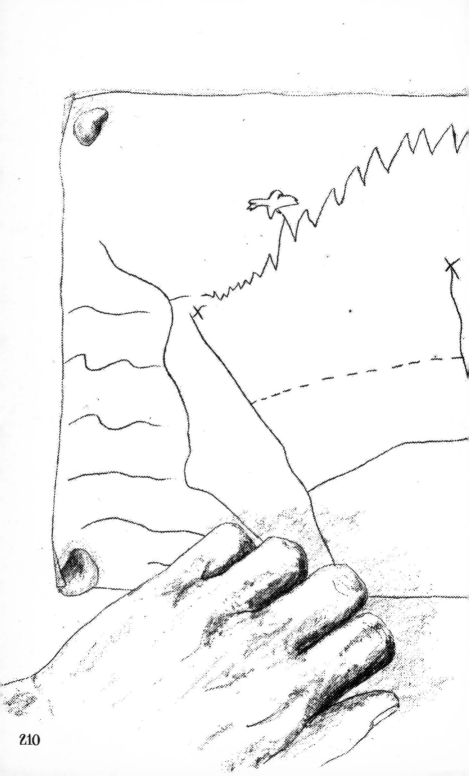

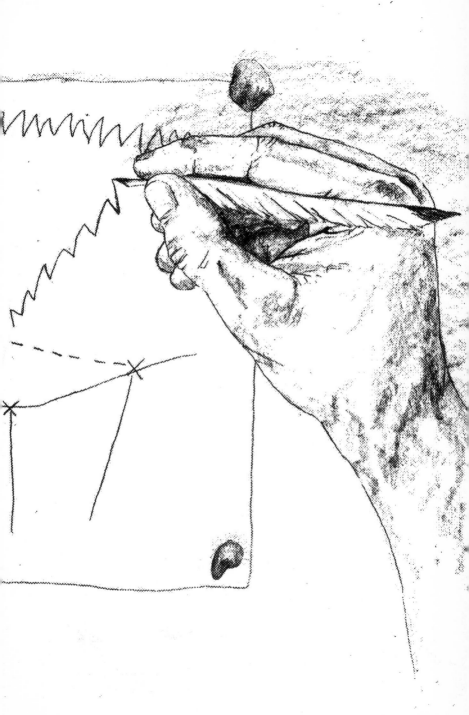

morning. You must get to him first.' He drew a line of dots from the cross that marked Trengam, heading a little north of west. 'Go here, up the track that leads towards Marstor. You will see the way because of the end of the first mountain ridge, here. Then due west, towards where the sun sets, as fast and as far as you can tonight. Tomorrow, or early the next day, you must reach the coast road ahead of Xela and warn him. You will know it because you will see the sea.'

'What's the sea?'

Marrak tapped the wavy lines on his map. 'It is a great deal of water, like a lake, only so big you cannot see the other side. The edge of the sea is called the coast, and this road is called the coast road. In case you have to ask anyone where you are.'

Marrak pointed to a straight line at the end of the mountains. 'This is the famous Westwall, and beyond it is the wilderness, where there is nothing but marsh and wild animals.' He prodded his feather just below the wall, making another black mark. 'Here, the last house in the kingdom, is the place he is going to. That is where danger lies for Xela. You must intercept him before he gets there. Can you do that?'

Lebasi memorised the shape of the land. He didn't know if he could, but he knew that he must. He tried to sound confident. 'Yes. But what will I eat and drink? Where will I sleep?'

Marrak considered. 'Best not to take anything. It will slow you down here in Trengam, where you are most likely to be stopped. And in the countryside, a boy with a pack is going somewhere, but a boy with nothing is just a boy. You can drink from the channels. The roadmen leave jugs of boiled water by the roadside in some places.' He stroked his beard, thinking. 'But for food, you must ask. It is the law of Xessus to help a stranger. Not the law of Riadsala, older than that. Think of a story to tell, and the people will give you food if you ask.' He paused, then emphasised his advice with a jabbing finger. 'Keep your story simple. Say too much and it is obviously a lie. Do not give away more than you have to.'

Knocking on someone's door in the middle of the countryside sounded risky to Lebasi. He wondered if he could get to the coast road without eating anything. He scanned the map again while Marrak pointed to different features, repeated their names and estimated the distance between them, then tested his recollection. It was perfect.

Marrak rolled up the map and looked deep into Lebasi's eyes. 'I hope this is the right thing. Your father will not be pleased, I think, but I can see no other way.'

Lebasi nodded. He didn't trust himself to speak.

'It is said where I come from, "a long journey is shorter when you have started it". Get ready. I will make you something to eat and drink.'

It was only a light snack. Marrak pointed out that trying to run on a full stomach wasn't sensible, and Lebasi agreed. His guts were squirming, anyway, and he couldn't eat more than a few handfuls of raisins. When he'd finished, Marrak led him up to the hall.

'Now. I think you had better go over the garden wall and up the track. None but children were minding it. I will cause a diversion in the street. I will wait for you to get out there.'

'How will I know when to go?'

Marrak smiled again. 'I think you will guess.' He put a hand on Lebasi's shoulder. 'Good luck. Please explain to your father I have done what I am sure is for the best.'

Lebasi wasn't sure whether that referred to calling for the Guard or sending him to take the warning. At least Marrak seemed to believe he would be able to pass that message to Xela, that he could make the journey and find him.

He put his head around the garden door to check that the boys in the pathway weren't looking over the wall, then scuttled across to stand with his back to it, listening. He could hear them talking quietly. He reckoned they were a few paces nearer the downstreet than where he was standing, but they'd surely catch him if he tried to climb over.

A shout from the right: Marrak's harsh voice, raised in anger. 'I am the magistrate's agent, and I wish to go to the bell tower. You are very foolish to get in my way.'

Lebasi couldn't catch the reply, but Marrak shouted again, saying that masks didn't fool him, naming the men, threatening them with Xela's wrath on his return. The response to that was perfectly audible: 'But he's not here now, is he, southrat? You're all on your own. So be a good boy and get back in your house, and no one needs to get hurt.'

Lebasi realised this was his moment. He found a good foothold and stepped up soundlessly to look over. As Marrak intended, the boys had gone to the street corner to watch the fun. Lebasi hoped he wouldn't take it too far and provoke violence. He wondered if the agent was threatening to use his sword, and what they would do if he cut someone. He dropped lightly into the pathway and started jogging up the hill, taking care to make no noise. If he could get to the first bend without them looking round...

'Hey!' A boy's voice, not yet a man's. But the men would follow.

Lebasi was ready. He set off at a sprint, around the corner into an alley between two workshops, left at the next junction, immediately right through the open doorway of an empty house. He didn't need to think: he'd practised escaping Sammas and Ruffur before Faya had called them off. He ducked through a broken doorway, out into the garden, scrambled over the wall and into yet another alleyway. That led to the eighth avenue: he ran straight across, hoping no one there would be looking for him. Glancing to left and right he saw only a few people in the distance. Straight uphill for sixty paces... at the bend he turned to look back – menk, the boys were in sight on the far side of the avenue, and they'd spotted him.

He chose a route with plenty of twists and turns, contouring around the hill to avoid tiring himself out. His legs felt tight, his heart was racing – this was as different from a game of chase as the story of Dennara was from the legends of Xessus. Most of his mind was concentrating on choosing the way, but a small part told him a surprising thing: *I'm enjoying this.* The air burning in his lungs, his heart thumping, the cobbles beneath his feet, the rough feel of the stones in the wall as he pushed against them for balance when skidding around a corner – he'd never felt so alive.

He didn't like to think what they'd do if they caught him, but he knew at best it would mean Xela wouldn't receive his warning. The thought of his father walking into a trap kept him going until he was sure he'd lost his pursuers. He crouched in a doorway, his chest heaving, and tried to work out how best to get out of town.

The north-west gate would be most direct. He was supposed to head for the end of the mountain ridge. He knew from the map that it lay between Trengam and Marstor – there was a road going in that direction. But he wondered if the rebels – even the word made him shiver, thinking about the likely reaction of the Guard – would guess where he was going. Marrak would tell them nothing. But they would realise that he had been in the house and had escaped from it. He had run from the stage when Perra had threatened Xela. They might work it out. Where else would the magistrate's son be running to, even if the idea of following his father was absurd? Maybe one of the other gates would be safer.

The emptiness of the town on the special day was in his favour. Maybe a few people had gone out early for a picnic, had missed the flag and had no idea what was going on; probably most people were on the Space. Apart from the small gang around his own house there was hardly anyone about. He crossed the eastern downstreet without being seen, then back across the eighth avenue to work his way towards the north-eastern gate. The downstreet there was straight: he could get a good view from the shelter of some beer barrels outside an inn.

He dug his fingernails into his palms. The gate was a hundred and fifty paces away, so he couldn't be sure what he was seeing, but there were three men with sticks instead of the usual single gatewarden. A boy and a girl ran into sight from the ninth avenue and spoke to them. The only reason for any of them to be there was to look for him. Perra had said that today everyone could walk out of the gates without question – everyone, perhaps, except for Lebasi. He jogged across the street, relying on the distance to conceal his identity, and headed further north.

He considered trying to climb the town wall, but he decided the jump down was too risky. It was a long drop into the ditch running around the outside. He might turn an ankle on landing, or worse. It would have to be a gate. He'd have to find one that was unguarded.

Peering out from the entrance to an alleyway on the northern downstreet, he realised he was clicking his tongue like his father. Another two men, more children. They were messing around with their sticks – banging them against each other. Practising to take on the Guard. What use were sticks? How many swords and longbows had Perra got his hands on? Did anyone know what to do with them? He stepped back into the shadows, trying to work out how he could slip by unnoticed.

'Gotcha!' A hand grabbed his shoulder. He jumped round, raising his fists, ready to fight in earnest. Mott and Akeme, two of Kara's friends.

'Woah! Don't worry, we're on your side,' said Mott. He put his hand on his heart and stood as tall as he could, coming up nearly to Lebasi's shoulder.

Akeme nodded vigorously, her blonde curls jiggling. 'We heard people are looking for you, we've come to help.'

Lebasi grinned at them. A moment ago he'd felt the whole town was against him. Two allies were welcome, even if they were small.

'Right. I need to get out of the gate, but there are people watching it. Any ideas?'

They all turned at the sound of ox-cart wheels on cobblestones. It crossed the end of the alleyway, trundling slowly down the street. The three looked at each other and touched their right ears. Catching a lift with a farmer was a standard game on freedays. If the gatekeeper was in a good mood, he would look the other way for children as young as Akeme and Mott to go outside and sneak back later. On any other Special Day, it wasn't even forbidden. On this day? It could work – as long as the load had something to hide under.

Mott and Akeme led the way. Lebasi glanced up the street before he broke cover. There was no one close by. In a moment he was behind the cart, hidden from the men below. There was nothing in it but a pile of empty sacks. Perfect. It was only moving slowly, but he needed to get in without the farmer seeing him. The back flap was hanging down, so it was easy to put his palms on the edge, lift himself up and roll forward. Akeme jumped up beside him, closely followed by Mott. Lebasi crawled under the sacks and felt the others piling more on top.

'Hey, what are you two doing?' The normal protest, not really angry.

'Just taking a ride, father. Looking at the view,' called Mott. *Father,* thought Lebasi, *he'll like that.* A term of respect.

He heard the man laugh good-naturedly. 'Don't you call me father or I'll be putting you across my knee like a son, you young rascal. Oh, go on then, the ox won't notice if he's going downhill empty.'

Through a gap in the sacking Lebasi could see Akeme's bare feet, the street beyond framed between the sides of the cart. They crossed the avenue. They must be close to the gate now.

'Hold up there,' came a voice. The cart slowed but didn't stop.

'What do you want?' The farmer didn't sound pleased to be challenged.

'We want you to stop your cart, old man.'

Lebasi heard a grunt of irritation. Maybe they should have called him father. 'It's a hard job to start him once he's stopped, lad. He's not going fast, talk to me.' The ox snorted and plodded on.

A younger voice said, 'We're looking for the magistrate's son.'

The farmer laughed. 'Why on earth would you be doing that?' His voice lowered a tone. 'Boys, what's with the sticks? You're not doing anything silly, are you?'

'Never you mind, old man. What are you doing driving your cart on a holiday?'

'I'd say that was none of your business – well, if you're going to be like that, I took some meat up to the Space yesterday ready to be roasted for the party. I stayed the night in a refreshment house on the fifth avenue. Got up late because it's a holiday, no one to give me my breakfast, there's thanks for you from the people of the town for a farmer giving them his best beef. And now I'm going home, and you're bothering me. Where's your respect, boys? I'll be talking to the elders, next time I see them.'

Lebasi closed his eyes. The old man didn't even know there was a revolution going on. The first voice spoke again. 'Elders! We've had enough of listening to the elders. Do this, do that. Enough of the outsiders, too. Time we made our own decisions.'

The old man muttered and sniffed. 'That's right dangerous talk, boys, you know that. You'll be bringing trouble –'

Another voice interrupted him. 'Who are these two?'

Lebasi hoped Mott and Akeme could act. He remembered Marrak's advice: don't say too much.

'I'm Mott...'

'... and I'm Akeme.'

'Where are you going, then?'

'We're just catching a ride. Nowhere, really.'

'Not far.'

'Out and back.'

The first man again: 'Have you seen Lebasi of Xela?'

'Not since yesterday,' Mott said.

Akeme contradicted him. 'That's not right. We saw him this morning. He was on the stage on the Space.'

'Oh yes, I remember. He was with Perra. I like Perra. Do you like Perra?'

The man sounded impatient. 'Never mind about Perra, I'm looking for Lebasi. Have you seen him since this morning?'

They chorused that they hadn't. Lebasi smiled. They're good. They sound innocent to me.

There was a sound of a stick striking the cobbles. The man barked an order. 'Stop the cart, old man, now, so we can look in the back.'

A girl spoke: 'It's all right, father. I can get on while you keep going.' Lebasi felt his eyes prickling. He bit his lip. Faya. He hadn't seen her in the group of children by the gate, but there was no mistaking her voice. He felt a tremor in the floor of the cart as she climbed up. He saw her legs through a gap in the sacks. Akeme and Mott had shut up. She was walking towards him. Could he jump over the side and run? Even the thought took too long – there was no time.

28
TO THE BORDER

Lebasi thought of grabbing hold of the sacking, trying to fool the girl that it was stuck on something – too late. She pulled it away. He blinked in the bright light. Faya glanced down at him, but her face showed nothing – no recognition, no triumph, no surprise. She dropped the cloth and called out, 'It's all right, he's not here.'

Lebasi stared at the rough brown material where Faya's green eyes had been a moment before. Had she not seen him? How was that possible? She was adjusting the sack now, making sure he was properly hidden. He felt the light bounce of the cart as she jumped off, he heard the guards telling the driver to carry on.

The last time they had spoken, he had shouted at her. She hadn't even acknowledged him that morning. She said she still supported Perra, still couldn't forgive Xela over Lakim. But maybe this was payment to him for the beating, or payment to Xela for Kara's life.

The ox kept going. Lebasi couldn't see out now, but he heard Mott and Akeme moving around and calling goodbyes to the gatekeepers. They started to play a hand-clapping game, repeating a nonsense rhyme and laughing at each other. Lebasi was aware of the plod of hooves, the old man muttering about a lack of respect, the crunch of wheels on the dry earth. He tried counting in his head to judge when he was safe, but time had stopped when Faya lifted the cloth and dropped it. He risked pulling a corner of a sack to make an opening. The wall appeared in the frame, then a tree, then more trees. They were out of town and out of sight.

Lebasi waited until he was sure the men weren't following. He pulled the sacks off his head and grinned at the children. He

mouthed, 'Is there anyone around?'

Akeme stood up and turned a full circle. She shook her head. Lebasi touched his nose and crawled to the back of the cart. He waited until they were passing through a grove of olive trees before dropping onto the road and stepping smartly into cover. The farmer didn't turn round. He heard the children thanking him for the ride and waited for them to join him.

Akeme fanned herself with her hands. 'That was close.'

Mott scratched his head. 'She was with them. Why'd she let Basi go? I thought we were done.'

Akeme laughed. 'She's Kara's sister. Maybe Basi's got a girlfriend.'

Lebasi grunted. 'I don't think so. I've no idea why she didn't turn me in. Anyway, no time to think about that now.'

'Where are you going?' asked Mott.

Lebasi was about to reply but Akeme interrupted him. 'Don't tell us. If we don't know, they can't make us say.'

'You don't think...'

Akeme opened her eyes wide. 'You didn't see, but they looked like they were going to hit the old man with their sticks. I heard someone say they were going to do horrible things to you if they catch you. That's why we came looking for you. Everyone's gone mad.'

Mott nodded. 'She's right, don't say. We'll go back in a different gate so we don't see them again. Everyone'll still be looking for you inside the walls. Like when Xessus the hero –'

Akeme put a hand over his mouth. 'Mott, you windbag, this is no time for stories. Come on, we'll head south, then Basi can go wherever he wants. Good luck.'

He thanked them as they crossed the road and disappeared among the trees. They should be all right – there was no reason for anyone to guess they knew where he was. He pushed his way through dense undergrowth to the northern edge of the wood until he could see how the land lay. Immediately in front, an open field, sheep grazing. Beyond it on the right, a farm, smoke wisping from the chimney. He scanned up and left, seeking out his first signpost – the end of the mountain spur that divided Trengam from Marstor. He glanced up to assess the position of the sun. Not good. The afternoon was already half gone, and it was maybe fifteen thousand paces to the border. There were any number of farms to get past. The revolution might not have spread out into the countryside, but he didn't want to have to explain himself. It would be easier to make progress if he didn't meet anyone.

He decided to put as much distance between himself and the town as possible. That meant going north first, west later. He set off across the field at a jog, looking for cover.

✻ ✻ ✻ ✻ ✻

At least so close to Midsummer there would be plenty of daylight. He worked his way through farmland slowly, keeping to the hedgerows that separated the fields, pushing through gaps to the other side if he saw anyone. He was scratched and bitten, and one encounter with a thorn bush all but cost him the right sleeve of his tunic. Stretches of woodland offered better cover, but there brambles and nettles slowed him down. He crossed several small streams by jumping from stone to stone, but the main water channel from the north was deep and wide, and he had to cast up and down the bank for a bridge. He paced himself so he wouldn't get out of breath in case he was spotted and had to sprint, but still he grew so tired that he could hardly remember why he was there: he only knew he had to keep going, he must make it to the end of that ridge before dark.

From time to time he glanced back across the open country

towards the town, its white walls and coloured roofs glowing peacefully in afternoon sunlight. He could pick out the avenues, could see the bell tower. He wondered if they were having the feast to celebrate their new freedom, or if they were practising with weapons for the coming of the Guard.

Whose side should he be on?

He couldn't work it out. Yesterday he'd told Xela that he thought Xessans should stand up against the king, and that was what Perra was doing. Xela enforced the brutal law, Xela had beaten him for something that was nothing. But Xela was still the da with whom he'd shared secrets, the doctor who saved lives. He couldn't abandon him to the trap that was being set. Apart from anything else, he still wanted an answer to his questions about Shelba, and if Perra meant what he said, the only way to get one would be to find his da and ask him, before... before the sparks hit the tinder. He wiped the sweat from his forehead and hurried on.

The sun had disappeared behind the distant mountains long before Lebasi reached the spur. For the time being it was still daylight, and even when the sun set, Lebasi knew that at Midsummer he would still be able to cover a good deal of ground in the dusk. For some time he had been able to see Nampetch on the other side of the hills that lay between it and Trengam. Now it was closer than his home. He still couldn't see Marstor, but he was almost at the edge of the mountains themselves, and was sure this must be the ridge Marrak had pointed out on the map. He was following a broad channel that flowed along the hillside. He'd never seen anything like it – cut out of the rock, at a gradient so gentle that the clear water in it moved without a ripple. He'd found it when he was forced to avoid a farmer and his sons driving their cows out into the fields after milking – their pastures were wide and open and he'd no possible business to be there, so he needed to keep out of sight. There was a good path beside the channel and the curve of the hill hid it from below, so he'd been stretching his legs. He was sure he must reach the border soon. He didn't know how he'd recognise it – there was a white stone on the road to Nampetch, but would there be anything up here in the foothills?

He stopped and sniffed the air. The light was definitely failing now, but he could still smell – there was woodsmoke, and... bacon. His mouth watered. He'd had plenty to drink from the channel, but hadn't had a thing to eat since the raisins at lunchtime, and he'd covered a lot of ground. He could ask for food, as Marrak said, but whoever was cooking was also a danger. He determined not to rely on the old law of Xessus until he was on Marstor land, at least. He wetted a finger and held it above his head: the light breeze was coming from in front. It was unlikely that there was a house up here. He bit his lip. Could someone be camping out to catch him? Had someone given him away – Marrak, Faya? Surely not – if Faya had wanted to, she'd had her chance. Had someone seen him running across the fields and guessed who he was?

He dropped down off the path into open woodland between the channel and the high pastures and ran from tree to tree, peering around them as if he was playing tag. The hillside ahead curved away to the right, which he took as a good sign of progress from what he could remember of the map. After two hundred paces he saw someone standing on a rocky outcrop high above, a man scanning the countryside. Lebasi waited, trying to breathe evenly. The watcher turned and disappeared.

Lebasi couldn't tell whether the man was one of many or alone, or whether he was on watch or there by coincidence. Anibor had mentioned the channelmen, another guild of waterworkers –

perhaps they spent the night up here while they were working. But if the man was there to catch Lebasi, were there others on the hillside below? He needed to know.

He ran in a crouch, keeping as well covered as possible, until he could see across the open country to the south. There were animals grazing, birds circling, and a farmhouse a few hundred paces away with lights in the windows and smoke rising from the chimney in a thin column that sloped gently towards the east. No men with sticks searching the fields. Lebasi let out a long breath that he hadn't realised he'd taken in. Maybe the man was nothing to do with him.

Still, he kept close to the bottom edge of the wood so the trees would hide him from view, and he kept low as he darted from one piece of cover to the next. He judged that he must have passed the man – the smell of bacon had faded. He peered out again. Where was the border?

A dog barked somewhere in the dusk behind him. It wasn't an unusual sound, but something about it sent a shiver down Lebasi's back. That dog meant business. A second dog joined in, a third, a fourth. He heard a man shout, then another. He looked round and opened his eyes wide in the gloom – yes, there was movement, on the edge of the woods a few hundred paces behind. The dogs were barking continuously now. He recognised the cry: they were hunting, and they wanted to be let off the leash.

He turned and ran. The tiredness in his legs vanished, but the tightness had returned to his chest. He seemed to be watching from above, like Marrak's bird looking down on the map: he could see himself tearing along the edge of the wood, he could see the pack bounding behind him, men running. Once again he forgot why he was there. There was nothing now but the hillside, the twilight and the yowling of the dogs.

An echo from earlier in the day jumped into his mind: *I'm*

not enjoying this now. He almost laughed, but he'd no breath left for that. In the dim light he failed to notice a low branch which caught him on the forehead, knocking him flat on his back. He swore, picked himself up and ran on out of the trees to where the light was better. There was a shout from behind: he'd been seen. The dogs were getting louder, their barks excited, high-pitched. They'd be on him in moments.

He burst through a prickly hedge and found himself on the bank of a brook. He'd grown used to the silent running of the channel: this was a proper downhill stream, wider than any he'd met so far. He looked to left and right. The light was almost gone. The dogs were yelping on the other side of the brambles, beside themselves, looking for a way through. He chose left, ran along the bank to get up speed and jumped, swinging his arms for distance, kicking with his legs. For a moment he hung in the air, remembering the swing across the drain-pit. No rope to hold onto this time.

His right foot hit the ground and turned on a stone. The rest of him followed with a thump, knocking the breath out of his chest.

Something cut into his right palm. He pulled himself up onto his hands and knees and started to crawl, realising his ankle hurt so much he didn't trust himself to stand on it. He reached the top of a low bank and rolled over the other side into a hollow scrape made by an animal. Lying on his back, staring up at the first stars appearing in the sky, he knew it was over. He couldn't run any further. There was nowhere to hide.

The dogs were whining, casting around on the other side of the stream. At least they'd lost the scent. But the men would follow. Lebasi wondered what they meant to do with him. At best, he supposed, they'd march him back to his house. At worst... what horrible things had Akeme heard?

Voices now. It was hard to pick out words above the burbling stream. They were coming nearer along the far bank. At any moment there would be the splashing of men wading across, or else the thud of feet landing. Would it be better to give himself up? He didn't have the energy to put up a hand or call out. They'd just have to come and find him.

29
WOUNDED

An angry shout. 'Menk it, he's got across the blegging border.'

Lebasi flattened himself against the ground, hoping nothing was sticking up above the rim of his foxhole. He was about as far across the line as he'd walked to get the stone for Faya, and it still felt no different to Trengam land.

Another voice: 'So what? We nearly got him, he can't be far ahead. The dogs'll run him down.'

There were murmurs that he couldn't catch. Then the second voice again, more distinct: 'Fine bunch of revolutionaries you are, this is what we're supposed to be fighting against. It's just a threbbing hillside over there, same as this one.'

More muttering. 'I'm not going on my own. We need the dogs. I can't search the whole flaming countryside, just one of me, while you chickens drag your yellow backsides home.'

Lebasi still heard only one side of the conversation. The others must be too abashed to speak up.

'Well the longer you stand there thinking about it, the further away he's getting.'

I wish. Lebasi lay motionless ten paces from the speaker.

At last one of the replies was loud enough to hear. 'I'm not taking my dogs onto Marstor land, that's flat. Who knows what they think of things over there? They might side with Xela.'

Lebasi wondered why Marstor people would be more likely to support his da than people from his own town. He held his breath, waiting to see whether the keen chaser would come over the border regardless.

'Well, I'm not getting myself wet on my own. You're a bunch of useless menkers. We come all this way...'

The voices faded. He heard a couple of final barks from the dogs as they left, then nothing but the sound of rushing water and his own heartbeat in his ears. The pain in his ankle gave a fierce throb. He touched his left hand against his right and felt warm blood on his fingers. He'd made it across the border, but what good would that do if he couldn't walk? He realised he needed the ancient laws of Xessus. He must find a farm.

He lay still until his heart had calmed down and he was sure the chasers had gone. He knew he was putting off the moment when he'd have to test his ankle. At last he raised his right leg and tried moving his foot – painful, but possible. Twisted, not broken. That was something. His right hand ached where he'd gashed it. He knew he ought to wash the wound, but he didn't want to go back towards the stream. Partly to keep low and partly to delay standing, he set off on his hands and knees across the hillside. Quickly he realised that was no good – he was getting more dirt in his cut. He thought of Kara, of Perra's mother. Not good.

He stood up.

He fell over. The darkness was full of shooting stars. Someone had jabbed a skewer into his foot and twisted it.

He sat up, breathing hard. He rubbed his hand over his face, realised he'd probably smeared himself with blood and dirt, and shook his head to try to clear his thoughts. His mind was fuzzy. Dimly he took in that he was in a bad way – he was exhausted from running, hungry, wounded. He searched the hillside below him for signs of humanity. There were none. The only hope was a copse three hundred paces downhill – that might hide a house. If so, it was also hiding any light.

Lebasi fumbled at the sleeve of his tunic with his good hand. The garment was well worn, and it didn't take much work to rip the seam. He wrapped it around his cut, tried to tie it, without success, and finally gripped it with his fingers to hold it in place. Then he set off to struggle towards the trees.

It took a long time. Once again his mind wandered. It was as if he'd always been here, grovelling in the dark, tired and aching. On the edge of his vision a glow told him the moon was rising, but he only had eyes for the wood ahead. At last he felt soft leaf-mould under his hands and knees. It was darker among the trees, even though they were well spaced. After another fifty paces he stopped to look around. Nothing but more trunks in each direction, seemingly growing closer together. He rolled onto his side and closed his eyes. He was so tired, he could just sleep here...

A dog barked. He was wide awake again. Was it the pursuers? He tried to get up and failed. The dog howled – maybe a different animal. Yes, two of them. Ahead and to the right, through the denser undergrowth. Surely not from the Trengam side. Dogs must mean a farm. He started to crawl. Then he stopped, wondering if there were wild beasts out here – could they be wolves?

He thought, *If they're wolves, they can eat me.* At least it would be over. He carried on making his painful way towards the noise.

'What're you barking at, you silly hounds?'

A man's voice, surprisingly close. A glimmer to his right through some bushes. Lebasi tried to go faster. The dogs whined, the man scolded them.

Desperately, Lebasi struggled to shout – no words came. He heard himself as if from outside, sounding more like an animal

than the dogs. If the man went back into the house, he didn't think he'd have the strength to follow. He groaned again and rolled on his side.

He heard the rustle of leaves being pushed back, the tread of heavy feet. Someone muttered something. Strong arms pushed under his legs and back, he was rising effortlessly, moving through the bushes. There was a house, a door, a large room. He was being laid on a table. Someone was lighting candles, saying something he couldn't catch. He smiled, and went to sleep.

❊ ❊ ❊ ❊ ❊

He woke up too soon. Surely it wasn't time to get up? Someone was hurting him. He turned his head from side to side and saw a tall man leaning over his right arm, a bushy grey beard hiding most of his face. His cheeks glistened in the candlelight. He glanced round, saw Lebasi's eyes were open, and reached across to rest a gentle hand on his forehead.

'There now, you rest. You're safe now. I'm cleaning you up a bit.'

A door creaked out of Lebasi's field of vision. A woman's voice: 'Oh, mercy – Barten, is it...'

The man growled, 'No, dear, of course it isn't. It's just a boy I found in the woods. He's in bad shape.'

There was a stifled sob, then the touch of softer fingers on his left arm. He turned his head and saw a kind, sad face gazing down at him, tears in her wrinkled eyes, white hair drawn back tightly.

'If you must be awake, dear, give me a hand.' The man spoke gently, as a father might coax a child.

She nodded and disappeared. Lebasi heard water pouring, logs being put on a fire. The farmer leaned over him and spoke slowly. 'I've bandaged your hand, lad. I'll clean up your face in a moment. Are you hurt anywhere else?'

Lebasi could only croak. 'My ankle – right ankle.'

The man nodded. Lebasi felt his fingers unlacing the boot, then touching – yow! He sat up, sharp knives piercing the joint.

'Sorry, lad. Sprained. I can do something for that, but it'll hurt while I do. Can you bear it?'

Lebasi nodded. He thought of Kara, lying silent as Xela cut her arm. The woman came back and held his hand while the man worked. He bound something hot and soggy around the foot and ankle. There was a strong, clean smell of herbs. The pain passed. The woman smiled at him, her face filled with some untold sorrow, and stroked his forehead.

Lebasi wondered if this was what it would be like to have a mother. He closed his eyes and let weariness take him. He felt those strong, gentle arms lifting him again, carrying him somewhere, placing him on something soft. A rough blanket was laid over him. The man's voice came from a great distance.

'What's your name, lad?'

The woman, scolding: 'Don't you bother him, Barten, let him be.'

'In a moment, dear. There's something I have to ask him.'

Lebasi had a vague notion he was supposed to tell the man a different story, but he couldn't remember why. Had he thought of another name? What was it? 'Lebasi,' he whispered.

He felt the man's hand on his shoulder. His eyelids were too heavy to open.

'All right, Lebasi, I'll let you sleep. But I need to know, is trouble following you? Should I stand guard?'

Lebasi shook his head. 'I don't think so.'

'Good. You rest now.' Lebasi didn't hear him. He was already asleep.

30
BARTEN'S HOUSE

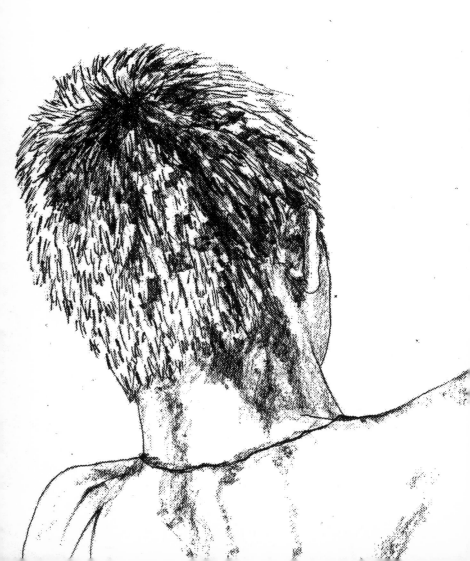

When he woke again, it took several moments to remember where he was. Lying on a battered bench, covered in a patchwork blanket. On his left, a wall made of logs. On his right, a curtain hanging from hooks in the ceiling, bright with sunlight from the far side. He'd never been anywhere like it. There were suppressed noises from beyond the screen – chinking, shushing, whispered words. The smell of bacon. His stomach reminded him that he'd run far and eaten nothing. He sat up and pulled the blanket off his foot. It was bound up in a large ball. He tried to wiggle it inside the bandages and was surprised to find how little it hurt.

The memory of why he was there came back in a rush. How long had he slept? He was only just over the Marstor border. He had thousands and thousands of paces to go in order to be on the coast road ahead of his father. His chest tightened. He lifted his right hand – noticing that it too was wrapped in a dressing – and pulled the curtain back.

There was a squeal of excitement. 'He's awake!' A girl bounded across the room and skidded to a stop right by his bed, her hands behind her back, grinning broadly. Lebasi guessed she was about ten, and she showed how pretty the old woman would be with fair curls for pulled-back white hair, no wrinkles at all, and no shadow of sadness in her eyes. He frowned: the girl looked too young, or the woman too old. Surely they couldn't be mother and daughter?

Behind her, a boy, a little older, also fair, also smiling. A much taller boy, dark hair, shyly peeking and looking away. They were standing in the middle of a large, open room, laying knives and forks on a table. Beyond it, without a separating wall, the kitchen – pans steaming and sizzling on metal racks placed over an open fire, the old woman bustling to and fro with plates. She turned to nod a good morning, then hurried out of a door on the far side of the room.

To Lebasi's surprise, the girl made the sign of respect to him. He smiled at her and touched his forehead in reply. She burst into giggles. 'Can you stand up? Da says your ankle's bad. Come and sit at the table if you can. We've got tea making and it's special breakfast. Happy Midsummer's Eve!'

The young boy came over to shepherd him to a seat. The older one brought a mug of tea, put it down clumsily in front of him and backed away as if he was scared. Lebasi thanked him, and received a nervous half-smile in response. He sipped the hot drink and looked around at the three of them, still wondering how quickly he could get on the road. The younger ones were like as two tomatoes, plainly brother and sister. The big boy – he didn't seem to fit. From the way he stood, the look in his eyes, his slow movements, Lebasi guessed he was brain-sick, like a few in Trengam. He wondered if that was the reason for the woman's sadness, but it didn't seem enough – the boy was clearly capable of helping in the house, and those children were usually kind and gentle.

The farmer came in, shaking water from his hands. He smiled at Lebasi. 'A beautiful day it is, lad. How's that ankle feel this morning?'

'Much better, thank you. I really ought to go –'

The farmer shook his head. 'It's still early. You're not going anywhere before breakfast. Come, everyone, sit.'

His wife returned and took the seat at the head of the table. The girl slipped into a chair beside Lebasi. She looked as pleased as if Xessus himself had come to visit. The boys helped the man bring pots and pans over. When everything was ready, they squeezed onto a bench opposite Lebasi. The farmer sat facing his wife and held out a hand to the youngsters on either side of him.

'Lebasi, you are our guest. We hope you'll join us in our custom.'

Lebasi nodded. The girl turned to Lebasi and shyly offered her hand, taking his fingers gently where they poked out of the bandage. He took the woman's on his other side, surprised by how small it was. They sat for a moment in silence. When at length he spoke again, the farmer's voice was cheerful.

'We are thankful for this meal. We are thankful for our lovely Harka who has made it' – smiling at his wife – 'and Preddo who has helped, and Dewen and Folla who have not got in the way too much' – beaming in turn at each of the children – 'and we are thankful that Lebasi is recovering from his injuries and is here to share with us.' He paused, then his tone became solemn. 'And we are thankful for Nerek, and we think of him and wish him safe and well.'

Out of the corner of his eye, Lebasi saw tears running down Harka's cheeks, even though she was smiling too. He looked quickly down so she wouldn't think him rude, but in any case her thoughts were somewhere else.

They let go of each other's hands and the meal began. There were eggs and bacon and newly-baked bread and creamy butter, milk and juice that must have been freshly squeezed from fruit picked that morning, cheese, tea, olives, raisins, nuts. Lebasi knew he had to go as soon as possible, but he told himself he needed to eat – he might not get another meal that day, if the one before was any guide. Barten talked about the cows that had to be driven out to pasture, holiday or not, and the younger children planned a picnic. When the meal was done, Preddo cleared the table, and Barten turned to Lebasi.

'Now, lad, I have to ask what brought you to our house in such a state in the middle of the night.'

Lebasi blushed. He hated the idea of lying to these kind people. He tried to keep it as near the truth as possible. 'I argued with my father. I ran away from home. I got lost in the dark, and then I fell and hurt myself. I'm sorry to cause you so much trouble.'

Barten looked at him shrewdly, sucking on a toothpick. He held it up, examined the end of it, then asked, 'Where are you running away from?'

Lebasi found another half-truth. 'My father's away west of here, near the sea. I've got to go to him now, to make up for the argument.'

'The sea? That's a long way.'

Lebasi nodded, not able to meet the man's eye.

'You came all that way yesterday? Nobody challenged you?'

'I kept clear of houses. I didn't want to have to explain what I was doing. I wasn't thinking properly, I was a bit crazy. I can see that now.' Lebasi glanced towards the door. 'I really need to go, you've been very kind. I've got to make a start, get to my da –'

Barten held up a hand. 'You can't go wandering through the country on your own, a boy of your age. It's not safe. It's a wonder no one grabbed you yesterday.'

'But I've got to –'

'Wait, I hear you. It happens that I'm going west myself today, a long way towards the coast, and I can walk with you. See that you don't get into trouble. How's that?'

Lebasi stammered his thanks, but he wondered how he could keep his secrets all day. It was bad enough over breakfast. There would surely be questions about his home, his family. Yesterday he'd prepared a story to tell, but it seemed transparent when confronted with real country people.

Harka asked her husband, 'You mean to go, then? Are you sure it's sensible?'

Barten stood up, walked around the table and caressed her hair. She closed her eyes and put her hand over his. 'Sensible?' he said at last. 'Not especially. But there'll be people a lot less sensible than me, and I think they need someone to put a different point of view. I'll be careful, my dear. You're not to worry about me.'

Lebasi pulled himself upright, testing his weight on his foot. It felt stiff, but the sharp pain had gone. 'When can we start?'

Barten smiled. 'Now, lad, I'm sure you're in a rush to make peace with your da. But I've a few things to attend to before I go, and I'm going to dress your ankle again as well.' He took in Lebasi's look of panic. 'Don't worry, you'll make good time – better time with me than without me. Now while I run an errand, can you make yourself useful? Do you know a story you can tell the children?'

'I suppose so. We learn the legends in school.'

'Well then, come outside in the yard and tell it. You're the most exciting thing that has happened in their lives in a while, and I think they should have as much as possible of you on Midsummer's Eve.'

⁂ ⁂ ⁂ ⁂ ⁂

Lebasi sat in a chair beneath a gnarled apple tree. Preddo, Dewen and Folla squatted on the ground around him. He'd noticed children doing this when his apprenticeships had taken him into the countryside: in Trengam they'd have been sitting cross-legged, but here they were comfortable perched with their bottoms on their heels, their arms around their knees. The big boy must be at least eighteen – he'd a red triangle tattooed on the back of his right hand, Lebasi noticed, so he'd come of age – but he was just as pleased as the younger ones to be promised a story.

'In a year without a number,' Lebasi began. Barten smiled approvingly, then strode off into the woods. He told them the tale of the hero's battle with the goddesses of drought and flood, Artay and Shasho, and how he'd built a great wall in the mountains to imprison them both. It was one of his favourites, and he enjoyed the opportunity to play Ivar. The children surely knew it already, but they hung on his words and clapped when he'd finished.

Barten joined in the applause. Lebasi hadn't noticed his return. He started to get up, but the farmer waved him back into the chair. 'Just sit there a moment longer and I'll bind up that ankle again. Then I promise you we'll go look for your da.' He smiled and winked, and Lebasi had a sudden conviction that Barten knew everything. Ridiculous, he told himself. He couldn't have guessed. In any case, Lebasi didn't have a choice. He'd have to go with the farmer.

Harka brought a pan of hot water and some herbs, and Barten bandaged Lebasi's ankle again with soothing ointment against the skin. He put aside the heavy ball-shaped poultice and instead bound his foot with strips of cloth thin enough to fit a boot over.

As he finished tying the laces he commented, 'These are a good piece of work. Lucky to have them, if you're going for a long walk. Probably saved you from breaking your ankle last night.'

Lebasi blushed. He suddenly saw that a child from the country would surely not have anything like them, any more than Faya or Sammas or Ruffur would. He waited for a question, but Barten simply stood up and declared that they were ready to go.

The younger children brought them each a mug of tea and a backpack with some food in. Harka hugged her husband and then Lebasi. For a moment she held his face in her hands and smiled, then kissed him on the forehead and wished him luck. All three children put their arms around him together and thanked him once more for their story. Looking back over his shoulder as they set off out of the farmyard, Lebasi noticed Preddo was crying. He glanced sideways at Barten, then back at the little group waving. He felt as if he'd breathed in too much air and might float away. This must be what it was like to have a family.

31
ACROSS COUNTRY

Lebasi waited until they'd turned a corner past a copse before asking, 'Why is Preddo upset? It's not my fault, I hope?'

Barten patted him on the shoulder. 'No, although in a manner of speaking it's down to you, I suppose. He's homesick. You telling him the story did that, I think. It was like he was back in school.'

'Homesick? But isn't –'

'No, he wasn't born here. He came from the town yonder, two summers ago.' The farmer pointed towards Nampetch, visible through a gap in the woods.

'But that's...' Lebasi started the question that formed in his mind, but stopped himself. He realised that asking questions might lead to more coming back. He wanted to keep the conversation simple, keep it safe.

It was too late. Barten raised his eyebrows, then ran a hand over the back of his neck. 'Aye, I suppose your da may not have told you.' He stared into the distance as he walked, the twitching of his beard indicating that he was putting words together. 'In a year *with* a number,' he began, reminding Lebasi of Xela starting to talk about history. 'We're not supposed to dwell on the past, you know that? But some of us do. Some of us remember. In the days before the prince came, six generations ago, it would have been nothing for my great-great-great grandfather to walk down to that town and sell his grain or his animals in the market there.'

Lebasi held his breath. Anibor had been afraid when he realised he'd talked about old rainstorms. Here was Barten going straight into the most dangerous history of all. Half the people in Trengam had gasped when the stranger said the name. Now Barten was talking about Dennara and the prince as if it was one of Ivar's stories.

He went on. 'Then we lost the war, and we were told we couldn't go from place to place any more. Riadsala's Mercy. Still, the wise scientists of Egator knew it isn't healthy for people to keep marrying in a small group – it's called inbreeding, it leads to problems with sickness and deformity if it's allowed to go on for a couple of generations. It happens in animals and it happens in people. They told Riadsala his rules would have this result, and he made an arrangement to try to avoid it. Every year, five young men move from each town to one of the others – from here to the east, from south to here, from east to south.' Lebasi worked out that Barten didn't name Nampetch and Trengam but only referred to their directions from his house.

'I don't understand,' he stammered. 'How can I not know about it?'

'Well, the ones who move have left school – seventeen years old, just before they come of age and have the tattoo. And it's five from the whole of the town and the land around, so it's not a great number. Just enough to mix things up a bit. Most everyone else lives and dies within a thousand paces of where they were born.'

'But don't people – how are they chosen?' Lebasi realised that this was dangerous ground. He didn't want to find out that this was part of his father's job as well.

'Don't people hate it?' Barten gave the boy a sidelong glance. 'They have no choice, lad. It's the king's law.' He shook his head sadly. 'And they don't mind too much, some of them. The ones who're sent away to mix up the bloodlines, often it's children their parents want to get rid of. Ones who've had an argument, maybe.' He winked again. 'I'm only teasing you, lad. I'm sure your da won't put your name up. But that's how it works.'

The farmer glanced towards Nampetch again as he went on. 'Preddo, now, he wouldn't have had much of a life in the town. He'd never be able to take care of himself, and his ma didn't think she could look after him forever.'

'His ma – what about his da?'

'I never knew him, of course, because he was from the town and I can't go there. When Preddo came here they told me a little of his story. His father killed himself when Preddo was just a baby.'

Lebasi shivered. He wished he could stop Barten, but that would lead to too many explanations.

'I don't know what they teach in your school. In old Xessus it was the worst thing you could do, it would bring a curse on your family. There are still some who believe in the old gods. I don't, myself, but when you've been brought up by people who've been brought up by people who believed something, it runs deep. I still have a horror of it. Suicide is a sin against Manaku the goddess of life, throwing away her gift. I reckon there were people in the town who imagined Preddo's like he is because of what his father did. Load of nonsense, of course. More likely his father did it because of how Preddo is – a stupid, unkind, needless thing to do, but maybe he was a weak man who didn't think he had the strength to raise a boy like that.'

Lebasi thought about his father. Was that why he was so reluctant to talk about Shelba, why he wouldn't even say her name? 'So his ma had to –'

'Bring him up alone, yes. With half her neighbours thinking she was cursed. And living with the memory of the man who let her down, when it was against the custom to keep a single thing that belonged to him, even to say his name, for fear of more bad luck.' He looked sideways at Lebasi. 'Have you been to a wedding, or the ceremony for a firstborn child?' Lebasi nodded. 'Well then, you know the promises we make. That's old Xessus, again, from before Riadsala. Same as helping a stranger. To love, protect, support and care for each other. To raise the child safe until it comes of age, to put your own life between it and danger. A young father, choosing to take the easy way out – a terrible thing for his widow to live with.'

Lebasi didn't think it sounded easy. But maybe it was easier to give up than to try.

Barten rubbed his chin. 'In the end, though, Preddo's done all right. Outsiders usually find it hard to fit in, torn out of their home and made to live among strangers. But he's a fine help to us around the farm, we treat him as one of our own, and you couldn't want for a nicer lad.' He shook his head sadly. 'He misses his own ma, though. He doesn't realise she sent him away. And he misses his friends, his school, playing the games he sometimes talks about even now. Of course, he's too old to still be playing in school. He'd be working in a trade, and he's better off with us, if only he could get used to the idea.'

✳ ✳ ✳ ✳ ✳

Lebasi was grateful to march in silence. For most of the time they walked on paths beside hedges as he'd done the previous day, but in Barten's company he didn't worry about running into people. He didn't have to: there were no workers among the crops today. It seemed everyone was enjoying the holiday. The landscape was empty apart from distant sheep in the pastures, a scattering of rabbits that scurried down their burrows when they approached, and flocks of birds – pigeons, starlings, and others Lebasi didn't recognise from the town.

He studied the land unfolding around him, new views that couldn't be seen from Trengam. To the north, he could now see Marstor rising on its hill, a similar shape to the other towns. Beyond it there were rolling downs with woods and fields, ending suddenly in the black wall of the mountains. Nearer at hand there were fields of growing corn, shining pale green in the bright sunshine, waving gently in the breeze. Criss-crossing the landscape was a maze of little water channels. Lebasi marvelled at the care that went into them – the dams and gates collected and diverted the precious liquid where it was needed. He glanced up towards the bottom of the rocky spur to the north-east, trying to pick out where the main channel might be. He guessed it was the source of all this water, somehow. He wondered where it came from, when it had been built, who built it – Xessus, he supposed, when he made the great wall in the story. When he tamed drought and flood, Artay and Shasho, by bringing water from the mountains to the irrigation ditches in the fields.

The sun was high overhead when Barten called a halt for lunch. They sat in the shade of a broad oak tree on the banks of a river. Its bed was ten times as wide as the narrow stream in the centre, and the span of the bridge that carried the road across seemed much larger than was needed. Barten explained, 'This is the river that comes down from the mountains behind the town yonder. In years gone by, it was a great torrent in the spring when the snows melted, and it carved out this big course for itself. But the watermen have made a dam and a lake up there, and they use it for farming and drinking. So all that's left is just a trickle.'

Lebasi felt a twinge of sadness that the river should be so tamed. He could see big boulders lying at random among the smaller stones, sticking out of the water, and wondered at the force that must once have rolled them down from higher ground. A wading bird flapped up from under the bridge and headed off silently upstream.

Lebasi found he was asking a question before he could stop himself. 'Barten, do you believe in the old stories?'

'What do you mean, believe in them?'

'Well, do you think there are dragons?'

The farmer laughed. 'Dragons? Where did that idea come from?'

'Our teacher in school has always told us stories about dragons and centaurs and other magical beasts. But I'm not sure they really exist. What do you think?'

'Well, I've never seen a dragon. That doesn't mean there aren't any anywhere, mind you – I haven't seen the king, either, but I think he's real enough. What do you think a dragon is like?'

Lebasi called a picture into his mind. 'Well, it's very big, maybe twice as big as an ox, with a long neck and wings and a tail with spikes on it. And it's got scaly skin and little ears and bright eyes and it breathes fire.'

'So you'd recognise one if you saw it?'

'Of course.'

'All right, we'll keep our eyes open. But I've never seen anything like that around here.'

Lebasi smiled. It was a change to find someone willing to answer questions. 'What about centaurs?'

'And what's one of them?'

'It's got the chest and head and arms of a man, but the body and legs of a horse, and it's very clever –'

'Just a moment, don't get ahead of me. What's a horse?'

'A horse is like a donkey, only bigger and – well, better. It's taller and it's got shiny skin and it's really strong and fast. It has big teeth and is very fierce, and it's got long hair on the back of its neck and a long tail.'

Barten made a show of looking carefully around. 'I've never seen one of those, either. So a centaur is a sort of horse, and a horse is a sort of donkey –'

'It's not a donkey! It's just, well, the same shape.'

'All right, all right. Well, as I say, I've never seen one, but that doesn't mean there aren't any. It only means there aren't any in Xessus at the moment. They may have lived here once, and they may live somewhere else now, but we don't know.'

'Well, what about spellmakers? Someone told me they don't exist, and there isn't any magic.'

Barten thought for some time before replying. 'No magic. Well, it depends what you mean by magic. If he means the sort where someone says some funny words and turns a person into a frog, then I've never seen anything like that and I've never met anyone who has. But of course, I may have met a few frogs who couldn't tell me I was wrong.' Lebasi laughed, but Barten grew serious.

'I've never seen any of that stuff, but there's plenty of magic around. It's just that people don't think of it as magic, because it happens all the time. If you're looking for something you can't explain and can't understand, just watch an egg hatching, or a baby being born and growing into a child. Or the way a flower opens, or the corn grows. That's all magic to me.'

'But it's not magic that people do, is it? It's magic that's just in the world and it happens.'

'Yes, I suppose that's true. You want some magic that people do? There are stories...' Barten stopped, shook his head, and packed up the remains of the lunch.

Lebasi protested at his sudden silence. 'What? What stories?'

The farmer swung his pack onto his shoulders and stretched his arms above his head.

'Dangerous stories, lad. Stories we aren't supposed to remember. Causing nothing but trouble. You'd best stick to Xessus the hero.' He started walking quickly, and Lebasi had to jog every few paces to keep up with the man's long legs.

Maybe Barten wasn't so different from Xela after all.

32
MEETING

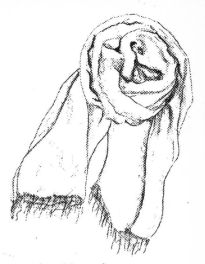

For a long time they didn't talk. Lebasi wondered how far Barten was going, and why he was going there, but he didn't dare ask. At least the direction was right: the mountains were closer now, and Lebasi judged by the sun that they were travelling almost due west. There was a distant haze between the horizon and the sky that could just be something else, something he'd never seen before – the sea. He had the sensation of being a bird again, imagining the map, soaring with the exhilaration of so many discoveries. He wished he could really swoop on ahead like the white birds circling above him. Marrak's picture of the land had covered just two spans' width of his material. Walking on real ground took so long.

Half-right ahead, the rocky peaks ended. Lebasi reckoned the rebels' farm must be at the bottom of that last cliff. It was still a long way, but he felt sure he could reach the road before nightfall. He'd be waiting for Xela when he came past in the morning.

There were more people about now. They appeared in the distance, walking in ones and twos. Lebasi glanced over his shoulder and saw some on the path a few hundred paces behind. There were others to left and right across the fields. Suddenly Lebasi guessed: they were all heading for the same place, for wherever Barten was going. At last the question wouldn't wait.

'What's happening, Barten? Are all these people going to a meeting?'

The farmer rubbed his chin. 'I think it's time we had a talk about that. Here, let's get off the path so we aren't bothered.' He led the way to a grassy bank beside an irrigation ditch. Lebasi knelt to splash some water on his face, then wiped his forehead on the sleeve of his tunic. He stopped, looking at the fabric in his hand.

'Barten, what happened to my clothes? I thought I tore the sleeve off last night.'

'You did. Your own things were such a mess that Harka and I cut them off you and put them aside for cleaning the floor. We had something your size, so we put it on you. You were so tired you didn't wake up.'

Lebasi opened his mouth but stifled the question. It couldn't be Preddo's. He must have been larger than Lebasi when he arrived from Nampetch. It couldn't be Dewen's. It must be Nerek's. Lebasi longed to ask who he was and what had happened to him, but he still didn't want to risk inviting enquiries. Instead he lowered his head in the sign of respect.

'Barten, thank you for everything you've done. I'll never be able to pay you back.'

The man waved a hand dismissively. 'Never is a long time, lad. Who knows when you might get the chance? Anyway, it's the law of Xessus to help a stranger. I'd do the same for anyone. For any father's son. I hope someone'd do the same for mine.' There was a challenge in the silence that followed: ask. Lebasi resisted the temptation, but he found a different question.

'But you said not everyone would help me, that it isn't safe to travel on my own.'

Barten nodded, gazing into the distance. 'That's why we've stopped. I'm only taking you a little further, and then you'll have to go on alone, because I don't suppose your da will be at the meeting. So I want you to know about the dangers.' He turned to look straight into Lebasi's eyes. 'Do you know about the boys who are sent to the army?'

Lebasi nodded.

'The best and the bravest of their age. Not like poor Preddo, whose ma wanted to get rid of him. The ones who go to be soldiers are a great loss.'

Faya's voice came into Lebasi's head: 'I miss him.' The angry flash of her eyes. 'I know,' he said.

'Most people can't bear to talk about them afterwards. They're here, they're gone: it's as if they never were. We don't dwell on the past when it's too painful.'

'Do they ever come back?'

'No, never. Too dangerous, I suppose. The king takes the best of Xessus to wage his wars for him, but he doesn't want to send back trained and experienced fighters to lead another rebellion. We don't hear of them again.'

'But what's that got to do with me?'

The farmer studied the backs of his hands. 'I don't know for sure, but I've heard tales. People who choose one law of Xessus over another. People who've hidden their own son, fearing he'd be picked for a soldier. Said he'd had an accident, presented the mayor with a body. Difficult, of course. Risky. Hard to bring the real one out of hiding later. And you need a boy about the right age, one no one's going to miss. A passing runaway, for instance.'

Lebasi's mouth was dry. 'You really think people do that?'

'I don't know for sure. I know they might. So when you leave me, you keep out of the way, all right? Don't stay the night with anyone else. Go find your father and make your peace.'

Barten lowered his voice. 'And you know who chooses the best and bravest?'

Lebasi nodded miserably. It wasn't supposed to be anything to do with him, but he couldn't help it.

Barten nodded solemnly. 'The elders, the mayor and the magistrate.' Lebasi's eyes were watering. Barten's words seemed to come from a great distance. 'They have rules to help them, to make sure no one can claim it was personal, or that someone else's child has been left because of a favour or a bribe.' He waited for Lebasi to meet his eyes before continuing. Lebasi tried to arrange his face to hide his feelings. Barten's tone became softer. 'Maybe you'll have seen the magistrate, Xela. Don't you think badly of him. He's a brave man, and a good one. Let me tell you a story. When I was a boy, my older brother was called for the army. This is thirty years ago, in the time of Drabo. Drabo didn't care to face the people whose children were taken. He sent the soldiers to collect them. I can still remember, I can picture it like you're sitting here beside me. Ten men with armour and swords, come to the farm to lead away my brother Merran, just a lad of eighteen. Last time I saw him.'

'And now?' Lebasi whispered.

'The soldiers haven't been in the Westwall District since Xela was elected. He promised he'd keep them out, as long as we obey the laws. So we do, and life is better.' He sighed. 'Except when it isn't. But Xela isn't Drabo. A year ago, he came himself to take Nerek, sat in that chair where you told the story to the children this morning, cried with us.'

Lebasi pressed his hands against the sides of his head, unable to take it in. 'How could he? How does he sleep?'

Barten laughed bitterly. 'I'm not sure he does, much. Not at the time of year when the levies are called, anyway. He feels it to the bottom of his soul, does Xela. But he knows, and most of the rest of us know, that if we break the laws then Riadsala's Mercy ends. The Westwall Guard comes and puts a torch to the place, and there's nothing we can do about it.'

Lebasi put his face in his hands. Barten gently touched his shoulder. 'You looked a lot like him, you know, sitting in that chair.'

Lebasi gasped. He dropped his hands and stared at the farmer. He couldn't think of anything to say. The man smiled.

'There now, don't fret. It's easier if I know. That's why I haven't been asking you all day about that farm you said you live on. I could see you didn't like lying to me so I didn't make you.'

'But how...?'

'Some of the things you told us didn't make sense to me. You couldn't have come all the way from the sea without someone stopping you. No one growing up on a farm ever had a pair of boots like those. And in the country we don't go to school, like you said you did. So it was more likely to me you'd run away from one of the towns. While you were telling your story I went to have a word with my neighbour to the east. He stands his side of the stream and I stand mine, and we've never shaken hands in all these years, but we talk most days. And he said a bunch of idiots out of the town, and some of his friends who should know better, were up across his land yesterday at nightfall chasing someone with dogs.' He made a snarling noise. 'They hunt a boy with dogs. Disgusting. I didn't tell him about you, but I asked what was afoot, and he said they were trying to stop the magistrate's son taking a message to his father about trouble in the town. And I minded the marks I saw on your back when I took your shirt off, and that brought back another story my neighbour told me in the spring, about Xela having to take the stick to his own son for a breach of the Mercy. And then it all made sense.'

Lebasi stammered, 'So you want me to warn my father?'

Barten nodded. 'Certainly I do. If there's trouble, the Guard will come, and it'll be worse. Xela will know what to do to keep the peace.'

Thinking of the boy whose clothes he wore, Lebasi couldn't meet the farmer's eyes.

'Don't you hate him?'

Barten reached out and lifted Lebasi's chin. 'If you understand someone, lad, it's hard to hate them. I know why Xela does what he does, and I can't say I'd do any different. He bears a lot for the rest of us. Hate him? No. He's a better man than Drabo ever was.'

Lebasi stood up and looked to the west. 'Maybe I should leave you now. I think I can see the way ahead.'

Barten tapped his fingers together. 'You know, I think it might be good if you come to this meeting too. You can still get to the coast tonight. I think Xela'll want to know what's happening, and you'll be the best person to tell him.'

Lebasi watched a group of four men pass on the path a few paces away. They'd all wrapped cloths around their mouths and noses. One wore a hood in spite of the afternoon heat. He turned back to Barten, who was digging two scarves out of his pack.

'A meeting this size is against every law, and the countryside is riddled with reporters,' he explained. 'No one should recognise you, because you're not from around here. But you'll stand out if you don't wear a mask.'

They put on their disguises and set off. In a moment they were back on the path. Lebasi followed in Barten's footsteps, his eyes fixed on the farmer's boots. He could feel his heart thumping again. Once he'd had a moment to think, he'd decided that the meeting in Trengam already gave him enough to talk to his father about, and maybe it wasn't worth the risk and the delay, but now masked men were close enough to hear. He'd have to look for a chance to escape, but he'd attract attention if he suddenly turned away from the path everyone else was taking.

They passed through a gap between dense woods and entered

a broad field, sloping down towards another dark forest a hundred paces away. There was a crowd of men – and some women – ahead of them, standing in small groups. They were talking with their heads close together, glancing around, shifting from foot to foot. The revolution didn't seem to be as far advanced in the Marstor countryside. Lebasi thought of the flint and the steel, and pictured sparks glowing in the tinder.

Lebasi pulled Barten's sleeve and pointed along the edge of the field nearest the wood. He felt safer when they found a place to stand at the back with the trees behind them. Barten was tall enough to see over most of the heads. Lebasi slipped his backpack off and stood on a tree-stump which raised him to the same height. They were facing south-west, the sun in their faces making the scarves hot and uncomfortable. At least there was a cool breeze coming from the same direction. Lebasi scanned the crowd. Everyone was in front of him looking the other way, so he hardly needed the mask. He pulled it down so he could breathe.

This wasn't the same as the throng on the Space in Trengam. There weren't as many people, for a start. This crowd was uncannily silent. There was no sound but the gentle rustle of the trees behind them. Lebasi shivered. He had an urge to run away before something bad happened. He only stayed because he didn't want Barten to realise he was afraid. He couldn't put into words, even to himself, what he was afraid of.

The speaker started without having to call for attention. It took Lebasi a moment to find him, a face across the rows of heads, a man standing on a bank at the far side of the field. He stood on tiptoe to be sure. This wasn't Marstor's Perra. He recognised the deep voice that carried on the gentle breeze, full of authority, not quite speaking as Xessans spoke.

'I am glad to see so many have come to hear me. I was told

Xessans were not brave enough to defy the law.'

Lebasi could see the crowd shifting, glancing at each other, shaking heads. The southerner took no notice.

'I understand the word has been passed secretly, that everyone here has been vouched for by the person who told them. So we are among friends.'

The heads rippled as people moved from side to side, trying to get a glimpse. The man was talking about Dennara, as he had in Trengam, and calling him the greatest Xessan. He punched the air. 'Who is ready to stand up for their freedom?'

Someone shouted from Lebasi's left, 'I'm ready. I've been waiting for years. What d'you say we start now?'

Heads turned, searching for the speaker. The stranger took a pace forward and the crowd pulled back. He called out, 'Start what, my friend?'

The other man again: 'The magistrate passed down the road yonder this afternoon. He'll sleep by the road tonight with nothing but an ox for company. Who's for doing something about it?'

Lebasi clenched his fists. He'd come to warn Xela about danger at the farm, but maybe danger was nearer than that.

Other voices joined in. There weren't many, but the rest of the crowd was silent. No one offered any dissent.

This was too much for Barten. He thundered, 'We've no cause to be arguing with Xela. He's a good man, one of us. Don't you think of harming a hair of his head.'

Some people shouted, 'Hear him, hear him!' Others muttered disagreement. People shifted, turned around, looking for the source of Xela's support.

The stranger raised his hands and the crowd fell silent again. 'Don't worry, my friend. It is not yet the time for that. I am here to see if you are ready.'

The first man shouted, 'I've said I'm ready. What are we waiting for?'

The stranger seemed to grow taller, his voice deeper. 'My master in Egator has been laying his plans for seven years. We require a little longer. We do not want the Westwall Guard to interfere, and Xela must be allowed to continue his walk.'

Another man, away to the right, objected. 'Why should we wait for you? What have the southerners ever done for us?'

Barten was about to speak again, but the southerner let out a roar of anger. 'You have no idea what you are dealing with. I have not walked twenty-four days from Egator to see my master's plans overturned by a bunch of witless farmers at the world's end. You will do as I say, or you will suffer appalling consequences.'

The crowd appeared to wilt in front of him. *No guts, no backbone*, thought Lebasi, and he was glad of it. He had been right about the stranger: he expected to be obeyed. The frightening thing about him was that Lebasi was absolutely certain that he, standing alone in front of a hundred or more, three eightnights from his home and his master, could make those appalling consequences happen, whatever they were. The farmers clearly believed it as well.

Barten muttered something inaudible. Lebasi let out a long breath. He shaded his eyes with his hand and peered across the crowd to left and right, trying to pick out the men who had wanted to attack Xela, but they had merged back into the mass of people. He turned towards the front again, wondering why the stranger wasn't speaking any more – he was no longer standing where he had been – there he was, pushing his way through the press. He was coming towards where Lebasi and Barten were standing. People were turning to look, trying to work out what the stranger was up to. Lebasi realised the man was staring straight at him. He realised in the same moment that his face was in sunlight, and his mask was down. It was forty paces rather than an arm's length – thirty paces – he wasn't even sure if the man had looked at him properly on the stage in Trengam – but his eyes were fixed on Lebasi as he worked his way through the crowd, and he was getting nearer. Lebasi stepped backwards off the stump, patted Barten's broad back, and walked quickly into the trees. Maybe the southerner wanted to say something to Barten, but he doubted it. He didn't wait to find out. He hoped Barten would understand. He wished he'd been able to say goodbye.

33
MIDSUMMER

There were bushes growing among the trees. As soon as he was properly hidden from the field, Lebasi tried to move quicker. It wasn't possible to run through the undergrowth, but he dodged left and right and pushed through gaps as fast as he could. If the man had spotted him, had recognised him... if he guessed why Lebasi was there... if the crowd were too roused up to listen to him, or to Barten... Lebasi feared that anyone coming around the outside of the wood would be able to head him off. He couldn't be sure of his direction – maybe he was going in a circle and he'd end up where he started. The air was still and humid. Insects buzzed, twigs cracked under his feet. Barten and the rest of the world seemed far away.

At last he detected a thinning of the branches ahead. Better still, the mountain ridge was visible in the sky beyond. He was on the far side of the wood from the meeting. Even so, he paused to wipe the sweat from his eyes and advanced cautiously, listening for signs that anyone was coming after him.

The trees ended. He crawled inside a hollow bush and peered out between the leaves. He pictured the map in his mind: north-west, there was the Eagle's Nest at the end of the ridge, then nothing. It still looked a long way. Immediately ahead was open land with scattered trees, a broad pasture rising gently for a thousand paces. Beyond it, more woodland. The evening sun picked out every blade of grass. He sat back and breathed slowly to calm himself. If anyone was searching for him, there was no cover – he'd surely be seen crossing that field. He couldn't take the risk. His ankle ached: he could still walk on it, but he didn't think he could run.

He'd have to wait for nightfall. He closed his eyes, grateful for an excuse to rest.

❊ ❊ ❊ ❊ ❊

When he opened them again, he was lying on the leaf-mould. He picked himself up and pushed the branches aside to take a look. The field was a ghostly white. The black bank of the mountains played tricks on his eyes. One moment it seemed near enough to touch, but when he blinked it was a great distance away. On his left a half moon hung in the clear sky, its brighter light dimming the stars around it.

He rubbed his arms and legs to warm himself. He realised he must have slept half the night: the moon was already on the way down to the horizon. Still, he felt fresh, and the pain in his ankle was less. Surely anyone watching out for him would have given up ages ago. He left the shelter of the undergrowth and started jogging in the direction of that last peak on the ridge.

As he came out into the open, he scanned the ground on either side. It was hard to be sure in the moonlight, but he didn't think there was anyone about. In the distance he could see some lumps in the grass that might be rocks, or cattle lying down. He could see nothing on two legs. He was hungry and thirsty – he hoped he could find somewhere to drink on the way, but food was too much to expect. He wished he'd thought to pick up the backpack when he made for the trees, because it still had the remains of lunch in it. He remembered the good breakfast he'd eaten that morning – yesterday morning, more likely – and felt hungrier still.

The distant woods came nearer, then suddenly he was among the trees. The darkness there was impenetrable, so he turned and headed west along the edge of the pasture. That was right, he decided – he wanted to strike the road that led to the farm and wait for Xela. There was a faint path to follow, narrow but even. He didn't want to turn his ankle again. At a stream flowing out of the wood he stopped to drink and wash the sleep out of his eyes, then settled down to cover the ground as quickly as he could.

✼ ✼ ✼ ✼ ✼

The light faded as the moon set, but his eyes were accustomed to the dark and the going was good. He slowed but didn't stop. The stars dimmed. At last he took a brief rest to watch the eastern sky grow pale. Through a gap in the trees he saw the top of the ridge glow a brilliant orange. A moment later it was as if all the birds in the world had woken and decided to celebrate the new day: the noise from the woods, from the field, from the air above him was astonishing. He turned and turned, closing his eyes and breathing it in, laughing with unexpected joy. Midsummer's Day. Special for the humans, but the birds must do this every morning.

In sunlight he doubled his speed again. Soon afterwards he crested a rise and looked down on what must be the road – a thin white ribbon running across his path in the bottom of a shallow valley, dead straight from away left to where it disappeared over a low ridge on his right. He ran down the slope at full tilt and almost fell as he tried to stop himself on the chalky surface of the track, worn out of the grass by the passage of feet and wheels over many years. He grinned. He'd made it: it was impossible, but here he was.

Now a problem struck him: should he turn left or right? Would his father have already passed this way with the ox? He stared first up and then down the track. He'd been concentrating so hard on getting here that he'd put yesterday's threats against Xela out of his mind. If his father hadn't reached this point, Lebasi should hurry south to warn him. If he was further on already, Lebasi should hurry north to catch him before he reached the farm.

The sun had only newly risen, so it was likely his father wasn't yet on the road. But he didn't know where Xela would have slept last night. When he left the town, he'd set out before first light – he might have started early again. He could see no fresh markings of feet or hooves on the dry ground. He took steps one way then the other, looking over his shoulder, banging his hands together. He knew he was wasting time, but he couldn't decide. At last he reasoned going south was riskier – he couldn't bear to have come so far and fail to deliver his warning by picking the wrong direction. If the Marstor farmers had followed the hotheads, he would in any case be too late. The road rose gently to a low saddle ahead – maybe he'd be able to see the land beyond and anyone travelling across it. He turned right and hurried uphill. His legs felt heavy and stiff after two days on the run.

There was a rough shelter at the high point of the road, no more than three walls and a roof. As he approached Lebasi thought he saw a movement inside, but his attention was distracted by the view ahead. There was another shallow valley on the far side, the road just as straight and even in the centre of it, running away for maybe fifteen thousand paces to a low hill that stood between the end of the mountains and...

'The sea,' he breathed, his eyes wide. Three days ago he hadn't heard of it: now he was looking at it, shimmering blue-green in the bright morning sunshine. A cool breeze from the west blew in his face, carrying a strange smell, tangy, exciting. He stood still and stared.

'Well now, who's this out on the road so early?' A low voice from behind made him swing round. A man stepped out from the shelter. Lebasi quickly took in a squat flat-faced dog strutting in front, its teeth bared in a growl. He ran his eyes over the man's well-worn cloak, his matted grey hair, a long stick, and the hand resting lightly on a knife in his belt. Barten's warning came back to him: but what could he do against a dog and a knife?

'Good morning,' he tried, taking a step back and keeping his eyes on the animal.

The man put his head on one side. 'I don't recognise you, boy. Where're you from?' He stepped to the right while the dog circled the other way. Lebasi couldn't watch both of them at once.

'I'm going to a farm that way,' Lebasi said, pointing down the road. He glanced down and took a step forward to keep away from the dog. He looked up again to find the man's leering face in front of his own. He'd drawn the knife now, a hunter's blade, a handspan long. It flashed in the sunshine.

'I haven't got anything worth taking. I haven't got anything at all.'

The man's expression didn't change. 'But you've got yourself, don't you?'

Barten was right. What was the man going to do? He tried the truth: 'I'm looking for the magistrate, Xela. He's somewhere on this road with an ox. Have you seen him?'

The man took a step back as if he'd been stung. He glanced quickly all around, then raised the knife again. 'Why would I have seen the magistrate, boy? What're you saying, I'm a reporter? Eh?' He waved the blade in front of Lebasi's eyes.

Lebasi held up his palms, trying to lean back without treading on the dog. 'No, not at all. He's my father –'

If he'd been stung before, now the man jumped as if burned. He lowered the blade and stared. 'Impossible! He can't be.'

Lebasi took a step forward. Nomara's voice echoed in his head: *bullies is cowards.* 'He is. I've come to bring him a message from his agent, Marrak. An important message. Have you seen him?'

The man studied his face. Lebasi wondered how to make himself look more like his father. It worked: the man nodded, put the knife back in its sheath, and snapped his fingers to bring the dog to heel. His voice became oily and wheedling.

'You should've said straight off. Old Verral wouldn't hurt no kin of Xela's, not at all.'

Lebasi tried to stand tall to keep his advantage. 'Of course you wouldn't. I'll tell him that. Do you know where he is?'

The man flicked his eyes from side to side again, then leaned forward to whisper. 'Yes, yes. He passed this way before the moon set. I spoke to him here. He'll be halfway to Gortan's now, maybe more.'

Gortan – that was the name Xela had mentioned when talking about his journey. Marrak had called him the awkward farmer. Perra had said he might be a friend. Maybe Perra could send messages as well as Marrak.

Verral pointed. 'Look yonder.'

Lebasi stared out over the plain. In the far distance, maybe that was something dark moving on the white road – it could be a man and an ox. More than halfway. Lebasi surely could not catch him. Why did Xela have to start so early? Why had he taken so long to make up his mind which way to turn?

'I have to go.'

'Of course, of course. Farewell, son of Xela. Tell him I...'

Lebasi didn't hear the man's final words. He was already running down the slope.

34
THE FARM

The fresh sea breeze faded as Lebasi descended into the valley. The air thickened, and the distant view became blurred. The speck that might be Xela disappeared into the haze. The morning grew hot under a cloudless, deep blue sky. Lebasi alternated between jogging and fast walking, but the gap between the mountains and the sea seemed as far away as ever.

The road dipped to ford a shallow stream. Lebasi stopped long enough to drink and wash the sweat off his face and arms. His stomach ached with hunger and fear.

As the sun rose higher, the white surface of the road started to dazzle him. He stopped by another water-channel and tried to clear his head. When he stood up he felt giddy and had to rest for a moment with his hands on his knees. Was that water lying across the road ahead? He screwed up his eyes, wondering if he was ill. Even if there was something wrong with his vision, he was sure the end of the ridge was closer now. He could see a wooded hillside above the heat haze: the road carried on up, a straight line cut through the trees. Dead ahead of him, a narrow tower was silhouetted against the sky. He wondered where the famous wall was – he could see no sign of it. He straightened up slowly: the dizziness faded. He set off again, trying to keep his pulse steady. No use making himself faint – he'd never catch Xela if he passed out.

He paused again by the first of a long line of tall trees which ran alongside the road ahead, spreading their branches over the track and cutting out the sun. He used his sleeve to mop sweat from his eyes and surveyed the land around. Between the road and the sea – visible now as a thin blue line beyond green fields – there was nothing but pasture. To the right, a group of buildings shimmered in the distance, maybe only two or three thousand paces away. He reckoned that a straight line to them wouldn't be a short-cut: too many irrigation channels to cross. He spotted another row of trees running west to east ahead, and guessed it must mark a side-road. Lebasi followed that track with his eyes until it disappeared into a small wood not far from the buildings. There was no sign of man or beast. He set off again, keeping in the shade.

A hundred paces short of the side-turning, a movement ahead made him duck behind a tree. As he peered round the trunk, the ox lumbered out onto the roadway, still burdened with its load of weapons. He was about to shout for Xela when a boy appeared behind the animal, about Lebasi's age, flicking at its backside with a thin stick. Lebasi pulled his head back. The burst of hope he'd felt on seeing the ox was overtaken by the opposite thought, that he was too late, the trap had already been sprung. Would his da have left the weapons unguarded?

He dropped to his knees and edged his head out at ground level. The boy was running his hands over the packages on the beast's back. The animal took no notice of him, pulling up a bunch of grass from the roadside and staring away towards the sea.

The boy suddenly turned and shaded his eyes. Lebasi stayed still. He knew that a quick movement was more likely to attract attention than a stationary head at ground level. Sure enough, the boy showed no sign of being aware of him. He also showed no sign of going away. He sat down with his back to a tree and pulled some sort of whistle out of his pocket. As he started to play, Lebasi slipped into cover and considered what to do.

Corn was standing chest-high in the field to the right of the road. A path disappeared in among the thick stalks. If they arranged their farm like the town fields, Lebasi reckoned that it would follow the water channel along the edge of one field, and meet another path crossing it in a hundred paces. He set off, crouching to keep out of sight, watching for an opening on his left.

In a hundred and fifty paces – they had larger fields than Trengam – the corn ran out. Ahead was open pasture. A track led leftwards towards the side-road, but there was no cover. Still, the farm was now hidden behind that wood, and he could see no one. He jogged up to the line of trees without hearing a challenge. He checked that the boy and the ox were still at the junction where he had last seen them, then kept to the cover of the trunks as he made for the wood.

No one came or went along the road. No one moved in the fields. The afternoon was heavy and silent. Even the birds and insects seemed to be asleep. The copse formed a green tunnel into which the road disappeared; Lebasi didn't want to risk meeting anyone, so he tried to find a way through the undergrowth a few paces to the right. He was well hidden from view, but it was hard to move quietly. He had to push low branches aside and winced at the swish as he let go of them. Dry twigs snapped under his feet. In the still air, the noise seemed enough to bring the whole neighbourhood down on him.

Even so, he reached the far edge of the wood and lay in the long grass on the border of another field, studying the farm from only fifty paces away. There was a solid wooden fence which hid the lower view, but he could see the tops of buildings – some wooden barns on the left, a row of two-storey houses on the right.

The road ran through an open gateway into a farmyard. Lebasi could see animals moving about, ducks, geese –

'Sindawatteryuduingear,' came a voice from over his head. He rolled over and scrambled into a crouch. A boy with short fair hair was sitting on a branch.

'Yorspostobewatchingtherowedarntcha.' He jumped lightly down and studied Lebasi curiously. There was something in the face, in the way the child moved, that told Lebasi it was a girl, not a boy. She only came up to his chest, but was clearly not in the least afraid of a stranger. Her tunic was shabby and patched, and her feet were bare. She reached out and pinched the cloth of his sleeve, then walked all the way around him. She stared at his boots. Lebasi twisted his head to follow her, then turned back to face her as she completed her inspection. Suddenly she broke into a brilliant grin, teeth showing white in her dirty face, bright blue eyes sparkling.

'Yorenotsinnederrarue,' she said.

Lebasi frowned. The sounds she made weren't familiar words, but they reminded him of something. He concentrated hard.

'Dooyoowunderstandmeornot?'

He tried to remember where he'd heard this sort of thing before. She spoke very slowly, as if she thought he might be dim.

'Do you understand me now?'

'Yes,' he nodded. 'I didn't know what you were saying before.'

But then he did. The sounds ran around in his brain and resolved themselves into proper speech. She'd thought he was someone called Sinder, who was supposed to be watching the road – that must be the boy Lebasi had seen with the ox – and then she'd realised her mistake, and asked him if he understood. But she'd said it all in Xela's private language. He was so surprised that he couldn't think of a reply. How did she know how to talk like that?

'Who are you?' She still seemed to be taking his expression as a

sign of stupidity. She emphasised her words by pointing at his chest.

'I'm Lebasi. Who are you?'

'Tik. What are you doing here?'

'I'm looking for my da.' His mouth was quicker than his brain. Still, she was only a child. Surely she wouldn't be part of the trap. She might even tell him something useful.

The girl raised her eyebrows. 'Your da? Is the magistrate your da?'

Lebasi nodded. She put her hands on her hips and looked him up and down, as if deciding whether to believe it. She made a decision: she nodded and smiled at him.

'You are a long way from home. Why have you come?'

'I've got to warn him – he's in danger...' His voice trailed off, as it struck him again that she might be on the side of the threat.

To his surprise, she grinned at him even more broadly and grabbed his hand. 'No he's not,' she called over her shoulder, pulling him along the edge of the wood. 'It's just what always happens, every year.' She turned and ran, making hardly any sound.

He followed her across the deserted road, through the undergrowth on the far side, and out into the margins of another cornfield. She turned right past the first rows of stalks and scuttled in a crouch below the level of the crops until they reached the fence. She turned to check that he was still right behind her, winked, and pulled aside one of the bottom planks. She rolled underneath. Lebasi followed, just managing to squeeze himself through the gap. He hoped this wasn't part of the trap. He checked for danger as he stood up, but there was no one in sight. They were in an open area between the buildings and the fence. He started to brush the dust from his clothes, but Tik was off again, sprinting for the back of one of the nearby barns. At the door, she put her finger to her lips.

'We can get close, but we don't want them to see or hear. You can meet him when he leaves, all right? I'll get you out the same way.'

There was no time to object. She lifted a wooden bar that held the door shut and slipped through into the building. Lebasi had to follow. She made no noise as she picked her way between sacks of grain and piles of wood. There was a large double door at the front of the barn with an ox-cart parked behind it. The girl pulled him to the left-hand side and ducked down to put her eye to a crack between the planks that made up the wall. Lebasi crouched beside her and peered out.

Xela was standing ten paces away. His boots were dusty from his long walk, but he appeared to be unharmed. He seemed to be waiting for someone. Lebasi squinted to the left and right. Three more men – farmers from their deep tans and strong arms – one behind and one on either side of Xela – all with their eyes fixed on him. Lebasi pictured the guards surrounding Perra at the meeting of the elders. Xela took no notice of them. He fanned his face with a straw hat. He was humming to himself.

The man at the back shifted his weight. Lebasi saw something resting on the ground, concealed behind his legs. A long, heavy wooden club. He almost called out a warning, but Tik seemed to sense what he was thinking. She put her fingers to his lips and shook her head. She mouthed, 'It's all fine.'

Lebasi turned to the crack in the wall again. It looked anything but fine to him.

35
TAKEN

The four men straightened up. Someone was approaching from out of sight to the left. Another farmer came into Lebasi's field of view, walking stiffly as if he wanted to put on a show. Behind him strode a man with long white hair and beard. He carried a stick, but did not lean on it. He looked old – sixty or seventy, maybe – but his back was straight and his steps sure. He was taller than any of his sons. Lebasi glanced at Tik, guessing this was her grandfather. The younger man joined his brother with the club. White Beard – Gortan, Verral had called him – came to a halt three paces from Xela. He said nothing: he stood with his head tilted back, looking down his long nose.

Xela made the sign of deep respect to him, not just bowing his head but bending from the waist. Lebasi gaped. He couldn't imagine anyone in all Xessus to whom the magistrate had to defer like that. Perhaps the captain of the Guard, but surely not a cantankerous old farmer out here on the edge of the world. He surely didn't mean it sarcastically. The old man made no movement at all in response.

Lebasi heard the greeting Xela gave him, speaking in the special language: 'Good afternoon, father Gortan, how do I find you today?' *Father*: yet more respect. What could it mean?

Gortan paused before answering. 'You know how we look forward to your annual visit, Xela.' He did not smile.

Xela nodded. 'I have no illusions. But if you would prefer me not to come. it would be better if you paid your taxes in good time. You know what's due. If the tallyman at Annessam tells me that he has received it an eightnight before Midsummer, we will not have to –'

Gortan waved his hand as if brushing away a fly. 'The king wants too much. We have had enough of paying.'

Xela shook his head. 'I cannot disagree with you. But you must pay, or the Guard will come.'

The brothers shifted from foot to foot. Gortan sniffed. 'Do you think they will march all this way for a few sacks of grain?'

Xela tapped his foot on the ground. 'I don't know. I only know that they say they will. I have kept the Westwall Guard out of this district for sixteen years. Do you want to be the man who brings them back?'

Gortan leaned forward. 'And what if you don't tell them?'

Xela spread his hands. 'You know it's not up to me. The tallyman sends a report with the goods. Egator will know we are short, and why. It might take half a year, but I believe they would send the soldiers.'

Gortan straightened up again. 'Perhaps you are right.'

Tik nudged Lebasi. He pulled back to see what she wanted. She grinned and winked. He could just hear her whisper, 'They always do this.'

Xela's voice, raised in anger: 'Fire and ice!' Lebasi and Tik pressed their eyes to the wall. Xela had been thrown to the ground. The two largest farmers each had hold of one of his arms. A third stepped up and forced a cloth between his teeth to make a gag. The fourth brother looped a rope around his ankles.

Tik's wide eyes told Lebasi that this was not what she expected. She gripped his arm, shaking her head. Lebasi pressed his palms against the wall, wishing he had run a little faster, wishing he had got away from Verral sooner. If he'd caught his da out in the open, he could have warned him – Xela might not have believed him, but at least he could have tried. There was nothing he could do against four strong men.

Gortan made no movement as his sons secured Xela. He folded his hands on top of his stick and watched without apparent interest. The man with the rope moved from ankles to wrists. Xela had stopped fighting against the gag. He stood between the two men grasping his arms, staring at Gortan.

At last the old farmer spoke. 'Perhaps you are right, but we have had enough. The time has come for us to stand up to the king. We will have to decide what to do with you.'

The tallest of the sons stepped away from Xela. He fell sideways. Unable to move his arms, he hit the ground heavily. Immediately he twisted himself up onto his knees, then jumped upright again. He continued to fix his eyes on Gortan.

'Nareb, please be more careful.' Gortan sounded no more cross than any parent correcting a clumsy child. 'Put him in the barn for the moment.'

Lebasi was still taking that order in when Tik pulled him away from the wall. She put her finger to her lips and pointed with the other hand towards the side of the building. Lebasi took long, silent strides. He heard the sound of the door opening behind him. They ducked behind a woodpile and lay still. There were heavy footsteps, then the heavier sound of a body being thrown on the floor.

'Not so high and mighty now, little Xela?' Lebasi heard the sound of someone spitting. He clenched his fists: only a coward would spit on his father, bound and helpless. *But there's no point fighting a bully if the bully will win.* He breathed in, breathed out. The door slammed shut.

Tik sat up and peeped over the logs. 'They've gone', she whispered. 'Let's see what we can do for him.'

Lebasi hesitated, then followed her towards the doorway. Xela was lying on his back, his eyes open. Tik knelt beside him

and wiped the spittle off his cheek with her sleeve. He nodded a thankyou. As Lebasi stepped forward to show himself, the door opened – there was Nareb, silhouetted against the light – Tik jumped up and ran, Lebasi close behind her – they dodged between the piles of goods and slipped through the back door. It happened so quickly that Lebasi hardly knew whether Nareb had seen them, but now he heard the man shouting, his heavy tread crossing the barn. Tik shut the door and dropped the locking bar in place, then led the way to the loose plank in the fence. She pulled it up; Lebasi didn't need her urging him to hurry. As he squeezed underneath with his head on one side, he saw the farmer coming round the corner of the building. Tik was too quick to be caught. She rolled a rock against the plank and set off into the cornfield. Lebasi glanced back to see hands appearing on top of the fence, then Nareb's head looking over – but they were out of sight among the crops.

Tik didn't speak until they reached the wood. She carried on, ducking under branches and between saplings until they were nearly at the far edge. Lebasi could see open sky ahead, and an opening on the left might be the track. Tik stopped by a thick, tall bush, and stood very still. Lebasi watched her turning her head sharply left and right, like a bird listening for danger. She bent down and pulled aside a branch, beckoning Lebasi to crawl into the space behind. After two paces of low tunnel, the middle of the bush opened up – it was like a small room with a smooth dry floor. His eyes adjusted to the dim green light as Tik appeared beside him. 'This is where Sinder and I hide out,' she explained, as the door closed. 'No one else comes here.' She gave him a fierce look. 'Deepest secret.' Lebasi nodded. After all, who would he tell?

They sat for a moment getting their breath back. Tik banged her hands together. 'This never happened before. He comes, they argue, they give in. He goes away.'

Lebasi realised she was crying. He put his hand on her shoulder. 'They're your family. Why are you on Xela's side?'

She wiped her eyes. 'Because he's kind to me, and they're not. They call me Little Bug. Even my own da does. Even Sinder's da, and he's not bad, most of the time. Nareb and Dareff, they're just horrible. I watch for Xela at the road, every Midsummer's Day. He always asks me how I am, tells me how much I've grown. Today he brought me this.' She held up a polished stone which hung around her neck on a thin leather cord.

Lebasi knew how she felt: it was how the others treated him at school. Even so, he couldn't help feeling a moment's jealousy. It seemed that once a year, every year, Xela showed this strange girl more affection than he did to Lebasi.

She stared into his eyes. 'What are we going to do?'

Lebasi realised that she expected him to answer. 'I don't know. I could try sneaking in at night and –'

She shook her head. 'Don't think so. You wouldn't get in or out without someone seeing you. And there are dogs.'

Lebasi shivered. He didn't want to be hunted again.

What did Gortan intend to do with Xela? They hadn't hurt him – much – they'd only tied him up. Perra had only said that Xela wouldn't be coming back. That could just mean that the farmers were only going to hold him prisoner. In that case he could... he could what?

Lebasi sat back, his mind emptying itself of all thought. He realised that he had no idea what to do next. He had focused only on reaching Xela and passing on Marrak's message. Xela would take over from there. But Xela was lying bound and gagged on the floor of Gortan's barn, and Lebasi was hiding in a bush in a wood at the edge of Xessus, hungry and thirsty, with nowhere to turn for help.

He covered his face with his hands. It was hopeless.

36
STRANGER

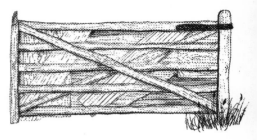

Tik sat up, her head turning from side to side. 'Hear that?'

Lebasi just had time to detect a high-pitched whistle before Tik muttered 'Sinder' and disappeared into the tunnel. He followed her out, taking a slap in the face from the door-branch swinging shut behind her. She ran ahead of him to the track. The boy Lebasi had seen on the main road was standing with his hands on his knees, breathing hard. He glanced up as Tik reached him, then straightened and stepped back.

'Who's that?'

'The magistrate's son. He doesn't understand how we talk.'

Lebasi raised a hand and said, 'Hello.'

Sinder stared at him for just a moment, then snapped round to point back the way he had come.

'He's coming, the one they told me to look out for. I fell asleep, he was right on me when I woke up.'

'Sinder, you idiot. You'd better run.'

'He was angry about something. Kept shouting after me to stop and come back.'

Tik pushed the boy towards the farm. She turned to gaze towards the main road.

Lebasi asked, 'Who's coming?'

She studied him for a moment before answering in the other

language. 'The man from the south.'

He wasn't sure why, but he decided to keep pretending he didn't understand. He shook his head. 'What did you say? Sinder looked like he was running away from someone. Is he in trouble too?'

The man from the south – it had to be the same one. Lebasi tried not to look interested. What was he doing here, on the edge of the wilderness, visiting the last farmers in the kingdom?

Tik took his arm and pulled him into the undergrowth. 'My da and uncles are all being very mysterious about someone coming to visit them. They don't think we know, but they get drunk and talk loud. He's from the south – not from Xessus at all.'

'Someone like that turned up in my town after my da left, and then again at a meeting on Marstor land yesterday. Why's he coming here?'

She shrugged. 'Come on, let's get a look at him.'

They hid in the bushes and waited. Soon enough the familiar figure of the southerner appeared, swinging his stick as he marched. He had a small pack on his back and a wide-brimmed hat. Lebasi pulled a branch aside to get a better view. The man turned his head sharply and met Lebasi's gaze over no more than twenty paces.

'You! What are you doing here?'

Lebasi ducked down and followed Tik further into the trees. They heard the man following, but she knew where to hide.

When the man had gone past, she hissed in Lebasi's ear, 'You and Sinder are both idiots. What did you want to let him see you for?'

Lebasi had no excuses. They crept round to the edge of the wood nearest the farm. They had a good view of the gate across fifty paces of short-cropped grass. Sinder had warned the farm: the gate was open, and Gortan was standing on the track with his four sons behind him, waiting to welcome the visitor.

'They don't come out like that for Xela,' Tik whispered. 'They make him bang on the gate, and then one of them goes off to fetch grandda.'

The southerner appeared out of the wood on their right, still brushing leaves off his tunic from his search of the bushes. When he was twenty paces away, Gortan made the sign of respect. Three of his sons went further and bent from the waist, as Xela had done for the old man. Nareb did something in between.

Tik nudged Lebasi. 'He must be really important. I've never seen them giving any respect to anyone before.'

The traveller only nodded acceptance. As he approached, he started talking to Gortan, gesturing behind him with his stick. Lebasi knew what he was saying. 'The magistrate's son – what's he doing here?' Gortan was raising his hands, the brothers were looking at each other.

Tik grasped his shoulder. Her mischievous grin was back, as if she had just thought of a good joke. 'I know what to do. But you need to get away, Lebasi of Xela. I'll make sure they don't come looking for you, but go home. It won't be safe around here. Goodbye.'

To Lebasi's surprise, she quickly hugged him, then disappeared in the direction of the cornfield.

Go home? How could he do that, leaving Xela a prisoner? Even if Xela had been free and safe, how could he manage it on his own? He had received help and food from Barten on the way, but now he knew more about the dangers of the countryside, and he didn't know who to trust. He decided to watch the group around the gate to see what they did. If they went inside, he would have a head start. If they started a hunt immediately, he would... what?

They were still holding a lively discussion. It was too far for the words to carry, but it was clear to Lebasi that the southerner was telling Gortan that he had seen the magistrate's son in the

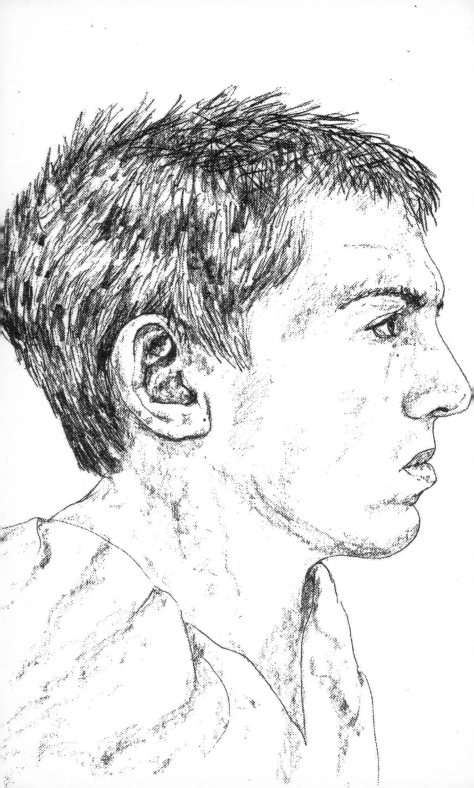

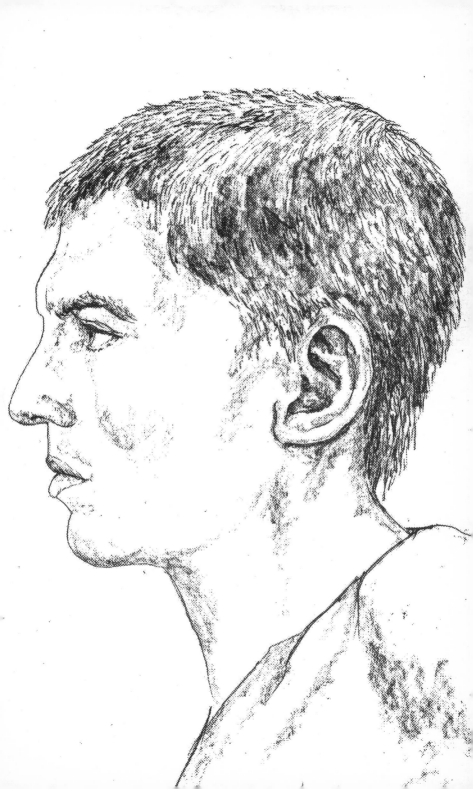

woods, and Gortan and the farmers didn't believe it. He kept low to the ground as the man waved his stick back down the road. For a moment he was pointing it directly at Lebasi's hiding place. Gortan turned and gave an instruction: the shortest of his sons went in through the gate. The others stayed where they were.

Barks and whines came from the farmyard. They were bringing out the dogs.

Lebasi dug his fingers into the ground. He should run, now, while he still had time – but what was the use? They would catch him. Lebasi felt the strength drain out of his legs. He was weary, hungry, thirsty, and lost. It was the end. Why run any further? He was so tired of having to work out what to do next. He felt a sudden longing to give in, to stand up and let them decide what to do with him. At least then he could rest.

Tik appeared in the gateway, pulling Sinder behind her. He clearly didn't want to be there. She jumped behind him and pushed him with both hands. Lebasi caught the sound of her voice across the meadow, but not her words.

The southerner turned. He stepped towards Sinder. He put his head on one side and examined his face. He glanced back at the woods, then at the boy again. He asked a question.

The farmer was standing in the gateway with four big dogs, each on a rope. He was struggling to hold them.

The words 'Sinder what are you doing here?' drifted into Lebasi's head. From three paces away, Tik had thought Lebasi was her own cousin. They must be really alike. The southerner had seen Sinder at the road, and no more than a glimpse of Lebasi's head among the bushes – it might work.

They were laughing now. The farmer dragged the dogs back through the gate. Gortan held out an arm and followed the visitor into the farmyard. The tallest son – Lebasi reckoned that was

Nareb – hit Sinder on the side of the head, sending him staggering across the road. When everyone else was facing the other way, Tik stared straight at where Lebasi was lying and moved her hands as if shooing a cat. The gate was pulled shut behind her.

Lebasi rolled over and stared up at the sky. His heart was threatening to burst out of his chest. He might make it, now – no one was looking for him. He could get back to the road, head south, hope to find someone friendly like Barten.

He could go back and join the revolution. Explain why he'd run away, tell Perra it wasn't because he wanted the Mercy to carry on, he did it to ask his father...

He still had to ask his father.

He closed his eyes and pictured Xela lying on the floor of the barn, Nareb standing over him. There was a little voice in the back of his head whispering that he deserved it, he should have stood up for Lebasi in front of the elders, he wasn't getting anything as bad as the beating he had been prepared to hand out to his own son.

But Lebasi didn't like that voice. The legends of Xessus told him it was wrong. He had to help him.

If the bully's bigger than you, you need someone to frighten them. It was useless. Four grown men, the southerner – and how many grandsons might Gortan have, who wouldn't all be like Tik and Sinder?

What had Xela said? 'The bullies here are frightened of me, but who frightens the Westwall Guard?' The question formed in Lebasi's mind: 'Who frightens Gortan?'

He twisted back to stare at the gate. He had an idea. A terrible idea.

37
ANOTHER PLAN

Lebasi sat in Tik's hideout and thought it over. It was risky, but what choice did he have? The only way Xela was going to leave that farm was if they let him go. Lebasi had to give them a reason. That meant he had to talk to them, show himself to them. Turning up at the gate so soon after the southerner had claimed he was there – and Gortan had replied that it was impossible – would be suspicious. But he had to do something.

The longer he could leave it, the better his story would be. He tried to judge the position of the sun through the branches above him. It was Midsummer's Day. He had met Verral early in the morning, reached the farm not long after midday. He wanted some daylight so he and Xela could put a good distance between themselves and the farm before they had to stop for the night – if it worked. He should go, but not yet. He told himself that the reasons for delay were good ones. He told himself that he was just making excuses for not wanting to knock on the gate.

At last, he decided it was time. He jogged through the trees to the western edge of the wood and scanned the track ahead. He hoped that the farmers didn't always have someone posted by the turning to warn them of visitors – that would give the lie to his story. Unless – he had come across the fields. That gave him another idea. He dashed across the road, hoping no one would see him appearing from the wrong direction, and threw himself into the irrigation channel running beside it. The water was lukewarm, but when he stood up his clothes felt clammy against his skin. He wiped a muddy hand across his face and through his hair. That might make him look a little less like the face the southerner had seen among the bushes. He took a deep breath and set off running towards the farm.

The gate was shut. It was made of solid planks, and there wasn't even a crack to peer through. Lebasi banged his fists on the wood and shouted, 'Is someone there? Please open up.' The dogs answered. Lebasi kept on hitting the gate and calling.

Footsteps approached. Lebasi stepped back as the gate swung towards him. He stared up at Nareb staring down at him.

'I've got an urgent message for the magistrate. I was told he would be here.'

Nareb leaned forward and looked in Lebasi's eyes. 'Who do you think you are, coming here and asking for the magistrate?'

Lebasi took a step backwards. He spread his hands. 'I'm sorry, I don't understand. I've come a long way. The magistrate's agent has called for the Westwall Guard, and the magistrate needs to know.'

'What?' The man grabbed Lebasi by the arm and dragged him through the gate.

One of his brothers was walking towards them. Nareb shouted, 'Get Gortan out here. Now!' The man turned and ran.

Nareb's fingers dug into Lebasi's shoulder. He had to run on tiptoe to keep his balance as he was marched into the middle of the yard. He tried not to look at the barn where he knew Xela was tied up.

Tik came running around the side of one of the houses on the right. He wondered how he could let her know that this was meant to happen. He hoped she wouldn't let on that she knew him. Her

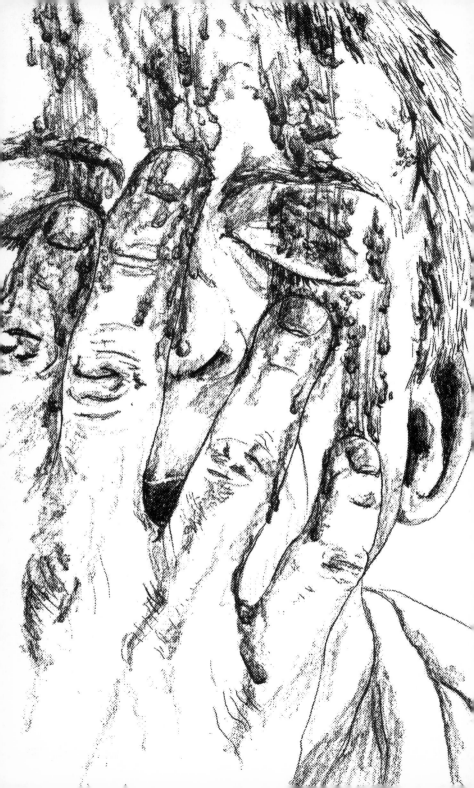

eyes flashed at him with anger and frustration, but she said nothing. Some other children, all larger than her – and, Lebasi noticed, all boys – appeared in doorways and from between buildings.

Ahead, Gortan was striding to meet them. Nareb's three brothers were behind him, but there was no sign of the southerner. Nareb shoved Lebasi forward so hard that he fell at the old man's feet. He struggled upright and made the sign of deep respect. Gortan made no response, just as when Xela had greeted him. He again had to resist the urge to glance sideways towards the wall through which he had watched the earlier meeting.

'Who are you, boy?'

'I'm sorry, I don't understand.'

Gortan's mouth twitched, as if he had eaten something unpleasant and was wondering where to spit it out.

'I said, who are you, boy?'

'I'm Lebasi.' He paused – he was going to add, 'of Xela,' but he had to gather up his courage to do so.

Gortan took a step backwards. The sons started talking in their own language, a jumble of words too fast and confused for Lebasi to follow them.

Gortan recovered. He used his stick to turn Lebasi's face from side to side, inspecting him.

Lebasi let words tumble out, trying not to give the old man time to think. 'I'm sorry I'm such a mess, I fell in a ditch. I was trying to take a short cut across the fields to get here quicker. I've been running for two days. Is Xela here?'

'What message do you have for him?'

Lebasi glanced to left and right. He had to judge this carefully. He needed to tell Gortan, but he didn't want to seem too keen to do so.

'I ought to tell only the magistrate. It's his business, between him and his agent.'

Gortan sniffed. 'Anything here is my business. If it is so important, I will see that the message reaches Xela.'

Lebasi made a show of indecision, knocking his knuckles together. Gortan banged his stick on the ground. 'Speak, boy!'

'There's trouble in our town. Marrak – that's the magistrate's agent – he's sent for the Westwall Guard. Xela said that if the Guard come, they'll kill everyone. I have to warn him. I ran away.'

'How did you know to come here?'

'I asked Marrak where Xela had gone, and he told me. He didn't think I'd do anything about it. He said the last farm in the kingdom, where the mountains come down to the sea. That's here, isn't it?' He pointed up to the cascading cliffs of the Eagle's Nest, then swept his hand around to the north, where the sky was empty of mountains.

Gortan nodded. 'Yes, that is here. But why is it important to me, that the Westwall Guard is going to Xela's town?'

This was the dangerous moment, where the truth ended and the lies began. This was where he had to hope his guesses were right. 'No, they're coming here, not to the town.'

At least that had the effect he wanted. The sons shouted at each other, the children gasped and babbled. Out of the corner of his eye, he spotted Tik, who had broken into a broad grin. Just as quickly she changed to an expression of shock and fear and started chattering with her cousins.

Gortan shouted for silence. 'Why are they coming here?'

'Marrak didn't tell me.' He paused. 'But I think I know.' He looked all around again. 'I really ought to tell Xela. Is he here?'

Gortan smiled. Lebasi tried not to shudder: he was sure it was not meant kindly. 'If you tell me what you think you know, I may be able to arrange for you to see him.' Lebasi guessed what that meant. Maybe this was not going to work, but he had to carry on.

'All right. I got Xela to tell me why he comes here every year. He says there's a big storeroom full of longbows and arrows and helmets and spears, and he brings some more on an ox. Marrak knows there's trouble in the countryside as well as in our town. I think he's sending the soldiers to make sure no one else gets hold of all those weapons.'

Gortan put a finger against his lips. Lebasi prayed that he would believe it. He had to believe it.

'And how soon will the soldiers arrive?'

'I don't know. Marrak sent for them two days ago, in the morning. I don't know where they'll be coming from, or how fast they march. But he said something about the day after Midsummer – that's tomorrow, isn't it?'

Once again, the children jabbered. Gortan and Lebasi stood silently staring into each other's eyes. Lebasi felt the ferocity of the man's gaze. He understood why Xela gave him deep respect. The will to lie seemed to drain out of him. Of course Gortan would know the truth, he might as well admit it.

A woman appeared at Gortan's elbow. Lebasi guessed that she must be one of the wives, one of the mothers. She stood on tiptoe to whisper in his ear. A muscle in the old man's cheek twitched. Lebasi was reminded of Xela trying to hold his temper in. Gortan whispered something back, then shouted, 'By the five tribes, will you all be quiet?' Silence fell as the woman ran back to the house at the far end of the farmyard. Gortan waved with his stick. 'You children, get about your business. You have jobs to do.' They started to drift away reluctantly.

Lebasi dared to ask, 'Please, can I have a drink?'

Gortan snapped his fingers. Tik ran to the nearest house and came back with a wooden beaker. She squeezed his hand as she handed it over. He tried to drink slowly, not wanting the feeling of cool water in his throat to pass too quickly.

The woman returned, her skirts flapping as she ran. She whispered to Gortan again. The old man took several deep breaths. His voice was strained.

'Nareb, bring Xela out. We will let him go.'

Lebasi tried to keep his face neutral. After all, he wasn't supposed to know that Xela was a prisoner, and he wasn't supposed to understand what Gortan was saying. And the old man was still staring into his eyes as if he could see every thought in Lebasi's mind.

38
FURY

Nareb started to protest, but Gortan roared something Lebasi could not understand in any language. The son turned and walked slowly towards the barn, casting furious glances behind him. He banged his palm against the door before pulling it ajar and slipping inside. His brothers gathered around Gortan as if to protest, but the expression on the old man's face silenced them.

Nareb reappeared, holding the end of a rope. Xela shuffled out after him, his ankles free but still bound at the wrists and gagged. There was blood on his cheek. Lebasi threw down the mug and ran towards him. He knew that he had to act as if he was shocked, but he was shocked anyway: he had never seen Xela looking so defeated.

'Da, what...'

Nareb put out his arm to block Lebasi. He felt the strength in the man's hand as he was thrown backwards. He stumbled and fell.

Gortan banged his stick again. 'Untie him.' In response to Nareb's glare, he shouted, 'Now!'

Lebasi picked himself up and watched Nareb loosen the ropes around his father's wrists. Xela was standing straighter now, staring at him, his eyes full of astonished questions. Nareb pulled the gag roughly out of his mouth. Xela spat on the ground and rubbed his sleeve across his face.

Lebasi moved towards him again. Nareb growled, 'Get back.

you little menker', and stepped in the way, his hand raised. Lebasi flinched and braced himself, but the blow didn't fall. Xela sprang across the space between them, a blur of motion, spinning around, grabbing the raised arm, twisting Nareb like a dancer twirling a partner – except that he finished with Nareb's arm bent high up against his shoulder blades. With his right hand Xela held a short wooden baton across the bigger man's windpipe. Lebasi had never seen it before and didn't know where it had come from.

'Behind me, son, now,' his father snapped. Lebasi jumped smartly and turned to stare at Gortan and Nareb's brothers, who were looking almost as surprised as Nareb himself.

Xela was whispering in Nareb's ear. 'Didn't expect that, did you? I've been practising.' Lebasi wondered when, where and who with... Nareb tried to struggle, but Xela pushed up with his left hand and pulled the stick tighter with his right. He growled, 'I'll gladly break your arm or your neck, man, just give me a reason.' He forced Nareb across the yard to stand five paces from Gortan. Lebasi followed behind him, hoping this wouldn't ruin the plan. He'd happily have taken a slap from Nareb if Xela had only agreed to walk away.

The other brothers moved to surround Lebasi and Xela, their arms spread out, their eyes wary. Lebasi turned to stand back-to-back with his father, glancing from one hostile face to another. One of them drew a short knife from his belt and held it out towards Lebasi.

Another muttered, 'Gone a bit too far, this time, little Xela. How are you going to get away?'

Nareb grunted as Xela tightened his grip again. 'If you want your big brother back, you'll –'

Gortan roared, 'Enough!' He raised the stick and pointed in turn at each of the three men. 'Stand behind me.' After a deep breath, he spoke to Xela. 'Release him. I give my word that you shall be allowed to leave.'

The sons obeyed, moving slowly and keeping their eyes on Xela. He kept hold of Nareb. Lebasi peered around him to watch Gortan.

'Your word? Should I trust your word, old man, when you've already had me tied up once? Setting traps for unarmed visitors, four to one, those are your ideas of honour.'

Gortan leaned forward, resting his hands on his stick. He seemed indifferent to the strangled noises coming from his oldest son. He spoke slowly, as if choosing his words with care. 'Things have changed. This boy has brought news that your agent has sent for the Westwall Guard. They are coming here.'

Xela glanced down, but did not relax his grip. 'Is that true, Lebasi?'

Lebasi stopped himself from answering the question. 'Sorry, da, I don't understand.'

'Has Marrak sent for the Guard?'

'Yes. There's trouble in the town. He ordered them to come here. I think he wanted to make sure that no one got to the weapons store.'

Xela narrowed his eyes. Lebasi hoped that his own father wouldn't tell Gortan that this was unlikely to be true. 'And you –'

'You told me that if the Guard came, and if anyone fought them, they'd kill everyone. I ran away to warn you. I thought maybe you can stop them.'

Xela turned back to Gortan. 'So why are you going to let me go, now the Guard are coming?'

Gortan curled his lip. 'I do not wish to have the king's soldiers at my door. I believe that you can tell them not to come.'

Xela laughed. 'So at last you think I could be useful. But why should I do that for you?'

'I have told you. It is worth me letting you go, that you should do this for me. If you do not agree to do it, then you will not leave. Nor will the boy. And if you do not send the signal as agreed, you will not get far away.'

Lebasi struggled to keep his face blank. His guess had been right: the southerner was in charge, and the southerner wasn't ready for the army to interfere.

Xela still wasn't convinced. 'And if I send a signal, what then?'

Lebasi decided that the old man's smile was the most frightening thing he'd seen since he escaped from the dogs. 'Then it will be up to you. Who knows?'

Lebasi silently willed his father to agree. He glanced up at Nareb, whose face was very red – whether with anger or being strangled, he wasn't sure. Suddenly, Xela released his grip and pushed his hostage forward so he fell at Gortan's feet. Nareb rolled over and jumped back up, raising his fists towards Xela, but Gortan rapped him on the ankles with his stick. He tumbled to the ground again, clutching his foot and swearing.

Gortan ignored him. He gestured towards Lebasi. 'This is your son?'

Xela put an arm around Lebasi's shoulders. 'Yes, and I'm not going to talk about him in a tongue he can't understand.'

Gortan reached out a bony hand to beckon Lebasi forward. He looked up questioningly at Xela, who nodded. He walked forward and made the sign of respect.

Gortan bent slightly, leaning on his stick, studying Lebasi's face. Lebasi stared back into his eyes, trying not to blink, determined that he wouldn't show how scared he was. The old man had the same brown eyes as his sons, but they were even fiercer, deep-set where his face had hollowed with age. His bushy eyebrows twitched up and down. Lebasi breathed in and made himself stand straight. After what seemed like a long time, the old man asked, 'Were you hiding in the woods earlier today?'

'I'm sorry, I don't understand what you're saying.'

Gortan regarded Lebasi shrewdly while he tried to look innocent. The old man translated the question, spitting each word out as if the language tasted bad.

'The woods? I... I came through some woods just before I got here. Before that I was on the road, then coming across the fields.' He wanted to give an impression of stupidity, to make it less likely that he could spin an elaborate lie. He looked down at the mud on his tunic as if remembering something important. 'I fell in a ditch.'

Gortan nodded and looked past him. 'He looks like a strong lad, Xela.' He sighed. A sudden sadness in his voice surprised Lebasi. 'I hope he is not a disappointment to you, as sons sometimes are.'

Lebasi walked backwards to stand behind his father, wondering who that was aimed at. Nareb, still rubbing his neck, scowling. The second biggest, still fingering the handle of the knife in his belt. All four of them younger, smaller versions of the old farmer.

Xela's cheek was twitching. He took a pace forward. 'There is the other matter, the one I came here for. I still need an answer.' Lebasi stifled an urge to pull at his father's sleeve. That wasn't important. But he wasn't supposed to know what Xela was saying.

Gortan glanced over his shoulder towards the house. Lebasi wondered whether he was acknowledging a message from the southerner, or simply casting his eyes in the same direction as his thoughts. He leaned on his stick and stood, drawing himself up to his full height. He looked down his nose at Xela and curled his lips into a sneer.

'Very well. To keep the Guard away, we will settle. I will send what is required to Anessam to be loaded onto the boats. You can turn back the cursed soldiers. You can send your report to the king that we are law-abiding citizens, here in this part of Xessus.' He paused to spit on the ground. 'I am sure it will make you happy to see the laws of Riadsala obeyed.'

This, finally, was too much for Xela. He drew in a deep breath, threw his arms out wide, his head back, and let out an animal's roar. He banged one fist into the other palm. He sprang forward and held his trembling fist in front of Gortan's nose.

'That is too much, you vile old man. Too much. I come here and I try to be civilised, and what do I get? Disrespect, threats, being tied up and thrown in the dirt, spat on. All that, I will walk away from, for the sake of peace. But I will not hear it said that any of Riadsala's laws make me happy.' He swept a hand around to take in the whole of the farm. 'What has the king ever done to hurt you, really? It's just the bitterness in your heart, old man. You know that I have far more reason than any of you to hate the king.'

Gortan started to say something, but Xela leaned forward and put his finger against the man's lips. 'No! You've said enough, more than enough. You know what? I don't care if you pay. I'm tired of protecting you. You pay if you want to, don't pay if you don't. I couldn't care less. I will tell the Guard to stand back now, but not for you. For me. For the sake of the sixteen years that I've kept them away from the people of this district. But if you don't pay, I'll send my report to say you speak Xessan here, and you all have five-pointed stars drawn inside the doors of your houses - oh yes, bravely on the inside, where you can see them but no one else can - and you think your rebellious thoughts.' He laughed scornfully. 'Yes, thinking, you're good at that. What have you ever done about it, eh? What in sixty-seven years have you ever actually done about your little grievance with the king?' He snapped his fingers in Gortan's face. 'That much. Less than that. You make me sick.' He swung his arm around again, and shouted so everyone could hear, in the yard and in the houses. 'You all make me sick.'

Lebasi stared at his father. He wouldn't have had to understand the words to know that Xela had lost control. He watched the farmer and his four hostile sons from the corners of his eyes. What would they do now?

The sons all started forward, but Gortan put up a hand to stop them. He still held himself in the same upright, arrogant stance, looking down at the magistrate. Then, to Lebasi's surprise, he stiffly made the sign of respect, the smallest flicker of a smile in the corners of his mouth. He held out a hand towards the gate. 'Go on your way, then. I trust that you will send your message to turn back the soldiers. Until we meet again, Xela.'

39
GUESSES

Xela didn't acknowledge the respect. He turned his back, put a hand on Lebasi's shoulder, and set off at a brisk pace. Lebasi had to put in a skip every few steps to keep up. He saw Xela was talking to himself, his cheek twitching, his mouth working, his face red. He didn't look round. Nor did Lebasi, even though he could feel the eyes of everyone in the farmyard boring into the back of his head. Xela pushed the gate open, passed through, left it standing wide.

At last, as they passed into the shade of the wood, Xela glanced over his shoulder. Lebasi did the same, and saw the four sons lined across the road in the gateway, arms folded, staring after them. Xela muttered, 'Looks like they're really letting us go. You'd better tell me what's going on, because I have no idea.' He turned his head as he walked to look at Lebasi properly, and smiled. 'Maybe you could start by telling me what in the name of Xessus you're doing here. And how you got here. I told you to keep out of trouble while I was gone. This counts as trouble.'

Lebasi wondered where to begin. While he was getting his thoughts in order, he pointed to the surrounding trees and tapped his ear. Tik had a hideout here – maybe others did too, who might not be so friendly.

He started to talk when they were between open fields. He began with the sight of the flag flying from the bell tower, and tried to keep to the most important facts – Perra's speech, Marrak's signal, the men with sticks in the streets of Trengam, the meeting of Marstor farmers, what the southerner said about his plans not being ready. He kept his eyes ahead, choosing his words carefully. Some things he would save for later – being chased in the tunnels, hunted with dogs, patched up by Barten, threatened by Verral. Finding out that Xela had taken Barten's son. Some things he hoped he would never have to explain, that Xela would never know – how he had helped Perra, how he was still not sure which side he was on.

To his surprise, Xela listened without interrupting. They reached the ox, still peacefully chewing the grass by the side of the main road, as Lebasi was explaining that he had guessed the southerner would tell Gortan to let Xela go, if he thought the soldiers would come and the magistrate could stop them. They turned to face each other. Xela put his hand over his heart and made the sign of respect. Then he put a hand on Lebasi's shoulder and smiled.

'Where have I been, while you were growing into someone who could do all that? I am sorry, more sorry than I can explain. Thank you.'

Lebasi didn't know how to reply. Instead, he glanced up at the sun and south down the road. 'How far away can we get tonight?'

Xela was running his hands over the ox's load, checking it was all still there. He picked up the leading rope. 'We're not going that way.'

Lebasi started to protest, but Xela shook his head. 'You heard what old man Gortan said. We have to send a signal to the Guard, tomorrow morning at first light, and the only place we can do that is from the top of that tower.' He pointed ahead to the silhouette on the hill.

'But they aren't really coming here.'

'Even so, we have to stick to your story. And there's another thing. You were right about the arms store. I want this lot' – he patted the sacking on the animal's back – 'safely locked away before Gortan changes his mind. Or those Marstor farmers get their courage up.'

'But after you've sent the message, won't they come after us again?'

'Oh, I think I can choose my signals carefully. I can tell the soldiers to meet me not far from here, so if I don't arrive, they'll look for me at the farm.'

'But they won't be anywhere near.'

'No, but I can make sure Gortan thinks they are.' He pointed up towards the Eagle's Nest. 'From the tower, I have to send signals to an old friend of mine who lives up there, and he passes them on to Marstor. And he passes them on to Gortan as well. Or Gortan believes he does. But he's not as reliable as Gortan thinks.' Xela tapped the side of his nose.

Lebasi gazed across at the cliffs, bathed now in the orange light of late evening, and wondered why someone would live there. And how, or why, Xela could have an old friend who did so.

Lebasi's mind wandered. He'd recalled the whole of the last three days while they were walking, picking out what to describe and what to leave out, and as usual the words people said came back to him exactly. Thinking about the main events and ignoring the spaces in between, he found he was putting together different phrases and reaching for something he couldn't quite grasp...

Xela interrupted his thoughts. 'So you understood what they were saying at the farm?'

Lebasi nodded. 'It took me a few moments to get back into it. I'd always thought the language was something you made up just between us – what is it?'

Xela smiled. 'How clever do you think I am? I couldn't invent all that. It's something you don't hear in the towns, because people have been afraid of being overheard for so long that hardly anyone knows it these days. But out in the countryside, especially around Marstor, a lot of people still speak it amongst themselves. Some of them are happy to use it with me, and they're friendlier to me as a result. People like Barten. Others are careful not to let on to me that they know it, but Gortan doesn't care. He doesn't think – well, he didn't think – I'd ever summon the Guard on him.'

Lebasi remembered his father's angry words, *I'll send my report to say that you speak Xessan here*. He gasped. 'It's Dennara's language, isn't it? Did Riadsala...'

'Forbid it, along with reading and writing and history, yes. He wanted all of old Xessus to be forgotten. What we're speaking now is how the southerners talked back then. Speaking Xessan is almost as bad as not paying your taxes.'

'But you taught me!'

Xela ran his hand over his face, suddenly looking tired. 'Yes. Maybe not very safe, not very wise. I was younger then, and sometimes I had views of my own, even as magistrate. I used to think these things shouldn't be forgotten. Xessus was a fine country, you know. We've lived – I've lived under the shadow of Egator for so long it's hard to remember that now.'

One word echoed in Lebasi's mind. 'Nareb swore in ordinary words, though. He called me a menker.'

Xela laughed. 'No, we all swear in Xessan. Marrak wouldn't say that – well, he wouldn't when he first came from Egator. Maybe he understands the words now. A menker's a cockroach to a Xessan. One of the milder ones. I didn't teach you those words when you were small.'

Xela rummaged in the packs on the ox's back and produced

some bread and nuts and a water-skin. Lebasi munched the food hungrily and washed it down.

His father put a hand on his shoulder. 'Careful with the water, we haven't got much between two. We'll eat properly when we camp. Top of the hill. We have to unload the ox first.'

They moved on without speaking, both deep in thought. Lebasi found phrases of Barten's spinning in his mind, settling, coming together. He stopped and stared at his father. Xela turned, his eyebrows raised.

'You were born on Marstor land. Not in the town. That's why you don't have any family in Trengam, isn't it?'

Xela took half a step back. His mouth moved, but no words came. Lebasi felt a stinging in his eyes. He turned and took two steps to the side of the road, gazing out over the fields towards the lowering sun.

'How could you not tell me that?'

Now the southerner's words entered his head so clearly it was as if he could hear his voice: *If you don't know where you've come from, you can't tell where you are.* He'd spent his whole life not understanding anything, wondering why the other children didn't accept him. Barten said that outsiders found it hard to fit in. He was an outcast because his father was. He wanted to roar as Xela had done in the farmyard, but he found he didn't have the energy.

Xela's voice was no more than a whisper. 'How did you guess?' The sadness almost made Lebasi want to forgive him. Almost.

'If you'd grown up in the town you wouldn't know Xessan. You said people still speak it in the countryside around Marstor. Barten told me some people get moved from one place to another when they're seventeen – that was you, wasn't it?'

Xela let out a long breath. 'Yes, it's true. I've always been an outsider at Trengam. Almost as much as Marrak. They like me better around Marstor, although from what they said at your meeting, not everyone does.'

Lebasi pressed him. 'Why didn't you tell me?'

His father hung his head. 'I hoped you wouldn't need to know, that you could belong in the town as I hadn't. You were born there, you went to the school. But I can see that was wrong. You'd have had a better chance to fit in if I'd explained, if you'd understood.' He met Lebasi's angry glare. 'Have you ever wanted to say something, known you should, but just thought you wouldn't do it yet? Later would be better?'

Lebasi felt a jolt. Telling Xela that he had helped Perra – it was the same. Not now, not soon. Maybe not ever. He realised Barten had been right: it was harder to hold onto his anger when he understood.

Xela glanced up at the sun. He pointed ahead. 'Come on. We need to get rid of this load, and we need to get to our camp. Maybe we need to have a long talk as well. That's the best I can do – say I'm sorry and try to put things right. I can't change what's past.'

Lebasi didn't trust himself to speak. He fell two paces behind and stared at Xela's heels as they walked.

✻ ✻ ✻ ✻ ✻

The hillside started to rise at the edge of the wood. The road carried on straight up the slope without any bends: they could see clear to the sky ahead where they'd come out into the open again, five hundred paces further on. The trees were tall, straight beeches, row upon row, forming a high canopy on either side. They didn't crowd the road, so there was still useable light where they were walking. It was already dark to left and right. As they began to climb, Xela spoke again. His voice was neutral now, as if he was trying to put aside the argument that they'd started earlier and must finish later.

'How did Perra get out?'

Lebasi opened his mouth, then closed it. He didn't dare to look at his father. His heart hammered. He was trying to think of something to say when he realised Xela was talking to himself.

'I thought I'd put him where he couldn't do any harm. Marrak and I heard rumours through last winter that he might be trouble. I wondered if his whole act, taking on your punishment, was part of it. But I reckoned that he'd be out of sight and out of contact, and I didn't think anyone else had the brains or the guts to start anything without him.'

Lebasi breathed out again. He tried to keep his voice even. 'Why did you suspect him, last winter?'

Xela rubbed his chin with the hand that wasn't leading the ox. 'People he was seen with. Conversations he was reported as having. The start of conversations that were likely to go on to other things in private later. He seemed to be a man looking for others of the same mind, being very careful not to let on too much until he was sure of the person he was talking to.'

They walked on in silence for a few paces. Those last words ran around Lebasi's head: Xela could not be sure of the person he was talking to.

'And he was good, too. I've a lot of reporters, more than most people know. Some of them aren't supposed to tell me anything except in a dire emergency. To keep secret, you see. So they get to hear about a dire emergency, because no one knows they're reporters, because they don't seem the type. And Perra never picked one of them to talk to. Or if he did, he persuaded them to join him, not to tell me.'

Lebasi concentrated on the ground under his feet. Pace, pace, pace. He didn't want to think too far ahead. He knew that, sooner or later, Xela and Perra were going to meet. Were going to talk. One of them would be winning and the other would be losing. He had no way of guessing which would be interrogating the other. But whoever was asking it, the question would be the same: *I thought I had dealt with you. How did you escape?* Lebasi had saved both of them, and he had betrayed both of them.

Xela's voice brought him back to the present. 'I need your brain, son. What do you think the southerner is up to?'

Lebasi was glad to change the subject. He thought for a moment. 'To stir up trouble. He and his master in Egator have been plotting something big for years, and this is part of it.'

'But how? It doesn't make sense. Gortan and his family would be on the side of anyone who wants to talk about rebellion, but why should a big man from Egator come all the way out here when talk is all they've ever done? If you want to overthrow the king, this is a funny place to start. I can't make it out.'

An idea occurred to Lebasi – he spoke before he remembered where it came from. 'Do you think his master from Egator could be the new captain of the Guard? The southerner's starting a rebellion so he can put it down and look good to the king?'

Xela pursed his lips, considering. Lebasi realised he wasn't supposed to have been there when his father suggested this theory to Marrak. 'It's possible,' he murmured, with a sideways look. Maybe he couldn't quite recall when he'd mentioned the captain before.

They reached a fork in the road, which distracted Xela from trying to work it out. He indicated the left-hand path, contouring across the hillside through the trees. He shook his head. 'Whatever he means to do, there's going to be blood. We need to find a way to keep Perra from fighting the Guard. How do you think we can manage that?'

This time, he did not seem to expect an answer.

40
STOREROOM

They followed the track as it curved around the hillside, then came out abruptly into a clearing. The ground flattened for forty paces or so of grassy meadow before rising steeply in a rocky outcrop, at the top of which the trees started again. Lebasi looked around for some sort of building, but as they neared the crags he dimly made out a large wooden double door set into the rock itself. It might be more obvious in broad daylight, but in the deep shadows of the dusk, it was hardly visible until he was standing right up close.

Xela reached behind a bush and drew out a stick as long as his arm. He produced a tinderbox from his pocket and struck sparks into the cup-shaped end. It ignited quickly and produced a flickering light. He fitted the torch into a hole in the rock, then turned to Lebasi and winked.

'Here's something clever, son. This door is very old – not as old as the Westwall itself, but built by people who knew how to do things we've forgotten. One thing they were good at was locks.' He opened a small wooden panel in the frame of the door to reveal a metal plate with round holes cut into it, ten across and ten deep. In the bottom row were ten pegs. 'I don't know how this works, but it does. Stand close, watch, and remember.' He briskly moved the pegs to different holes. Lebasi tried to fix the positions in his mind. Then Xela put them all back to the bottom row, and said,

'Your turn.' Lebasi reached up and tried to do exactly as his father had done. 'Let's see if you got it right,' Xela said, turning towards the centre of the door.

They each took one of the great iron rings which hung halfway down the inner edges and pulled. Lebasi was surprised at how easily they moved. He'd expected squeaking hinges, grinding over the rough floor, rust – but both sides swung open smoothly and silently, with little effort. Inside there was complete darkness.

The ox gave the impression that it didn't like the way things were going. Its eyes shone red, reflecting the torchlight. Xela clucked at it, 'Oh, come on, we aren't going to cook you – we're going to unload you.' He moved around behind the beast to encourage it to walk forward, holding the torch high so the light could show it what was ahead. Inside, he lit other torches on the walls, and in a few moments Lebasi could see what sort of a place they were in.

He gasped as he stared to right and left. The doorway was narrow and the cave didn't go far into the mountainside ahead, but the space was huge, disappearing into darkness on both sides, the ceiling a full manheight above them. Against the further wall were rows and rows of spears, leaning neatly against pegs stuck in the wall to make them stand up. He turned to the left, and saw a line of longbows and baskets of arrows running further than the torchlight reached. On his right there were stacks of wooden helmets. 'How many...?' He remembered Xela's conversation with Elmass before leaving the house. A hundred years of magistrates bringing the annual requirement. 'Are they all still good? Don't they rot?'

'The air's very dry. Probably some of the bows need new strings, the older ones at least. But the helmets and spears and arrows are all fine, just as the day they were first put here.'

Lebasi helped with the unloading and arranging of the

weapons. 'What are they all for?'

Xela finished piling up a stack of helmets, brushed his hands against the front of his tunic, and surveyed their work. He shrugged. 'I haven't the least idea. It's one of those rules we follow just because it's the law and no one has told us to stop. I suppose it's meant for use if Dennara ever returns and tries to cross the Westwall, but that reason was out of date a hundred years ago and more.' He patted the ox on its rump, turning it around and driving it out of the cave. 'I don't think he's coming back now.'

Xela handed Lebasi a metal douser to put out the torches. Their eyes had grown used to the orange light: back in the open air it seemed almost as dark now as the cave when they first opened the door. Xela found a glass-cased lantern in a corner, lit the candle inside it, and handed it to Lebasi while he pushed the doors shut. 'Last thing – you have to lock it again.' Lebasi went to the panel in the frame and moved all the pegs back to the bottom row. Then he tried the handle. There wasn't a tremor: it was like pulling a wall. Xela smiled. 'You could tie ropes to those rings and have a hundred men heaving on them and they wouldn't budge. As I said, they were good at locks. I'll show you an even better one in the morning.'

Xela hung the lantern on a fallen branch so he could hold it higher and cast light on the road ahead. Lebasi took the rope; they led the ox back to the main road and up the hill, walking in the glimmer of the guttering flame. Lebasi glanced uneasily to right and left at the dark woods. He heard the hoot of an owl and the faint calls of other birds he couldn't name. He whispered, 'Are there wild animals?'

Xela's face looked sinister with the candlelight flickering across it. 'Well,' he said softly, 'I have heard tell that in the depth of the forest there's a pack of – squirrels.' Lebasi punched his arm.

Xela laughed. 'No, there's nothing dangerous around here. In the mountains up north there are wolves and bears, but there's too much farmland between us and them. Farmers hunt down all the beasts that kill livestock. There's nothing bigger than a fox here, and a fox won't hurt us.'

Lebasi stole a sideways glance at his father, searching for a change in his face. He couldn't remember the last time Xela had cracked a joke.

41
GHOSTS

In spite of the reassurance, Lebasi was happy to reach the end of the trees and come out into an open field. There was still a touch of pink in the west, and the stars weren't yet out. There was no moon. Ahead of them stood the tower, tall and thin on the very top of the hill. He could see it only as a silhouette, blacker than the night sky. They stopped and gathered firewood at the edge of the trees, loading it onto the ox for the last few hundred paces up to the foot of the building.

Lebasi scanned the field in the gloom. 'Where's the wall? I can't see it.'

Xela pointed ahead. 'It's on the other side of the hill. Whoever built it used the slope to make the barrier bigger. We'll have a proper look in the morning, when it's light. Let's just get our camp set up for now.'

Standing on the ridge by the tower, Lebasi could make out a dark shape a hundred paces lower down. He was disappointed that he'd have to wait to see the wonder of the world, but he felt a thrill to think that he was looking out beyond the edge of the kingdom. There was the wilderness, empty but for marshes and wild animals, the place of banishment. He couldn't distinguish any details. The dark bulk of the cliffs leading up to the Eagle's Nest loomed on his right, and he knew the sea would be on his left, but ahead there was a wide flat nothing. Stars were coming out low down above the distant horizon, so he knew there were no hills in that direction. Xela pointed out one particularly bright light to the north-west: 'The evening star, the first to appear. You can't see it from Trengam because the mountains are in the way. I always look out for it when I'm here.'

They unloaded the firewood, food and Xela's bedding bundle in an enclosure that had been built for shelter around the base of the tower. They left the ox to graze outside. They made a fire. Xela handed Lebasi a blanket and laid out a thinner one for himself. When they'd eaten, they sat with their backs to the tower wall, gazing up at the stars.

An owl hooted as it flew past. They heard the sound of something moving out in the darkness. Lebasi half-stood to look out, but he could see nothing. He felt a sudden shiver, and shifted closer to his father. 'Do you believe in – ghosts, da?'

Xela was lost in thought again. He snapped out of it. 'Ghosts? No, I don't. If there were such things as ghosts, then I'd surely have seen them here, of all places. And I never have. I'll tell you a piece of history, to keep you happy. I think it's something you ought to know. Or are you too sleepy? You've had a tough couple of days.'

Lebasi claimed he wasn't sleepy at all, which wasn't true, but he certainly wanted to hear something his father offered to tell him without being asked.

Xela waved an arm out into the darkness. 'I'm not sure if you've realised, busy as we've been with unloading the ox and making camp and having supper and being tired, that this is where Dennara and his army made their last stand on another Midsummer, a hundred and thirty-five years ago today. Just down the hill over there, straight ahead, is the Westgate. We'll go down and have a look at it tomorrow.'

He fell silent, but Lebasi was sure this wasn't the whole of the important thing he was going to say. Eventually Xela went on. 'Dennara had five sons. Each of them had a wife and children. Each of them commanded troops in the rebel army, and they'd all fought bravely in the war. They were all here, with their soldiers, the survivors, at that last fight. Rather, at that last surrender, because there wasn't a fight.'

Xela tossed another branch into the fire, sending up a shower of sparks. He held his hands out to the flames and rubbed them together.

'When Riadsala made his offer, that anyone could choose to go with Dennara or stay and live in Xessus, the four older sons went straight to their father, and their wives and children too. But the youngest son, he looked at his wife, expecting their third child. And he looked at his son, four years old, and his daughter, a baby in his wife's arms, and he decided he couldn't take them into the wilderness, and he couldn't leave them behind. He was torn; he knew he'd have to betray his father or his wife. He'd made promises to her, promises to his children – he couldn't break his word.'

The owl called again. Lebasi closed his eyes. When he was telling himself a Xessus story, he liked to take part in the action. But he knew how the action ended in all the legends – the hero would win. History was different. Even so, he found himself joining the story in his mind's eye, sitting here at the base of the tower as the prince decided the fate of the defeated army.

'Riadsala knew who the sons of Dennara were, and he saw one of them was wavering. So he called for a decision: those who would go must go now; those who would stay must get behind the tower. Riadsala lined up his soldiers between the two groups. The four older brothers saw the youngest on the wrong side, and they were furious. The story has it that Dennara himself forgave him, but who knows? That could be something the people who stayed behind told themselves so they could sleep at night.'

Xela's voice became bitter. 'You've heard that Riadsala was merciful. Well, he wasn't without a few cruelties of his own, even if he was nothing compared to his father Rednaxela. He thought up the idea of the branding, and he thought up an even better one to go with it. He sent his soldiers to fetch the youngest son from

the group of stayers. "You are Dennara's son," says Riadsala. "I am," says the young man. "Yet you are not going with him." "I have a wife who is pregnant, and I have two small children," he replies. Riadsala's dilemma was this: he wanted to get rid of anyone who might be a problem, out through the Westgate forever. He was concerned that a son of Dennara, who had been a rebel general, might be a focus for future trouble in Xessus. He didn't want to harm the man, because that also might make people rally to him later; Riadsala didn't want to kill him either, because that might stir people up to fight in his memory. So instead he ordered his soldiers to take the man down to where the branding was going to happen, and they made the youngest son press the hot iron on his father and his brothers, one by one, in view of the crowd who were going to stay.'

Lebasi gasped. 'He had to brand his own father?'

Xela nodded. 'Riadsala reckoned no one would follow him after seeing that. And he was right. In fact, the man was so disgusted with himself that he wouldn't have caused any trouble anyway. He wanted to hide away from the people he'd grown up with and fought with. He didn't go back to Trengam. He stayed in this part of the country instead. He built a house at the bottom of the hill, near the Westwall, and he raised his family there.'

Lebasi's eyes opened wider. 'The farm...'

The fire was burning down, and Xela's expression was hard to see in the darkness. His voice was without emotion. 'He had five children in the end, and in spite of the shame of what their father had done, they found wives and husbands in the countryside round about, but the oldest stayed in the farm, and he had a family, and the same happened again, another generation. And his eldest son stayed in the farm, and had more children in his turn, and the oldest was called Gortan. You met him today, Dennara's great-great-grandson.'

Lebasi frowned. 'But he's a rebel, he'd be on Dennara's side.'

'Indeed he would. It tears him apart, what his own great-grandfather did. It's torn him apart all his life, and it's made him bitter and twisted like King Rednaxela was twisted by his wounds. I don't know whether his father and his grandfather were the same, but Gortan feels the shame of the branding with every fibre of his being in every waking moment, and when he sleeps it haunts his nightmares, and he wishes he could make up for it somehow. He daydreams of a rebellion in which the rebels win, and the five-pointed star is restored, and everyone speaks Xessan again, and the branded people return from the wilderness. It's an idle dream, but it's a dangerous one, particularly with the mystery man from Egator involved.'

Lebasi peered over the wall again. Xela shook his head. 'Oh, don't worry about them here and now. Whatever it is, they aren't ready for trouble yet, and they don't want the soldiers turning up before their plans are in place. The southerner must have wanted me to go on my way and give my signal, and he seems to be able to give the orders.' Lebasi wasn't completely reassured, but he tried to have faith that his father knew what he was talking about.

Xela fell silent, gazing into space as the fire crackled. They sat warming their hands. Once again, phrases were spinning around Lebasi's head as he drifted towards sleep. The history his father had just explained mingled with something else he'd said, eightnights ago... *my own da told me the story, and it was clear to me that it filled him with nothing but hatred.*

Suddenly he was wide awake. Xela felt him move and asked, 'What is it, son? Did you hear something?'

Lebasi jumped to his feet, throwing off the blanket. Xela stood up, scanning the darkness. The red glow of the fire left dark shadows where his eyes should be. Lebasi pointed an accusing finger at his father's face.

'Which part of the Marstor countryside did you come from, exactly?' he shouted.

'Basi, I – it's late, tomorrow...' Xela reached out to try to calm him.

Lebasi turned away. 'Don't you think I've done enough yet? I got you out of the farm, maybe saved your life. What else do I have to do? Tell me now, or don't bother at all.'

There was silence. He breathed in, out, in, his eyes closed tight, his whole body tensed.

His father's voice came, tired, defeated: 'Very well. Sit down again. You know the answer already, but you're right. You should hear it from me.'

Lebasi threw himself on the floor with his back to the tower, staring at his hands. Xela put some more wood on the fire and prodded it into a blaze. He took a deep breath. They both gazed into the flames, not meeting each other's eyes.

Xela's voice was hardly above a whisper. 'This is what you've clearly guessed. Gortan, the great-great-grandson of Dennara, had five sons like the old rebel himself. He taught them the history, with all the details filled in of Dennara's heroism and the prince's cruelty. He taught them to speak Xessan, he taught them to read and write, to fight, all the forbidden things. He taught them to curse the name of Riadsala, filled them with the hate that flows in his veins in place of blood. Four of them shared his views about Dennara, but the youngest one didn't, even when he was a little boy. He believed even talking about rebellion was dangerous, it would get the Guard to come and crush the whole of Xessus. Xessans couldn't fight the soldiers – it would be pointless, an empty gesture, to defy the king. Gortan despised him, and gave him all the dirtiest jobs around the farm, and wished he could get rid of him.'

Lebasi found he was holding his breath. His father's voice

had taken on a sharp, bitter edge again. 'So when the mayor of Marstor came looking for the five young men who would move to Trengam according to the rule, Gortan was delighted to offer his youngest son. When he was born, he was called Lebasi, the same name as you. But since he was six years old everyone on the farm had called him by the name of Dennara's fifth son, because they thought of him as the same sort of traitor.'

Xela gave a humourless laugh.

'Xela, that was his name. Dennara's youngest son was called Xela.'

42
TRUTH

Lebasi stared into the embers. For a moment, he felt nothing at all. He tried to take it in: Gortan, his grandda. Tik and Sinder, his cousins. Nareb and his stony-faced brothers, his uncles. The farm, his home, as Trengam had never been.

I hope he is not a disappointment to you...

The numbness gave way to anger. He stood up again and circled around so the fire was between him and Xela. His father seemed not to notice, lost in his thoughts.

'Do people know that, in Trengam? That Xela means traitor, that you're – we're – Dennara's family?'

Xela started, glanced at Lebasi, then studied the backs of his hands. 'Some, maybe. No one talks about it, not in front of me.'

Lebasi stared out into the darkness. 'Perhaps they know and they tell their children. Keep clear of Xela's son. Not from the town, that's one thing. Related to the man who branded Dennara, that's something else.'

'I'm sorry. What can I say? I wanted to protect you from the bitterness that poisoned my own father.'

'Protect me? Is that what you call it, leaving me not knowing anything about anything? I should have left you in Gortan's barn. You've never even explained that my mother killed herself –'

'WHAT?' Xela's voice was as loud as his roar in the farmyard.

He strode round the fire, clenching and unclenching his fists. Lebasi found he was no longer afraid of his father's anger. He took half a pace forward. Xela held out his hands as if to grab Lebasi's arms, then dropped them to his side.

'Who told you that? It's a filthy lie. Tell me, I'll make them eat it.' Lebasi tried to read Xela's face, but his expression was lost in the shadows. He pressed a finger into his father's chest. 'You did.'

Xela stepped back sharply. 'Me? I did not. Why would I say that?'

'You told me it was her choice. She abandoned you, she abandoned me, like Preddo's da. She died by her own choice. That's suicide, isn't it? Barten told me –'

Xela staggered as if Lebasi had hit him. He crouched down and put his hands on his head. Lebasi could hear him sobbing, but felt no pity. 'Well? If you won't explain, I have to work things out for myself.'

Xela wiped his sleeve across his face. He raised his eyes and stared at Lebasi as if he hardly knew him. At last he sat back and put his hand on the ground beside him. His voice was drained of emotion. 'The truth, then. Sit by me, and I will tell you the truth.'

Lebasi hesitated, wondering what more was left to discover. Perra had suggested that Xela might have killed her or had her killed, but surely... he sat down slowly, keeping a space between them, looking straight ahead.

'I have never told you because I was ashamed. If I told you one thing about Shelba it would lead to everything else. What I have done, why I have done it. When you were small you trusted me. On which day could I say now, this is the time, today I will destroy that? But silence rots trust slowly, as surely as the truth burns it quickly.'

Xela held his hands together, working at the knuckles with his fingers.

'When Drabo the last magistrate was nearly seventy, his agent looked for someone to replace him. I'd treated him for a sickness that year, and we'd talked. He knew what I thought about things. There was a vote in the town, and I suppose Drabo put my name forward. The townspeople of Trengam chose me as their candidate. An eightnight after you were born, the soldiers came and told me I was to go to Egator to meet the king. I didn't want it – I was beginning to get some sort of acceptance from the people of Trengam because I was curing their illnesses. But I didn't have a choice.'

Lebasi was so surprised that he almost forgot where this story was leading – to go to Egator to meet the king? He opened his mouth to ask the first of a hundred questions, then closed it again.

'There were two others, one from Marstor, one from Nampetch. I walked there hoping that the king would pick one of them. The strange thing was that both of them wanted the job. So I was sure that it wouldn't come to me, that I was safe.'

Lebasi glanced sideways. Xela's eyes were wide open, but it seemed he was seeing the streets of the capital city long ago, rather than the fading glow of a wood fire on Westwall Field.

'I had to go in and talk to the king, just me and him and his bodyguards. He asked me what I would do if I was magistrate, how I would make the place better. I told him I would get rid of the soldiers: they were a plague on the countryside, robbing people, abusing people, doing what they liked with no comeback. I thought that would rule me out straight away. But the king listened, and he smiled at me, and he said perhaps it could be arranged. I don't know what the others said. Rednaxela chose me, and I had to swear an oath of allegiance to the fourth king of that name. I never saw the others again. They didn't come back from Egator. I thought that was something – at least as I'd got the job I could go home. I was introduced to Marrak, told he would be my agent, had the agent's job explained to me. My helper, but the king's eyes and ears on me at all times. We walked home with an escort of soldiers, and by the time we reached Trengam you were nearly a quarter of a year old. I told Shelba that they had made me magistrate and the king had agreed to withdraw the soldiers from the district, and we were happy for one whole night.'

Xela paused. He made a fist and tapped it against the other palm, working at the knuckles with his fingers. He let out a deep sigh.

'In the morning Marrak told me the king's price. The soldiers would go, but I had to give a hostage, to make sure I kept my oath and maintained the law. One of the only two people who mattered to me: my wife or my child. I tried to back out, to resign as magistrate, to say the soldiers could stay and never mind the abuse. But once again I didn't have a choice, or only a choice I didn't want. If I didn't agree to one of you, the soldiers would take both.'

A cold, hollow feeling spread through Lebasi's stomach. The ashes of the fire gave no heat.

'Marrak said the king promised to look after the hostage in Egator, but I would never see or hear of them again, until I retired at the age of seventy. I wouldn't know if they were alive or dead, because if they were dead, where would be the king's hold over me?'

Xela's voice ran out. His eyes closed, his shoulders were gently shaking. Lebasi put a hand on his arm. He began to ask, 'So Shelba decided –'

Xela's eyes snapped open again. He turned sharply and stared at Lebasi. 'No! That is what I have to tell you. That is what I have never brought myself to admit or explain. It was my choice, not hers. The magistrate's first decision. I chose to give them – you. The most painful day of my life. But I did not think I could live without Shelba.'

Lebasi felt he was dreaming. He imagined himself, a baby, being handed over to the soldiers to take with them to Egator.

'She agreed that it was the right thing to do. We would have other children. She was calm. She held you in her arms and fed you, and shed a few tears, then put you to bed. She prepared an evening meal, and I ate it.' Xela shook his head. 'It never occurred to me that she would lie. She raided my medicine store for things I gave people to help them sleep, and put the whole lot into my food. I woke up three days later. And she had gone. Marrak told me she gave him our decision and went with the soldiers the next morning. I told him it was not our decision, that it was wrong, that she had to come back. And he said no, he could tell that the king was getting a better hostage.'

Xela knitted his fingers together and tensed them as if they were around someone's neck. His voice was quiet but hard. 'I'll pay him back for that. I'll have to wait, though. When I'm seventy, when I finally find out if Shelba's still alive and what I do to Marrak can't hurt her any more, he'll be sorry for that cruelty. Until then, I have to bury the thought, and work with him as if nothing lies between us.'

All Lebasi's questions had disappeared. His mind was empty. The thing that he had been most sure of all his life had been taken away: his mother had died. But she had not died. He had been angry at Xela for all his secrets and lies, but the truth left him numb.

At last, Xela spoke again, quietly, staring away into the night. 'I'm sorry. You have every right to hate me. I have always loved you more than I can say, but you have always reminded me of what I lost. I cannot look at you without thinking of her. I cannot think of her without pain. When you were little, somehow I managed to cope. I was younger, the years hadn't worn me down so much. But now...' He took a deep breath. 'I have no right to ask you to forgive me. I should have been a better man. I certainly can't ask you to understand, when I've never dared to tell you what happened. All I can say is that I will try to start again, to look at you and think of what I have left, rather than what was taken from me.'

Lebasi could not think of anything to say to that. He didn't know how he would feel once the shock had passed. A question appeared out of the darkness. 'Do the people in Trengam know what happened to Shelba? Some of them put stories around that you killed her. They all seem to believe she's dead.'

Xela too had run out of anger. 'She left in darkness. No one saw her go. I couldn't bear to explain the choice that was put to me, or the choice that either of us made. So people decided what they wanted to believe, and I let them. I didn't care. But I should not have let you do the same.'

'So she's still alive?' Lebasi held his breath.

'I don't know. Marrak made it clear that I would never be told, and said that asking more than once might lead to trouble for her. I can only hope that she is.'

'What about Drabo? Did he give a hostage?'

'I don't know. He never said. He had a wife when I moved to Trengam, and she died before he retired. I don't know if she was his second wife, or if they had a child who grew up in Egator.'

'But when he retired –'

'He came with us on our journey, and he didn't come back either. I don't know whether there's a home for old magistrates in the capital, or maybe just a burial ground. It's still a few years before I get to find out.'

✳ ✳ ✳ ✳ ✳

Lebasi's mind was too full for sleep. For some of the time, he watched the stars: he'd never before lain under the vault of the open sky and taken in their countless number, twinkling and circling coldly in the black distance. For some of the time, he closed his eyes and recalled everything he'd discovered in the last few days. It seemed like more than he had known in his whole life. The stranger had said they had to know their history in order to understand their present. On his sixteenth birthday Lebasi didn't know any history, he didn't have any history – now he found he was connected to the past, to this place, to Riadsala's Mercy, more closely than he could have imagined in his most fanciful daydreams. He worked out that Dennara must be his great-great-great-great-grandfather. Was that the right number of greats? He kept counting them to see if he had it right – Lebasi, Xela, Gortan, someone, someone, Xela, Dennara, four greats or three or five?

He'd never had a family of any kind before. He wasn't sure this one was better than nothing. He'd rather have Barten and Harka. Still, Tik and Sinder were all right. He wondered if they knew – did Gortan and his sons admit to the children that the hated magistrate was their own kin?

He stared at the stars and thought about the stranger's other saying: *if you don't know where you are you can't control your future.* He had learned where he had come from, but he couldn't see where he was going. He couldn't even see the way back to Trengam, past the farm, through countryside where the revolution might be winning.

He tried not to think about Xela and Perra fighting. He was caught in the middle. Was there any way they could be on the same side? Xela hated the king, hated the Mercy. If it wasn't for Shelba.

Lebasi's thoughts wandered far beyond the border. On that apprentice day, he had daydreamed of a road that led out of the gate and kept going. He was floating over the kingdom, like Marrak's bird above a map that no one had drawn, all the way to Egator. The king appeared in his half-dream, wearing a crown and robes and the face of the stranger from the south. There was a woman beside him; he could not see her face. He tried to call to her, but he couldn't make a sound.

The owl's soft call drifted over the camp again as it flew back from hunting. Lebasi was too far away to hear it.

Read the first three chapters of the
next instalment of the story...

XESSUS II

THE WARNING

1
THE HERMIT

Tik stopped at the foot of the cliffs to catch her breath. She scanned the fields below, backtracking with her eyes the five hundred paces she had run. The half-moon rendered everything a uniform pale grey. No lights showed from the farm buildings. There was no sign of movement in the open ground, no hurrying lanterns. The silence was broken by a dog's single bark. She tensed, turning her head from side to side, testing the sound for direction, for distance, for meaning. She shook herself as if flicking off an insect – it was just an animal stirring in the night, not a sign that she'd been missed. Her heart slowed, each beat throbbing in the weals on the backs of her legs.

She felt her way along the rocky wall until she found the gap she was looking for. She squeezed inside, already feeling safer, knowing none of them could follow her now, and reached up for the jutting ledge she knew she'd find just above head-height. The moon-glimmer that had guided her across the fields couldn't penetrate in here. She'd often thought she could make this ascent with her eyes shut – now she'd have to find out if it was true. She took one deep breath, then another, readying herself, reassured by the familiar mixture of smells, flower-scent and damp mould, noticing that they seemed stronger in the dark; then she climbed without pausing, right hand, left foot, left hand, right foot, seeing the holds clearly in her memory. Even so, she had to concentrate: it took her mind off the pain in her legs. If she slipped, there'd be nothing to break her fall before the bottom.

Her heart pounded again, the rhythm matching the strokes of her uncle's belt. With nothing else to see, her mind's eye conjured the fury in his face like a dream. She heard his laboured breathing all around her. She told herself it was only her own, echoing from the stones. She gripped the handholds harder. She knew it made him worse, that she said nothing, made no sound. If she only cried out, begged him, he would stop. But she wouldn't give him that satisfaction. She wouldn't give him anything.

Her arms ached. It was harder at night – the handholds, greasy with dew, needed a stronger grip. She took a moment or two longer on each one to be sure of it before pulling up. Something fluttered past her face, nearly dislodging her as she put up a hand to fend it off. Unseen thorns scratched her, the bushes that grew out of the smallest crevices plucked at her hair and her clothes.

She tried to turn part of her mind to where she was going. She pondered what to tell. She couldn't hide much from Mallam, whatever her father and her idiot uncles said about him. He saw more than they did. Would he be up at this time of night? She didn't think he'd mind her waking him.

A broad ledge gave her a chance to rest. Crazy thoughts raced through her mind. Should she keep going, run away? Where, how? Was that maybe what they wanted? She bit her lip. Why should she have to leave the place she knew and loved? They wouldn't drive her out. She was stronger than they were, they'd see. She clenched her teeth and climbed on.

The familiar shape of a twisted root in her hand told her she'd arrived. She pulled herself out of the chimney and scrambled away from the drop behind her. She rubbed her arms, suddenly cold in the light breeze. She took another glance back, the farm now nearly as far below as far away – nothing yet to show pursuit. If they'd noticed her absence – if they'd guessed where she'd gone, which they might – they'd still have to come the long way. In the dark, she didn't think they'd bother. After all, they'd be expecting her back in the morning for another whipping. Maybe she would surprise them by going missing for a bit. She could spy on them, find out from their reactions if they really wanted her gone. She'd have to ask Mallam's advice about that. He'd always told her how to survive.

The moon shone full onto the ledge, silvering the grass. It seemed bright as day after the darkness of the closed-in crack, but soft, without details. The hermit's house merged into the cliff-face. She padded towards the doorway, her bare feet making no sound.

Out of the blackness there came a spark, a flare, a lamp lighting: the old man's face appeared, clear among the shadows. She shook her head. How could he know? But he always did. She couldn't take him by surprise, even in the middle of the night.

He held the lamp high towards her, smiling fondly. As she came close, the wrinkles around his eyes moved to his forehead. He hung the light on a hook and leaned forward to rest his hands on her shoulders. He studied her face, turned her round to look at the backs of her legs, gently lifted her hands to examine the palms. There was no fondness in his eyes now. His hands formed the question, 'Which?'

She tried to grin, and started to sign back, 'He's looking worse than me.' But halfway through the movement, her will crumbled. She leaned forward into his arms and let out the sobs she had held inside through the beating, through the evening shut in the cupboard, through the rough march to her room, through the climb out of the window and the run across the fields and the scramble up the cliffs. They would never see her cry, but with Mallam it was different.

He held her for a long moment. She wiped her sleeve across her eyes and sat on his bed as he set to work on the fire. While his hands were busy, he couldn't talk to her. Once the flames were crackling under a kettle, he turned to her again. He beckoned, 'Tell.'

She tapped two fingers on her left forearm, saying the name at the same time. She wasn't sure whether Mallam was better at reading lips or gestures. 'Nareb.'

He nodded, and signed back, 'Why?' Then one finger on the forehead and four tapping together on the left biceps. 'I know! The magistrate. He came today, they were angry.'

She waggled her hand: 'Yes and no.' How to explain? She repeated the sign for Xela, then for a child.

Mallam leaned forward. With his bright eyes searching hers, she could almost forget they weren't speaking. She watched his fingers moving, but imagined that she could hear his voice.

'Xela's son was with him?'

'Yes.'

'And the son made trouble?'

'I brought him into the farm to watch Xela arguing with Gortan. Then they went mad and tied Xela up. We had to run away.'

'And Nareb saw you?'

'He wasn't sure. The boy looks like Sinder. But Sinder was down by the road waiting for the stranger from the south. So Nareb thought it might have been Sinder with me in the barn.'

'You didn't admit that it was Xela's son?'

'Of course not! I didn't say anything.'

'But he beat you anyway.'

Mallam sat down beside the fire and checked the kettle. For a moment he seemed to be seeing something else, a smile crossing his face as he stared into the steam; then he shook himself, made two cups of herb tea and handed one to her. He poured boiling water into a basin and threw in leaves from a bunch hanging on the wall. The fresh smell raised her spirits and calmed her heartbeat. She lay on the bed, propping herself on her elbows so she could sip her drink, while he cleaned the cuts left by Nareb's belt. The warmth spread through her chest and made her drowsy.

He laid cold dressings on her legs, then moved around so she could see his hands again.

'Your father and Gortan let him do this?'

She jerked awake. 'My father, yes. Not Gortan. He didn't know.'

Mallam shook his head, running his hands through his long white hair. His fingers seemed uncertain what to say.

At last he signed, 'You always have excuses for Gortan.'

She closed her eyes. *Of course*, she thought, her hands still. She pictured her grandda: always smiling at her, offering her his hand as they walked together in the woods, telling her legends of Xessus the hero. Holding her tight as she stood on the battlements of the Westwall, looking down the dizzy drop into the wilderness, whispering in her ear the name of Dennara and the story of the exiles. *He's the only one I care about. Him, and you.*

2
THE WESTGATE

He lied to me my whole life. He still tried to lie to me yesterday, after all I'd done. My mother is still alive.

Lebasi pulled the blanket tighter around his shoulders. Thoughts scurried through his tired mind, too many to organise, jostling for attention. Round and round, going nowhere, solving nothing, beating with his pulse. He couldn't sleep. He was too angry.

He opened his eyes to check that Xela was still there. The moonlight played tricks: the grey lump in the grass on the other side of the dying fire could have been a rock. Lebasi resented that as well – his father didn't seem to have any trouble with wakefulness.

He rolled onto his back and stared at the stars. He counted the patterns he knew, trying to imagine the shapes that gave them their names – the Eagle, the Turtle, the Bow. It didn't help. His limbs were heavy with exhaustion, but he could tell sleep was not coming back. The rolled-up sacking itched against the back of his neck. Warmth leached out of his body into the ground. The breeze seemed to pass straight through the thin blanket. He wondered how long it would be until morning. He listened for any sound of animals stirring, for the birds getting ready to greet the dawn. He remembered hearing them singing in the woods to bring in Midsummer. The memory seemed like something in a story, long ago and far away, in a year without a number. He had to go over everything in his mind to be sure that it was only yesterday.

There were noises from outside the shelter, but no birdsong. In the deep quiet, he could not tell what the sounds were – something large moving in the distance, or a mouse the other side of the wall? The ox, tethered a few paces away, or a wild animal prowling? He didn't want to get up and look. Xela had told him the story of this place, and had said he had never seen a ghost even here – but Lebasi wasn't so sure. In sunlight, he didn't believe in them. In the dark, on an open hillside where terrible things had happened – wouldn't some of that misery remain? Take shape?

He rolled onto his other side, turning his back on his father. He closed his eyes and tried to think of nothing, but ideas seemed to burst into his head from nowhere. Two voices that were both his own argued with each other.

If she's still alive and in Egator, then I have to go to Egator and find her.

How can I do that? It's so far, and I don't know the way.

'Basi?'

Xela had whispered his name so softly that Lebasi guessed he wasn't trying to wake him, but was checking to see if he was awake. He didn't want to speak to his father, so he lay still. He heard soft footfalls – breathing – the click of stiff knees bending – Xela must be crouching right behind him. There was the sound of his boots turning on the short grass, then steps going away – six, seven, eight, further than where he had slept – a crunch from the stones in the low wall of the shelter as he climbed out – then silence.

Lebasi rolled over and untangled himself from his blanket. The fire was dead and cold. He stood up and scanned the hillside. The sky was definitely lighter in the east now, but night seemed to be lingering on the slope that led down towards the Westwall. He could just make out Xela's figure moving through the gloom, striding quickly downhill.

He felt another rush of anger. After everything Lebasi had done, after risking his life and rescuing Xela from Gortan, his father was still keeping secrets from him? Where was he going? He turned his head towards the south, wondering where Egator lay, thinking for a moment about setting off immediately, starting the long journey. That would serve Xela right, to come back and find him gone. But he didn't feel ready. He needed a little more... he wasn't sure what he needed, but he didn't have it in him to set off now, in the half-dark, with empty pockets and an empty stomach. He turned north again. Xela was out of sight. Lebasi was angry with himself for his indecision. He needed to do something, anything to stop the little voice murmuring in his head that he wasn't starting because he was afraid. If he wasn't going to go south, he would have to find out what his father was up to. Another shouting match would take his mind off what he knew he ought to be doing. He ran across the enclosure and scrambled over the wall.

The ground was firm and smooth and covered in short grass. The last light of the setting moon picked out the trail of his father's footprints in the dew. He could see that Xela was following a track – a slight dip in the turf that might once have been a road, now long overgrown. From five paces away it would appear to be just part of the hillside. Lebasi guessed where it was leading, and shivered. This was the way the exiles had gone, out through the gate into the wilderness, never to return. Why was Xela following them now?

On his right, the massive bulk of the Eagles' Nest showed up as a black hole in the sky, blocking out the stars. He knew that the emptiness far to the left must be the sea, but the only sign of it was that strange salty tang in the air he had smelled for the first time yesterday. Ahead, the wilderness stretched out in a featureless expanse. There wasn't even a clear horizon – just different shades of grey. Xela had told him a little about the empty country out there – marshes for thousands upon thousands of paces, no roads, nothing to eat, disease-ridden insects. And, somewhere, maybe separately, maybe all together, the bones of Dennara, his two hundred and fifty branded followers and their women and children. No, surely there would be nothing left, so many years later... Lebasi shook himself and ran on.

At last, he could see the famous wall – a darker line in the foreground, rising and falling with the shape of the hill, running to right and left out of sight. He felt a pang of disappointment – it was supposed to be a wonder of the world, but it was not as big as he had expected. Long, certainly, but only two or three manheights tall – it must have grown in the telling of the legend, like the hero Xessus himself who was supposed to have built it.

Lebasi scoured the hillside ahead for Xela. It seemed to be getting darker rather than lighter. He realised that the track was no longer a gentle depression in the slope. He was descending into a deep defile between steep sides. He could no longer see his feet, and had to slow down. He reached out and brushed his fingers against a cold stone wall. Ten paces on he glanced up and saw only a thin ribbon of sky, a lighter shade of dark, still sprinkled with stars. Ahead, there was the glimmer of his father's lantern.

The track opened out into a paved space maybe forty paces square, closed in by stone walls on three sides and by the gateway on the fourth. Lebasi looked up. This was more what he had expected: the top of the wall was now eight or nine manheights above him. His eyes took in the lantern, hanging from a hook on the right, above something like the box on the wall outside the weapons store that he guessed was the lock. His father was standing in the centre of the space, hands on hips, facing the other way, apparently unaware of him. Ten paces beyond him, through the thickness of the wall... there was the gate. He was surprised how well he could see it. The faint beginnings of daylight surely couldn't reach all the way down here, and the lantern only contained a single candle. It was as if there was moonlight in the gateway and nowhere else. Lebasi guessed that the two huge doors were made of wood and iron, but in the soft glow they could have been silver.

Xela was rubbing the back of his head. Lebasi recognised the sign: he was trying to make a decision, and finding it difficult. All at once Lebasi guessed what that decision was: at the weapons store, Xela had told him there was another lock to look at in the morning, a better one. He must be thinking about opening the gate. He had not spoken of it, but that meant nothing – he didn't say much about anything. Lebasi felt another rush of feelings – astonishment, that his father knew how to open the gate and would even think of doing so, surely against Riadsala's law; a burning curiosity to stand in the opening and look out at the wilderness; and anger, rising to overtake everything else, that Xela would come here without him, on maybe the one day in his life that he would be at the Westwall, and leave him out of something so exciting.

He walked forward silently, fixing his gaze on the back of his father's head. Xela took half a pace, then stopped and ran his hand through his hair. He didn't look round. Lebasi stopped below the lantern. It was as he expected: a framework with ten rows and columns of holes, ten pegs in a pattern. He fixed the arrangement in his mind, looked away, looked back to check: if Xela knew how to open the gate, now he did too.

Lebasi started walking backwards, trying to make no noise as he made for the shadows outside the lantern-light, keeping his eyes on his father. Xela seemed to come to a decision. He took a purposeful step forward. Lebasi stopped, willing him to open the gate. As he did so, Xela suddenly tensed, looked sharply to left and right, then turned and searched the darkness. Lebasi stood still, but there was nowhere to hide.

'Basi!' Xela walked towards him. 'I thought you were asleep. I didn't –'

'You didn't think I'd want to see this?'

Xela held up his hands. 'I'm sorry. Of course –'

Lebasi's anger had the upper hand. 'Secrets! Always secrets.' His shout echoed and re-echoed from the walls. It was as if a crowd of invisible people had gathered around them, all joining in the argument. Lebasi felt the presence of the long-dead exiles again, and spoke more quietly.

'You're going to open the gate.'

Xela shook his head. 'No.'

'Don't lie to me. Why else have you come down here?'

Xela's eyes flicked between Lebasi and the lantern, Lebasi and the lock. He strode the ten paces across to it and stood with his body in in the way as he moved the pegs to the bottom row. He closed the door on the frame and turned around, leaning his back against it.

'Not this year. Not now.'

Lebasi's voice wakened the ghosts again. 'You mean you've done it before, but you're not going to do it because I'm here?'

Xela unhooked the lantern and crossed the space between them. He reached out a hand towards Lebasi's shoulder, but Lebasi stepped away. Xela clenched and unclenched his fist.

'Yes, I open it every year. My own little act of rebellion. No one knows I do it. No one knows I can. If Marrak found out, I would be a dead man.'

'Then why do you?'

Xela seemed to swell up. Lebasi could tell his father was on the very edge of his temper, but he didn't care.

'I came here all the time when I was a boy. Before he decided I was good for nothing, when I was his youngest and dearest son, my father brought me to the wall to look at the wilderness, to hear the story of the exiles. We came down here to see the gate. He taught me that it's dangerous – if you step on the threshold, you die. And it wasn't just a story to scare the children – he made sure we knew he meant it.'

Lebasi glanced across towards the gate. His eyes had grown used to the strange glow, or else the daylight had started to penetrate – he could see the regular flagstones ended two paces from the door itself. The threshold was a single piece of stone that ran from one side of the room to the other.

Xela hadn't finished. 'Gortan thought that no one knew how to open the gate safely. But the magistrates of the Westwall District have passed the secret down. It's even a secret that there is a secret. Drabo told me on the way to Egator – he drew me a picture of how to arrange the pegs, here and at the weapons store. He learned the patterns from Arkon, and Arkon would have had them from Tebak, and I suppose Tebak would have had them from Dennara himself. Drabo watched me burn the picture. I don't know if he expected the king to choose me, or he did the same thing with the other two candidates. We didn't speak about it.'

Lebasi had never heard the names, but he recognised the way of telling a story. It was like some of the legends of Xessus: I heard it from my father, who heard it from his father, who heard it from his father, who was there. Only those stories were from a year without a number, and this was another impossible connection to a man who walked out through this gate with a fresh brand burned into his forehead, a hundred and thirty-five years ago.

'So I open it because I can. Because this place is important to me. Because of everything my father told me, and everything he did to me. He wants the exiles to come back, and he sits down there in his farm plotting. I come up here once a year and I open the gate, and remember. My father is a hateful, bitter old man, but Dennara was a hero, and I stand here and honour his memory.'

Lebasi glanced back at the box on the wall. Maybe now there were just two people in the world...

He turned back. 'But you're not going to open it today? Why not?'

Xela rubbed his beard. 'It's one thing if it's just me. But you can't be part of it. You can't know...'

It was Lebasi's turn to take a deep breath and let it out. 'You're trying to protect me again. Dennara's my family too, I'm part of this. Open the gate.' He hadn't thought of Dennara in that way before he said the words, but he knew immediately that it was true – he felt a connection with the exiles in the wilderness that seemed stronger than any tie he had ever known in Trengam.

Xela shook his head. 'All right, it's not just that. I'm worried. The stranger from the south at the farm, Gortan and his sons creating trouble, your friend Perra starting a revolution back home – this year isn't like the other years.'

Lebasi flinched at the mention of his friend Perra. Xela seemed just to be using a figure of speech. He had no reason to know that Lebasi had freed Perra from jail and acted as his messenger. No reason to know that Lebasi had betrayed him, as well as saving him.

And he had betrayed Perra, by saving Xela.

Sooner or later, they would meet. They would talk. A winner and a loser in the revolution. One asking questions, one giving answers. Telling each other what Lebasi had done.

Another reason to go to Egator...

Lebasi tried to drive those thoughts out of his head. He raised his voice again. 'You're scared of something happening if you open the gate? What can possibly happen? You said there's nothing out there. There are no ghosts.' The word echoed around them.

Xela breathed out slowly. 'Yes, I'm sure there's nothing out there, the same as every other year. But I'm not taking any risk, not today, and not with you here.'

Lebasi banged his fist against his palm. 'Do you think I'll ever have the chance again?'

Xela shook his head. 'I'm sorry. But we can climb up on the wall to look at the wilderness, if you like.'

Lebasi raised his hand to protest, but then he had an idea. He dropped his hand and shrugged in resignation. 'No,' he said. 'If you're too frightened to open the gate, let's just go. Let's go home.'

Xela clicked his tongue. He opened his mouth to say something, then relaxed his shoulders. 'I'm sorry. That's all I can say. I'm the magistrate. Sometimes I have to do the right thing.'

He tried once again to put a hand on Lebasi's shoulder, but Lebasi twitched if off. He was distracted by his new plan, but he wanted Xela to think he was still just angry. As they set off up the track, Xela said, 'I have to climb the tower to signal to old Mallam up on the hill. You can pack up the camp and find something to eat. It'll take me a little while to get up and down the stairs.'

Perfect, thought Lebasi.

3
HIDING

Tik woke from a dreamless sleep. Mallam was tapping her hand. He signed, 'You should be getting back. You need to be home before it gets light.'

She raised herself up on her elbows. She glanced down and bit her lip. Then she fixed her eyes on his and shook her head.

Mallam's hand hardly moved, but his eyes asked, 'What do you mean?'

'I can't stand them any more.'

He pursed his lips. He rubbed the back of his head. He lowered his eyebrows. Again, the question formed more in her mind than in his gesture. 'What do you have in mind?'

She thought hard, moved her hands slowly. 'I don't know.' She stared into his eyes, willing him to help her. 'You told me once that when I'm bigger I will have learned the secret of dealing with them.'

He nodded. 'Yes, I remember.'

'I can't wait until I'm bigger. I need to know now. You have to tell me.'

The corners of his mouth turned down. He studied the backs of his hands, as if hoping they might know how to answer. He moved them wordlessly, then replied, 'It's not that kind of secret. Not something I know, that I can tell you and you will know it too.

It's something you learn as you go along, and only you can learn it.'

She looked down at her feet, determined not to cry again. He put a finger under her chin and gently tilted her head up so he could talk to her. 'Look at me. If I knew that secret, I would still be living down there, not up here.'

Her mouth opened and closed. It had not occurred to her that Mallam had once lived on the farm. He was part of the mountain.

He smiled at her surprise. 'My dear girl, I was not born here. I have lived on this hillside for nearly forty years –' Mallam stood up, cocking his head to one side as if listening for something. That was impossible, she told herself. But he always knew when she was coming, so he must have some way of sensing – she jumped to her feet – he beckoned her to follow him outside. They hurried across his garden to the edge of the cliff and looked out. The stars were beginning to fade. Not yet morning, but the end of night. Too early for milking, too early for the cockerel to rouse the farm.

But there were lights. From the way they were spaced out, Tik guessed that more than one house was awake.

She forced herself to lower her eyes to the nearer ground, and felt an unfamiliar wriggling in her stomach. There were lights in the field as well, two lanterns moving quickly, almost at the foot of the slope.

Mallam put his hand on her shoulder and firmly steered her back to his cave so she could see his hands. As soon as they were in the lamplight, she signed to him, 'I'll climb down the chimney. If I start now, they'll pass me while they're on the path.'

He cut across her with a flat palm. 'You would kill yourself.'

She thought about protesting, but she knew he was right. She didn't even climb down in daylight. Up the chimney and down the path, that was the way. Downhill, the extra distance made no difference – she could run. It was difficult climbing down anything, and the chimney would be treacherous. In reverse, she wouldn't know automatically where the next hold would be.

Mallam was signing again. 'You must hide. You must stay very quiet. Whatever happens, you must not come out. However bad it seems, it will be worse if you do.'

'Where?'

The cave was small. There were no cupboards, no doors to other rooms – just tiny nooks and ledges cut out of the rock to hold the hermit's few possessions. There didn't seem to be anywhere to conceal anything, let alone a person. Mallam pointed to his bed – a mattress stuffed with straw resting on a rough wooden frame. Each quarter year she brought him fresh straw to stuff it. Now she helped him drag it forward. The rock wall behind it wasn't straight – even if the bed was pushed in as far as it would go, there was a narrow space behind it. Mallam glanced over his shoulder and waved her in. She pressed herself into the wall as he pushed the frame back into its normal position. The mattress slid over her, cutting out the light.

Tik felt the sides of her hiding-place pressing against her. Those lanterns had been hurrying. They would be here soon. If they knew she was with Mallam ... if they even thought it... surely they wouldn't leave without searching everywhere? It wouldn't take them long. There wasn't anywhere else, after all. She tried to take a deep breath. There wasn't enough room to fill her lungs. She clenched her fists and forced herself to be calm.

She wished she had chosen to climb down.

'You awake, old man?' Her uncle Yacul's voice. Sinder's da. Pointless, she thought. He can't hear you.

'Still playing dumb, are you?' She tensed. Dareff. Almost as bad as Nareb.

There were sounds she couldn't interpret – she guessed Mallam would be trying to make signs to them, and they wouldn't be able to understand.

'I don't believe it, old man. You've got a voice. You're just pretending.' She heard the sound of a slap. She clenched her fists. *Whatever happens*, Mallam had told her. And what could she do? He was right. It would be worse if they found her. But would they find her anyway?

'Leave it, Dareff. Let's just give him the message and go.' There was an undertone of fear in Yacul's voice.

'This is part of the message, idiot. Making sure he pays attention.'

'He doesn't look too good. Don't push it too far, or he won't be able to...'

'He's just pretending. Always pretending.'

'I'm not so sure.' Yacul's voice slowed down. 'Sit down, Mallam. Nod if you understand me.'

'Told you.' Dareff sneered.

'He can lip-read, if you talk slowly. Tik told me.'

She heard Dareff mutter her name with a swear-word. But he let Yacul deliver the message. He spoke slowly, as if Mallam was stupid.

'Xela is going to send a signal to Marstor. We'll send the little bug up to find out what he says, and what the reply is.' Tik let out a breath she hadn't realised she was holding in. They weren't looking for her. They didn't even know she was missing.

Dareff interrupted. 'And we know what he's supposed to be saying, so don't think you can tell us something else. If we don't hear what we're expecting to hear, we'll be back, and we'll be angry.'

There were more noises. More swearing. The bed jolted, pressing her harder against the wall. Yacul's voice was pleading now: 'If you hit him again, he's not going to be able to send the signal.' Tik couldn't stand it. Whatever he said, she couldn't just let Dareff beat him up. She started to push against the bed frame, but she couldn't shift it.

Dareff laughed. 'I don't really care. If he can't, then Gortan will have to let us deal with Xela and his boy. I don't believe the army's coming, anyway. Gortan's losing his grip, to fall for that story. We've waited long enough.'

Tik pushed harder, furious now. How dare Dareff go against Gortan's plan? Whatever it was, Gortan had been working on it for years. The arrival of the stranger from the south meant that everything was about to happen, and Dareff was thinking of wrecking everything. What did he know about anything? She was on the point of shouting out loud, but she realised she would be as bad as Dareff – she had to trust Mallam, as her uncle ought to trust his father. She let herself go limp.

Yacul didn't reply to his brother. He was speaking to Mallam again, his voice unusually gentle. 'Here, have some water.' More swearing from Dareff. Then Yacul again, speaking very slowly. 'You understand? Tik will be here after first light to bring back what Xela sends.'

There was no more noise. The cold of the stone wall spread through her body. Mallam should be pulling the bed back. She was sure they had gone. She pressed her knees and elbows against the frame and pushed. It shifted a little. She braced her back against the rock and heaved. Why wasn't Mallam helping? She changed her position and tried again. She made a space at the end just big enough for her to squeeze out. The lamplight seemed bright after so long in darkness.

Mallam was lying on the bed, his eyes open, staring at the ceiling. One hand was resting on his chest, the other hung loose, his fingers trailing on the floor. He didn't move at all.

Acknowledgments

The people I want to thank fall into two main groups – those who encouraged me to keep going because they said they liked the story, and those who told me it wasn't good enough yet. There have been many of both, so if I have forgotten to name you here, please forgive me.

My early readers: Zoe and her friends from the Queen's School, Sarah and Alice Brown, Struan Hogg. The good people of the Arvon Foundation and the Society of Children's Book Writers and Illustrators, for so much learning about how to tell a story. Jeannie, Kathy and Catherine, for many writers' group meetings in which we have tried out our different worlds on each other. The children of the Latymer Prep School and the Hawthorns School and their teachers Ed Pugh and Alex Woodard for their feedback, and particularly Ffion, who said she loved the story. All the people who entered the illustration competition, who brought my imagination to life in different ways. Mike Cook, who convinced me that there are people out there who are as keen to inhabit Xessus as I am, and gave me good advice about fantasy worlds. Chris Lavy, for advice on surgery. Jane Moss, for advice on English. Neil Brown, the Evil Publisher, without whom none of this would be possible. Johanna, whose illustrations transform this book into something my words alone could not be. Luisa, for putting the pictures and the words together so well.

And, of course, my wife Kathy, who has had to cope with a husband living much of the time in a country in his head.

About the Author

I have always loved listening to stories, reading stories, making up stories. For me, the best ones come with a map – a new world to get lost in. I started writing Xessus when I couldn't find exactly the kind of book I wanted to read to my daughter Zoe – an extended tale set in an imaginary country and time, about people who have to deal with real world problems in a real world way. I've got nothing against magic, but I wanted to see how my characters would manage without it. I gave the first few chapters of the first version to Zoe, who came downstairs half an hour later to ask, 'Is there any more of this?' And so it began...

Along the way, I took some time out to write What happened to the Hippy Man? This is a true account of the hijacking of Pan Am flight 073 on 5 September 1986 in Karachi, Pakistan. I was returning from a mountaineering expedition held in memory of my brother Pete, who died in northern Pakistan in 1983. I boarded the plane just before it was taken over by armed terrorists of the Abu Nidal Organisation, who held some 380 people hostage for the day. They collected passports, looking for an American. The brave and resourceful flight attendant, Sunshine, concealed all the Americans with white faces and western names, and convinced the hijacker that there were only Indians and Pakistanis among the US nationals. So he picked a British passport instead – mine. I spent the rest of the day at the front of the plane, waiting for the authorities to refuse a demand. In the end, as the power generator failed and the plane went into darkness, they put me back with the others – before throwing hand grenades and spraying the cabin with automatic fire from their Kalashnikovs. Twenty people were killed and more than a hundred injured, but I jumped off the wing of a jumbo jet and ran away to tell the tale. The book has recently been published in India under the title This is a hijack, after the 2016 Hindi film about PA073, Neerja, was a box office hit.

When I had finished writing The Magistrate's Son, I realised that another thing the younger me loved about stories was pictures. So Neil the Evil Publisher and I decided to hold a competition to find an illustrator. Seeing other people turning the images in my head into pictures was inspiring and moving. The best four entrants submitted detailed pitches and we chose to work with Johanna. I love the illustrations she has created for this book, and I'm looking forward to her visions of the rest of the series.

The only map in this book is the one Marrak draws for Lebasi – to start with, he's not allowed to know any geography or any history. There's some of both on the website www.xessus.com, for anyone who wants to explore.

Onward to The Warning...

ABOUT THE ILLUSTRATOR

I was born in 1995 in a little mountain village in the South of France. I grew up surrounded by the smell of ink and linseed oil, both my parents being engravers. I was homeschooled for most of my schooling which gave me time to wander the Pyrenees, with our horse, dogs and sheep, to read quietly for hours, and to become independent. I was also lucky enough to be able to travel to various countries with my mother, and then on my own, which allowed me to discover new cultures and to learn English. I completed my secondary schooling in Belgium, where my family was originally from. A couple of years ago I was accepted at Middlesex University in London where I am now completing my third year as an illustration student. Winning the second prize in the Lanista Partners Ltd competition, then being chosen to illustrate this book is a really promising start to my career, and I would like to thank Mike for the trust he has placed in me. I would also like to thank my family and teachers for their support.